**In Copper Ridge, Oregon, lasting love
with a cowboy is only a happily-ever-after away.
Don't miss any of Maisey Yates's
Copper Ridge tales, available now!**

From HQN Books

Shoulda Been a Cowboy (prequel novella)
Part Time Cowboy
Brokedown Cowboy
Bad News Cowboy
A Copper Ridge Christmas (ebook novella)
The Cowboy Way
Hometown Heartbreaker (ebook novella)
One Night Charmer
Tough Luck Hero
Last Chance Rebel
Slow Burn Cowboy
Down Home Cowboy
Wild Ride Cowboy
Christmastime Cowboy

From Harlequin Desire

Take Me, Cowboy
Hold Me, Cowboy
Seduce Me, Cowboy

Look for the first of the new Gold Valley series

Cowboy Christmas Blues (ebook novella)
Smooth-Talking Cowboy

For more books by Maisey Yates,
visit www.maiseyyates.com.

MAISEY YATES

Christmastime Cowboy

HQN™

HQN™

ISBN-13: 978-1-335-01331-6

Christmastime Cowboy

Copyright © 2017 by Maisey Yates

The publisher acknowledges the copyright holder of the additional work as follows:

Cowboy Christmas Blues

Copyright © 2017 by Maisey Yates

Recycling programs for this product may not exist in your area.

www.HQNBooks.com

Printed in U.S.A.

Dear Reader,

Christmas has always been my favorite time of year. The spirit of the season—love, joy and togetherness—makes the winter seem brighter and miracles seem possible.

Liam Donnelly and Sabrina Leighton are in need of a miracle. Years ago Liam broke Sabrina's heart, and she hasn't been able to move on. But now that she and Liam have to work together to make a new business venture a success before Christmas, they might end up with a holiday miracle of their own.

In this book I'm excited not only to welcome you to Christmastime in Copper Ridge, but also to spread the cheer to the neighboring town of Gold Valley—home to true-blue cowboys, family-owned wineries and rustic ranches. More Gold Valley novels are on the way in 2018, but don't miss the special bonus novella included in this volume, which introduces you to the town and some of the people in it. In *Cowboy Christmas Blues*, Cooper Mason dreads going home for the holidays—but when he reunites with childhood friend Annabelle Preston, his future in Gold Valley has never looked brighter.

I hope you'll enjoy these two festive new holiday reads, and keep an eye out for a new Gold Valley book, *Smooth-Talking Cowboy*, coming soon to a bookstore near you.

Happy reading,

Maisey Yates

CONTENTS

CHRISTMASTIME COWBOY

CHAPTER ONE

LIAM DONNELLY WAS nobody's favorite.

Though being a favorite in their household growing up would never have meant much, Liam was confident that as much as both of his parents disdained their younger son, Alex, they hated Liam more.

As much as his brothers loved him—or whatever you wanted to call their brand of affection—Liam knew he wasn't the one they'd carry out if there was a house fire. That was fine too.

It wasn't self-pity. It was just a fact.

But while he wasn't anyone's particular favorite, he knew he was at least one person's least favorite.

Sabrina Leighton hated him with every ounce of her beautiful, petite body. Not that he blamed her. But, considering they were having a business meeting today, he did hope that she could keep some of the hatred bottled up.

Liam got out of his truck and put his cowboy hat on, surveying his surroundings. The Grassroots winery spread was beautiful, with a large, picturesque home overlooking the grounds. The winery and the road leading up to it were carved into a mountainside. Trees and forest surrounded the facility on three sides, creating a secluded feeling. Like the winery was part of another world. In front of the first renovated barn was a sprawling lawn and a path that led down to the river. There was a seating area there and Liam knew that during the warmer months it was a nice place to hang out. Right now, it was too damned cold, and the damp air that blew up from the rushing water sent a chill straight through him.

He shoved his hands in his pockets and kept on walking. There were three rustic barns on the property that they used for weddings and dinners, and one that had been fully remodeled into a dining and tasting room.

He had seen the new additions online. He hadn't actually been to Grassroots in the past thirteen years. That was part of the deal. The deal that had been struck back when Jamison Leighton was still owner of the place.

Back when Liam had been nothing more than a good-for-nothing, low-class troublemaker with a couple of misdemeanors to his credit.

Times changed.

Liam might still be all of those things at heart, but he was also a successful businessman. And Jamison Leighton no longer owned Grassroots Winery.

Some things, however, hadn't changed. The presence of Sabrina Leighton being one of them.

It had been thirteen years. But he couldn't pretend that he thought everything was all right and forgiven. Not considering the way she had reacted when she had seen him at Ace's bar the past few months. Small towns.

Like everybody was at the same party and could only avoid each other for so long.

If it wasn't at the bar, they would most certainly end up at a four-way stop at the same time, or in the same aisle at the grocery store.

But today's meeting would not be accidental. Today's

meeting was planned. He wondered if something would get thrown at him. It certainly wouldn't be the first time.

He walked across the gravel lot and into the dining room. It was empty, since the facility had yet to open for the day.

The place was totally in keeping with current trends. Old made new. A rustic barn with a wooden chandelier hanging in the center. There was a bar with stools positioned at the front, and tables set up around the room. Back when he had worked here there had been one basic tasting room, and nowhere for anyone to sit. Most of the wine had been sent out to retail stores for sale, rather than making the winery itself some kind of destination.

He wondered when all of that had changed. He imagined it had something to do with Lindy, the new owner and ex-wife of Jamison Leighton's son, Damien. As far as Liam knew, and he knew enough—considering he didn't get involved with business ventures without figuring out what he was getting into—Damien had drafted the world's dumbest prenuptial agreement. At least, it was dumb for a man who clearly had problems keeping it in his pants.

Though why Sabrina was still working at the winery when her sister-in-law had current ownership, and her brother had been deposed, and her parents were—from what he had read in public records—apoplectic about the loss of their family legacy, he didn't know. But he assumed he would find out. About the same time he found out whether or not something was going to get thrown at his head.

The door from the back opened, and he gritted his teeth. Because, no matter how prepared he felt philosophically to see Sabrina, he knew that there would be impact. There always was. A damned funny thing, that one woman could live in the back of his mind the way that she had for so long. That no matter how many years, or how many women he put between them, she still burned bright and hot in his memory.

That no matter how he had prepared himself to run into her—because he knew how small towns worked— the impact was like a brick to the side of his head every single time.

And no matter that this meeting was carefully orchestrated and planned, he knew it was going to be the same.

And it was.

She appeared a moment after the door opened, looking severe. Overly so. Her blond hair was pulled back into a high ponytail, and she was wearing a black sheath dress that went down past her knee, but conformed to curves that were more generous than they'd been thirteen years ago.

In a good way.

"Hello, Liam," she said, her tone impersonal. Had she not used his first name, it might have been easy to pretend that she didn't know who he was.

"Sabrina." The word came out neutrally enough, but he couldn't ignore the fact that he could taste it. Like honey on his lips. Sweet. Enticing.

Something he hadn't tasted in far too long.

Sabrina didn't seem to feel the moment at all. Her expression remained cool. Her lips set in a flat line, her blue eyes looking through him.

"Lindy told me that you wanted to talk about a potential joint venture. And since that falls under my jurisdiction as manager of the tasting room, she thought we might want to work together."

She finally smiled.

The smile was so brittle it looked like it might crack her face.

"Yes, I am familiar with the details. Particularly since this venture was my idea." He let a small silence hang there for a beat before continuing. "I'm looking at an empty building at the end of Main Street in Copper Ridge. I think it would be a great opportunity for both The Laughing Irish and for Grassroots. A tasting room that's more easily accessible to the tourists who come to Copper Ridge."

"How would it differ from Lane Donnelly's store? She sells specialty foods."

"Well, we would focus on Grassroots Wine and Laughing Irish cheese. Also, I would happily purchase products from Lane's to give the menu a local focus. It would be nothing big. Just a small lunch place with wine. Very limited selection. Very specialty. But in a town like Copper Ridge, that works well. People want to wander the historic main street and shop in boutiques. A place that offers the chance to sit and have a short break is perfect."

"Great," she said, her smile remaining completely immobile.

He took that moment to examine her even more closely. She was more beautiful now than she had been at seventeen. Her slightly round, soft face had refined in the ensuing years, her cheekbones now more prominent, the angle of her chin sharper.

Her eyebrows looked different too. When she'd been a teenager they had been thinner, rounder. Now they were stronger, more angular.

"Great," he returned. "I guess we can go down and

have a look at everything sometime this week. Gage West is the owner of the property, and he hasn't listed it yet. Handily, my sister-in-law is good friends with his wife. Both of my sisters-in-law, actually. So I've got the inside track on that."

Her expression turned bland. "How impressive."

She sounded absolutely unimpressed. "It wasn't intended to be impressive. Just useful."

Her lips twitched, like she was holding back a smile. But not a particularly nice smile. "Well, aim for what you can achieve, I suppose."

"I didn't say I *couldn't* be impressive if I had the mind to be," he said, unwilling to let that dig go.

Her lips twitched again, but this time he sensed a lot more irritation than he had before. "That won't be necessary." She cleared her throat. "Lindy and I had discussed a shop front in Gold Valley, since it's slightly closer to the winery, and at the moment retail space is cheaper there. Why are you thinking Copper Ridge? Aside from the fact that it's closer to your ranch."

"I just told you. I have the inside track on a good deal. Plus, Gold Valley isn't as established a tourist spot as Copper Ridge. It's definitely on its way, but it's not there yet."

"But it's on its way like you said. Property values are only going to go up."

"Property values in Copper Ridge already have. And oceanside real estate isn't going to get cheaper. At the price Gage is willing to sell for we'll come in with equity."

She looked irritated, but clearly didn't have another argument ready. She sighed slowly. "Did you have a day of the week in mind to go view the property? Because I really am very busy."

"Are you?"

"Yes," she responded, that smile spreading over her face again. "This is a very demanding job, plus, I do have a life."

She stopped short of saying exactly what that life entailed.

"Too busy to work on this project, which is part of your actual job?" he asked.

She looked calm, but he could sense a dark energy beneath the surface that spoke of a need to savage him. "I had my schedule sorted out for the next couple of weeks. This is coming together more quickly than expected."

"I'll work something out with Gage and give Lindy a call, how about that?"

"You don't have to call Lindy. I'll give you my phone number. You can call or text me directly."

She reached over to the counter and chose a card from the rustic surface, extending her hand toward him. He took the card, their fingertips brushing each other as they made the handoff.

And he felt it. Straight down to his groin, where he had always felt things for her, even though it was impossible. Even though he was all wrong for her. And even though now they were doing a business deal together, and she looked like she would cheerfully chew through his flesh if given half the chance.

She might be smiling. But he didn't trust that smile. He was still waiting. Waiting for her to shout recriminations at him now that they were alone. Every other time he had encountered her over the past four months it had been in public. Twice in Ace's bar, and once walking down the street, where she had made a very quick sharp left to avoid walking past him.

It had not been subtle, and it had certainly not spoken of somebody who was over the past.

So, his assumption had been that if the two of them were ever alone she was going to let them have it. But she didn't. Instead, she gave him that card, and then began to look...bored.

"Did you need anything else?" she asked, still looking determinedly cheerful.

"Not really. Though I have some spreadsheet information that you might want to look over. Ideas that I have for the layout, the menu. It is getting a little ahead of ourselves, in case we end up not liking the venue."

"You've been to look at the venue already, haven't you?" It was vaguely accusatory.

"I have been to the venue, yes. But again, I believe in preparedness. I was hardly going to get very deep into this if I didn't think it was viable. Personally, I'm interested in making sure that we have diverse interests. The economy doesn't typically favor farms, Sabrina. And that is essentially what my brothers and I have. I expect an uphill fight to make the ranch successful."

She tilted her head to the side. "And yet, our winery is well established and very healthy."

"But Lindy wants to expand, I'm not incorrect about that. She was very interested in this proposition, and not only that, she's started hosting weddings and farm-to-table dinners, right?"

"You know you're right," she said. "Like you said, you do your research."

Her friendliness was beginning to slip. And he

waited. For something else. For something to get thrown at him. It didn't happen.

"That I do. Take these," he said, handing her the folder that he was holding on to. He made sure their fingers didn't touch this time. "And we'll talk next week."

Then he turned and walked away from her, and resisted the strong impulse to turn back and get one more glance at her. It wasn't the first time he had resisted that.

He had a feeling it wouldn't be the last.

As soon as Liam walked out of the tasting room Sabrina let out a breath that had been killing her to keep in. A breath that contained about a thousand insults and recriminations. And more than a few very colorful swear word combinations. A breath that nearly cut her throat, because it was full of so many sharp and terrible things.

She lifted her hands to her face and realized that they were shaking. It had been thirteen years. Why did he still affect her like this? Maybe, just maybe, if she had ever found a man that made her feel even half of what Liam did it wouldn't be so bad dealing with him. The feelings wouldn't be so strong.

But she hadn't. So, that supposition was basically moot.

Everything that had been beautiful about him then had only magnified in intensity since. That square jaw more firm. Gold-tipped hair she wanted to run her fingers through. Green eyes that seemed to see directly inside her.

The worst part was the tattoos. He'd had about three when he'd been nineteen. Now, they covered both of his arms, and she had the strongest urge to make them as familiar to her as the original tattoos had been. To memorize each and every detail about them.

The tree was the one that really caught her attention. The Celtic knots, she knew, were likely a nod to Irish heritage, but the tree—whose branches she could see stretching down from his shoulder—she was curious about what that meant.

"And you are spending too much time thinking about him," she admonished herself.

She shouldn't be thinking about him at all. She should just focus on congratulating herself for saying nothing stupid. Well, except the thing about the can opener. So, she had almost said nothing stupid. But at least it hadn't been specific. At least she hadn't cried and demanded answers for the night he had completely laid waste to her every feeling.

So, that was that.

"How did it go?"

Sabrina turned and saw her sister-in-law, Lindy, come in. People would be forgiven for thinking that she and Lindy were actually biological sisters. In fact, they looked much more alike than Sabrina and her younger sister, Beatrix, did.

Like Sabrina, Lindy had long, straight blond hair. Bea had freckles all over her face and a wild riot of reddish brown curls that resisted taming almost as strongly as the youngest Leighton child herself did.

That was another thing Sabrina and Lindy had in common. They were predominantly tame. At least, they kept things as together as they possibly could on the surface.

"Fine."

"You didn't savage him with a cheese knife?"

"Lindy," Sabrina said, "please. This is dry-clean only." She waved her hand up and down, indicating her dress.

"I don't know what your whole issue is with him..."

Because no one spoke of it. Lindy had married her brother after the unpleasantness. It was no secret that Sabrina and her father were estranged—even if it was a brittle, quiet estrangement. But unless Damien had told Lindy the details—and Sabrina doubted he knew all of them—her sister-in-law wouldn't know the whole story.

"I don't have an issue with him," Sabrina said. "I knew him thirteen years ago. That has nothing to do with now. It has nothing to do with this new venture for the winery. Which I am on board with 100 percent." It was true. She was.

There had been no question about whether or not she was going to side with Damien or Lindy in the divorce. And unfortunately, what Damien had done necessitated picking sides. Though, more accurately, the ensuing legal battle over the winery had been the major thing that necessitated taking sides.

It had been a simple thing in Sabrina's mind. Her relationship with her father was so difficult already that aligning herself with Lindy had really only confirmed more of what he thought of her anyway.

Part of her understood her parents' reactions to all of this. She did. In their minds, Grassroots was theirs. But they had foolishly given the entire thing to their oldest son, not considering their daughters at all. And then, said son had gotten married, and they had drafted a prenup designed only to protect him. Of course, that prenup, with its clause about infidelity, had backfired on Damien, not on Lindy.

Yes. Sabrina had a hard time feeling sorry for her older brother or her parents.

"Well," Lindy said. "That's good to hear."

She could tell that Lindy didn't believe her. But, whatever. "It's going to be fine. I'm looking forward to this." That was also true. Mostly. She was looking forward to expanding the winery. Looking forward to helping build the winery, and making it into something that was truly theirs. So that her parents could no longer shout recriminations about Lindy stealing something from the Leighton family.

Eventually, they would have made the winery so much more successful that most of it would be theirs.

And if her own issues with her parents were tangled up in all of this, then...that was just how it was.

"Looking forward to what?" Lindy's brother, Dane, came into the room, a grin on his handsome face. A grin that had likely melted even the iciest of women into puddles. For her part, Sabrina was immune to him. He was like a brother to her.

He was only back at the winery to offer Lindy support during his off-season. Sabrina could tell that he was more than a little antsy to get out of here about now. Shockingly, handing out small samples of cheese was not in his wheelhouse.

"The new tasting room venture," Sabrina said, doing her best to make sure that her words sounded light. It was starting to feel a little bit crowded in here. She needed a chance to have a post-Liam comedown. Which was impossible to do with Lindy and Dane looking at her so intently.

"Oh, right. That's going well?"

"Well, it's getting started," she said to Dane.

Those thoughts swirled around in her head, caused tension to mount in her chest, a hard little ball of anger and meanness that she couldn't quite shake. Didn't really want to.

"I guess that's good news," Dane said, rocking back on his heels.

Lindy and Damien had been married long enough that Dane felt like family to Sabrina too. He'd been in her life for ten years, and he really did feel like a brother to her. In some ways, more than Damien did. Even more so now as it was difficult to reconcile with a brother that had betrayed someone she cared for so much.

"Great news," Lindy said brightly. "It's exactly what we need. More forward motion. More… _More_."

"Until you have a swimming pool full of gold coins like Scrooge McDuck?" Dane asked.

Lindy narrowed her eyes. "This has nothing to do with money. It's about making the winery successful. And okay, it has a little bit to do with money, because I do like food. And having a roof over my head."

"And sticking it to your asshole ex by living underneath the roof that used to be over his head?" Dane grinned.

The corner of Lindy's mouth quirked upward, and Sabrina could clearly see the resemblance between her and Dane. "It's not unpleasant." She cleared her throat. "I really want the goal to be that we have this tasting room up and ready to go for the Christmas festivities this year."

"That is…awfully quick, Lin," Dane said.

"Sure," Lindy said, waving a hand. "But it isn't like we're a start-up. It's just a new, extended showroom. And with the plans that Lydia West has for Christmas this year, we can't afford to not be open. It's going to be a whole Victorian Christmas celebration this year with carolers and chestnuts roasting on…well, probably not open fires because of safety. But we need to be there with hot mulled wine and cheeses and goodwill toward men!"

"Did you want to add world peace too?" Dane asked. "Because with all that you might as well."

Dane wasn't wrong. It was a very tall order. But they knew exactly what they wanted the showroom to have, and they already had stock at the winery. They would just be moving some of it to town. So it might be tricky, but not impossible.

And suddenly Sabrina wanted it all to work, and work well. If for no other reason than to prove to Liam that she was not at all the seventeen-year-old girl whose world he'd wrecked all those years ago.

Sabrina had to admit she envied the tangible ways in which Lindy was able to get revenge on Damien. Of course, her relationship with Liam wasn't anything like a ten-year marriage ended by infidelity. She gritted her teeth. And she did her best not to think about Liam. About the past. Because it hurt. Every damn time it hurt. It didn't matter if it should or not.

Didn't matter if it was something she should be over. It was stuck there, a thorn in her heart that she wasn't sure how to remove. If she could have figured that out, she would have done it a long time ago.

At least, for a while, she hadn't thought about him all the time.

She had tried to date. She'd really tried when she'd been working in Gold Valley and had been exposed to men she hadn't known as well at school in Copper Ridge. But it just hadn't worked. Inevitably, there would be

comparisons between the way Liam made her feel and
the way those guys made her feel. Which was... Well,
there was no comparison, really.

But now that he was back in town, now that she sometimes just happened to run into him, it was different. It
was harder not to think about him. Him and the grand
disaster that had happened after. The way it had ruined
her relationship with her father. And that thorn in her
heart constantly felt like it was being worked in deeper.

That first time she had run into Liam when he had
come back...

She had walked into Ace's bar, ready to have a drink
with Lindy after a long day of work, and he had been
there. She hadn't even questioned whether or not it was
him. He looked different, older, deep grooves bracket-
ing the side of his mouth, lines around his eyes.

His chest was broader, thicker. And there had been
tattoos covering the whole of his arms. But it was Liam.
It was most definitely Liam, and before her brain had
been able to process it, her body had gone into a full-
scale episode.

Her heart had nearly lurched into her throat, her pulse
racing and then echoing between her thighs, an immedi-
ate reminder of how it had always been to be near him.
A tragic confirmation that her memory had not blown
those feelings out of proportion.

Because, after enough years of unexciting good-night
kisses and attempts at physical relationships that hadn't
gone any further than a man putting his hand up her shirt
while sitting on his couch, she had started to wonder if
she had really ever felt anything close to the intensity
that she'd associated with Liam. For sure, she had started

to think, her memory had exaggerated it, and was actively sabotaging her now.

But such hopeful notions had been demolished when she had seen him again.

And with that attraction had come anger. Because how dare he? How dare he show up in her part of Oregon again, after abandoning her the way that he had. How dare he come back to Copper Ridge and invade her space like this? He was supposed to stay away.

Mostly, she was angry that he had the nerve to come back even sexier than he'd been before. If there was any justice in the world he would have lost his hair, gotten a beer gut and had his face eaten off by a roving band of rabid foxes. Yeah, those things combined might have worked together to make Liam Donnelly less appealing to her.

But there were never any rabid roving foxes around when you needed them.

The door to the winery tasting room opened again, and in walked her sister, Beatrix, who was holding a large cardboard box that she was staring down into worriedly. Her hair was sticking out at odd angles, a leaf attached to one of the wayward curls.

At twenty-two, Beatrix sometimes seemed much younger than that, and occasionally much older. She was a strange, somewhat solitary creature who defied any and all expectation, and was a source of incredible frustration for their parents.

Sabrina had spent a great many years trying to be exactly what her parents wanted her to be. Beatrix had never even tried. And somehow Bea wasn't the one their father wouldn't speak directly to.

Not that she could hold it against Bea. No one could hold *anything* against Bea.

"What do you have in the box, Bea?" Dane asked.

"Herons," Beatrix responded. "Green herons. They got kicked out of their nest."

Lindy's forehead wrinkled. "Beatrix, could you not bring wildlife into the dining room? We have *food* in here."

"I just wanted to see if you had an extra dropper. I have one, but I can't find the other one."

"I don't think I have a dropper in my dining room," Lindy said.

"The kind you use for medicine," Beatrix pressed.

"Yes," Lindy said, "I actually did understand what you meant."

Beatrix looked fully bemused by the idea that Lindy did not have a dropper readily at her disposal.

"Okay. I guess I'm going to have to go down to town." Which, Sabrina knew, Beatrix didn't like to do.

"I have to go down later," Dane said. "I'll get one for you, Bea."

Beatrix brightened, and her cheeks turned slightly pink. "Thank you."

Sabrina occasionally worried that Beatrix did not see Dane as a brother, which was fair enough, since he wasn't even actually their brother-in-law. But Dane was not the kind of guy for a sweet girl like her, and anyway he was far too old for her. About ten years and a whole other lifetime of experience.

She would worry more than occasionally if she thought that Dane returned Beatrix's feelings at all. Fortunately, *his* attitude toward *her* was entirely appropriate. He saw her as a younger sister, as he should.

But that didn't seem to change the fact that Beatrix's entire face illuminated whenever he spoke to her.

"Come on, I'll help you find a safe place for your herons so you can stick close to them today." Beatrix followed Dane out of the tasting room, leaving Lindy and Sabrina alone.

Lindy didn't say anything, but she did lift one eyebrow. Sabrina had a feeling she wasn't the only one who had observed Beatrix's response to Dane.

In some ways, it hurt Sabrina to see it. She had to accept the fact that she might actually be projecting. Because there had been one summer when she had followed a man around like that. Looked at him like the sun rose and fell on his broad shoulders.

And she had confided in him. Her hopes, her dreams. Her secret fears. And they hadn't mattered to him at all.

In the end he had made a fool out of her.

She looked at Lindy again, and noticed that her sister-in-law had some fresh lines on her pretty face. She had to wonder if she was having similar thoughts right now too.

"Good thing we know better," Lindy said finally.

"Huh?"

Sabrina laughed, and even she thought she sounded a little bit bitter. "I suppose so."

But that was the thing, she did know better. It was the one good thing about everything that had happened with Liam all those years ago. She had trusted her heart's wants. Fully. Completely.

And no matter how her body might react to him now, she had learned her lesson.

She would not be making that mistake again. Ever.

CHAPTER TWO

BY THE TIME Liam pulled back into the Laughing Irish Ranch he was feeling pretty good about the venture with Grassroots. As far as he could tell Lindy was a good businesswoman, and she had something to prove, which would help fuel the fire.

Liam wasn't immune to the need to prove things. He'd come back to town and swung by Jamison Leighton's lake house—which had turned out to be a home built near a man-made lake, in a neighborhood along with about twenty other homes, not a cabin set in the pristine wilderness, and it was splitting hairs to notice, but Liam did, because he was pissed and willing to be petty—to write the old man a check. To pay him back, with interest, for the money he'd gotten to leave in the first place.

The look on his face had been worth the trip out to Copper Ridge all on its own.

He pulled up in front of his family's ranch house and his truck skidded to a stop, the fine coating of ice over the gravel making traction a bit of an issue. He got out and looked up to see his brother Finn standing by the porch smiling, a gold wedding band gleaming on his left hand.

Liam had never seen anyone so happy to be tied down. Except for maybe his older brother Cain, and his younger brother, Alex. They were pretty damn happy to be tied down too.

Liam was…well, kind of ambivalent about all the romance he was surrounded with at all times.

Alex and Clara had moved to her ranch, though Alex continued to work at the Laughing Irish. Cain and his wife, Alison, and Cain's daughter, Violet, lived in another house on the property that Cain had refurbished for them out of an old barn.

Which left Liam, Finn and Finn's wife, Lane, in the main house.

It wasn't really bad. Lane was a fantastic cook, and Liam got all the benefits of having a wife without actually having to have one. Well, except for the sex.

Not that he wanted to have sex with his brother's wife. Even Liam Donnelly had his limits.

"How did it go?" Finn asked.

Of the four of them, Finn had been at the ranch the longest. He had worked with their grandfather from the time he was sixteen years old. The place was in his blood. And this expansion both excited him and made him nervous. Mostly, Liam felt like Finn wanted to kill him with his bare hands.

If Finn had his way, he would essentially keep the status quo. But between Lane and Liam he'd encountered a constant push for change. For growth.

He knew that Finn hated that. But Liam was good at it. He was good at start-ups. He was good in investments. And, if the expansion of the Laughing Irish went to hell, he had a shit-ton of money to back it all up.

Money that just kind of sat there now. Money that didn't seem to mean anything or accomplish anything. He didn't have much else to offer. He had capital. Which, when you were kind of an asshole, was always the smart thing to lead with.

"It went well. I'm going to be working with Sabrina Leighton on the project."

He started to walk past Finn up the porch and into the house, then turned and caught sight of his brother's expression. It was just a little too hard. A little too insightful. "Did you have a comment, Finn?"

"I have a lot of comments. But because I'm not entirely sure what went down with you and Sabrina—or really, what went on in your life at any point when you weren't on the ranch—it's tough for me to pare it down to the most effective one."

"Good. You're easier to deal with when you're at a loss for words." Liam let out a breath. "I'm not going to pretend that I don't have a history with Sabrina. I do, in that she hates me." It wasn't that he didn't know why. And, no matter how committed he was to the denial of having led her on, he did have to admit at least to himself that he hadn't been *neutral* about her.

No matter what she'd thought, when he'd left he'd done the right thing. He couldn't regret the way he'd done it either. She might be mad at him, and he could even understand that. But it had been the right thing to do. The fact that she was still angry at him thirteen years later for about the most honorable damn thing he had ever done didn't really seem fair.

Honorable and self-serving, maybe. But the honor was definitely present.

"And you're going to be able to work with her in spite of that history?" Finn asked.

"I don't think it's the history you think it is. When I worked for Grassroots she was seventeen, Finn. I never slept with her. She got her hopes up that I would. That's it."

"So she turns and runs the other direction every time she sees you coming because she had a crush on you thirteen years ago? That's it?"

Liam gritted his teeth and spread his hands. "That's about the size of it. Apparently, I'm ruinous to women even when I don't have sex with them."

"I feel like you meant that to sound badass, but mostly, I just think it's true."

Liam shrugged, not even caring if his brother was insulting him. Not even caring if his words had been chosen poorly enough that he'd insulted himself. "We had a meeting today, and everything seems like it's going to be fine. I don't think she's going to spend the entire time plotting my downfall." He took a few more steps and walked into the house. Then stopped and turned. "Unless this is all an elaborate ruse to get revenge on me by destroying the Laughing Irish. In which case, Finn, I'll go back to New York and leave you here in the smoldering wreckage."

Finn glared at him and slammed the door behind them, enclosing them in the large entryway of the custom log cabin their grandfather had built about five years ago.

"The funny thing, Liam," Finn said, sounding like he found nothing at the moment funny at all, "is that I think you believe that. But I know you wouldn't. I know that you actually want this to succeed. Maybe not because you love the ranch. Maybe not because you love me. But most definitely for your damned stubborn pride."

Liam rubbed his chin. "I do like my pride."

"Yeah, you do. And I don't think you would ever

allow a ghost from your past to be responsible for your failure."

They were just ribbing each other, and Liam knew it. But there was something a little too close to the truth in those words, and they gouged him in tender places. "Whatever the reason," he said, "I'm not going to hang you out to dry."

"You've gone soft."

"If I have, it's because of your wife's cooking," he responded. Then he slapped his hand against his stomach—which was still rock hard, thank you very much—for good measure.

"What's your timeline to get the shop up and running?" Finn asked, crossing his arms over his broad chest, clearly done with the banter. Finn had limited patience for banter when it came to discussions of the ranch.

"I'm not sure. We're going to look at property sometime this week. I have to get in touch with Gage West. I think once we start in on it we should be able to get the sale to go through quickly. But if something happens with the loan, I have the cash to front it."

"I'm not having you do that, Liam," Finn said. "I'm not putting your finances at that big of a risk."

Liam bit back a frustrated curse. His brother didn't understand because to him, that amount of money had more value. And Liam could understand that. He'd come from poverty. But now he had money. And he didn't know how the hell else he was supposed to contribute. "What do I care? Do you see me spending money?" He looked down at his boots and lifted them up, tapping them on the floor, a sprinkling of mud landing there on the hard wood. "How old do you think these boots are?"

Lane, Finn's wife, appeared from the kitchen, her dark hair pulled back in a ponytail, her brown eyes glittering. "I don't know how old your boots are, Liam Donnelly, but if you want to live to be any older than *you* are, I suggest you clean up that mud mess because I sure as hell am not going to do it. I'm not your maid."

He bit back a comment about her being the cook. He had a feeling that right now, she would launch rockets from her eyes and leave him reduced to nothing more than a pile of ash. He didn't know what the hell Lane's problem had been lately but she'd been in kind of a mean mood for a while.

"I'll clean it up," he said. Though, not anytime soon. "I was just telling your husband that I don't need all the money I have sitting in my bank account. I can afford to invest in the expansion of the ranch."

That turned Lane's focus to Finn.

Finn shot him a deadly glare. "Just because you can doesn't mean I'm going to let you. This venture is ours, it's equal. We can all put the money back into the storefront that we're making on the ranch. We don't need you to invest that much capital up front."

"But I can," Liam said.

And damn it, there had to be some use for that money. For that money that just felt like a weight. He had busted his ass, worked himself blind from the time he had been given the money to go to college. Twenty years old, coming in late, working up from a deficit, and he had done every damn thing he could to make sure that he succeeded. He didn't graduate early. He didn't graduate at the top, but it didn't matter, because when it came to work, nobody was more willing to beat their knuckles bloody pounding the pavement than he was.

He worked long, and he worked hard. And he had amassed a fortune for himself working at large corporations and major cities. Investing in start-ups that became wildly successful, funding businesses and increasing profits.

And then one day he had stood in that corner office and looked out over Manhattan, in a position in life a boy from the sticks certainly had never imagined he'd be in, wearing a custom suit and honest-to-God Italian leather shoes and he had felt...

Exactly the same as he had twelve years earlier.

He didn't feel better. He didn't feel different. He didn't feel healed. He didn't feel any different from the boy who'd been stuck in his home. Afraid to make too much noise. Afraid to breathe wrong in case it brought his mother's wrath down on him.

That was when he had gotten word that his grandfather had died and left him a quarter of a ranch in Copper Ridge, Oregon, and he had thought it might be time for him to go back.

For him to go back for the first time since Jamison Leighton had sent him packing with a bribe.

There was more here. More here than in that corner office. He wasn't exactly sure he liked it or wanted it, but at least it offered a change of pace.

And his brothers.

He hadn't grown up with Finn or Cain, and living with them, getting to know them had been... Well, there was something in that. Being around Alex again, the brother he had been raised with... That was always a little bit of a mixed blessing.

Not because he didn't love Alex, he did. Alex's happiness was the proof that he had done something right early in his life.

Their life growing up had been awful. But Alex's had been a little less awful. Because Liam had been the lightning rod. And Alex had never even known it.

So yeah, he felt like he was on the right track here. And after all that emptiness, that seemed like a pretty good deal to him.

"Fine," Liam said, "using my money won't be the plan. But if loans or anything like that hold stuff up, let me do it."

Finn opened his mouth to argue.

"Let me, Finn," Liam said. "Let me give you this."

His brothers seemed to give with themselves all the damn time and he couldn't figure out quite how they did it. He knew how to create things. Knew how to make money. And he knew how to give money.

That was what he did.

"Fine," Finn relented. "If we get into dire circumstances, I'll let you throw some cash at it."

"What's the point in having a rich brother if you don't use him?"

"I do use you. For hard labor. Which frankly I find more useful, Liam. I can earn more cash. I can't grow another pair of hands."

Liam shrugged, then started to walk toward the stairs. "Liam!" Lane called after him. "Clean up the mud! I'm trying to plan a Thanksgiving menu and you're tracking mud all over the place." She whirled around and went back into the kitchen, leaving a trail of sulfur in her wake.

"Boy," Liam said, "she's about as fun as a bee-stung wolverine at the moment, isn't she?"

Which wasn't fair. He knew that Lane was putting a lot into her and Finn's first married Thanksgiving. Even though he was a jackass, Liam understood that.

"Hormones," Finn said.

Liam's eyebrows shot up. "Hormones?"

A slow smile spread over his brother's face. "She's pregnant."

"Holy hell."

Finn laughed. "Definitely putting that one in the baby book. What your uncle Liam said when we told him you were going to be born."

"Why haven't you told us yet?"

"Lane wanted to wait. You know, something about the second trimester, or something. But it's close. And, I don't want to keep it a secret anymore. So, congratulations. You're going to be an uncle."

"I'm already an uncle," Liam said. "It's just that my niece is almost an adult."

"I wonder what Violet is going to think," Finn said with a grin.

"A baby cousin might be something she can't play it cool about." Cain's daughter was in the throes of teenage snark and angst, so it was difficult to guess how she'd react to much of anything.

As far as Liam went, he was happy for his brother. But it kind of underscored the fact that everyone around him was living in a completely different phase of life than him. A different phase of life than he was ever going to live. Marriage. Family. Babies. None of it was his cup of tea. Not at all. All that happy family stuff was just a load of crap as far as he was concerned.

Yeah, he knew some people were happy. But it had never been him. And he didn't know why he would sign on to that kind of thing. Not again. He had grown up in a house with a mom and dad. They had been in love.

And it had been awful. Vile and toxic.

Full of drama and cheating. His mother taking her anger out on her sons—most especially him—and eventually the inevitable meltdown of the relationship.

Still, he hoped that Lane and Finn would be happy. They would keep being happy. As far as he could see, they were. And it wasn't some kind of *Leave It to Beaver* fantasy. Where everybody acted like they had a lobotomy just because they had fallen in love and gotten married. No. They were real people still. They were just people who seemed committed to making a life with each other. People who really loved each other. But Finn and Lane had been best friends before they had fallen in love.

As for his brother Cain and his wife, Alison, it was a second marriage for both of them. They both knew what hadn't worked the first time around, and they seemed settled this time. He figured if you were going to do it again, you had to be pretty damn sure.

And Alex… The youngest of the Donnellys had recently gotten engaged to his fiancée, Clara. And Liam thought that Clara particularly was a little young for all of that. But like Alex always was, he was happy. Reckless and certain. Liam was glad that Alex had that certainty even after their growing-up years.

Liam didn't. More than that, he didn't want it.

It didn't mean that watching all this happiness unfold in front of him didn't make his chest feel weird though. Didn't make him feel like he was in a strange space of longing for something he knew wouldn't actually suit him. Like being allergic to peanuts and wanting a Snickers bar.

It was a reminder. A reminder of that small, bright window of time where he had thought that maybe, just maybe, he could have something more. More than what he had ever imagined. More than what he had thought someone like him could ever hope to touch.

That summer with Sabrina.

He'd made the right choice then. He was confident in that.

And he didn't like dredging up all this old crap.

But, since he was trying out having a family rather than existing in isolation, he figured he had better smile and say something that wasn't profane. "Congratulations," he said finally. "That's great."

"I'm not sure you really think it's great," Finn said, a slight smile on his lips.

"It's great for you," Liam said. "I want a wife and kids like I want a suspicious rash."

"Given your behavior, the suspicious rash is a lot more likely."

Liam flipped his brother off, then continued up the stairs. He needed something. To change before he went outside and worked. To take a hot shower. Something. Something to keep his head on straight. He had to call Gage West and figure out when he and Sabrina could meet up to deal with that real estate stuff. Which meant seeing Sabrina again.

He had gone thirteen years without seeing her, and it had worked out pretty well. Seeing her, he supposed, didn't really have to mean a damn thing.

If he kept repeating that to himself, he might just start believing it.

CHAPTER THREE

SABRINA WAS SURE that Liam was out to ruin her life. Because not only did he manage to make their appointment to go look at the building the very next day after she had already shared the same airspace as him, but he made the appointment at 7:00 a.m.

Scowling, she charged into The Grind and shook the dampness from her boots, curling her toes and trying to stave off the chill. The coffeehouse always had a warmth about it, with its exposed brick walls and rough-hewn floor. It created a stark contrast with the stormy gray outside.

There was a line, because it was six forty-five, and she supposed that everybody was rushing to get their caffeine fix before they went about their days. Though there were also some retirees sitting, using social media on their tablets or playing crosswords in the newspaper. As if they had all the time in the world. Sabrina supposed they did.

There were a few people that look like they might be students, or graphic design types, wearing flannel with messy buns tied high on top of their heads. Men and women alike.

She envied them. She wanted to sit in the coffee shop all morning by herself on her computer. She did not want to contend with reality. She did not want to deal with

Liam Donnelly, and yet, here she was about to be dealing with Liam Donnelly at far-too-early-o'clock.

She wrapped her arms around herself and hopped in place, distracting herself with her movements more than actually needing the warmth.

When she reached the front of the line, the girl behind the register smiled. Sabrina didn't think she possessed the ability to smile at the moment. "Just a coffee," she said. She was tempted to add that the girl was welcome to hold the cheer. "Room for cream." She made no comments about cheer.

That was the worst part about living in a small town. You really couldn't let yourself have a bad day. Because if you did, inevitably the person whose head you bit off today was the daughter of someone you needed to approve a permit tomorrow. Or the person writing up your bank loan.

Or just uncomfortably, someone you had to see day in and day out forever after and pretend that you never had a tantrum wherein you acted like a petty child that one time.

Small-town politics were a thing. A thing that left very little room for cranky faces and sharp remarks.

Though she was ever grateful for the etiquette that allowed two people to ignore each other as long as they could successfully not make eye contact. The tacit understanding that you could both pretend you hadn't seen each other so that you could get on with your day.

That brought to mind the shock of running into Liam. That first time. They had definitely made eye contact. There was no way she could pretend she hadn't seen him. And so she had fled Ace's bar like a scalded cat.

Her pride had yet to recover from that. Because she

had some difficulty explaining it the next day to her sister-in-law.

Not that she had given much explanation.

Frankly, the whole story with Liam was just more embarrassing than anything else. Embarrassing because she had been an idiot. Embarrassing because it still hurt. Because she had gone all-in on what her teenage heart had imagined was love, and caused a permanent rift with her father that hadn't healed yet.

Just looking at Liam hurt. She didn't know why, but it was all as tender as if it had happened yesterday.

Because when he had broken her heart, he had truly broken it.

She would love it if there was a more dramatic story. If she could claim that he had callously taken her virginity and ruined her for all other men, etc. etc.

Sadly, all she could really say was…that he had humiliated her. Made her feel like a fool. Made her feel as though she couldn't trust a single instinct that she had. It had been the gutting loss of a friend and first love all in one. She'd laid herself bare to him—literally—and then he'd rejected her and disappeared. From her life. From town.

Then, not content to let that be the last of it, she'd confronted her father, who had confessed to her he'd told Liam to go. That he'd paid him to leave her alone.

Discovering that Liam had put a dollar amount on their friendship had been intensely wounding. Almost more so than his rejection.

But not even that had been enough for her in her seventeen-year-old despair. No, no. She'd had to get wasted at an event at the winery for the incumbent mayor of Copper Ridge and make a total ass of herself in front of every influential person in Logan County.

And loudly revealing her family's worst secrets to hurt her father the way he'd hurt her…

Well, that wasn't really about Liam anymore. Even if he was the root cause.

Of her estrangement with her dad and her eternal humiliation over playing the part of wounded opera heroine so publicly. As she put her pain and the depth of all her feelings on display for everyone.

Just remembering it made her skin crawl with humiliation.

She took a deep breath, trying to dispel the tightness in her chest. Trying her damnedest to smile when the girl behind the counter handed her her cup of coffee. She took the lid off, and the dark, scalding liquid spilled over the edge and onto her skin. She growled and stuck her thumb into her mouth, trying to alleviate some of the burn.

"Not a great morning?"

She bit down on her thumb, then jerked it out of her mouth, not wanting to turn and confirm what she already knew. But she had to.

She turned slowly, curling her lip upward into what she hoped resembled a smile. "Liam. I thought we were meeting down the street."

"We are," he said. He smiled. "I just had the same idea you did, apparently."

Today, he was dressed in a button-up shirt that was open at the collar and a pair of dark-wash jeans and a belt. His shoes were…nice. Very nice.

"You look like…well, like you're headed to a business meeting." She wanted to bite her tongue off for that. Because of course he was headed to a business meeting. They were having a business meeting. And, she too was dressed up. It was just that yesterday he had not been so dressed up. Which meant he was dressing up for Gage, but didn't see the point in dressing up for her.

That was fine with her. She didn't want him to dress up for her. She didn't want him to do anything for her except maybe jump into the sea and float way the hell out of town.

She, of course, had simply dressed up because it was what she did. Not because of him. Never because of him.

"I could say the same about you," he said, deadpan. "I'm just going to order a coffee. We can walk over to the building together."

She wanted to tell him that wasn't necessary. Actually, she wanted to hit and spit and act like she was choking so that he could fully understand her displeasure. But she wasn't going to do that, because she was mature.

So there.

"Great," she said, adding a sugar packet to her coffee and stirring it absently while Liam walked over to the counter. He placed his large hands flat on the surface, leaning in slightly, making rather intense eye contact with the girl behind the register as he proceeded to order.

Sabrina felt something curl in her stomach, and she continued to stir her coffee absently, tearing open another sugar packet and dumping it in without thinking.

The girl fluttered, her cheeks turning a particular shade of pink as she tucked a wayward strand of dark hair behind her ear.

Sabrina blinked, her upper lip curling without permission as she grabbed another sugar packet. She was stirring when she realized what she had done and sighed. It was too late, and now her coffee was two packets of sugar too sweet, and she was standing there acting like an idiot watching Liam flirt with a girl who had to be twenty-two.

At thirty, Sabrina did not find that amusing.

Of course, she shouldn't care, because she shouldn't care about anything that Liam Donnelly did. She should be more than happy to watch him flirt with another woman. He could crush somebody else's self-esteem underneath his extremely nice shoe sole. He was not going to crush hers. Not ever again.

She deserved better than that.

She deserved…

Well, she deserved to get this tasting room up and running for her sister-in-law before Christmas. She deserved to have a lovely, cozy place to work in town where she could extol the virtues of Grassroots Wine and interact with customers, which was what she really liked to do.

Of course, that would mean not hanging out with her friend and fellow winery employee, Olivia, as much, because Olivia lived in Gold Valley and would definitely not be working the Copper Ridge tasting room. But they could still get together after work sometimes.

Her other friend, Clara, had quit working at Grassroots shortly after she had gotten engaged to her boyfriend, Alex. Which had been shortly after the bison had arrived at their ranch, and they had gotten busy with their new venture.

She was happy for her. She really was. But it meant she didn't see her as often. But then, considering she was now the only single friend in that group, maybe it wasn't so bad.

Olivia was perennially dating Bennett Dodge her boyfriend of several years, whom Olivia seemed convinced was about to propose at any moment.

Definitely for Christmas, she had said.

Privately, Sabrina was afraid that Bennett had no plans to propose anytime soon. But since Sabrina was an abject failure at relationships she was never even tempted to voice that concern.

Though a woman standing there with a stomach that had gone acidic while watching a man who had never been into her flirting with somebody else had no call giving commentary to anyone.

Liam took his coffee from the register girl's hands and their fingertips brushed, and Sabrina couldn't stop herself from rolling her eyes. She smoothed out her expression as Liam made his way over to the cream and sugar. He dumped one packet of sugar in his cup, stirred it slightly, then popped the lid back on. "Ready?"

"Yes."

They walked out the front door and back onto the wet, frigid street. In a couple of weeks, it would be decorated for Christmas, and there would at least be some glittering lights to pierce the eternal fall gray that had descended upon the coast. Right now, it was just cold and wet. Sabrina lifted her shoulders to her ears, trying to brace herself from the chill, and not at all trying to fortify herself against Liam's presence.

"You should be careful," she said, unable to keep the words back.

"With…what? I'm not running with scissors, I'm walking. With coffee."

"It's hot coffee. I burned myself when I opened the lid."

"Sorry about the burn. But I think I can handle walking and drinking. Maybe you were just distracted."

"Me? Hardly. More like you were the distracted one. That girl was making a fool of herself over you," she said, keeping her eyes determinedly fixed straight ahead on Main Street. Most of the shops weren't open yet, and wouldn't be for a couple of hours. Right now, only Pie in the Sky bakery was also up and running. The other shops, full of artisan gifts, vintage clothing and specialty foods, wouldn't open until closer to ten, when the tourists were up and around.

"I didn't notice," he said.

That made her want to take the lid off her overly sweet coffee and splash it in his face. Because of course he didn't notice. That was his MO. Make a young girl fall in love with him and then act like he hadn't realized. Act like it was shocking and horrifying when she propositioned him.

"Right," she said stiffly.

"Sabrina," he said. "Are you going to spend our entire working relationship acting like you want to cut me open and feast on my liver?"

"Don't be an idiot, Liam. I don't like liver."

"Are you going to spend our entire working relationship—"

Sabrina stopped walking and turned to face him. "If you lecture me on my behavior, Liam Donnelly, I really will kill you. I have no problem working with you in a professional capacity, because I am a professional. But the fact is, you don't know me. You knew me thirteen years ago. And even then, you didn't know me that well.

So, you have no idea whether how I'm behaving is just the way I behave, or if it has something to do with you. Because you don't know me. Remember that before you lecture me again."

THE THING WAS, he *did* know her. At least, he had back then. He wasn't going to say that though. But the fact of the matter was, there was a point in time when he had known Sabrina better than just about anyone. Because they had talked. At first, because she had followed him around with an obvious crush, but then gradually because he had come to enjoy her company.

That had been the problem with Sabrina from the beginning.

It was part of the problem with her now. Because, no matter that he should feel nothing for her, she was far too beautiful for her own good, for his own good. Just like always.

And when she'd kissed him...

Well, when she'd kissed him he'd felt like the sun had come out from behind the clouds for the first time. Something about that kiss had made him feel deep, Far more raw, far more real, than he was prepared for.

He was older now, and he doubted she could conjure up that stunning response in him again if she tried. He was also a little more jaded when it came to arousal, and still, she got to him.

Even though she was vibrating with irritability, her hands shoved deep into her coat pockets, her posture rigid, as if she was doing an impersonation of a very indignant plank of wood, he still thought she was beautiful.

He wasn't sure what the woman he'd ordered his coffee from had looked like. The woman Sabrina had accused him of flirting with. That was the funny thing. Sabrina had been seething at him about how he could never know her, all the while assuming she knew him.

He wouldn't point out the hypocrisy, though, because there was no point. She was already mad at him. He would wait to throw something like that at her when she was relaxed and fine. That, at least, would result in a little more amusement.

Not that he should try to make Sabrina angry, or enjoy it in any fashion. But he found that he did.

"Sorry," he said, not feeling sorry in the least.

"I don't believe that."

"That's okay. A healthy dose of skepticism is a good thing."

She made a strange scoffing sound and tapped the top of her coffee cup. "Oh, I know. Believe me."

They walked on in silence. Until Sabrina cleared her throat. "So, what have you been up to for the past…well, since I've seen you?"

He chuckled. "I don't actually think you're interested in that, Sabrina."

"I am interested in that, Liam. Do you know how you can tell? Because I asked. If I wasn't interested, I wouldn't have."

"Well. You have seen me a couple of times in Ace's bar, and you didn't ask me then. In fact, if memory serves, you just left."

"Right. Well, I remembered that I had somewhere else I wanted to be."

"Where?"

"Anywhere? Root canal?"

"Surprisingly, you're not the first woman to say she'd rather get a root canal then be around me."

Sabrina laughed, a short, somehow-unamused sound that was more than a little bit forced. "Well, I do hate to be unoriginal. Maybe not a root canal then. Maybe getting towed behind a fishing boat by my big toe?"

"That I haven't heard."

He didn't answer her question, and she didn't press. And then they had reached the end of the street, arriving at the vacant corner building he thought would be the ideal location for the showroom. They would catch most of the traffic as it came through Copper Ridge, and quite a bit of foot traffic too.

Anyone headed down to the beach would most likely come this way, and anyone headed out toward the winery itself, or to the town of Gold Valley, would pass through as well.

He could tell Sabrina all of that, but she was smart enough to figure it out on her own, and to see the advantages the location would bring to Grassroots. He had a feeling that any resistance she was putting up was just for the sake of it. Because she was still pissed at him. Which he had known, because of the aforementioned running out of the bar when she had seen him. Not that his own reaction had been neutral.

But that was the thing about her. The thing that he could never quite figure out.

He could forget women he'd had sex with. He had forgotten women he'd had sex with. More than once. He wasn't exactly proud of his behavior in that particular arena, but it was what it was.

And before Sabrina, he had never gotten close to a woman without getting naked with her. And even then, there had been a limited emotional connection. He had his reasons for that, and they were good reasons, in his opinion.

Still, Sabrina had defied everything he'd known about himself. At least, in the end that was what it had added up to.

He hadn't seen it coming. Not from the beginning. That was the important part. Meeting her hadn't felt like anything special at all. It had seemed safe. Easy. If he'd had any idea what his feelings for her would turn into, he would have pushed her away a hell of a lot sooner.

But then he probably wouldn't have gotten a full ride through school, so he supposed everything happened for a reason.

Still, he had not expected seeing her to feel like a punch in the chest. She had walked into Ace's, those beautiful blue eyes widening as they had met with his. Like a magnet. The moment she had walked in he had looked, and she had found him.

As if there was no space between them at all. As if there weren't thirteen years between them. Thirteen years and some hard decisions and some hurt.

And then, just like that, the moment had snapped in half, reality coming down on it like the fall of an ax. And she had run right out the door.

It had damn well ruined his night. He had been determined then that he was going to break the dry spell that he'd been in the midst of since he'd come back to the ranch. But then, of course, all he had been able to think of was Sabrina.

"This is it," he said, reaching into his pocket and pulling out the keys.

"Are we meeting Gage here?"

"Nope." He jammed the key into the lock and turned it. The lock was gold, ornate and old-fashioned. Not original to the building, he didn't think. But possibly from the 1930s. Which was an odd thing to be focusing on, but it was that or continue to ruminate on Sabrina.

He pushed the cranberry-colored door open and gestured for her to go in first. She did not. Instead, she stood there, staring at him.

"I got the keys from Gage last night. He said it was fine if we had a look around."

She was still staring at him.

"He's not a real estate agent," Liam said, walking into the building since it didn't seem like she was going to. "He has other things to do that don't entail hovering over us while we look around. Anyway, I thought you might appreciate the chance to speak freely."

He could tell by the tentative steps that Sabrina took inside that she had been hoping Gage West would be here to act as a buffer between them. Liam had been hoping for no such thing. He didn't want her to have a buffer. He didn't want a buffer at all.

He didn't need one. He was more than capable of dealing with the situation. Actually, he relished the chance to do this. Because he might have taken a deal a long time ago to stay away from Sabrina, but now, no man owned him. Least of all Jamison Leighton.

Which meant he could be here with her if he wanted to be. And actually, she was the one who had to play nice with him. The Leighton family didn't hold a single damn thing over his head anymore.

He turned a slow circle and looked around the room. It was clean and in good condition. There was no furniture in it of any kind. It was just big and empty. Picture windows looked out over Main Street and out toward the Chamber of Commerce, the Crab Shanty and, beyond that, the ocean.

It was the best of Copper Ridge, all visible there from the shop.

They would need a counter, some coolers and a seating area. But, given that they planned to keep everything simple, it should come together pretty quickly. He had done a lot more with less.

"It's perfect," he said.

And then, a moment later he realized his mistake. Because there was no way Sabrina was going to let this be that simple. If he had voiced a complaint, he would be much more likely to get her on board.

Her lips twitched, and then her left shoulder. "I don't know about that. And really, I think that Lindy should come and look at everything before we make decisions."

"I was under the impression that Lindy had enough on her plate, and that she wanted you to handle it."

He could see that Sabrina wasn't used to being challenged directly. It was another thing that was interesting about her. Another difference. When he had known her she had been a lot more open. Sweeter. A lot more likely to crumple if pressure was applied.

Now she might be more outwardly brittle, but he had a feeling it would take an iron squeeze to get her to crack.

And when she did… Yeah, he was afraid she would shatter. And he had no intention of shattering her. Messing with her a little bit while they worked on this project was one thing. But he wasn't a total dick.

"It's a big decision though," Sabrina said, "so, I think it's definitely something she should be a little more involved in, no matter what she might think now. Right now… She's just very focused. Very, very focused."

"On?"

"Making my brother sorry he crossed her, I think."

Liam frowned. "Yeah, what happened with that?" Lindy Parker hadn't been in the picture back when Liam had worked at Grassroots, so he had no idea about the history between her and Damien Leighton.

"He cheated on her," Sabrina said simply. "Ten years of marriage, and he had an affair. I'm not happy with my brother, Liam. Not at all. Lindy is like a sister to me, not just in law. Just because she and Damien got divorced doesn't mean my connection with her is gone."

"Hey, I'm all for a little revenge and retribution."

Sabrina's expression turned to stone. She was thinking about them again, and he knew it. He hardly thought it was fair for her to compare what he had done with what her brother had done to his wife. Because Liam had never cheated. Mostly because he had never made any promises.

"Go ahead," he said, crossing his arms over his chest.

"What?" she asked, blinking rapidly.

"Go ahead and yell at me. You want to. You're mad at me. I get it. So we can keep on tiptoeing around it, or you could just go ahead and shout at me. Here and now. The room is empty, and I bet it has great acoustics."

Sabrina's eye twitched. She looked…well, she looked completely torn. And a little bit shocked. Both like she really wanted to take him up on his offer, and like she was wishing there was some furniture she could scurry underneath.

"Okay. How about I go first?" If there was one thing

he didn't mind, it was facing something head-on. "I saw you naked, I turned you down and you're still mad."

"I... That is not... You make it sound like..."

He shrugged. "I'm going to go ahead and make it easy for you. I've seen a lot of women naked. Before you, after you. I'm not picturing you naked when I look at you now." That was a lie. But he didn't really mind lying either. "So whatever you imagine is happening on my end, it's not."

"You're an asshole," she said.

She turned away from him and began to pace the perimeter of the room, paying closer than necessary attention to things like crown molding.

"That's it?"

"I'm going to do exactly what we came here to do. Which is evaluate whether or not the building is suitable for our purposes. I wouldn't say that it's perfect," she said, giving him a hard glare. "But I suppose it will work."

"You're ready to do this, then?"

"I still think that Lindy should drive down and have a look before we confirm, but I can't imagine finding a better place." She seemed almost downtrodden about that. Probably because this had been his idea.

Actually, she was capitulating much more easily than he had imagined, and it occurred to him that it was probably because she just wanted to get this project moving so that she could put any interaction with him behind her.

"What's your timeline?"

She looked slightly sheepish. "Lindy wants it open before Christmas. She wants us up and running to take advantage of the festivities that are going to be happening around town. The sooner the better."

That would mean long, intense days in Sabrina's company. Whether she wanted that or not.

"We can do it," he said. "But you are very busy, so I hear. So, you need to clear your schedule a bit so you can actually devote your time to serving my needs."

The look she gave him was so dry it could've sapped all the moisture out of the heavy coastal air. "Poorly phrased. But then, I have a feeling you did it on purpose."

"And you're still not willing to clear the air between us."

"There's no air to clear. I don't feel comfortable around you, Liam, and I would think it was fairly understandable why. You humiliated me. You were cruel to me. At the very least, you should have treated me like a friend. Because even if I did have the wrong idea about what was happening between us, we were friends. I...I told you about my relationship with my father and you still... I trusted you."

Those simple words cut through every ounce of bullshit in him. He couldn't give her a hard time, not after that.

"We were *friends*," she reiterated. "I had a hard time connecting with people because of my family's position in the community, and you knew that. I got close to you, closer than I was to anyone. And I made a fool of myself in front of you and then you disappeared."

And when she found out exactly why, she wouldn't be any happier with him than she was now. So, he wasn't going to say a damned thing.

"I did," he said. "Because that's what I do. At least, that's what I did. But I've spent the past few years figuring out how to finish what I start. And I've done a good job with it. I'm still terrible with people, to be clear. The emotional part. But I know what I'm doing in business. And I'm going to make this successful. I promise you that."

"Are you going to apologize to me?"

In that moment, she looked like the Sabrina he had once known. Young, vulnerable and far too innocent for the likes of him. Like someone who actually believed that he was going to apologize. He almost felt bad.

Almost.

"I'm not going to apologize," he said. "Because leaving you like that was probably one of the nicest things I've ever done. Because if I hadn't left you then, I would have left you after. And I stand by what I said."

Her cheeks turned scarlet, rage glittering in her blue eyes. "Right. Well, it's emblazoned in my memory. So, there's no reason to revisit it."

"What exactly are you mad about? That I didn't have sex with you? Or that I left?"

She sputtered. "That you… That you *left*. That you left and you didn't say anything to me. I cared about you."

"And you're still mad at me."

"Not every day of my life. But having you come back to town has been awkward."

"Well, I never imagined I would end up back here either. But here I am."

"Because of the ranch?"

"Yes and no. I never intended to come back. Not even with part ownership of the ranch on the table. I had a big job. I liked what I was doing. Until one day I realized that I actually didn't."

"Is that what happened with us? You were my friend until one day you realized you weren't?"

"I was twenty years old, and I was an asshole. That's about it."

She looked...deflated by that.

"*Was*, as in past tense? As in you aren't one now?"

He could tell she really didn't want to let go of her anger. "I still am. But I would probably call before leaving town now." That was a lie. He absolutely would not. And particularly not under those circumstances.

She looked begrudgingly amused. "Well, as long as we both know the score. Which is the real difference between now and thirteen years ago."

"Which is exactly why I'm not the villain that you seem to think I am," he said. "Because you didn't know the score, Sabrina, and I didn't take advantage of that."

"Fine. Let's let it go then, okay? I'm Sabrina Leighton, I work for Grassroots Winery. It has recently changed hands and is under new ownership, and I am helping the new owner realize her vision."

"Liam Donnelly," he said, sticking out his hand. She shook it reluctantly, those delicate fingers curling around his, and it shocked him how visceral the response was to that contact with her. "I've been living in cities for the past thirteen years. Chicago, mostly New York. I had what was arguably an early midlife crisis and decided to take my inheritance and live in a small town. But, apparently, I can't just get used to ranching work, so I decided to take on this venture. Something to keep me busy. Idle hands are the devil's workshop." He released his hold on her. "Or so I hear."

She didn't say anything, but he noticed that when she lowered her hand back to her side she brushed her fingers against her pencil skirt, as if she was trying to wipe the impression of his touch off her. "That's very interesting. And it seems like we should be able to work well together."

He looked around the space. "I think we should. So, leaning toward this place?"

"Yes," she confirmed. "I'll see if Lindy can come down and have a look. Can I hang on to the keys? So that I can open it up when she has time?"

"I don't know," he said. "Gage gave them to me."

"Come on. Do you honestly think he'll care?"

He smiled and then held the keys out. "No."

She took them, quickly, being careful not to make any contact with him this time. "I'll let you know what she says. I'm guessing she'll be on board. And once she is we can start making plans. We're going to need shelving and…"

"Seating. Refrigeration. Yeah, I have a fair idea. How elaborate is the menu going to be?"

"For now? Nibbles only."

"Nibbles?"

She raised a brow. "Yes. Nibbles."

"Okay. I suggest we maybe don't call them that on the menu."

"We call them that at the winery."

"What's wrong with *appetizers*?"

"Look, Donnelly, you can name your cheese whatever you want to name your cheese. But this is primarily a Grassroots venture. We are going to own most of it. Controlling share and stuff. So, I get to call them nibbles."

"If you want to die on the hill of nibbles, be my guest."

"I do, thank you. Surrounded by nice cheese platters."

"Now, where cheese platters are concerned, I think we are on the same page."

"Have you ever done this before? I mean, restaurants. Or, things like this."

"No. Not specifically. But hotels, and there were restaurants in the hotel. So while I didn't oversee food service specifically, I've definitely seen what works and what doesn't. Though I'm sure that what works in Manhattan won't necessarily be the gauge for what works in Copper Ridge. And there, you get to be the expert."

"Because I'm so exceedingly local?"

"Yes."

"Why does that not feel like a compliment?"

"I don't know," he said. "Sounds like your baggage to me."

She snorted. "All right. I'll get in touch with you once Lindy gives her opinion."

She moved past him, and he caught the scent of her. Vanilla. Just like always. And suddenly, he was thrown back to a different time, to warmer days...

He shook his head, ignoring the tightening in his gut.

"Do that."

The sooner she did that, the sooner they could get started. And the sooner they got started, the sooner they could be done.

CHAPTER FOUR

MUCH TO SABRINA'S CHAGRIN, Lindy was ecstatic when they arrived at the shop later that afternoon. It was perfect as far as she was concerned, everything about it. She had absolutely no qualms and was ready to get the ball rolling immediately.

It was funny, because Lindy seemed to be fueled by her enthusiasm to make the winery a complete and total success and throw in Damien's face the fact that she didn't need him at all, and that in fact, she could do more without him around.

Sabrina, on the other hand, was fueled by something altogether different and that was her desire to work with Liam and emerge unscathed. She felt like she was continually reevaluating that situation. At first, she had wanted to avoid him, but if avoidance was the primary goal then it was difficult to make the case that she was all right. Difficult to make the case that she had moved on in any regard.

Not that she had ever pretended she had. Not to herself. And to other people? She just didn't talk about it.

Maybe *moved on* was the wrong phrase. It was just… She didn't trust herself. Her father had always told her to be cautious. To lead with her head, and not with her heart.

Back when he'd talked to her.

He had said that passion was faulty, and feelings were lies. And she had worked so hard to comply with that. To be quiet so that she could spend time with her dad, since he couldn't handle endless chattering. To be the one who took after him. Not like Damien, who was always volatile like their mother.

She had rebelled once.

The first time she'd set eyes on Liam Donnelly—when he'd come to work at the winery—she'd been sure her chest would crack open and her heart would spill right out in front of him. Like every feeling, every need, every desire she'd shoved down all of her life had risen up to the surface and begged for release.

And then he'd looked at her. She had been certain, utterly certain, that he was the first person to truly see her.

She had known it was wrong. But he made her feel *right*, and after so many years of feeling like an alien in her own body, vying for her father's attention the only way she knew how, it was magical to her.

Until the end. The end when everything had fallen apart, and then she'd set about to make everything around her as wrecked as she'd felt inside.

But it was over. She wasn't that girl anymore. She really never had been. She'd had a moment of insanity, and that was done and never happening again.

Sabrina was going to handle being around him now. She was not going to give her sister-in-law any extra grief. Lindy had had enough. She didn't need to deal with Sabrina's baggage on top of everything else. Especially since Sabrina's baggage was…well, stupid in a lot of ways, she supposed. Nothing was worse than having Liam confront her with what had happened between them. With him making her voice everything.

Because it made what had happened between them feel small. And in her mind it was so large. But she was reluctant to admit that he had a point. It wasn't like the situation would have been any better if he had slept with her and then disappeared.

But that was the worst part, actually. It was the part that was so hard to explain to people, including him. Maybe especially him, because if she did it would make her sound even more like she was a pet-boiling whack job.

The lingering tenderness made sense to her though. And it hurt all the way down. She had trusted him with all of herself, and more than that, she had trusted in her own feelings for him. They had been wrong.

And that was the bitterest pill to swallow.

That the one time she'd decided to believe in herself, to trust her gut, her gut had been nothing more than a fluttery case of hormonal butterflies.

"This is amazing," Lindy said, walking slowly across the wooded floor, her high heels clicking on the surface.

Sabrina pressed her fingertips against the door, right where Liam had put his hand earlier. She pulled it back.

"It is," she said, stepping inside after her sister-in-law.

They had brought along the other tasting room employee, Olivia Logan, who was a funny little woman even though Sabrina quite liked her. She was a prim creature, with a lot of very lofty ideas about right and wrong, and sometimes got a little too judgmental for her own good, but she'd become a good friend to Sabrina over the years.

"This will be too far for me to drive every day," Olivia commented, sniffing.

"It's fine," Lindy said. "Nobody will expect you to

come down here. You're welcome to continue working up at the winery. But, just in case, I did want you to come down and see it. Because I want everyone to feel like they have input."

Lindy almost overinvolved the winery staff in her decision-making, in Sabrina's opinion. Though she knew the whole "we are all in this together" thing was kind of part and parcel with her gaining control over the winery.

Damien had been much more about it being a Leighton family business. And only Leightons got a say in what happened. Her family was all about their standing in the community, all about their money.

Perhaps that was one reason she was sympathetic toward Olivia, even when she was a little bit difficult.

Olivia Logan was a member of the founding family of the county. The Logan family had been here since the 1800s, the first to settle both Gold Valley and Copper Ridge. They had come from Independence, Missouri on the Oregon Trail. And Olivia still carried their name.

Sabrina didn't have a famous name, but she knew how family pride, a lot of interest and concern with family reputation and standing could shape you.

And what happened when you demolished said reputation.

Of course, Damien hadn't exactly helped the reputation. But she'd always had the feeling their dad didn't expect as much from Damien as he had from her once upon a time. As if he was given a pass because he was never supposed to do well. Sabrina knew her dad felt like the fact that Lindy had ended up with the winery was ample evidence that their son had made a mistake marrying outside of his class. That she had somehow taken advantage of him.

Sabrina just hadn't been able to understand their take on it. Not in the least. Not when Damien was the one who couldn't keep his dick in his pants.

Knowing what she did about her parents' marriage made it all the more confusing in some ways, though not in others. Because what her dad believed in above all else was doing the right thing to avoid making waves. And that was where Lindy had sinned.

She had made a tsunami when she'd discovered her husband's affair. And after the ground had dried from the storm, she'd left it scorched in her wake. She hadn't just gotten mad, she'd gotten it all.

That unchecked emotion was what Sabrina imagined really irked her dad.

Sabrina hadn't been able to imagine a scenario where she cut off a relationship with Lindy to preserve the fractured one she had with her mom and dad. So the choice—and she'd had to make a choice—had been pretty clear. What had surprised her was that Bea had ultimately sided with Lindy. It was possible that Bea's attachment to Dane had played a role in all of it, but she doubted that her parents paid close enough attention to understand that.

"That's nice," Olivia said. "I mean it. It's nice to feel part of something."

Sabrina often wondered if Olivia didn't feel much a part of her life in Gold Valley. Even though she had a boyfriend that she loved, she always seemed somewhat lonely. Distant. She was a funny, repressed little bird.

"I think that we can make this something," Lindy said, turning a circle in the large, vacant room and holding her hands out. "It's like girl power."

"No one has said girl power since 1996," Sabrina said, but she couldn't help but smile.

"*I'm* saying it," Lindy said, slapping her hands down at her sides. "Because I feel it. Because I'm optimistic."

It was nice to see Lindy smile like that. Nice to see her excited. Nice to not see her heartbroken by Sabrina's douchebag brother.

"I'm glad," Sabrina said.

"I notice you didn't say you're optimistic too," Lindy said.

"It's not my *job* to be optimistic, Lindy," Sabrina said. "It's my job to make it happen. You don't want optimism from me anyway. You want realism. Active realism."

"Okay, my little active realist." Lindy reached out and patted her shoulder. "Can you get everything accomplished in time for us to take advantage of the holidays?"

"I think we can," Sabrina responded. "I think we can and we will. Because I'm determined."

And because it regrettably seemed like Liam Donnelly knew what he was doing. Though, Sabrina supposed that since she did have to have her wagon hitched to him, it was best that he be a competent wagon partner. Because if she had to work with him and he sucked, it would be untenable.

Realizing he had grown into an adult man who was responsible, smart and resourceful was goading in other ways.

She was going to focus on the business aspect though. And from a business standpoint, Liam was exactly who she should want to work with. And really, what better way to strike back at Liam? To show him how competent and amazing she was.

She had just thought earlier that she and Lindy had

different goals. That Lindy wanted to do this to stick it to Damien, and that Sabrina just wanted it done to get away from Liam.

But they were more similar than she had initially imagined.

Why not use this as an opportunity to show him that she was a kick-ass woman and not a *girl* he could just walk away from while she wept on the floor of the cabin he'd been staying in on the winery property.

"We can even get a Christmas tree. Christmas lights. It will be festive. The most festive grand opening Copper Ridge has ever seen!" Lindy said.

"Wait," Olivia said, looking suddenly envious. "I kind of want to work here if there's going to be a Christmas tree."

"I'm sure we can schedule you for a shift. I bet Bennett won't mind coming down to pick you up and see the new location."

Olivia smiled. "You're right about that. And I'm thinking he might even propose before Christmas. So that means he could do it here. It would be so picturesque. The photo you would, of course, take of the moment would be so perfect."

Sabrina exchanged a glance with Lindy, and in that wordless exchange, Sabrina could tell that her sister-in-law thought much the same thing about Olivia's boyfriend. That the proposal was likely not as forthcoming as the other woman hoped.

Still, neither of them said anything.

Lindy walked across the space, rubbing her hands together. "This is what I've always dreamed of doing. And Damien wouldn't consider it. Not at all. He wouldn't entertain any of my ideas." She shot Sabrina a glance. "I'm sorry. I know he's your brother."

"Yeah, he's my brother. But you know that I'm mad at him for what he did. You know that I don't support him. I love him, I always will. But I can't be comfortable around him and that woman. Whatever her name is." Sabrina knew Brandy's name. But she didn't like to acknowledge it. Especially not in front of Lindy.

She could tell Lindy appreciated that. Even if she knew it was a put-on.

"Thank you. But you know it's not like you have to choose between the two of us. I'm actually just happy that you still want to be in my life at all."

"Family is about more than blood," Sabrina said.

It was a difficult thing for families like hers, families like Olivia Logan's, to acknowledge anything other than blood. But everything she'd been through in the last thirteen years had taught her that blood really wasn't the be-all and end-all. It wasn't even half of it.

"You know," Olivia said, her expression turning mischievous—a side of her Sabrina thought she didn't express enough. "Instead of putting up the first dollar we earn here at the tasting room, we could always put up a picture of your divorce papers. Since the loss of Damien is what made this possible in the end."

Both Sabrina and Lindy let out a shocked laugh. "I suppose we could do that," Lindy said. "Oh, your parents would have a fit."

"Don't worry." Sabrina waved a hand. "You know that Jamison and Suzanne Leighton are never going to darken the door of this establishment. They have washed their hands of the winery and all it entails."

"Unless they can get ownership back somehow. You

know your parents' lawyer called me again the other day. Asking if I was interested in selling."

Sabrina's mouth dropped open. "I'm completely shocked that my parents would broach the subject of buying something they believe is rightfully theirs."

"They probably shouldn't have given full ownership to Damien in the first place. And he shouldn't have signed that prenup." The corner of Lindy's mouth lifted. "Not that I'm sorry about any of it. But why on earth he decided that in the event of infidelity the wronged party would get most of the assets is beyond me."

"Well," Sabrina said, lifting her shoulder. "You are the *undesirable* one. I mean, the one from the wrong side of the tracks. I'm sure that he assumed you would be the one to stray. Or that you wouldn't be smart enough to know that he had."

Lindy snorted. "Right. Of course. How could I forget that pedigreed Damien Leighton would never be so foolish as to get caught with his penis in the wrong honey jar."

The color heightened in Olivia's cheeks. "That's descriptive."

Lindy smiled. "I can be much more descriptive if the occasion calls for it. Believe me."

"I trust you," Olivia said, holding up a hand.

Then they all stood there for a moment, taking in their surroundings, and Sabrina suddenly felt wholly optimistic. Perhaps it was the vision of this place bedecked in Christmas decorations. Perhaps it was just being here with these women, determined to accomplish something. Whatever the reason, it didn't feel as hard as it had earlier today. Right now, it felt possible. More than possible.

Liam Donnelly thought that he knew her. But he knew

an insecure girl who had been easily wounded by his rejection. She wasn't that girl anymore, and she wasn't going to allow being around him to make her backslide. No. It was time for her to take a step forward. Time to shake it off, and all that.

She was going to make sure this was the best damn opening any business had ever had in the town of Copper Ridge. She was going to knock Liam Donnelly on his ass—metaphorically—with her awesomeness.

And if he was the one who left with a sense of unfulfilled longing after all this? All the better.

CHAPTER FIVE

"DON'T YOU LOOK FANCY!"

Liam looked over at his sister-in-law, Alison, and lifted a brow as he simultaneously raised his coffee cup to his lips. "Unlike your husband, I know how to dress for the venue."

Alison smiled and looked over at Cain, who was currently scowling into his coffee. "If I had occasion to put on a monkey suit I would. In fact, I believe I even wore a tie when I married you, woman," he said.

"Under such extreme sufferance you would have thought that I was asking you to put on a tie and then place your testicles in a jar for me to keep under my bed."

Cain snorted. "Well. We both know that's not true."

"I keep them in my purse," Alison said, grinning widely at Liam.

"Great. I feel much better now that I know the location of my older brother's testicles. Why aren't you two at your own house?"

"There's an extremely teenage music situation happening," Alison said. "Apparently, someone has late classes today."

Liam grimaced. It was difficult for him to believe sometimes that his older brother had a daughter who was closer to being an adult than being a child. Considering the fact that Liam was not in a headspace to ever consider having children at all.

"A paperwork situation is about to be happening with me, so I'm not entirely sure that it's better than being exposed to pop music." It was only eight forty-five, but as far as Liam was concerned it was getting late. He and his brothers got up so early to take care of the ranch every day that it was a routine now.

At first, it had fully kicked his ass. He was used to a fairly early routine, but not getting up and outside by five. Now... After all this time, it was just part of life.

A life that felt tangible in a way his previous life had not. And yeah, he pretty much did think of them as two separate lives. When all was said and done, Liam Donnelly felt like he had lived quite a few lives. One of them, once upon a time, had been in Copper Ridge. Had been working at Grassroots Winery. Had involved Sabrina Leighton. And somehow, Sabrina Leighton was involved again.

Just thinking about her made his gut tight. Unfinished business. That's what it was. Because he hadn't slept with her back then, and it made him wonder what he had been missing. Especially considering the degree to which she had wormed her way under his skin without him ever getting inside of her.

A subtle thing. A closeness that had occurred in inches. With each bit of confidence and trust she had put in him. He had never told her much about his life, about his past. But he'd let her talk about her own.

About how hard she found it to have friends. How it was tough for her to relate to other girls her age because they were allowed to go to parties and stay out and she wasn't. There was something about that. About her isolation, her vulnerability that he'd related to.

He sure as hell had never expected to relate to a sweet little rich girl from the right side of the tracks. And yet he had.

"I have to go." He stood up and nodded once at Alison and Cain before heading out of the kitchen and toward the front door.

He grabbed a black cowboy hat from the peg by the door and pressed it onto his head. There was a strange sense of rightness that settled down to his bones as he did that. As he walked out onto the deck wearing a pair of black jeans, boots, button-up shirt and a black tie. Of course, to his older brother, that was a monkey suit. It made Liam laugh.

It was a far cry from the custom suits he had once worn, but he figured that this was dressing up for a cowboy. Farmer. Rancher. Whatever the hell he was these days.

The hat itself was not custom-made. He had bought it at the Farm and Garden when he had come to town. But in a great many ways it felt a lot more made for him than one of those suits ever had.

He got into his truck and fired up the engine, heading down the long gravel driveway toward the main road that would take him into town. And the whole way he wondered what mood he would find Sabrina in. Whether or not she would have her pretty pink lips pursed together in irritation already. In anticipation of his arrival. Anticipation of having to deal with him.

And he wondered if her blond hair would be pulled back in a prim little bun. If she would be wearing one of those pencil skirts that he imagined was supposed to be demure, but instead put him in the mind of pushing it up her hips, or grabbing hold of the zipper and working it down, leaving it in a heap of demolished modesty on the floor of his bedroom.

He had not let himself have fantasies like this about her thirteen years ago. No way in hell. At least he hadn't indulged them.

But she was a woman now, not a seventeen-year-old girl. So all bets were off.

He wasn't going to do anything about it, of course. Same as back then. Because while she might be a grown woman, she was still off-limits. They needed to get through this business venture with minimal drama.

It felt right. Being here. Wearing the cowboy hat, and heading to the bank to sign a stack of mortgage documents that was probably about as tall as he was. Like he had finally found some way to reconcile the pieces of himself. To repair the parts of him that had been deeply uncomfortable and always displaced living in major cities. And to deal with that restless, unsatisfied part of him that had felt trapped in small towns.

He had gotten an opportunity to better himself, and he had taken it. To become something more. To add layers of importance to himself. To get all the money and status that his mother had sure as hell been convinced would have made her happy. Rather than her children.

And then, he had happily written her a check so she would finally shut the hell up.

He had taken immense satisfaction from the fact that he had been the one to provide her that money. He, the one who had been responsible for her sad, stale life, as far as she was concerned. Her most hated son. The one who had been beneath her notice at the best of times, going without food and water for extended periods. And the one who had been subject to her expressions of rage at other times.

But it didn't matter. Not now. He had made good. He had gotten his own back.

Life was pretty damn good, all things considered.

On that note, he pulled into the parking lot of Copper Ridge Credit Union and killed the engine on his truck. He recognized Sabrina's little silver car in the lot already. It was very her. Sleek, contained. Then he wondered what had happened to that pretty, reckless girl he had once known who ran barefoot and let her blond hair fly free.

You happened to her, you asshole, or have you not listened to anything she's said to you?

He snorted. Listening had never been his strong suit.

Sabrina chose that exact moment to pop out the front door of the bank, her expression tight and her hand wrapped around a Styrofoam cup that was steaming, and full of coffee he assumed.

Bank coffee was not his favorite.

"There you are," she said. "You're late."

He lifted his arm and looked at his watch. "Like two minutes late. Are they waiting?"

"No," she said. "But I was."

She turned sharply and went back into the building, and he shook his head as he followed her in.

The credit union building was new, at least new to him. With high ceilings and glossy floors. It was much larger and a bit fancier than anything he typically ascribed to the aesthetic of Copper Ridge. Though, there was also a touch of that rustic Oregon flair in the wooden crossbeams on the ceiling, and the supports throughout the lobby area. There were large windows that made the most of the view of the rocks, scrubby pines and the ocean out back.

The mist was clinging to the top of the gray waves today, the sky blending into the water.

And Sabrina stood out in bright contrast to that.

She surprised him today, wearing a pair of black pants that conformed to her slender legs, bright pink shoes and a neutral-colored sweater. Her blond hair was up. He hadn't seen it down once since he had come back.

It made his fingers itch.

He found the coffee station and decided to make himself a cup, even though it involved powdered creamer. It was something to do. Something other than reaching up and taking Sabrina's hair out of its bun.

He imagined that he probably shouldn't harass her right before they went in to sign paperwork. He should wait until after. When it was too late for her to pull out.

He had already faxed over all the legal agreements for the business partnership, and they had been signed by Lindy. For this, Sabrina would be signing on behalf of the winery.

"Have you ever done this before?" he asked.

She jerked, like he had shocked her with a cattle prod. "I'm sorry, what?"

"Have you ever signed mortgage documents?"

"Yes. I bought a house four years ago."

"Good." That kind of surprised him. He wasn't sure what he had expected. That she lived on the winery property, or that she perhaps still lived with her parents. Which was ridiculous, considering she was thirty years old.

But rich girls like her, they often did continue living

with their parents. At least, in his head they did. Otherwise, they were sent to some fancy school by their parents. And then subsequently had their housing paid for.

"Where did you go to school?"

She looked at him blankly. "What?"

He realized that he had skipped a step with her. But in his head it had made sense. "School. I was just wondering where you went to college."

"Oh. Just… I went to Oregon State."

"I figured you would go somewhere a little bit…bigger of a deal."

"It's a great school," she said, visibly bristling. "Go Ducks."

It was fine enough, he was sure. But he had gone to a top-ranked university with her father's money. He had assumed that she would do nothing less.

"I figured that you would go somewhere further afield," he said. "That's all."

She stiffened. "Things change."

"All right. I guess that's true. So, what kind of house do you have?"

"What, is this interrogate Sabrina hour?"

"In fairness, it's basically interrogate Sabrina five minutes. Hour is vastly dramatizing the situation."

"Have you ever bought a house?" she asked, clearly looking to turn the spotlight onto him.

"Not a house. But a penthouse. New York City."

She blinked rapidly, her pale eyebrows knitting together. "But those cost…millions of dollars."

He just let the implication of that hang between them, and watched as her skin went slightly waxen.

"Grassroots Winery and Laughing Irish?" An older

woman with dark hair peeked out of one of the glass corner offices with a smile pasted on her face.

"That's us," Liam confirmed.

For some reason—instinct, something—he reached out and pressed his palm against Sabrina's lower back to guide her toward the office. She stopped dead in her tracks, her gaze sliding over to him, irritation glittering sharply there.

"Do you touch men you're doing business deals with like that? Because I'll tell you, that's some mental image."

"No," he said, lowering his hand slowly.

"I don't mind a little *Brokeback Mountain* fantasy, Liam."

"After you," he said, waiting for her to walk into the office before he followed behind her.

It had been a stupid thing to do, touching her like that. Normally, he would never do something so asinine with the woman he was doing a business deal with. He would normally never do that with anyone.

There was just something about Sabrina that pushed him to do things he was usually way too smart to do.

They took a seat at the table with the banker and with another person who was introduced as the notary. Gage West had apparently signed his end of the deal already.

The stack of papers was indeed massive, and both Liam and Sabrina were given pens before the banker handed him the first page, which Sabrina promptly took. "We're the first name on the documents, as we own a larger portion," she said crisply.

She signed quickly next to a sticky tab, then passed the paper back to him. As if it mattered which order they signed in as long as they signed on the right spot. But he could tell she was compelled to make an issue out of it, so he was going to let it go.

They carried out the signing in relative silence, the only real conversation happening when the banker explained a page that he was certain both he and Sabrina already understood, but that she was legally bound to verbally expound on.

Sabrina passed one paper to him, and he pressed his fingertips down on it, brushing the tips of them against hers. She jerked back, trying to look composed as she moved on to signing the next document.

"There," the woman said, smiling through the tension that was making the air crackle, "all finished. Congratulations. You are now the proud owners of some very nice property."

"Thank you," Sabrina said. "I hope that you'll come down for the grand opening. There's going to be wine, cheese and all manner of festivities."

"Definitely," the banker said, and Liam really couldn't tell if she was being genuine, or if there was just no other polite response to give.

Considering they had just signed a considerable amount of their lives over to this establishment, she did have to be polite.

Well, it was a considerable amount of Grassroots' life, and Lindy's, he imagined. It wasn't so much to him. Even if Finn was being adamant that it all be paid for with Donnelly ranch money, and not Liam's.

As they walked out of the bank, Sabrina still had a large, fake-looking smile plastered on her face. But as soon as the glass door closed behind them, she chucked the Styrofoam cup of coffee in the trash beside the building. "That was disgusting coffee."

He grimaced and sent his cup the same direction. "Agreed."

"Well, I need more coffee. Better coffee. So I'm going to head down to The Grind and grab some, and then I'm going to go to the shop."

"I'll go with you."

She looked...not shocked, but a little bit like she wanted to argue. "I don't really have any plans. I just want to make a quick sketch of the floor plan so that I can get a rough idea of what we need to get, and you know, layouts and things."

"Right. Do you have a tape measure, anything on you?"

"I can buy one," she said, looking mulish.

"I have a toolbox in the back of my truck. Why don't you ride down with me?"

He knew that she was annoyed. And he also knew that she would rather ride with him than protest. Because he could tell that she was caught between wanting to spend less time with him and wanting to act like it didn't matter.

For his part, he wasn't really sure why he cared either way.

Really? You don't know why you care?

As if his stomach didn't clench tight when he smelled vanilla, which was a scent that he had always associated with her. Like he hadn't quit a job because he'd worked closely with a woman who shared her name, and he couldn't hear it without thinking of her and that devastated expression on her face when he'd left her that night.

As if he didn't have a tattoo on his body that was dedicated to her.

He could admit that now. He had been in pretty deep

denial even when he had gotten the ink. But, as it had taken shape, as he had laid out what he had wanted, it was pretty hard for him to deny that the barefoot blond figure that rested beneath the tree that stretched over his shoulder and around to his back wasn't inspired by her. That she wasn't the picture in his mind when he'd thought of it in the first place.

"Great. Let's go. I suppose I should be grateful for you and your tape measure."

She stepped gingerly toward his truck and got into the passenger seat without waiting for him. He hadn't bothered to lock it. There wasn't really much point in Copper Ridge.

He jerked the driver side door open and got in, starting up the engine. "Yeah, you probably should be a lot more grateful for me than you are."

They pulled out of the lot and headed back into town. There was one lone spot that he was able to parallel park in just in front of The Grind.

"Two hour parking," he commented as he got out and rounded her side. "We could walk from here." He finished that sentence when she hopped out onto the sidewalk.

"Sure," she said. "If you want to lug your tools all the way down there."

"I think I can handle it."

He held the door open for her, but this time, did not put his hand anywhere on her body. She said nothing, but walked into the café in front of him. They got in line together, and he could tell that she was annoyed that they were together in public, and not just running into each other by happenstance.

"What's your poison?" he asked.

"Just a coffee."

"That's not at all exciting."

"You don't find a strong jolt of bitter caffeine exciting? I do."

He laughed. "I suppose I do. A little more exciting with a double shot of espresso poured over the top."

When they got up to the front he ordered just that, and then ordered her regular coffee. She glared at him as he got his wallet out and paid. "What?"

"I didn't say you could buy me a coffee."

"I don't recall asking you."

The girl behind the counter handed them their order with a slightly glum expression on her face. Sabrina snatched her coffee out of his hand and headed over to the cream and sugar station.

"I hope you're happy," she commented, pouring a little bit of cream and a packet of sugar into her cup and stirring. "You've broken that little girl's heart."

"That little girl?" he asked, gesturing back toward the counter.

"Yes."

"First of all, she's like five years younger than you. Second of all, why? Because she thinks I'm with you?"

"You bought my coffee."

"Well. I was unaware that was small-town symbolism for a marriage proposal. I thought that you still had to give a couple of oxen to get a woman. I didn't know you could get her with one cup of coffee."

She laughed reluctantly, and the two of them walked out of The Grind and onto the rain-soaked sidewalk.

Sabrina looked both ways, and didn't bother to go to the crosswalk. She just did half a jog across the street, conveniently forgetting the lecture she'd recently given him on the dangers of walking with hot beverages, and he followed.

They walked past his sister-in-law Lane's Mercantile, full of specialty foods, and then past Pie in the Sky, his sister-in-law Alison's bakery, which was now across the street from them.

"Main Street is becoming quite the Donnelly affair," he commented.

"The tasting room is not primarily Donnelly," she said. "Not that there's anything wrong with it being part Donnelly, I suppose."

"Sure, sure." He smiled at her, and she looked away from him.

He shook his head.

They rounded the corner to the front of their new store and Sabrina produced the keys. "Officially ours," she said, jingling them before jamming the key into the lock. "After you."

She held the door for him and he went in ahead of her.

She pulled a pad of paper out of her purse and paced around the room studying their surroundings. "So, we've already figured a few things out. But, we need to figure out how much seating we can put in here versus floor space, and of course there needs to be a bit of space for preparation. And for merchandise."

"Great. I'll do some measurements and we can do a little Googling to figure out how big some refrigerated display cases are and standard table sizes."

"Thank God for smartphones," Sabrina commented.

He chuckled, setting his toolbox down and taking out his tape measure. "I hear that. We didn't really have those last time you and I hung out."

She snorted. "I guess not."

"It's funny," he said. "All the things that have changed. That credit union for example. The building was not like that when I lived here."

"They built a new one about six years ago," she said.

"And another example. Your brother has been married and divorced," he said.

"Yes. Dramatically. And of course, the ownership of the winery has changed."

"True. And if it hadn't, you wouldn't have to work with me. Because there's no way in hell your father would have let me in on a venture involving his precious winery."

It was her turn to laugh, an icy sound. "Well, if the ownership of the winery hadn't changed you wouldn't be working with me anyway. I mean, I wouldn't be here. It would be a moot point."

He frowned. "What?"

"I've only been back at the winery for two years."

"Really?"

"Yes. I've been doing other things. Worked in banking for a while. I managed a bed-and-breakfast in Gold Valley and then I managed the hospitality portion of a dude ranch there called Get Out of Dodge. That's where I met Olivia Logan. I'm not sure if you've met her yet. She works at Grassroots. She used to work at the same ranch that I did, but they scaled back when the owner had a heart attack. Quit taking as many guests and running as many touristy things."

"You did all that just for...for fun?"

Her shoulders twitched, and her face went tight. "What do we have so far?"

"For what?" he asked, frowning.

"For the dining area. How many tables and chairs?"

He gestured toward the picture windows. "Two with two chairs here. And maybe we can do one with four chairs here. Probably five or six additional tables here in the center of the room. But we need to keep enough space available for the wine."

"Right. Right. I'm thinking of talking to somebody around town who might have an idea of where we can get shelving made. Something that's a little artisanal…"

"You can talk to Lane. But don't think I didn't notice that you derailed the conversation. Why haven't you been working at the winery?" he asked.

"It's been thirteen years since you were back in town, Liam. Did you really think I was only going to have one job for my entire life?"

"Hell no. Not for one second. But I also figured that you would go to some big East Coast school. And I certainly didn't think you would have come back to the winery after it had passed out of your parents' control. What does your dad think of that?"

"He thinks poorly of it," she said stiffly. "But that's fine. He thinks poorly of me."

Liam huffed out a laugh. "Now that isn't true. Your dad thinks you're everything. Believe me."

"Right. Is that some coded reference to the fact that he paid you to leave?"

Liam felt as though he had been punched in the stomach. "You…"

"I know. I know why you left. I know that my father offered you money to leave. You didn't just run away because my naked breasts offended you. In hindsight, I was never sure if it was better or worse that you had an incentive." She swallowed hard. "I have to say, it's actually good to know that you did something with that."

"That I did something with what your father gave to me?"

"Yes. Because whatever we were about... Our friendship, whatever you want to call it... If you were going to sell it, Liam, I'm glad that you got something out of it. I'm glad you went to school. Not because I'm happy for you, but because at least I know I got traded for something bigger than a really fast car that you were just going to crash in the end, or something."

"I already told you that what I did was a kindness to you. You were seventeen years old, Sabrina." He crossed his arms and watched her. She was agitated, her shoulders twitching, her lips pressed into a thin line.

"Right. Right. And you were protecting me from your big bad penis. I know. And you know what? Maybe if you had just left I would believe that. But you took a payoff, and then you left. Mostly, I think that my virginity wasn't worth however many thousands of dollars my father paid you. I think that for you sex was cheap, so you might as well go have it with someone else with a flush bank account. Why not? But you know what, it doesn't matter anymore. Because I don't regret that we didn't...you know. I just don't. But I don't need you up on any high horses about it."

"Why did I end up at the big university and you didn't? I swear to God, if that bastard gave me your money..."

She looked stunned. By his anger, but he didn't know why. As if he didn't have any conscience at all? Yeah, he hadn't been the nicest guy where she was concerned. Or in general, but he didn't think he was entitled to money that had been earmarked for her education. No way in hell. If he had been told that, he wouldn't have taken it. Bottom line.

"No. That's not what happened. My family had more than enough money to send you, me and a few Dickensian street urchins to the university of our choosing. My father and I had a falling-out after you left."

She looked so arch, so stiff when she said the words. And at the same time, so immeasurably fragile. He wanted to reach out and touch her. Not the way that he had done earlier in the day, unthinkingly placing his hand on her lower back. Even if he wasn't in the habit of doing that with women, it was still something of a generic touch.

No. He wanted to trace the line of her high cheekbones, down the edge of her jaw, to explore the changes in her face.

The new hollows in her cheeks, the slight little crinkles at the corners of her eyes. To learn the thirteen years he'd missed through touch, as well as through talking to her.

She had always made him want things like that. Things he didn't understand. Things he had certainly never wanted with anyone else.

Liam had not been…chaste. Not in the last decade, and certainly not before. But Sabrina had never been about sex. At least, not entirely.

"What happened?"

"It doesn't matter," she said.

"The hell it doesn't. Your father is a puppet master," he said. "If he can't control it, he doesn't like it."

She shook her head. "No. What I did wasn't okay."

"What did you do?" he repeated the question.

She closed her eyes, looking pained. "I got drunk

and shouted something… Something I shouldn't have. In front of the most influential people in the county."

"What did you say?"

She met his gaze, looking somewhat defeated. "Oh. I just revealed to all in attendance that my mother was having an affair."

CHAPTER SIX

SABRINA WAS MAD at herself for telling him any of this. She was mad at herself for walking into this discussion. For letting him know that she had made herself vulnerable like that, that she had been so affected by losing him.

But honestly, she had been angry at herself for thirteen years. For detonating a bomb in her life because she had lost what she could see now was simply a crush. At the time, it had felt like love. Destroyed, broken love. As if her heart had been pulled out of her chest, still beating, and dashed to the rocks to be pounded by the surf. No one had ever suffered as she had, she had been certain.

It hadn't just been about love. She had been taught at her father's knee not to give trust. Not to friends or anyone. To hold her emotions close. To keep walls in place to stay protected, and she'd done that. With everyone but him.

When she'd lost him, she'd not only lost the man she'd fallen in love with, she'd lost her first real friend. The only person who knew all of those things about her. How hard she tried to please her father. How she felt continually caught in the middle of being a good daughter and trying to fit in with friends. Trying to have friends at all.

Then he'd left. Proved all those things her father had told her right.

She had willfully, defiantly and almost gleefully destroyed her relationship with her father then. Had done her best to hurt him as she had felt he had hurt her. Because of course at seventeen she hadn't seen the difference between her feelings for Liam and her father's pride. His relationship to his wife of twenty-five years. No. Of course, teenage Sabrina had seen none of that.

It was as if her seventeen years of sensibility had simply dissolved, leaving behind no sensibility at all, leaving behind nothing but a mass of unguarded, unprotected, senseless feeling.

And that Sabrina—that ridiculous, emotional Sabrina, seemed to be making a reappearance. Because she was certainly able to be goaded by Liam. Though she supposed, since he was the one who had brought her out in the first place, it stood to reason that he would make her reappear now.

"What?" he asked his green eyes sharpening.

"Yes. You look about as shocked as everyone else did."

"Back up. Where was this? When was this?"

What she hated was that it felt like a simple thing to tell him. How was it that three months of her life had affected the next thirteen years so profoundly? And how was it that this man, the one that had always been so easy to talk to, still was, even when he was the root cause of all of her problems?

"A few weeks after you left. Remember, my father was hosting a campaign event for Richard Bailey. He was running for mayor for like the three hundredth time, or something. Everyone influential from Copper Ridge came. Everyone influential from Gold Valley, from Portland, from everywhere, they all were there. Our function at things like that was to simply smile and pretend we were working at the party. Make it all look like a glossy, classy family event."

"Sabrina, I knew you when you were seventeen. You did not drink."

She squared her shoulders. "Well, I decided that I would start that night. I took a bottle of wine into one of the barns and sat in the corner. I guess I should back up and let you know that I had a confrontation with my dad after you disappeared. I thought that he fired you. I thought that he had found out about me going to the cabin that night. Because when I came to see you the next day, after I recovered from being embarrassed and upset, you were gone. I was going to apologize. I was going to tell you that I wanted to preserve our friendship... But you were gone. And I knew that you wouldn't have just... I thought that my father had to be involved."

"You were right," he said, his voice hoarse.

"Yes. I was." She closed her eyes.

She would never forget that. Tiptoeing into her father's office, because quiet was always demanded if one was going to enter Jamison Leighton's inner sanctum. She had been fighting back tears, fighting down panic.

She couldn't cope with the idea that Liam might actually be gone. But none of his things were back in the cabin, and he had taken his motorcycle. And for her, Liam had been...freedom.

The first and only person in her life to ever pay attention to her when she was just being her. Opening up to him had felt easy, and there had never been another time or another person in her life that had made it feel that way.

In order to have her father's attention, she had to be quiet. She had to be good. She could hardly ever command her mother's attention, and her older brother didn't care. Beatrix had been too young for Sabrina to care, and of course, that irony had been lost on her at the time.

"I was just so angry," she said. "And I felt like I had escaped a box, and when you left I thought I was going to have to get back inside of it."

He frowned, the brackets by his mouth deepening. "I'm not sure I understand."

"Of course not. It's not like I explained it to you. But the me that you knew then was not the person that I was for most of my life. I was seventeen, so I met you and I got giddy. I won't pretend it was anything else. I made an idiot out of myself following you around. But you gave me attention. And you never made me feel stupid. You never made me feel like I had to be different. It wasn't like that with anyone else in my family. With anyone else at all. You made it seem like being me might be easier than I had thought before I met you. It wasn't just you I liked. I liked who I was when I was with you. Braver. Funnier." She shook her head. "I was afraid that when you left I would lose that."

The terrible thing that she had to contend with, even as she spoke the words, as emotion threatened to crush her chest like a pair of snapping iron jaws, was that it had changed her to lose him. That she had lost something she'd found over that carefree summer, where she had learned what it meant to smile so much her face hurt for the first time.

She hadn't lost all of it though. Because while she was angry about a lot of what had happened, it had also shaped her into who she was. She was definitely stronger. Definitely more independent. But lonely sometimes too. And cautious.

She could never be as innocent as she had been. But that was the cost of growing older. It happened to everyone. It wasn't like she was a special case, even if, when she got lost in her own personal darkness, it started to feel like it.

"Anyway. My father used your taking the money as an example of the fact that he had been right and I was wrong. That what he had done had been to protect me, that I had committed the unpardonable sin of being led around by my unstable emotions."

She blinked rapidly. "Again, he wasn't necessarily wrong. But I was so wounded by it. By all of it. And I let it fester over the next week. And when the party happened… And everyone was happy. Having fun. Putting on that polite, calm face that people in our position always do. I just couldn't do it. I couldn't do it, I couldn't support it. I couldn't be part of it. I went off by myself, and I was just going to…well, to soak my misery in alcohol for a while. I'd had tastes of wine, of course, you don't grow up in a winery and not have samples here and there. But I had never gotten drunk before. So, I made it my goal."

She spared him the finer details. Of her sitting in the corner of the barn, the cold soaking through from the floor to her clothes, chilling her, as tears rolled down her cheeks. As she wept pathetically in the corner, drinking straight out of the bottle like a mortally wounded soldier trying to blunt the reality of her upcoming death.

Truly, there had been no less elegant expression of heartbreak in the history of the world.

But then, as she'd had more to drink, her grief had begun to fade to something else altogether. To anger and righteous rage. And she had begun to feel bold again, not so crushed and defeated. All of that bravery, all of that recklessness that had fueled her to leave her bedroom in the middle of the night, to go down to Liam's cabin wearing nothing but a trench coat, fueled her again.

She had stood up on wobbly legs, and taken herself down to the big outdoor seating area where everyone was standing, drinking and socializing in the most civilized of ways.

She could remember clearly the way the lights had looked, strong over the party. Double, tripled in her vision, and hazy. Everything was so hazy. A blessed relief next to the sharpness she had experienced ever since Liam had left her.

It made her feel strong. Made her feel like the most bright, distinct thing there. Like she was owed the floor. Like she was owed this moment.

"After I was…compromised, I walked down to the party and I found my father. And I started yelling at him. And believe me when I tell you that every eye in the place was on me. And I was thrilled. I wanted that attention. I had always earned my father's favor, his notice by being good. And I was ruining it all then. And getting all the attention I could ever want. It was the best thing. The most amazing, empowering thing. So I kept going. I yelled at him for ruining my life. For sending you away. For thinking he was so much better than everyone else, even though his wife was sleeping with another man."

She closed her eyes, pain washing through her. "I didn't think he knew. Isn't that terrible? Telling my father that his wife was cheating on him in front of all those people…"

"When did you find out?"

She swallowed hard. "The first time I saw my mom with another man I was maybe six? But I didn't understand then. What it meant that she had a visitor in the middle of the day, that they disappeared for a couple of hours. Everything looked like friendship in my eyes. I think it first hit me when I was thirteen. I started to suspect that she had affairs then. But it was confirmed a couple of years later when I saw her kissing someone. I came downstairs one night, and heard people down there, so I hid in the hall. My father was out of town on a sales trip. I knew that she wasn't down there with him. I looked around the corner and into the living room and I saw them together. I don't know who it was. I had never seen him before. And I didn't see him after."

"You just kept that secret to yourself?"

She shrugged. "What else was I going to do with it? If I told, it would destroy everything. Destroy our family. I couldn't do that. Until I was drunk and wounded, and destroyed myself, so I figured I might as well ruin everything around me too." She sighed heavily. "He knew. He told me later."

Tears filled her eyes, and she tried to blink them back. Liam Donnelly had had enough of her tears. She didn't want to give him any more tears. Particularly not in front of him. But it was hard to talk about this without feeling emotional. Mostly because she had never talked about it. She had never told anyone this whole story.

She had been angry at her father, and she had humiliated him in an unforgivable way, but not just him. She hadn't even considered what it would mean for her mother to announce that. What it would mean for Damien. And poor Beatrix, who had of course been shielded from everything up until that point.

"After the party my mother went to their room, wailing like I'd personally cut her open. My father dragged me into his office, white-faced. It's the closest I've ever seen my father to losing his temper. But even then, he kept his tone completely calm. He asked me if I thought he was stupid. If that was all the respect I had for him. He said he had tried to protect me. To protect me by instilling in me the importance of control. Of doing the right thing. Being led by that sense of morality and not by feelings. Like him. Because the alternative was being like my mom. And of course he knew her shortcomings, but he honored his vows. He was never unfaithful. And he refused to divorce her."

Liam crossed his arms over his broad chest, angling his face upward. "Sounds like a martyr to me. Not a saint."

"Same thing, historically speaking."

"Maybe historically, but not so much in practice. What does he want? Accolades for sticking it out, even though it sucks?"

"No," she said. "Because nobody knew. Nobody knew but him. Until I uncovered it all. He said... He knew that Damien was just like our mom. He knew it. He never expected him to be better. And Beatrix... She was wild, then and now. Kind of untamed, marches to her own beat. But me... He was sure that I was like him, but when I met you, he could see me going down the same road he had gone down."

"With your mother?"

She nodded. "Yes. And so, he had tried to protect me, and I had refused to allow it. And that it was too late to fix."

"He cut you off."

"I lost my job at the winery. He didn't kick me out of the house, but he didn't speak to me anymore. I don't know if he would have paid for me to go to school, I never asked. I just started arranging all of it by myself. I moved out. I went and got my own work. My mom forgave me," she said. "Which I've always found so strange, because I didn't humiliate her any less. But, I think she's in general a lot more forgiving of uncontrolled emotions. Damien never cared either way, because Damien has never cared what anyone thought."

"I imagine his marriage to Lindy wasn't a popular decision on his part?"

She shook her head. "He met her while he was traveling with the rodeo, which was another unpopular decision. Her brother, Dane, also rides, and he and Damien became friends. Of course, my father considered them a class of people that we were far too good to associate with."

"So you've stayed around, stayed close to the rest of your family, and your father just…doesn't speak to you?"

"He asked me to pass him the potatoes at Christmas one year." She wasn't kidding.

"Well. That's bullshit."

"Says the man who left town and never spoke to me again?"

"That's different."

"Right. Because you were protecting me. You know what, my father thinks he was protecting me too."

"I didn't have anything to give you, Sabrina. I didn't. And I shouldn't have encouraged our friendship, whatever it was, I shouldn't have done it. But I was being an idiot. I already told you, I was young, and I wasn't any smarter than you. And I'll tell you something, I wasn't a virgin. So when I met you, and I thought you were cute and funny, and I wanted to listen to you talk more than I wanted to see you naked, I figured that maybe it was all right to get to know you better. I didn't think I would be tempted to do anything."

"You weren't," she said.

Something shifted then, his stance, the light in his eyes. She was suddenly very aware of the fact that even if he was dressed like a civilized man, he was still a very large one. Muscular. That the tattooed bad boy was underneath the long-sleeved shirt and tie.

Her heart was beating rapidly, her palms starting to sweat a little bit. "You're an idiot," he said.

She hadn't expected that. "Was that your version of an apology? Because it sucked."

"No. I'm not apologizing to you. You think that I didn't want you? With all of your wisdom gained in the last thirteen years that's really what you think?"

"Yes, asshole. Because that's what you told me. You said you didn't want me. You said you didn't do… Well, you remember. I'm not going to recite your screed back to you."

"If I hadn't wanted you, I would have wrapped you in a fuzzy blanket and set you down on my bed. I would have explained to you why it wasn't a good idea. I wouldn't have had to get your naked ass out of my house as quickly as possible before I threw you down on a rug and had my way with you."

Involuntarily, her fingers drifted upward, and she grabbed hold of her necklace. "On a rug?"

"Or just the hardwood."

"Then why? Why did you leave?" She shook her head. "Never mind. I don't really need the breakdown on how that would have been really expensive sex, all things considered."

"It's funny, Sabrina, you've done a lot of lecturing me about how I don't know you, but I think you didn't know me very well at all. It's been thirteen years. I've never had a long-term relationship. I'm not married. This doesn't surprise me. I'm not the marriage and family type."

"Well, I'm not married either."

"You'll find somebody. I don't want to."

She sniffed. "Maybe I don't want to either."

"I don't think that's true."

"Well, my father is an icicle who has spent the past thirty-six years being cheated on. My mother is a cheater. My brother is a cheater. He cheated on the most wonderful woman in the world. Lindy is amazing, and she did nothing but love him. Not exactly advertisements for love and happiness, my family."

He lifted a shoulder. "Fine. Maybe we didn't know each other. But the last thirteen years… Everything I've done, I had to do. I'm not going to apologize for taking your father's money."

She shook her head. "I didn't ask you to."

"But you wish I would."

"The fact that you're actually not very nice doesn't surprise me."

"It has nothing to do with being nice. I didn't have any opportunities in my life. I was raised by a mother who had no money, and if she had money, she wouldn't have spent it on me. I got the opportunity to get a leg up, and I was sure as hell going to take it. Just so you know… he offered me the money before you came to the cabin."

Sabrina's heart jerked forward, slammed against her

breastbone. "He offered you money before," she said, not a question, just trying to get confirmation.

"Yes. He had noticed that you were...fascinated by me." The corner of his mouth tilted upward, and she wanted to punch it.

"I was not."

"You were. And it was obvious. To everyone."

That old shame, that old embarrassment, washed over her. She had exposed herself like that to everyone. Anyone who cared to look.

"Why were you still there? If he'd already offered you the money, why were you still there when I came to you?"

"Because of the kiss."

CHAPTER SEVEN

FIRE WORKED ITS way through Liam's veins. Neither of them had spoken about this. And there was a reason for that. At least, on his part. He wasn't sure he could get into this without...without doing something they were both going to regret.

Her pale cheeks turned red. She pressed her lips into a thin line. "The kiss is why you didn't leave?"

"I had just met with your father. I came out of the house, and there you were, standing by the barn."

"He offered you money, and then what?"

"I told him I would think about it. I told him that there was nothing between us, but if he was really concerned I would think about taking his offer and leaving, but it wasn't that simple... Because of my grandfather."

It had been a lie.

He had told himself it was because of his mom. Because if there was one thing he had never wanted to do it was hurt people the way that she had. By simply not thinking. By only thinking of herself, only looking out for herself and how she might be able to get ahead.

So he had told the old man he would think about it. And he had walked out of that house and seen her there, the sunlight shining behind her like a halo. She was standing next to that big old oak tree... That image of her lived in his head, was inked on his skin.

He had wanted to talk to her, to tell her what was happening. Three months, and she had become a friend to him. And something deeper. Something more. It wasn't what he had wanted, but it was true and in that moment he hadn't been able to deny it, not to himself.

His memories of Sabrina were funny. Because he didn't let himself think about them. Not in one continuous rush. He remembered bits and pieces, and he did that on purpose.

Let himself have images, moments. That was how he had managed to get that tattoo without being completely honest with himself about what it was.

But whatever he remembered, he rarely let himself remember those feelings. That friendship.

Liam was a lonely bastard, there was really no sugar-coating that. He didn't have close friends. He loved his younger brother, had spent his life shielding Alex from the worst parts of their home life. But shielding someone meant never really being close to them. Keeping a wall between the two of you, and he'd been fine with that.

He had felt close to Sabrina. Had felt real with her.

It was why he hadn't taken the money without thinking.

"I came out and saw you," he reiterated. "And then you asked me to walk out to the grapevines with you."

They had done that often, walked through the rows of vines, concealed from anyone who might be in the house. Just to talk, that was what he always told himself. And it was what he told himself that day too.

She had looked up at him, those blue eyes glittering, and whatever words he'd been about to say had evaporated and blown away on the breeze. He could smell sun, the earth, the damp river and the sharp pine trees. And, under all of that, vanilla. She always smelled like vanilla.

Then she had done something he hadn't expected. She had launched herself into his arms, wrapping herself around him, clinging to him as she pressed her lips against his.

And he knew that he should push her away. Knew that he should grab hold of her hips and set her back, break her hold, break the spell. But he didn't. He just stood there and let her kiss him.

It was a sweet kiss. He couldn't remember ever getting one like it in his life.

Affection, desire, feelings, all caught up in one simple gesture that had nothing on the kind of physical intimacy he was used to sharing with women. And it lit a fire in his stomach that he could no more combat than he could put out.

"I remember," she said, the words scratchy.

"That's why I didn't say anything. Not then."

"Because you felt sorry for me? And then you let me make an even bigger idiot out of myself because I thought that… I thought you liked it. Kissing me. I knew that you were too nice…too good to ask me for more."

She looked away from him, and he did what he'd been itching to do since this morning. Hell, maybe it was something he'd been itching to do for thirteen years. He put his hand on her cheek, slid his thumb along her silky skin, down her jaw, along her lower lip.

He wasn't sure what he expected. Maybe to get hit. But she didn't hit him. Instead she froze, standing there looking at him with those blue eyes, just as she had on that day so long ago before he had held her in his arms.

But she didn't fling herself at him. Not now. She

didn't possess that kind of abandon anymore. That kind of fearlessness. She had bound it all up, just like her hair. He could feel all her repressed...*everything*...bubbling to the surface. And yet, she still stood frozen, not making a move.

"I wasn't too good to ask you for more," he whispered. "I was never as good as you thought. Hell, the fact that I took your dad's money and left? That's evidence enough. I should have talked to you. But I thought it might be better if you hated me." He shook his head. "That was my version of a kindness, Sabrina."

He let his hand drop down to his side.

Her eyes fluttered closed, and she swallowed hard. "Admit it then. I mean, really admit it. Not the double-speak and name-calling, and talking about how you did the right thing." She opened her eyes, and when they met his this time they were blazing. "Tell me that you wanted me. That you're a liar. That you pushed me away because you didn't want to have to talk to me. So you just hurt me instead, because it was easier. You admit that. Don't lie to yourself about how honorable you are. Honor would have been admitting that you didn't want the responsibility of having a virgin, not that you didn't want her at all."

Liam took a step back, grinding his teeth together. This was a pointless conversation. One that made him ache in strange places, and in expected places too.

"Coward," she said.

He didn't have any words. Not a single fucking one. Instead, he closed the distance between them, grabbed hold of her face and held it steady. He hadn't kissed her back when she had been seventeen. He had simply let her kiss him. And then, when she had come into his cabin, the one that he lived in on her parents' property, and stripped her coat off to reveal all that pretty pale skin, he hadn't even touched her.

But she wasn't a kid anymore, and he doubted she was a virgin.

Hell, there was no point pretending they were going to be professional at this point. That ship had sailed. It had sailed far beyond the horizon line, and it wasn't coming back.

So he was going to do what he hadn't done then. To hell with the consequences.

He lowered his head and pressed his mouth against hers. Gentle, just for a fraction of a second. Just gentle enough so that when she gasped in shock he could take advantage of those sweetly parted lips, press deeper and slide his tongue between them.

She was frozen. As he had been that day long ago. This time, she was the one who was shocked. If he hadn't been so intent on kissing the hell out of her he might have smiled.

But it wasn't time to smile.

He wrapped his arms around her, gathering those slender curves up against his body. And it was like something in him sighed. As if he'd been holding a breath for thirteen years and it had finally, finally been released.

There had been other kisses. Other women since then. But until now he hadn't realized that there had been a whole part of himself left untouched. A part of himself that only Sabrina had ever come close to.

Were you protecting her then? Or running from this?

He pushed that question aside, and pushed himself more firmly against her, backing her up against the wall. Her hands were trapped against his chest, and he wasn't entirely sure if she was clinging to him or trying to get a hold so she could shove him away. But he didn't give her a chance to do either. Instead, he gathered both wrists in one fist and lifted her arms, pinning them against the wall above her head.

She wiggled, arching her back, pressing her breasts more firmly against his chest, a frustrated sound on her lips.

Yeah, he was frustrated too. Thirteen years' worth of frustrated.

And this time... *This time...*

Well, he didn't know how to finish that any more than he had back then. But at least now if there were consequences, when it ended, she would be an adult. Relationships ended, that was part of life. He'd just had no desire to be the first relationship that ended for her. Had wanted nothing to do with that kind of responsibility, with inflicting that kind of pain on her.

You hurt her anyway, jackass.

Yeah, he had. And so had Jamison Leighton.

Basically everyone she trusted.

He pulled himself away from her, his chest heaving, his breath coming in sharp, short bursts.

He released his hold on her wrists, and it took her a moment to slowly lower her arms back down to her sides. She blinked, looking dazed.

And then suddenly, she seemed to come back to herself, the color mounting in her cheeks as she looked around the room, picked up her purse. She must have dropped it on the floor at some point when they had been kissing, along with her notebook. He hadn't even noticed.

He had a feeling some walls could have collapsed and he might not have noticed that either.

"Let's just… We don't…" She waved a hand.

He nodded once. "Fair enough."

Her eyes met his, and then she looked away again, brushing her fingers through her hair, which was still bound up in that tight little bun. He should have dealt with that first thing. Should have released it, so he could see that long blond hair flying free again.

She was so skittish. The Sabrina he'd known had not been skittish.

The Sabrina he knew had flung herself into his arms with abandon.

But he supposed he didn't deserve to be mystified by the lack of it now. He had been part of destroying it.

Had had a hand in creating this cautious, repressed creature that seemed so different than the girl he'd known.

But as they silently gathered their things and headed out of the shop, he could think of only one thing. That she might be completely different in many ways, but she still smelled of vanilla.

And she still tempted him in ways he couldn't afford to give in to.

"YOU HAVE TERRIBLE AIM," Clara Campbell said, looking at Sabrina with disdain.

"I said I was terrible," Sabrina said, walking over to the dartboard and collecting her ill-thrown dart, which was listing sadly to the side, barely sticking into the edge of the corkboard. "You wouldn't listen. You said you wanted to come to Ace's and play darts."

"We should have played for money," Clara commented.

Olivia, who had been standing there relatively quietly, holding her own darts, simply shrugged. "Oh, I wouldn't like to gamble. Plus, I would lose badly."

"Maybe we should make a wager," Clara said. "How about it? Losers buy the winner's drink?"

Olivia nodded. "That sounds fair. I guess it's my turn."

Olivia took a timid step to the green line that was painted on the scuffed wooden floor. She looked around, seemingly distracted by the chaos around them. It was Friday night and Ace's was packed full of people letting off steam at the end of the workweek, or, just drinking because they had to work over the weekend.

A lot of the men in the bar were fishermen, or they were ranchers, and they didn't get Saturdays and Sundays off. Of course, that meant they drank every night.

Sabrina watched a couple of college girls approach Ferdinand the mechanical bull. They were drunk and giggly, and the group they were with was egging them on. Sabrina shook her head. She was glad she was more sensible than that.

And she refused to think about her moment of nonsense earlier. That door was closed. Firmly. Completely.

She turned her focus back to Olivia, who lifted an unsteady hand, cocked it back and let the dart fly. Straight into the bull's-eye.

An impish smile tugged at the corner of Olivia's mouth. "Beginner's luck?"

Clara narrowed her eyes. "Why do I doubt that?"

"I have two more throws," Olivia commented blandly.

And she took them, getting a bull's-eye each time.

"How?" Clara sputtered.

"My dad had a game room in the basement," Olivia said simply, shrugging. "I used to get bored and go downstairs and throw darts. Do you guys want to play pool next?"

"No!" Sabrina and Clara said in unison.

Clara shook her head, as the three of them walked over to the bar. "I would never have thought that you, Olivia Logan, were a secret game shark."

Olivia batted her eyes. "I contain multitudes."

"Okay," Sabrina said. "Your drink is on us. Whiskey?"

"Diet Coke, please," Olivia said.

Sabrina shook her head. "Fine. I'll have a whiskey."

"I'm just getting a Coke," Clara said, handing Sabrina a five.

"I didn't figure I would be coming to a bar just to drink alone," Sabrina said despairingly. She signaled for Ace, who wandered down to their end of the bar.

He flashed her a smile, the kind of smile that had been known to bring women to their knees, and up to his room above the bar, for years. But not anymore. Now Ace was happily married to town princess Sierra Thompson, née West, and the proud father of two little girls.

He was still good-looking, but definitely a one-woman man.

"Whiskey," Sabrina said, "on the rocks. And a Coke and a Diet Coke with nothing fun in them."

He laughed. "You got it."

Sabrina turned around and scanned the room, hoping in vain to find one man in the place that made her feel even an iota of what Liam made her feel. A man who might be a fifth as good-looking. She was desperate enough to take that measly of a fraction.

"What's up?" Clara asked, lifting her hand and fiddling with the rather sizable engagement ring there.

"Nothing," Sabrina said.

The fact that Clara was now engaged to Liam's younger brother made things…well, tricky. Because she knew that Clara was curious about Sabrina and Liam. And that she was very curious about how they were getting along. And Sabrina had no desire to talk about it.

She had even less of a desire to talk about it now that she and Liam had kissed.

Really kissed.

Her throat felt tight and scratchy, and her face felt hot just thinking about it.

"Really?" Clara asked.

"Really," she said, turning as Ace brought the drinks. She gave him the cash and handed out the beverages.

She lifted her whiskey tumbler to her lips, relishing the burn. And then the door to the bar opened, and she nearly killed herself breathing in that golden fire.

"You did not tell me that Alex and his brothers were coming tonight," she said, putting the glass down quickly, trying to keep herself from visibly gasping and wheezing.

There they were. The whole pack of Donnelly brothers. From broad-shouldered, muscular Cain, the oldest brother, to Alex, who was so very like Liam, with the same green eyes and slightly darker hair. Then there was Finn, brown haired and blue-eyed, designed to break hearts with one of his hard-earned smiles.

They were all hot. Every last one of them.

But it was only Liam who made her heart feel like it was running a marathon it could never, ever win.

Clara winced. "I'm sorry. I didn't know."

"Is it…Liam?" Olivia asked.

"Yes," Sabrina said, "it's all of them. Every Donnelly."

"I mean, is he the reason that you're making that face?"

Sabrina grimaced. "Yes. Yes, he is the reason I'm making this face. I just spent half the day with the man, I don't need to see him again."

Plus, after that kiss, she had scurried off like he'd tapped her ass with a branding iron. And he had let her. Frankly, he'd seemed like he had regretted what had happened just as much as she had.

And she had. Regretted it. There was absolutely no part of her that had gloried in it. That had shouted *finally* and leaned in to it. That had been thrilled to have Liam Donnelly at last see her as a woman.

That had been so damned happy to discover she wasn't actually broken. That a kiss could light her on fire the way that one had long ago.

And even if there was a small part of her that had felt that way, it had immediately been quashed by the realization that apparently it was only Liam that could make her feel like this.

She had kissed other men. Had gone on dates. Had tried. She had tried to want someone else. She didn't. She never had. Another way that she felt irrevocably scarred by damned Liam Donnelly.

CHAPTER EIGHT

"I REALLY DIDN'T KNOW," Clara said, looking apologetically at Sabrina, who did nothing more than take a larger gulp of her whiskey than she would have otherwise. She said nothing. Because there wasn't really anything to say.

She couldn't yell at her friend, even if she wanted to, because she knew that it wasn't like Clara had set her up for failure. Or for disaster. Clara would never do that.

Olivia looked wide-eyed, and potentially a bit too interested in all the drama. But then, she imagined with Olivia's history—her one, steady relationship—this was well outside her sphere.

All things considered, Sabrina found it borderline laughable that she had man drama. It was only ever the one man. Just the one.

And he was coming right toward them. Well, in fairness, he wasn't leading the pack. Clara's fiancé, Alex, was, with a sharp and determined look on his face.

He approached the group, putting his hands on Clara's hips, leaning in and kissing her neck. "Fancy meeting you here."

Sabrina had to look away from the two of them, because it made her chest feel like it was too full.

What they shared wasn't casual intimacy, it was far too intense for that, but it was…assumed. That kind of deep familiarity, where a man could walk right up to a woman and know that his touch would be well received. Sabrina had never had anything like that. Not ever. It made her ache a little bit, and she wasn't entirely sure why.

What she hadn't had—romantically—had been her own choice. Not really at the forefront of her mind, but she had just never gotten involved. A few dates here and there, but not a relationship.

The bottom line of it all was a fear of rejection, she supposed. The top layer simply being that if she didn't want someone even half the way she had wanted Liam, what was the point of risking exposure? What was the point of putting herself in potential harm's way?

She looked away from Alex and Clara, and immediately regretted it, because her eyes locked with Liam's. She squeezed her knees together tightly, trying to do something to ease the restlessness between her thighs.

"Yes," Sabrina said, "Fancy seeing you here."

Liam shrugged. "Finn decided we should all go out tonight."

"I did," Finn said, "because we are celebrating."

"What are you celebrating?" Olivia asked.

Sabrina didn't actually want to know. She just wanted them to go away. But Olivia wasn't picking up on the tenseness, and now that Clara was being held close by Alex, Clara didn't care. Because there was no one else in the room besides Alex. Sabrina could tell, based on the other woman's expression.

Her heart seized tight. What must that be like? To look at someone like he was the only person in the room. On earth. To have him look at you the same way?

She cleared her throat and turned her face away.

"Yeah." She gathered herself and looked back at Liam. "What are you celebrating?"

"The new store," Liam said. " And a new generation of Donnellys. Finn is going to have a lot less free time coming up in about seven months."

She blinked, then shifted her focus to Liam's older brother. "Congratulations."

Finn grinned. "Thank you. It isn't only me with news." He cast a glance at his other brother, who Sabrina didn't know all that well, but had interacted with a few times prior to his wedding at the winery.

"Yeah," Cain said, "Alison is pregnant. Kind of a surprise. But I'm not unhappy with that." In fact, he looked ecstatic. There was an irrepressible grin on his handsome face, and even though she didn't know Cain, it was impossible to not feel his excitement radiating from him.

"*Not unhappy?* He ran in and told everybody about five minutes after they found out."

"Not my first time at the rodeo," Cain said, looking downright smug. "And, since Violet is going away to school next year…"

"You don't even get a minute to have an empty nest," Alex commented.

"Alex, you're always up in my shit," Cain said. "I wouldn't have an empty nest either way. I've got you knuckleheads around constantly."

"You could move," Finn pointed out.

"Hell no. Especially not with Alison having a baby. Now we're going to need you guys on night shift."

"How's that going to work?" Finn asked. "Lane and I are having a baby too."

"How about it?" Alex asked, his eyes on Clara. "Should we hop on the bandwagon?"

"No way," Clara said, poking him in the chest. "You have to marry me first, Donnelly. And even then, I think you're also going to have to take me on a honeymoon. And get this current crop of bison out of my hair."

Clara and Alex had a bison ranch, where Alex spent most of his time at now, Sabrina knew from talking to her friend.

"That's harsh," Alex said. "I offered to give you my seed."

Clara made a hideous face, and Olivia's cheeks turned bright pink. "Call it that one more time and it's never getting near me again. To make a baby or not."

Alex smirked. "Well, there you have it, the Donnelly clan increases."

Liam chuckled. "We never did have a problem with increasing in our family. We were always pretty damned prolific."

"True," Cain said. "But, this will be different because we'll all stick around to raise our kids."

Alex snorted. "I'll drink to that."

"None for me," Finn said. "I promised I wouldn't. You know, since Lane can't drink."

"Harsh," Cain said. "I get to drink."

"Just wait," he said. "Just wait until she has morning sickness. You're not there yet."

Cain laughed. "Don't lecture me like you're the old hat at this. I've already raised one. This is round two for me, and on that note, I will buy *this* round."

He started ordering drinks from Ace, and Sabrina was thinking that she might need to have a drink or ten to deal with the situation. Because it seemed like, whether she wanted to be or not, she was partying with the Donnellys.

"Do you want to play darts?" Olivia asked Liam.

"She'll win," Sabrina warned, her chest getting a little bit weird and tight, and she told herself it wasn't jealousy at all, the thought that he might play with Olivia.

Olivia had a boyfriend, anyway, and Sabrina had never gotten the impression she had an extremely active sex life with him, so she imagined she didn't need to worry about anything with Liam.

And Liam isn't your boyfriend. So, maybe you shouldn't worry about if he wants to play darts with Olivia, or "play darts" with her. It's not your business.

She squared her shoulders, stretching out her tense muscles.

"You know, it's tough to be a dart shark if somebody gives away your secrets," Olivia pointed out.

"Well, I need Liam to hang on to his money. I'm in the middle of a business venture with him, and I don't need you taking all of his capital."

Olivia smiled. "Fair enough."

Sabrina turned to Liam. "Congratulations. On the uncle thing." Because she wasn't a totally petty cow, and she did have some manners.

"Thanks," he said. "Nothing has motivated me more to get moving on building my own place on the family property. I mean, I'm happy for them, don't get me wrong. But a crying baby in the house doesn't really sound like fun to me. I like to hold them for a minute, then give them back."

Sabrina ignored the twinge in her stomach. "Same."

If she had been told just a few months ago that she would be standing in a bar talking about babies with Liam Donnelly she would have told the bearer of the news that they were nuts. But here she was. Trying to pretend that when the people around her announced pregnancies it didn't make her ache in strange and terrible ways. Trying to laugh as he reiterated that kids and family weren't for him. Trying to sort through the mess of feelings that she had for him. The past, the present and the even more distant past, when she had burned for him.

"I'll get us a table," Cain said, after ordering the drinks, and Sabrina really wanted to tell him that was okay, but it was too late. He was already pushing furniture together and gathering up chairs.

Sabrina sighed heavily. Leaving Olivia would be mean. Her boyfriend, Bennett, wasn't coming for another half hour and taking off and abandoning her with just the Donnelly brothers and Clara, who was now firmly glued to Alex, seemed like the wrong thing to do.

It had absolutely nothing to do with the fact that she viewed Liam a bit like she did a giant spider that she wanted to run from and stare at in equal measure. Fascination and fear winding its way through her.

Except, unlike a giant spider, Liam Donnelly did not disgust her physically in any way.

Would that he did.

She took a seat, and Liam just went ahead and took the one right next to her. Then Cain started to pass out drinks. Liam took two from him, handing one to Sabrina, their fingertips brushing.

Heat burst in her stomach like a flame doused in kerosene and she did her best to get a handle on her breathing.

Whatever was happening between them, everyone around them was oblivious to it. It was between the two of them. Or maybe it was all in her head.

Maybe she was the only one who felt it.

But then she looked up, meeting his green eyes, flashing back to the kiss from earlier today, and she knew that wasn't true.

She looked away.

She kept silent, mostly letting conversation swirl around them, discussions about babies, nurseries and the new shop washing over her. Her head was buzzing, and she felt strange and weightless. Like she was watching this happen to someone else. Which all seemed a little less weird than the reality that she was currently sitting with Liam and his brothers like they were old friends, and not like he was her old, oversize baggage.

When she looked up and saw Bennett Dodge walk through the door of the bar, she let out a near audible sigh of relief.

There was a woman trailing behind him, though, one who looked nothing like pretty, petite Olivia at all.

She had reddish-brown hair that was tied back in a braid draped over her shoulder. She was only about three inches shorter than the very tall Bennett and was wearing blue jeans with a hole in the knee and a plaid work shirt. Sabrina doubted Olivia owned anything with a hole in it, even if it was meant to be fashionable. And she had a feeling that this was not a fashion statement.

"Who's that?" Sabrina leaned over toward Olivia.

"Oh, that's Bennett's friend, Kaylee. She's nice, but I don't really have a lot in common with her."

Sabrina wondered how she would feel if her boyfriend had a close friend who was a girl, but she supposed it wasn't really any of her business. And she also supposed she wasn't really able to gauge that, since she had never had an actual boyfriend.

"You all hang out?"

"Sure." Olivia shrugged, clearly unperturbed by the presence of the other woman. "Like, at Gold Valley Saloon sometimes. They own a veterinary clinic together, so we'll go out when they're done with work. They're super into animal stuff. I mean, they'd have to be. Vaccines, deliveries, surgeries. Not really my thing," Olivia said, stirring her drink with a manicured hand.

Bennett and Kaylee crossed the room, joining them at the table. Bennett was more than a little bit handsome, tall and broad chested with dark hair that looked like he'd just run his hands through it. His clothes were dirty, like he was coming in off a hard day of work at the ranch. Sabrina could definitely see why Olivia liked him.

"Hey, princess," he said, leaning down and giving Olivia a kiss on the cheek. "How was your day?"

Olivia blushed prettily. "Good."

"Are you ready to go?"

"Can we stay for a little bit?" Olivia asked.

Sabrina frowned, and so did Bennett's companion.

"Sure, for a bit."

With much chair scuffling and handshaking, Bennett and Kaylee soon took seats at the table with them.

Sabrina supposed that she could leave now. At least Olivia had people there. But then she would be very obviously extricating herself and she wasn't sure she wanted to do that either.

Or you could just admit that you want to stay near Liam, because as much as he bothers you, he makes you feel things that you haven't felt in so long you can't walk away.

Okay, maybe she could admit that. But she didn't particularly want to.

"Anybody want to play darts?" Kaylee asked, grinning in a warm, broad way that was irresistibly likable. Sabrina took against her fresh-faced, universal appeal.

"Are you a dart shark too?" Liam asked her, leaning in, returning the smile.

And suddenly, Sabrina was very, very bothered by the whole situation. "I'm not as good as Olivia," Kaylee said.

"Okay. I'll play."

"Me too," Olivia said.

That prompted Bennett to stand and nod, clearly all on board for the dart business.

"Me too," Sabrina added, the words slipping out before she could think them through. She was both terrible at darts and theoretically did not want to be anywhere near Liam, so she had no idea what the hell she had been thinking.

Before she was fully cognizant of what she had consented to, Sabrina was up and headed over to the dartboard with Kaylee, Bennett, Olivia and Liam.

Liam passed a handful of darts around, and they laid out a light wager of drinks for the winner. Kaylee went first, the taller woman taking her position and throwing a few darts effortlessly, hitting one bull's-eye, and some high-ticket rings with the others.

Sabrina felt swollen with inadequacy.

Especially when Olivia stepped up and hit the bull's-eye three times.

"It's really not fair," Sabrina commented.

"It's not," Bennett said with a grin. "I can't beat her. Nobody can."

"Too bad there are no real-life equivalencies to this," Olivia said.

"You could be a sniper," Liam said. "Or, just a professional dart player."

"Yes. I'm sure both of those things would go over really well with my father," Olivia commented.

Bennett chuckled, then lazily cocked his arm back and threw his first dart. Sabrina felt slightly mollified when it landed on the outer edge of the board. At least she wasn't the only one who wasn't great at darts. Except, then his second two didn't suck. And it was apparently her turn.

She cocked her arm back and let the dart fly, and it hit the wall, bounced off and landed on the floor.

"You need help?" Liam approached her, moving next to her, his green eyes intent on hers.

She sniffed. "No."

She went to retrieve her sad, fallen dart from the floor. And Liam just looked at her. She practically twitched. "I don't need help."

She moved back to her place at the line, and Liam moved up behind her, then wrapped his hand around her wrist and lifted it up. "Do you want me to show you how to throw the dart?"

She sucked in a breath, holding her stomach tight, her entire body tense. "I don't need your help for that," she said.

"Really?"

"Really," she insisted.

He didn't release his hold on her; instead, he shifted his thumb to a different position on her wrist, and she had a horrible feeling that he was taking her pulse. That he could feel just how rapidly her heart was beating.

His hands were rough, calloused from all the work, and all she could think in that moment, stupidly, was that if she had left, it might have been Kaylee who managed to finagle a tutorial out of him.

Except she doesn't suck at darts.

No, Kaylee did not suck at darts, and apparently sucking at darts was something of an asset if you wanted a man to touch you.

Except she wasn't *supposed* to want Liam to touch her. But then, if she didn't want him to touch her, if she wanted to keep distance between them, then she should have left in the first place.

He put one hand on her hip, straightening her so that she was square to the dartboard. "That was your first problem," he said. "Your second problem being that you're throwing across your body at an angle. So when you let go, it's flying at an angle. And the tip can't get in."

Her head felt light and fuzzy, and her face felt warm. It took all of her strength not to simply lean back into his touch. Liam Donnelly possessed some kind of black magic over her body. He had cast a spell on her when she had been seventeen years old, and it had never lifted.

The real question now was whether or not there was any point in fighting it.

With his guidance, she let the dart fly, and this time, she actually landed on the outer ring and it stuck.

"Wow," she said. "That was…not terrible."

"Not even a little bit terrible," he said, smiling.

Liam Donnelly was smiling at her. A real smile.

She tilted her hips slightly to the left and took her position again. And she realized, when he placed his hand back on her hip, when he squared her up to the board again, that she had done that on purpose.

She despised herself a little for that. For that silly move, where the woman pretended to be less competent than she was to get a little bit of male attention.

But frankly, it was a move that had been underutilized in her life thus far, so she felt somewhat entitled to it.

"My turn," he said, his breath on her neck when he spoke the words. She shivered, then moved away from the dartboard, casting furtive glances at Olivia to see if the other woman had noticed her and Liam.

Olivia seemed blissfully unaware, happily hanging on to Bennett's arm.

Kaylee, on the other hand, did not seem unaware. Either of the tension between Liam and Sabrina, or of every minute action taking place between Bennett and Olivia.

It was subtle. But there was something in the way that she looked at them. The way her eyes would move over Bennett, and then to where Oliva's hands gripped his arm. Before darting away, quickly. Very quickly.

Sabrina felt a sympathetic pang. If she was reading the situation correctly, she was a platonic bunny as far as Bennett was concerned, and as far as Olivia was concerned absolutely no threat. She possessed none of the sweet, feminine charms Olivia had, and had probably been a fixture in Bennett's life for years.

And clearly thought of Bennett as a fixture not at all.

Sabrina felt a lot more kinship to the other woman now. Attraction was such an unwieldy bitch.

There was ample evidence of that all over the place tonight. She realized that she hadn't really paid attention to Liam's throws. Because she had been so lost in her general ruminations, her eyes fixed on his forearms, and not where the dart had flown.

She took a deep breath, tried to regain her composure and cleared her throat. They went a few more rounds. Olivia predictably beat everyone then demanded nothing more than another Diet Coke. Sabrina declined to have another drink, and instead, excused herself.

She expressed happiness over having met Kaylee, waved fondly at the Donnellys and scooted herself out the bar door. She breathed in deeply, the cold salt and sea air burning her lungs. But her relief was short-lived. She heard the door open and close behind her and she knew exactly who it was.

She paused, closed her eyes and took a deep breath, trying to ease the tension in her chest. Then she turned around. "Your brothers are still here," she commented.

"Yes, they are."

"Come to think of it, so is Kaylee, and I bet she would like a little bit of dart coaching."

"She doesn't need dart coaching. And anyway, she wouldn't want it from me."

"But, she's not going to get it from the person she wants it from. So…"

"Doesn't work like that, Sabrina. At least, not for some people."

"Does it work that way for you?"

Liam took a step toward her, the harsh, pale blue streetlamp above illuminating his hair, backlighting him, showing off that broad, muscular frame. Mist hung in the air, not quite fog, not quite rain. It swirled around them, damp little crystals dancing in the light.

She might have thought it was pretty if she didn't feel so restless. So edgy.

"No," he said, his voice rough. "I mean, it used to. When I was younger. But I came back to town, and I saw you in the bar. Even if it was only for a minute. After that…"

"What does that mean?" She was tired. Tired of

guessing. When it came to her own motivation she was guessing at this point; she really didn't have the energy to guess at his too.

"I haven't been with anyone since I came to town. And that was quite a while ago."

"Oh," Sabrina said. "Oh."

She did not want to turn this into a discussion about other partners and things like that. It was a conversation she was not equipped to have.

Still, she couldn't deny that she felt somewhat mollified by that bit of news. That Liam hadn't actually been carving a swath through the female population of Copper Ridge since he had returned.

"So. Wait," she said. "You haven't been with anyone else because you wanted to be with me?"

"That is what I said."

"Kind of. But to be clear. You have been celibate because you wanted me. You couldn't be with anyone else. Because you wanted me."

It was so damned close to the story of her life that it made her want to cry as much as she wanted to laugh.

He shifted, shoving his hands in the pockets of his jeans. "It's a problem."

She raised her brows. "I guess so."

Of course, she supposed it didn't have to be a problem. They could… Well. They *could*.

Excitement, illicit and intense, twisted low in her stomach. If she wanted to…she could have Liam Donnelly. In her bed. In her body.

She could have him. There was nothing stopping them now. Not an overdeveloped sense of chivalry on his part, or edicts from her father. Nothing.

She could hardly breathe. He wanted her. He wanted *her*, and he was in a state of discomfort over it.

She held the keys to his celibacy.

Well, what a twist that was. And it felt a whole lot like compensation. Compensation for her humiliation. For her separation from her father... And for the past thirteen years of lingering virginity.

Not that she was going to tell him that. Absolutely not.

"You want me. And it keeps you from wanting anyone else. From having anyone else."

He grimaced. "I think we're a bit of unfinished business."

She let out a started laugh. "And who the hell's fault is that?"

"Don't do that. We both agreed that there was no point in me taking what you offered back then."

She crossed her arms. "What if I don't want you now?"

His expression was dark, shadowed, and she couldn't read it. He took a step toward her and her heart stuttered. "Well, baby, we both know that's not the case."

"No," she insisted, "we don't."

"The way you kissed me back in the tasting room..."

"You kissed me, jackass. You...you held on to my wrists. You held me still."

"And you had your tongue in my mouth."

"It seemed...polite," she sputtered. "You put your tongue in mine."

"So that was all it was. Courtesy tongue?"

"Yeah. Courtesy tongue." This was faintly ridiculous. But she had this one shot. This one little moment of pride. And she just... She just wanted it. He'd bruised it, fatally wounded it all those years ago, and right now she was in an unexpected position of power with him and she couldn't pass this up.

"And if I kissed you again?" he asked. "Would I get a little bit more of that courtesy tongue?"

"Don't you dare," she said. She took a step back, taking a deep breath. Wondering what the hell she was doing, and why she couldn't be consistent, even in her own head. "Don't kiss me."

"Why not?"

"Because if I kiss you, you're going to want to have sex with me." The words felt flat, and stupid, and so did she.

"Yeah. Probably. But then, I already do."

"You can't just do that. You can't just come back to town all... More muscular, with more tattoos, being more... More of all the everything that you used to be back then, and demand that I pick up right where I left off."

"I can't?" he asked.

"No. You can't. Also, for all you know, I could have a boyfriend."

He crossed his arms over his chest. "*Do* you have a boyfriend?"

"No," she snapped. "But that's beside the point. I could."

"But you don't."

"My point is this. Everything has been on your terms. Everything. You let me get close to you back then. Then you were the one who threw me out. You were the one that took money and left. I was just reacting. To everything. Even in the tasting room you kissed me. And now, you think because you've declared your celibacy that I'm supposed to flutter and fall over and be thrilled that you finally want me after all this time. But I'm not going to do that. I'm going to… Dammit, Liam, I'm going to make a decision."

He spread his arms. "Well, I am all fucking ears."

"Later," she said. "Not now. Patience is a virtue, Liam Donnelly, and you appear to be short on virtues. So maybe this will be good for you."

She turned on her heel, with a vehemence that she had no idea she possessed, and headed toward her car, her hands shaking, her breathing unsteady.

And she called herself about a thousand different kinds of fool because she was walking away from something that she wanted.

But even though her body felt largely unsatisfied, another part of her felt so good. She had turned him down. Or she had at least put him on hold. She had put him on hold and it was up to her now. Fully up to her.

That was what she told herself on her drive back to her little cabin that was nestled just outside the Copper Ridge city limits. That was what she told herself as she put on her flannel pajamas and got into her bed. Her very empty bed, which had been empty all this time, because there had only ever been one man she had wanted to share it with.

And now that he wanted to share it with her, she was keeping him waiting.

She felt both powerful and idiotic in that moment.

But maybe that was how this always felt. If she recalled correctly, thirteen years ago she had felt much the same way.

But this time, it was different. This time, Liam Donnelly wanted her back. She might be burning, but she knew she wasn't burning alone.

CHAPTER NINE

SHE HAD REJECTED HIM. That little minx had *rejected him*. It was the last thought in his head before he had fallen asleep, and it was the first thing on his mind when he got up the next morning.

By the time he made his way to the kitchen, his brothers were already set to go outside and start their chores. Finn handed him a cup of coffee and gestured to the front door.

"Let's go," he said.

He grabbed hold of the coffee and took a quick, fortifying sip. It was easy, apparently, to get out of the habit of going straight to work before the sun was up. Just a few days of running other errands, and he had been dragging. But then, that could also be because he had been kept awake most of the night with thoughts of her.

He took another sip of coffee and grimaced as the cold, early morning air bit into his face, sinking down through his coat and to his bones. "It is fucking cold," he said.

"Really?" Cain asked, shooting him a skeptical glare. "I'm the Texan. I'm the one that should be whining about the bitterness of impending winter and saying folksy things like 'it's colder than a witch's tit out here.'"

"What does that mean?" Finn asked. "I didn't know witches were renowned for having particularly cold tits."

"They must be. It's a saying," Cain said.

Liam rolled his eyes and continued on with his brothers toward the barn.

"What's on the list of chores today?" he asked.

"The usual," Finn said. "And then I want to make sure we ride the fence line in the south pasture. Just to be sure everything is good. It's been really wet out there. Soupy. And I have to be sure that the fence posts aren't going to fall right the hell over because the ground is so soft."

"I'll do that," Liam said.

The opportunity to get out and ride, to clear his head, was a welcome one.

It was funny, because he had hated working on the ranch when he had been a teenager. Every summer, he and his brothers would come stay with their grandfather and work the land. Mostly, he figured it was to get out of his parents' hair.

He hadn't liked the work. But he had enjoyed the chance to get away from his mother. To get three square meals. Though, by the time he was older, he was getting his own food, and was too big for his mother to do any serious physical damage to.

He had dealt with most of his starving kid baggage, really. And if he had a little bit of a plate-cleaning compulsion, nobody noticed. They just figured he worked hard, or didn't like to waste, or something. And all of that was true enough.

Of course, the real reason was that he had spent so long being not quite sure when his next meal would come, that he had gotten in the mode of never wasting an opportunity to eat as much food as was on offer.

Still, as surly and messed up as he'd been as a teenager, and as much as he'd bitched about the early mornings and hard work, he had liked being here. Had found solace in it. It was one reason he'd decided coming back here was his best option when he'd hit that dead end in New York.

As much as he'd hated the work as a punk kid, he relished it now.

And right about now, he needed a little bit of physical punishment to take his mind off Sabrina. Sabrina and their kiss. Sabrina and her rejecting him last night.

He still couldn't believe that.

"We'll all do it together," Finn said. "Mostly because I think you're looking for a chance to get rid of us."

The three of them crossed the large gravel lot, the only sound the rocks beneath their boots as they went into the milking barn to get everything started for the day.

"I'm not avoiding you," Liam said, bending down and checking gauges on the milking machine.

"Right. I really want to know the story about Sabrina," Cain said.

"Like I already said, there's nothing to tell. I knew her once. A long time ago. And now, I know her again."

"And you look like you'd want to get to know her a little better, judging by the way you were coaching her with her dart throwing. And she was letting you."

"Friends don't let friends suck that badly at games. Not when they can help."

"You're honestly telling me that you want to be friends with her?" Finn asked.

"No," Liam said. "I don't particularly want to be friends with her. But that's all that's happening. I am doing a business deal with her. I have to work with her. She's hot. But a lot of women are hot."

"But you've admitted that none of those women are leaping into your bed right now."

Liam bit back the truth. Which was that he wasn't jumping at the chance to have any of *them* in *his* bed. He had closed off every near hookup he'd had since coming back to town. He was the one who had shut it down. Because every time it got close he pictured the woman he really wanted. And he just didn't have the stomach for that kind of game anymore.

Sabrina Leighton was a ghost. One that he really, really needed to lay to rest. He could think of only one way of doing it. He was certain of it. But she was *thinking* about it.

"Very professional," Finn said. "As you know, both Cain and I are very good with boundaries."

"Says the guy who ended up banging his best friend about the other guy who started sleeping with his daughter's boss?" Liam asked.

"Hey," Cain said. "We married them. So clearly, it was worth playing with some boundaries."

Liam snorted. "Right."

They continued to work in silence after that, and once they were finished, they stepped back out into the cold. "How many cheese varieties do we have now?" Liam asked.

He was pretty well versed in what was happening with the Laughing Irish products, but Lane experimented with new flavor combinations faster than he could keep up with, and she was continually refining things.

"Well, with Lane overseeing that, it's all gotten very artisanal. Cranberry and herb infusions and things like that. Softer cheeses. And some aged ones."

"Great. I think we need to work on coming up with some pairings for the wine and the cheese."

Finn grimaced. "Yeah, that's not really my wheelhouse. Mostly, I just eat the cheese. More with beer than with wine."

"Your wife must despair of you," Cain said, smiling.

Lane's tastes ran much more toward foodie than her husband's did. Liam certainly appreciated Lane's cooking skills, and the fact that her tastes were somewhat refined. It was one of the consequences of his time in larger cities. He had gotten accustomed to good food. But what he had learned was that with the farm-to-table movements being what they were, small towns actually had nicer food on offer than it might seem at first.

And Liam really liked nice food. He had gone so long in deprivation that he saw no point in denying himself now. Gotten a more active job. Now that he was edging into his midthirties, it was definitely more of an effort to make sure he kept his body the way his casual hookups liked it.

Not that there were any at the moment.

"Don't look at me," Cain said, "I don't know the first thing about putting all that together. I just know how to put it in my mouth."

"Lane would help," Finn said, "but she's currently knocked up, so wine tasting is kind of off the menu. Plus her taste buds are off, according to her."

"It's fine," Liam said, already starting to formulate an idea. "I'm sure Sabrina will want to be involved anyway."

"I'm sure," Finn said, looking interested.

"Why do you care?" Liam asked. "It's not any of your business what happens with me and Sabrina."

"You're the only one without somebody," Cain said. "It is kind of our business."

"We have family meetings about this," Finn said. "Alex comes over. We talk about how sad it is that you're alone."

"While watching chick flicks and talking about which member of the Backstreet Boys is your favorite?"

"I liked *NSYNC," Finn said, deadpan.

"You guys don't talk about me," Liam said.

"We have," Cain said. "I'm just saying, you're the only one that's single."

"Because I like to be."

"Right," Finn said. "Frankly, if you were getting laid, I would believe that. But you aren't."

"It's even weirder that you care about that than that you care about my love life."

"I'm going to say something," Finn said. "And you're probably going to give me shit about it for the rest of for-ever. But I want you to be happy, Liam. We spent way too much time coping with the sucky hands that got dealt to us by life. By Dad mostly. And I spent a lot of my life lonely. A lot of my life pushing people away because of all that crap. I just don't want to see you do it too."

"There's no danger of that. I'm not going to say that I'm not going to hook up with Sabrina, but I'm not in a *happily ever after* space, and I don't think I'm going to be. But that doesn't mean I'm miserable. Not everybody finds rainbows and puppies in a marriage license, Finn. It's not the only way to be happy."

"No," Finn agreed. "It's not. It's certainly not the way to be happy if you're not in love. Love, I think, can make you pretty happy."

"Not on my agenda. Alex and I... Our parents really

sucked. And I know that you didn't have Dad at all, and I would feel sorry for you, but believe me when I say he wasn't an asset. He didn't do anything. He didn't pay any attention to us. He was just the thing our mother obsessed about. When we were the things that trapped her with him. Even we couldn't make him love her. And she hated us for it." One of them more than the other, but he wasn't going to get into that right now. "We were broke a lot of the time, things were hard. So I went out and I made money. Maybe you guys needed to find love to compensate for what you didn't have. I needed to go get some cash. I did it."

"And it made you so happy that you came to take your quarter of the ranch?"

"It didn't make me happy. I didn't expect the money to make me happy," he lied. "I just expected to enjoy it. And I do. So now I have money, and I get to live on the ranch. And I get to hook up with whoever I want."

"But only theoretically," Cain said.

"You're an ass."

"Never said I wasn't."

"Great. So," he said, directing his focus to Finn. "Instead of riding the fence line today, why don't I put together a little wine and cheese tasting situation. I'm going to need to get into the storage, and if I can get a list of the types, that'd be great, so that I know I'm not missing anything. Whatever you want the tasting room to carry."

"Yeah, I actually know that Lane has some inventory spreadsheets. I'll have her give them to you."

"Great."

"So," Finn said. "You think this is going to make you happy?"

"What?"

"Opening up the tasting room. You've definitely attacked this project with more enthusiasm than I've seen you do other things."

"It's what I know," Liam said offhandedly. "I like dealing in what I know."

"Sure."

He could tell that his brother didn't believe him. He didn't really care. He knew that Cain and Finn had had it hard. So had Alex; he had been there for it. But Liam had had a few times when he'd missed school because he'd been locked in a closet instead. Alex didn't know that stuff. Nobody did.

So maybe for Finn and Cain and Alex the end goal was happiness.

Liam had learned to simply prioritize surviving. And now? Well, now he just wanted to keep the demons pushed away.

Money might not make him happy, but he found it a pretty successful demon deterrent. And so were women, though he'd been sadly lacking in women recently.

But that would change. He was confident that it would.

Sabrina Leighton was unfinished business, and the good thing was he was her unfinished business too.

Which meant that sooner or later, no matter how long it took her to get there, she was going to say yes.

Come to think of it, that would make him pretty damned happy. At least for as long as it lasted.

CHAPTER TEN

SABRINA WAS LEANING over the counter in the dining room at the winery when her phone buzzed. She looked up from her inventory sheet and her heart leaped into her throat when she saw the name flash across the screen.

Liam.

Do you have time to meet up tonight?

She looked around the room, at the guests that were currently dining there, and then looked back down at the phone.

I told you I wasn't ready to make a decision yet.

I promise this isn't a booty call.

Her heart fluttered, and she took a deep breath.

Obviously. It's a booty text.

No. I want to work on the menu. I think we need to fig ure out some pairings.

She felt flushed, her cheeks getting warm. Of course.

It was about work. And not at all about him pressuring her into sex.

She had hoped a little bit that he was trying to pressure her into sex.

She looked furtively around again, because for some reason she felt like her thoughts, and her texts, were being broadcast to everybody in the room. Which was ridiculous. It was just her extreme embarrassment and guilt. She imagined that if Lindy knew she was engaging in any kind of flirtation with the man that they were currently trying to do a business deal with she would be unamused.

Yes. I have time. When? Where?

Meet me at the tasting room? 6 o'clock?

She swallowed hard. Sure.

She hit Send before she could second-guess herself.

"How's it going today?"

Sabrina startled, and then turned, knowing she looked guilty when her eyes connected with Lindy's.

"Great," she said. She had a feeling that her smile looked off, that she might resemble a dog that had gotten caught with her nose in the trash.

"You don't *look* great," Lindy said, staring at her a bit too incisively.

"I'm just thinking," she said, shaking her head, trying to clear the visions of Liam out of her brain.

"Okay. How is everything going? With the tasting room?"

"It's going really well," she said. "That's actually

what I was thinking about. I'm meeting up with Liam tonight to work on the menu."

Lindy lifted her eyebrows. "I'll probably want to have a hand in that."

Sabrina couldn't tell if she was relieved or disappointed. Her stomach twisted, almost as if it was going in different directions. Like the rest of her seemed to be.

"Well. If you want to come tonight, we're meeting at six. He's bringing cheese. I'm bringing the wine."

Lindy grinned. "That sounds like a great time, but I'm not going to be able to make it tonight."

"Have a date?" Sabrina asked.

Lindy laughed. Really laughed. "I have absolutely no interest in dating, imagine that. And if I did, I would not sacrifice work for a date."

That just confirmed what Sabrina had thought earlier about Lindy and her approval—or disapproval as the case may be—of Sabrina getting romantically entangled with Liam.

Of course, romantic entanglement wasn't necessarily on the table. It was more physical, *naked* entanglement.

A little thrill slipped down her spine and right between her thighs.

"Of course," she said.

"Actually, I'm having a night with myself," Lindy said. "Which sounds lamer than a date, I admit. But I just need a little time to relax. I do want a hand in the menu planning, but why don't I wait until you guys get it past prototype stage?"

"Sure," Sabrina said, knowing she sounded a little bit breathless. "That works for me. Hey, if we hit on some winners, we can always incorporate some of it here too."

"I'm counting on it. Why don't you bring some fruit

and meat down too," she suggested. "It would be nice to have a few charcuterie trays down at the tasting room. Also some breads. I've been talking to Alison Donnelly about that."

"That would be great. It would be really nice if we could have some of Alison's bread."

"And I'm going to order all of the oil from Lane Donnelly also. It will be nice to have a lot of the local businesses supported in each other's various shops."

"We're steeped in Donnellys," Sabrina said.

"They aren't so bad," Lindy said, smiling.

"Not all of them."

"Uh-huh."

Sabrina cleared her throat. "We should consider bringing some of it up here. I mean, the winery could regularly stock Alison's bread. And maybe some things from Lane's shop. Since we are a bit out of town, we could be a good representative, and a good way for them to get extra eyes on their products."

"Also a good idea," Lindy said. "I really like being in charge."

Sabrina laughed. "I'm glad. I know that Damien didn't allow it."

"Damien definitely had his ideas about how things should work. And then, oddly, would suddenly deviate from those ideas when it concerned him."

"He's a jackass."

"Agreed. I wish I hadn't loved him so damn much." Lindy smiled ruefully. "He pretty much cured me of it though."

"Definitely an idiot," Sabrina concluded.

The devastation that people could wreak when they were so determined to please only themselves never ceased to shock her. Looking at the way Lindy's life had been devastated, at the way she had to rebuild, all because her brother had decided that marriage vows didn't matter, was continually alarming.

The ways in which her mother had constantly hurt her father. The way she had hurt her parents by acting out because of Liam…

Emotions were a mess.

And her father was the stony, silent calm at the center. The one who built up barriers when people interfered with his sense of order. His sense of right. He didn't let people destroy anything around him. The walls he put up were too high, too thick.

"I really wouldn't go back," Lindy said. "I mean, if it was an alternate scenario where we could head trouble off at the pass, where we were both better at communicating, and I could more effectively get what I needed out of the relationship…then maybe. But it's not an alternate universe. I can't romanticize the marriage that we had just because it's gone."

"Well, why would you? I'm certainly not going to romanticize his behavior. Sometimes I wonder how we managed to turn into such a mess. We were a pretty happy family once. I think Beatrix is the only one of us who isn't ridiculously damaged."

Lindy huffed. "Well, whether or not she will be depends on how doggedly she clings to her crush on my brother."

"Give her more credit than that," Sabrina said. "She's more likely to be destroyed by the loss of a sickly vole she was trying to nurse back to health." She tapped her pen on the counter. "Anyway, as far as Dane goes… she's young. She'll get over it. Eventually she'll figure out that nothing could ever happen with him. Anyway, the rodeo season will start again soon and he'll be on the road. And she'll get a break from her exposure to him."

It almost physically hurt to dismiss Bea's crush like that. If only because Sabrina knew how real those things could feel. But the fact of the matter was, trailing around after an older guy just because you had developed a fascination for him when you were young was not love.

And thank God, because as much as Sabrina liked Dane, he was essentially family. But he was definitely a bad bet as a lover.

"Yeah," Lindy said, sighing heavily. "Plus, he knows that I would shank him if he ever hurt her."

"He wouldn't," Sabrina said. "He has so many Buckle Bunnies throwing themselves at him all the time he's hardly going to seduce my baby sister who he's known since she was twelve."

"Good point," Lindy said.

Really, Sabrina did not need to be thinking about seduction right about now, but Lindy's next words didn't make that any easier. "Everything going okay with Liam?"

"You don't need to worry about me," she said to Lindy. "I'm pretty realistic about relationships. And I'm exceedingly realistic about business."

Both of those things were true, but neither was a direct denial of anything happening between Liam and herself. Mostly because she didn't feel like she could make that guarantee at the moment.

"Okay," Lindy said. "Did you and he used to…date?"

Sabrina smiled sadly. "No. I just had a crush on him once upon a time. But like you said, Bea will survive hers. And I definitely survived mine. I will keep on surviving it."

By the time her shift ended and Sabrina got in her car to drive over to the tasting room her nerves were decidedly frazzled. Which was silly. She had done enough things with Liam since he had come back that she should be inured to his presence. And anyway, it wasn't like they were going to do anything on the floor of the tasting room in front of the large picture windows.

Except, suddenly, she could imagine only that.

Right. And you're going to...entice him to take you on the floor when you've literally never enticed a man in your life?

She huffed and turned out onto the road that would carry her toward Copper Ridge. She knew each curve on the highway by heart. She'd driven it a thousand times before. Often enough that the stately pines that stood sentry on the shoulder blended together in an indistinct blur of green.

She passed the road that led to her own house, and kept on driving until she reached the turnoff sign that proclaimed Copper Ridge to be only two miles away.

A smile touched her lips as she drove down Main Street. She did take a moment to pause and look at the little buildings. All done up in brick and rich cranberry colored paint with crisp white trim.

There was a small group of people marching down the sidewalk helmed by the town's mayor, Lydia West. Lydia had a clipboard, and was gesturing broadly, indicating lampposts and eaves on the various buildings.

Sabrina wondered if they were planning holiday decorations. Since Thanksgiving was only a week away, she figured it was time, as she had a feeling the moment the turkeys were cleared away from various dinner tables Christmas lights would be blazing in the tiny town.

She parked right in front of the tasting room and gripped the steering wheel tightly as she looked inside. The lights were on, the shop illuminated. And then Liam walked into view. She just sat there for a moment and stared at him, her heart thudding painfully against her breastbone. He was so beautiful. Would he ever not be beautiful to her? Would he ever not be the one and only person who made her feel like this?

She wouldn't know, she supposed, unless she went ahead and had him. How could she? To get rid of a demon, you had to exorcise him. And she had tried all the ways that seemed smart. All the ways that seemed illogical. She had tried going on dates with other men and she had tried burying herself in work. She had tried throwing a drunken fit in front of all and sundry. The one thing she hadn't tried was actually allowing herself to have him.

So perhaps that was the answer.

She sort of despised the idea that her virginity had been hanging around for the past decade plus simply because Liam Donnelly had been the first man she'd wanted all those years ago. That somehow her body was waiting for him.

But she couldn't deny that it was starting to seem that way.

That the moment he had come back to town her hormones had roared to life.

Yeah, definitely difficult to deny that.

She turned her car off and slowly made her way out of the vehicle, grabbing a wooden crate with wine in it and a tray of meat and fruit, and heading toward the door.

It was unlocked, and she let herself in.

"Hey," he said, a half smile curving his lips.

She felt the impact of it all the way down.

"Hi. There are more crates in the car. Want to get them?"

"I have a feeling that's not a question so much as a command."

"Take it however you like," she said.

"Okay. I'm going to take it as a command. Because I like the idea that you think you can tell me what to do." He winked, then walked out of the tasting room, and she snarled at his retreating form.

Her heart tripped over itself when she looked around the room. There was a blanket set out on the ground, because there was still no furniture in the place. That had been an oversight on their part.

But he had brought a blanket. And suddenly, that earlier vision she'd had of the two of them on the floor of the tasting room didn't seem so far-fetched. Hell, they were starting on the floor, she wasn't sure there was any other way it could end.

She swallowed hard and set the crate down, and Liam appeared a moment later with two crates stacked on top of each other. There was a box on the corner of the blanket that had various cheeses and suddenly all of this felt a hell of a lot like a date.

She cleared her throat. "There are wineglasses in one of the crates."

"Great."

He set the crates down and sat next to her, pulling out the first bottle and a wineglass. "Tell me about this one," he said, uncorking the top and pouring a measured amount into the glass.

"That one is a pretty standard table red. It goes with a lot of things. It's a safe bet, basically. I think it would go really well with a stronger cheese."

"All right," Liam said, looking through the box. "This is an aged cheddar. Sharp."

The cheese was wrapped in wax paper, just a small portion, and he broke off a piece and handed it to her. "Try a little."

She took a bite and smiled. "That's good."

"I think so," he said. "Have a little bit to drink with it."

"All right." She took the glass from his hand and took a sip. "That's good, but it is kind of an intense wine. Tell me what you think."

He took a sip, and then had a bite of the cheese. "You might be right."

"I'm not sure that it's the best one to have on the menu when you're having anything less substantial than red meat. We might want to go with…" She looked in the crates and twisted the labels until she came up with a merlot. "Something like this."

That, they both agreed, was more successful. They moved through the different varieties, going from the bolder flavors, and working their way to the sweeter, more delicate ones.

"Have you ever considered making gelato?"

The question seemed to take Liam off guard. "No."

"You should look into it. They make red wine ice creams."

"Now there's a thought. That's a real partnership."

"Exactly."

She smiled at him, and took a sip of the sauvignon blanc that was now in her glass.

She was feeling much less stressed now. A little tipsy from the amount they had been drinking. Just enough that she wasn't sure why she had been so worried about tonight. Why she had been so stressed about coming in and doing this with him. It was all going fine. He was charming, and she just…liked being with him.

She always had, really.

"Okay," he said, "this is a softer cheese, and it has ginger and mango in it."

"That sounds strange," she said.

"I promise you it's amazing."

"I'll try it with this," she said, lifting her glass.

"I think I might try it with a dessert wine," he said, rifling through one of the crates until he produced a rosé. He poured a measure of it into the glass and took a taste.

"Verdict?" she asked as she watched him take a long, slow sip.

She had the vague thought that she would pay a good amount of money to be that wineglass about now, and she wondered when her running internal monologue had become a construction worker.

But watching his lips curve around that fine crystal, masculine, firm, and everything that she craved, then watching the strong column of his throat shift as he swallowed… Everything in her had gone tight, completely bound up with her need for him. With her need for something she had never experienced before. Something she had only ever felt the promise of.

She was suddenly starving. The intervening years between when she had last been naked with him and now seeming endless.

And sure, the last time she had been naked with him she hadn't touched him, and he hadn't touched her. But she craved it again. Being before him like that, without barriers, without hiding.

"Good," he said, his voice rough.

His eyes met hers, then dropped down to her lips, and she felt…weightless. Breathless.

"You should have a taste," he said.

She reached out, making a move toward the wine-glass, but he set it down, moving it out of her grasp, and then he leaned forward, resting on his elbow as he brought his lips up against hers.

If his mouth tasted of wine, she didn't know it. Couldn't make any sense of it all. Because the only thing she was aware of, the only thing that she tasted, the only thing she was conscious of, was Liam. Liam's mouth. Liam's hand, coming up to cup her face, that calloused thumb running over her cheekbone, down to her chin, holding her steady as he deepened the kiss, as his tongue slid over hers.

A shudder went through her. A deep, unending sigh of satisfaction that seemed to come from somewhere deep inside her.

He moved away from her, his thumb still pressed against her chin.

"I told you that I was…" Her words came out thick, slurred, and it had nothing to do with the wine. She swallowed and tried to finish her thought. "That I wasn't sure yet."

"It was just a kiss," he said.

He smiled, too smooth, too easy.

And she knew then that he was a liar. Because there was no such thing as *just a kiss* between them. There never had been. Not thirteen years ago and certainly not now.

He could talk all he wanted about how that kiss out in the vineyard hadn't meant anything. He could say that it was nothing now, that it wasn't leading to anything, but it was a lie. That kiss, that *first* kiss, had always been leading to this one.

There was nothing simple about the two of them. Nothing simple about when they touched. About when they were sharing the same space, breathing the same air.

Their connection with each other had been instant from the start. Electric. Everything. It still was.

A flame that had been smoldering for years, never effectively put out. So why not let it burn? Why not see how bright, how hot it could get? Instead of simply letting the coals sit there, refusing to die.

This passion between them was like a campfire that she had been keeping an eye on for the past thirteen years. Minding it closely, making sure it didn't flare back up, but never quite letting it die.

So now she just wanted to let it rage. All the way. To see how high, how hot those flames could get before she thought that was the only time she would be able to let it go. It was the only hope she had of being able to let it go. Letting him go.

To either prove that it had no potential, that it was never going to burn at all, that it was only ever going to be embers, or to prove that it was as hot and destructive as she had expected, as she had always suspected.

It was this in between... That was what couldn't be endured. Not anymore. Not for one more second.

But she wasn't seventeen, not anymore. And she wasn't going to let him get away with his oh-so-patented charming brand of bullshit.

"Liar," she said against his mouth, the tip of her tongue touching the top of his lip.

"What?" he asked, those green eyes burning into hers.

"It's not just a kiss. It's never just a kiss. Not with us. It ends in scars. In nakedness. In tears. But it doesn't end in a kiss."

"Maybe this time it will," he said.

"Maybe," she said. "But I don't want it to."

"You want scars and tears?"

"Those I would rather avoid. But…I was naked in front of you, Liam Donnelly, and you were never naked in front of me. I think I'm owed a little bit of nakedness."

His gaze slid to the picture window, to the darkened streets outside. "You want to put on a show for the neighbors?"

Her heartbeat quickened. "Not especially."

"Then maybe it's best if it doesn't happen here."

"Take me home," she said. "I'm buzzed, anyway."

"A few sips of wine doesn't do much to me," he said.

"Take me home," she reiterated.

"I don't think you want me to take you back to Finn's place."

"No. You can come to my house. I have a place. Just outside of the town. About ten minutes past Copper Ridge. Before the winery. I live by myself."

"Okay," he said, the words coming out slowly.

"Don't reject me," she said. "Not again. I will end you, Donnelly. I swear it."

He shook his head, his green eyes intense. "I am not capable of rejecting you right now," he said. "Not this time, babe."

"Good. Because I swear to God if you got me all worked up for this and it's some kind of joke…"

"It's not," he said. "It's not."

He grabbed hold of her hand and jerked her upward so that she was standing with him, and then they started to head toward the door.

"Wait!"

"What?" he asked, those green eyes suddenly looking hazy, and she knew it wasn't from the wine. Gloried in that realization.

"We can't go wasting all that cheese," she said.

He looked down, and her eyes were drawn to the very obvious bulge in the front of his jeans. "I'd rather waste the cheese than this."

Heat bled into her cheeks, spread down her neck. "Do erections have some kind of short shelf life I'm unaware of?" she asked, giving thanks for that little bit of buzz she did have, since it was making her feel bolder, and a bit less awkward than she otherwise would.

Or, it was lying to her, and she was actually behaving awkwardly, and what she had just asked him wasn't funny at all. But she didn't know which it was. Because wine.

He rolled his eyes, then went back and grabbed the box of cheese. "The wine will be fine," he said.

"Yes," she said emphatically. "It will."

They went outside, and she waited for him to unlock the truck. He opened the passenger side door and she got in, casting a glance at her car, knowing this meant it would be here all night.

They were on the very end of the street, at least, so maybe people wouldn't notice. Or, if they did, maybe they wouldn't jump to too many conclusions.

He started the truck and headed down the main street,

and suddenly, Liam cursed. "Do you happen to have condoms at your place?"

The question jarred her, made her cheeks even hotter. Duh. She should have thought about condoms. "No," she said.

"Why not?"

She turned to face him, but his eyes were fixed on the road, his jaw set. "Don't you have them in your wallet?" she asked.

"No," he said, "I don't."

"Men are supposed to carry them in their wallets," she insisted.

"Actually," he said, "men are not supposed to carry them in their wallets because it's bad for the latex."

"Oh," she said, blinking, "I didn't know that."

"Well, a lot of people don't know that," he said. "But I've kind of made it my business to know about contraception."

"Right," she said, folding her hands in her lap. "I guess that makes sense."

"I was not going to be like my father," he said. "I'm not going to have a bunch of random kids and not take care of them. Hell, I don't even want a bunch of random kids that I *do* take care of."

"Totally understandable." Her stomach sank, not sure what all this meant.

He hung a sharp right and swung into the grocery store parking lot. "I'll just be quick."

"Wait," she said, tumbling out of the truck with him, not willing to let him out of her sight in case their separation broke the spell that had settled over them.

She followed him into the grocery store, and belatedly realized her mistake. "Oh," she said. "You're buying…"

"What did you think? That I was going to take you home and just leave you there to sleep by yourself? Hell no. You said you want me, so I'm going to have you. And no lack of condoms is going to stop me."

They walked through the automatic doors and into the small store, moving quickly past the produce and on to the aisles of packaged foods and everyday necessities.

She looked around, feeling edgy. The store wasn't crowded, but she still didn't trust that they wouldn't run into someone they knew. Well, they probably wouldn't know Liam, but they would most definitely know her. She grabbed a little handheld shopping basket and took a bag of Cheetos off the shelf, then continued walking behind Liam.

He turned and glanced at her basket. "Cheetos?"

"If we're hungry." She straightened and met his eyes. "After the sex."

He blinked. "Right."

They kept walking toward the aisle that read Family Planning on the little sign that hung over the top of it, and she grabbed a few more items along the way. Oreos and a jar of pickles. "You realize that that basket makes it look like we don't need the condoms."

She blinked. "What?"

"I mean, it looks like they're too late to be effective. Oreos and pickles?"

She scuffed her toe over the pale, mottled tile floor. "I figure we might burn calories."

"What do you think we're going to do? Run laps around the bed?"

She bit back the honest answer, which was that she honest-to-God *didn't know*.

Well, she did. She was thirty years old. She knew

what people did in bed. Theoretically. She just hadn't done it.

She followed him down the aisle, and they stopped in front of the condoms, which was an item she had never bought before. It was an item she kind of avoided looking at whenever she came near this aisle for pads or tampons.

"I hear the ribbed ones are supposed to be good," she said, the words sounding inane.

"You hear?" he asked, the corner of his mouth quirking upward.

"Yeah," she said, trying to sound casual and sophisticated and very much in the loop where condoms and their various attractions were concerned.

He lifted a brow, then grabbed a box that was not ribbed. She held out her basket, and he put the box inside, and she arranged the bag of Cheetos over the top of it.

He smirked, but didn't say anything as they made their way over to the checkout. Her face got hideously red as they approached because she realized that no matter how well-concealed the condoms were beneath the Cheetos, the high schooler currently working the register was going to have to ring them up.

"You could have waited in the truck," Liam said, noticing her discomfort.

"Well, I wasn't thinking."

"And you needed Oreos and Cheetos. And pickles, apparently."

She wrinkled her nose, then looked behind them and nearly jumped out of her skin. Clara was standing there with a speculative look on her face and a shopping basket that had frozen macaroni and cheese and a couple of cases of Coke.

"Hi," Sabrina said.

"Hi," Clara returned.

"What are you doing… I mean… It's a weird time to be at the grocery store," Sabrina said, knowing she sounded faintly accusing.

"It can't be too weird, since you're here," Clara pointed out.

"I just thought…" Sabrina waved a hand. "You bison farmers went to bed early."

"Usually," Clara said. "But we were out of Coke, and I can't abide by that. I need it in the fridge and cold by lunch tomorrow. And I'm not going to have time then. So. Important things."

"Sure," Sabrina said. "We were just at the tasting room."

"Okay," Clara responded. Meanwhile, Liam had moved up to the front of the line and was unloading their items onto the conveyor belt. He said nothing to Clara, and placed the Cheetos, pickles and Oreos on the conveyor belt casually. Then the condoms.

She cast Clara a glance.

"Just running some errands," she said, the words thin.

"Cool," Clara responded, her eyes most definitely on that very telling gray box.

"Stocking up on the essentials," she continued.

"Clearly," Clara said, nodding.

"How are the bison?"

"The bison are good," Clara said.

As small talk went, theirs was fairly ludicrous. Talking bison and ignoring the magnum elephant in the room.

Liam finished paying, and blessedly, all of their items were then put into a bag. Concealed from sight.

Sabrina breathed out a sigh of relief. "Well, we're going to go."

Clara nodded. "You should. Get those Cheetos in the fridge."

She bristled, but kept a smile on her face. "Sure. And…maybe don't mention that you saw me buying Cheetos to anyone."

"Okay," Clara said, putting her mac and cheese on the conveyor belt. "Have…a good night."

"I will," Sabrina said.

She really hoped that was true.

She looked up at Liam, who was looking at her with an intensity that made the rock in her chest feel possibly heavier, larger.

She looked back at Clara one more time, and then followed Liam out of the store.

Suddenly, panic was the prevailing feeling. That rock sliding down into her stomach, sending sparks of confusion and nerves skittering through her. "Maybe you should just drop me off at home," she said.

He said nothing, instead, he just turned onto the road that led out of town, his forearm resting on the top of the steering wheel, the streetlights illuminating the determined set of his jaw.

"I just… That kind of messed up the mood."

He didn't respond to that either. She watched him until they drove out of range of the streetlights, until the only light came from the headlights on his truck, those same trees that had almost been beneath her notice earlier today suddenly looking dark and ominous.

"Is this the right way?" he asked.

"Yes," she responded, twisting her hands in her lap.

What was she doing now? She was afraid. That's what was happening. She was scared of what all of this meant. Of being rejected again. Of not knowing what she was doing. Of him discovering that she didn't know what she was doing. That was the problem. With all of this.

Because once she was naked with him again, once they were together, he was going to know. That she wasn't just wounded, that she wasn't just angry, but that she was stalled out. And that it was because of him.

Now that the buzz from the wine had faded, all of her bravado was gone with it. Evaporated into the ether, impossible to retrieve.

The silence was as oppressive as the darkness, crushing in around them, like a weight that she didn't have the power to lift back off. She didn't know what to say to him. Didn't know what to say to any of this.

She was *never* like this. She was never panicky. Except when it came to him. He was the one that made her do things like this. That made her walk into Ace's bar and run out like a scared little girl. He was the one that made her feel uncertain, where she had otherwise learned to stand on her own feet and be competent. She'd had to do that, because her own father had cut her off and everything in her life she'd been so certain of had gotten destroyed at seventeen. She had to make her own way, she had no choice.

And Liam made her feel like… Well, he made her feel like a seventeen-year-old. Like the feelings inside of her were too big for her skin. She wanted to unzip it. To escape. To be someone else. Anyone else. Just not Sabrina Leighton. Sabrina Leighton who would never be woman enough, would never be sexy enough or interesting enough for a man like Liam Donnelly.

He made her feel immature. Like everything she did and said was wrong.

Not because of him, but because she just wanted to do the right thing, the seductive thing, so damned much.

And now it was all ruined again. What the hell had she been doing? Pickles and Oreos. She was a world-class dumbass. And most definitely a virgin.

She was going to continue to be one.

She continued to spin out her self-flagellation as they carried on down the highway, until they came to the road that led to her house.

"Turn here," she said softly.

"Left or right?"

"Left," she said.

He turned sharply, then continued on down the road until she indicated a narrow dirt driveway. Doom. It felt like they were headed toward doom. Or the very least the end of something. Something she wasn't sure she wanted to see the end of.

She had made her decision, and she was upset about it. But she couldn't go back now. He didn't want to be jerked around, she was certain of that. She had done a fair amount of it, all high-and-mighty and full of her own power when he'd admitted that he wanted her.

And right now, she did feel stupid. As stupid as she had felt that day at the winery when she had caused a drunken disaster in front of all and sundry. When she had destroyed everything she held dear.

She had been a teenager then, demanding that she be treated like a woman while acting like a child.

Now she was a woman, acting like a child, feeling like a teenager.

She just couldn't get all the pieces of herself to play nicely. To line up.

"This is it," she said softly, when they reached the

end of the road and her small home came into view, the porch light on, typically a cheery and welcome sign, and now less so.

"I'm sorry... I just... Bye." She put her hand on the door, and then suddenly found herself being called back toward the driver side.

"Where do you think you're going?"

"Into... Into my house," she said, her voice trembling.

Suddenly, she was in his arms, crushed up against his chest awkwardly, her back against the steering wheel. And he was kissing her. Hard, fierce, his tongue staking a claim, branding her with a fire that burned away every worry, every thought, every little panic she had experienced just a few moments before.

There was nothing. Not a single year without him, let alone thirteen. Not a giant gulf between their experience levels. Nothing. Nothing but his lips. Nothing but his kiss.

It went on and on, for she didn't know how long, and she reveled in it. Gloried in him. Was so damned grateful for it.

He lifted his hand, cupped the back of her head, then curled his fingers around her hair, jerking her back, separating their mouths.

"I want you," he said, his voice hard. "And I don't care about moments. How many damn moments have passed, Sabrina? Since I've known you, too many damned moments have passed. We let them pass. I'm done with it."

"You're the one who let it pass the first time," she said.

"That's true. I did. And I regretted it, a lot more often than I care to admit. Damn, did I regret it. I'm not gonna let it happen again."

"But… It just… It kind of did."

"Then I'll make a new one. A new moment."

"I don't…"

And then he was kissing her again, each drugging pass of his tongue against hers, that slick slide of flesh, carrying her closer to something she couldn't put a name to.

They parted and he was breathing hard, just like she was.

"Get your ass in the house," he said.

"Liam…"

"Otherwise, this is going to happen in the truck, and after all this time I think we deserve a little bit more room than that, don't you?"

"I…"

"If you want to stay in the truck, that's fine with me. The first time can be in the truck, we'll make the second time in the bed."

"The bed would be good," she said, moving away from him and stumbling out of the cab of the truck, her heart hammering.

She was shaking, she realized. Not because she was afraid of him. But because she was just… Overwrought. Overwhelmed. She couldn't believe it was happening, and she knew, to a degree, that she hadn't told him the moment was over because she was trying to put a stop to something she had a feeling had been inevitable from the start. An inevitability that scared her now.

It wasn't about Clara, or conversations of bison. It was about her. About being terrified of risking the kind of exposure this would cause her. About feeling silly. About doing the wrong thing.

About revealing so much of herself.

It was all fine in theory, but in practice… It was so much of her worst nightmare.

This stripping away of layers, this unguarded emotion. This need that would be a thousand times more naked than they were.

Maybe that was the real reason she had avoided men and sex all this time. Maybe it wasn't because of Liam, and how much she wanted him.

She could have lain back and taken second best at any point in time. Maybe it was just the idea of being out of control. Of being at the mercy of someone else and what they might make her feel.

Because she *hated* it. Because she had done it once, and it had wrecked her entire life. No, Liam hadn't made love to her ever, but he had taken control of her. Bewitched her. Her emotions, her actions. She had felt beyond herself, completely and totally out of control after he'd left. He had demolished all of her carefully cultivated defenses from day one. She was so afraid of that happening again.

So afraid of so many things.

She opened the front door and walked inside, waiting for a moment until he came in after her before closing it behind them. She wished that she had cleaned. She didn't think her bed was made. She was pretty sure she had left her pajama bottoms and her panties lying on the bathroom floor. Was most definitely not ready for this. Not ready for him.

She turned to him, turned to him to say something, to protest. But then he gathered her up in his arms and kissed her deep and hard. Kissed away her thoughts. Her concerns.

Just as he had done in the truck. And it left behind nothing. Nothing but desire. Nothing but need.

She felt like she was standing on the edge of a cliff, on the brink of making a choice. And she realized then that she was going to have to be more afraid of turning away from the cliff than jumping off.

When he pulled away from her, cupping her cheek and gazing into her eyes, she felt like maybe she was. Like it would be worse, more terrifying, to avoid the jump than to simply take it.

He dropped the plastic bag on the ground, reached inside and pulled out the box of condoms. He left the rest. Then he wrapped his arm around her waist and kissed her again, sweet, consuming kisses that went deeper each time. Kisses that made her shake, that made her ache between her thighs, a hollow feeling spreading out from there.

She had come too far not to jump.

"Take me to bed," she mumbled against his lips.

"With pleasure."

Suddenly, she found herself being swept up off the ground, held against that hard, broad chest. "Which way?" he asked.

"Back that way," she said, gesturing wildly toward the hall. She grimaced as they passed the tiny kitchen, the sink piled high with dishes.

Yeah, definitely not the sexiest thing.

"Where'd you go, Sabrina?" he asked, his voice rough.

"What?"

"You're not here with me. You're thinking about something. Worrying about something."

"Just... My house is a mess."

He stopped walking, then he gripped her chin, holding her face steady and forcing her to meet his gaze. "Look at me, baby. I don't give a fuck about how your house looks. Whatever other things you're worried about? I don't care about them either. I want you. There is nothing else on my mind. Nothing else I'm thinking of at this moment. I want you. Just you. Exactly as you are. Whatever it is you're afraid I won't like, afraid you won't like, don't be afraid of it."

"Just like that?" she asked, her voice wobbling. "Don't think about anything else? Don't worry?"

"Yeah," he said, his voice calm. "Just like that."

"It's not that easy for me," she said. "I have a…a busy brain." And all those thoughts kept her from feeling too much. As long as she was thinking about everything that was happening, it didn't feel quite so big.

"I think I can handle that," he said. "By the time I've got you in bed, I'm going to erase every thought from that head. Until all you can do is feel. My hands on your skin. My tongue. My cock."

Shock stunned her for a moment, her stomach twisting sharply. She said nothing, did nothing but stare at him.

"That's more like it," he said, clearly taking her silence as a victory.

And then he was walking again, carrying her toward the bedroom, toward a moment that had been in the making for thirteen years.

There was so much between then and now. So much hurt. So much worry. So many good things, and so many bad things. So, so much. But it didn't matter. Not now.

It was only them. Only this.

They moved into her bedroom and she tried very hard not to imagine what it was he saw when he looked around the place. At her bed with the little pink duvet with the little gathered bunches of fabric that made it look like roses. At all the girly pillows on her bed that clearly announced a man did not live here, never had, and had likely never even been anywhere near the mattress.

But he didn't pause. Instead, he crossed the room and set her down at the center of the bed, straightening and leaning back to flick the light on. She bit her lip.

"What now?" he asked, way more in tune with her than she'd like him to be right now. If only she could save all that instinct of his for the actual sex, and have him be totally oblivious when it came to everything else.

"Are we going to do it with the light on?" she asked.

"*Do it?* You mean am I going to make love to you with the light on? Yes. I damn well am. Because I want to see your body."

"It hasn't improved since I was a teenager." She shifted restlessly on top of the covers, leaning back against the pillows.

"Well, I don't believe that," he said. "I maybe haven't seen you naked since I've been back, but believe me, I have taken stock of the situation."

"My hips are bigger," she pointed out.

His green eyes swept her up and down and her whole body went hot. "I've noticed. I like it."

"My breasts are not as perky," she added, making sure he was aware of the grave reality.

"Do you honestly think any man cares about how perky they are? You're a woman. You're built like a woman. The hell do I care if your breasts are up by your eyeballs? I don't. I just care that I get to see them. That I get to touch them. Taste them."

She shuddered. "Oh."

"And I figure, that what you said is true. I have seen you naked, even if it's been a long time. And you haven't gotten to see me. I thought you might want to."

He gripped the hem of his T-shirt and pulled it up over his head, his ab muscles rippling with the motion. Her throat went dry, her entire body seizing up as she watched the play of his muscles, the way his tattoos shifted and bunched with the motion.

He was beautiful. So much more than she had imagined. Her heart felt like it had been crunched up in a fist and she forgot to breathe. Forgot to do anything but stare at that incredible body that was everything it had ever promised to be. Those glorious muscles and those incredible tattoos. She was trying to read them, trying to take it all in, trying to figure out what they all meant.

She could see the rest of the tree now, the one she had only just gotten a glimpse of peeking from the short sleeves of his T-shirts since he had come back.

It wrapped around his shoulder, wrapped around his back. She couldn't see the whole thing, not yet.

Though, now that she could see as much of it as she did, it reminded her of that large tree at the winery, the one just in front of the house where she had grown up. The one she'd been standing under when he'd come out of the house after talking to her father...

She swallowed hard.

"I do want to see you," she said, her breath catching. "I really do."

"Good."

He smiled, walking over to the bed, tossing the box of condoms onto her nightstand. Then he leaned over, placing his hands on either side of her head, pinning her down to the mattress as he kissed her deeply. She lifted her hands, then curled them into fists, dropping them back down at her sides.

"You can touch me," he said.

She was embarrassed he had realized how nervous she was. Had definitely picked up on her hesitation. Rat bastard and his selective insight. He was going to pick up on her inexperience too.

She could tell him, she supposed. Except, she didn't want to talk about it. She didn't want to say anything. She didn't want to think. For the first time in a long time, all she wanted to do was feel.

Wanted to feel his hot skin against hers, wanted to finally know what it was to have him inside of her.

Yes, she wanted all of that. All of that and more. She wanted to escape that prison she had built inside of herself. Those walls. All those walls.

That thought jarred her. Hadn't she just been thinking about the way her father built up walls between himself and everyone around him? The way he closed everyone off from him.

She did it too. She had spent the past few years slowly barricading herself behind reason and sense, hiding herself away from strong emotions, from anything that might challenge her, that might take her control.

She might not cut people off, but she cut off feelings. And she cut them off ruthlessly.

But if this was her chance to explore passion, perhaps it could be even more than that. Maybe it was her chance to destroy that fear. To destroy those walls.

To get back what she had lost all that time ago.

Liam had made it perfectly clear that nothing was going to happen between them, not permanently. But there was no reason that it couldn't be something more than just sex.

No reason it couldn't rebuild what had been lost.

So she reached up, pressed her palm against his chest, felt his skin, so hot and delicious beneath her touch. The hair there tickled her palm, sent an arrow of need down between her thighs. He was so different from her. So much harder. So much larger. It was intoxicating. And so, so sexy.

"Your turn," he said, his voice rough.

He grabbed hold of her sweater and wrenched it up above her head, so that she was exposed to him, wearing only her very plain white bra that had not a single bit of lace or anything sexy to recommend it.

She was going to try to not worry about that, was going to cling to what he had said earlier. That he didn't care about much of anything as long as he got to touch her breasts. And taste them.

She shivered. She very much wanted him to taste them.

He gripped her chin, held her face steady as he kissed her, and somehow, he removed her bra from her body without her even realizing what he was doing, somehow, her bare breasts were now crushed against his chest, her nipples tight. From the cold air, and from the intensity of her arousal.

She was so turned on. So desperately needy for whatever he could give her.

It was terrifying. Most definitely like falling off that cliff she had been poised on the brink of only moments ago. But she wanted it. Wanted to embrace the fear, wanted to take this moment to be a woman untamed.

Out of control. To be nothing but feeling, and no hesitation at all.

She wanted to be new. Wanted to be different.

Perhaps it wasn't so different than that earlier feeling of wanting to crawl out of her skin. Wanting to be someone else. Feel something else.

Wanting him. Just him. With a kind of desperation that stunned her.

He moved away from her, gazed at her body, his eyes unashamedly fixed to her breasts.

"Damn," he said, reaching up and sliding his thumb over her nipple. She gasped, arching her back. "Sensitive."

He leaned down, tugged the tightened bud between his lips, sliding his tongue over it, then drawing back and blowing across it. She shivered, shocking jolts of need rocking her. Her internal muscles pulsed, bringing her to the edge of climax with just one touch. Oh, she was going to embarrass herself. She was going to come so quickly he was going to know that she was inexperienced. He was going to know no other man had ever touched her like this. No other man had seen her naked.

But then, she couldn't worry about it. Not when he brought his lips down on her other breast, on the tender skin just above her nipple, before lowering his mouth and taking it in deep, sucking hard, making her moan.

"Very sensitive," he murmured against her skin.

She was dying. Coming apart. Each touch, each kiss a brick removed from one of her walls. Undone. *She* was undone. Or at least, about to be.

Nothing left but need. Nothing left but feeling. So much feeling. Feeling she had turned away from, denied, shut out for so, so long.

He reached up, palming her breast, squeezing her hard and she arched against him, begging for more of his touch without words, because she didn't have words. She had nothing. Nothing but a deep, intense desire to have more of him, all of him. Everything he would give. She grabbed hold of his shoulders, slid her fingertips down his back, the interplay of those hard muscles beneath her touch a sweet kind of torture that had her feeling hot and slick between her legs.

This was nothing like anything she'd ever felt before. Nothing like wanting him at seventeen had been. She had wanted to be close to him. Wanted intimacy. And she had been turned on, but mostly nervous. She had been innocent. A girl.

Now she was a woman. And she felt every inch a woman. Responding as a woman, needing as a woman.

Her lips curved into a smile.

She matched up. *Finally.*

His hands lowered down and he flicked the button on her jeans open, drawing her zipper down, then he pushed his calloused fingers beneath the hem of her panties, sliding one finger down between her slick crease, moving the pad of his finger back over her clit. She jerked against his touch, that intensity of her longing so shocking she was powerless to hold back her gasp of need.

She wanted him so much. Wanted this *so* much. Finally, Liam Donnelly. *Finally.*

She looked up at his face, and memorized the sameness. Those green eyes, those wicked lips. And the differences too. The hard grooves that had been carved next to his mouth, the lines between his eyebrows, by his eyes. Representative of a thousand smiles she hadn't seen. A hundred different frowns. Moments of stress and tension that she hadn't been a part of. So much life that she had missed. So much of him.

It made her ache. Made her feel desperate.

And it made her reckless. Made her determined to seize this moment, to seize what they had now. To grab every little thing that she could. Every last groan, every breath, every beat of his heart against her hand as it lay pressed against that bare chest.

They couldn't have the past thirteen years back, and she knew they couldn't have forever. But they had right now. And she would take it.

Oh, would she ever take it.

He stroked her, bringing her close, so close to the edge of orgasm, and then drawing back. She shifted restlessly beneath his touch, and he pressed a finger deep inside of her as he continued to stroke her with an extremely talented thumb.

She couldn't believe how easy it was. How quickly he was accomplishing this, when typically on her own it took a whole lot of time and an extreme amount of concentration.

He was drawing out her climax with ease. As if he knew her body better than she did.

He shifted, pressing another finger inside of her, the slight burning pressure stealing her pleasure for a moment before he pressed the heel of his hand back to that sensitive bundle of nerves. He rocked his hand slowly, back and forth, his fingers stroking something sensitive and untouched deep inside of her. And then she lost herself. Lost everything in an extreme explosion of pleasure, lights bursting behind her eyes as she gave herself over to her climax. Her internal muscles tightened around his fingers, her whole body releasing as pleasure washed over her like a tide, endless, unchecked.

When she came back to herself she was breathing hard and he was gazing down at her with those fierce green eyes glittering.

"Beautiful," he said, kissing her lips. "The most beautiful."

He withdrew from her, grabbing hold of her pants and pulling them the rest of the way down her legs, casting them down on the floor, along with her underwear. She was naked, but now she didn't care. She simply felt boneless, pliant. She had already come, so there was nothing more to worry about, really. Whatever happened now, she felt like she was floating, felt like she was about to sail away on a breeze. Or something. She couldn't exactly think straight. And she didn't have anything she could compare this to.

That first touch of Liam's hand. That first time being brought to the peak of pleasure by someone else.

Of giving over that control.

He moved away from her, standing on the edge of the bed, undoing his jeans and shrugging them down his muscular thighs.

She could see the outline of his arousal clearly through the black boxer briefs he was wearing. So big, so thick, so much more than she had imagined it could be. She had gotten the gist of it when she had looked down at his jeans earlier in the evening, but this was a much more explicit preview.

And then, he pushed them off without ceremony, leaving him naked and exposed to her hungry gaze. To her hungry, curious gaze, because she had never seen a naked man in person before. And he was quite a lot of naked man.

He was quite a lot in general.

He moved to the edge of the bed and she scooted toward the end of it, reaching up and pressing her hand against his hard-cut abs. She trailed her fingertips down each ridge of muscle, hesitating when she reached that gorgeous cock. She wanted to touch him. Wanted to taste him.

And so she did.

She wrapped her fingers around his hard length, stunned for a moment how hot it was. And how soft the skin was. Then she leaned in, touching her tongue to his shaft, gratified when he jerked. She looked up at him, and he was gazing down at her, his jaw held tight, his lips pressed into a grim line. The evidence of his tested control in each distended tendon in his neck, in the way he stood completely immobile.

She pressed her lips against that wide head, then wrapped her lips around it, drawing each glorious inch of him into her mouth, as far as she could take him. She curled her hand around the base, dragged her tongue along his length.

He breathed out a curse, reaching up and grabbing hold of her hair, his hips bucking forward.

It was crass, but she didn't care, because she knew that he enjoyed it. Knew that he was this close to losing it because of her.

Because a virgin had her mouth on him.

That at least made her feel satisfied. Whatever came after this, she had that.

She might be inexperienced, but he wasn't immune to her. Not even a little bit.

She dragged her mouth from him slowly, sliding her tongue along his length as she did, then she licked him like a lollipop, and found herself being lifted up, held against his chest, her breasts crushed against him as he claimed her mouth with his.

And then she was falling, back onto the bed, beneath all that hard, hot wall of man. He pressed her thighs wide, settling between them, pressing the head of his erection against the entrance to her body before dragging it up to where she was most sensitive, sliding that hard length through her slick folds.

Then he reached to the side, fumbling until he grabbed hold of the box of condoms. The condoms that had nearly kept this from happening. That had nearly given her the out that her fear so desperately craved. She could not remember what she had been thinking then. It seemed like another day. Seemed like another person.

That girl who had nearly let her fear, let her embarrassment, talk her out of claiming something she had wanted for so long.

She could hardly *remember* that girl.

He opened the box quickly, taking out a gray packet and tearing it open. Then he quickly rolled the latex over his length before moving back between her thighs, kissing her deeply, stealing her nerves, stealing any hesitation she might have felt.

She arched against him as he pressed into her, slowly, achingly slowly. She felt each agonizing inch as he stretched her, as he reached that barrier, the burning, stretching pain strangely welcome. Then he jerked his hips forward, finishing it, burying himself in her completely.

She cried out, unable to stop herself, because that hurt like *fucking hell*.

He lifted his head, his gaze burning into hers, and for the first time she was sorry they had left the lights on. Because she knew that he could see her expression perfectly. That he could see the pain etched there, the uncertainty, the nerves, the embarrassment.

That it was all written there in a flush stained over her cheeks, in the way she was biting her lip, in all the raw uncertainty she was sure he could see in her eyes.

She didn't know what to expect. For him to get angry. For him to stop.

Instead, he lowered his head for a moment, first pressing his forehead against hers. Then he kissed her lips, kissed her neck. He murmured something she couldn't understand, jerking up against her body, sliding his hands down beneath her butt as he lifted her up to meet him.

He whispered something that sounded a lot like an apology before withdrawing from her slightly and thrusting back home.

He rolled his hips against hers, that thick, uncompromising length sliding in and out of her as he made short, fractured sounds that sounded somewhere between pleasure and pain. And it took a while for her own pain to fade. For that restless buzz of desire to return. But it did. And when it did it built deeper, more intensely than it had before. When it did, she couldn't be concerned about anything. Not about her lack of practical experience or what he thought of it, not about what he wanted, not about what he felt.

Everything in her world was reduced to her own need,

to her own desire. To the restless command of arousal that overtook her completely.

She was close. *So* close.

She rocked her hips against his, instinctively meeting his every thrust with a movement of her hips.

He reached up for her breast, sliding his thumb over her nipple, pinching it, teasing it. And then he kissed her, taking her mouth hard with his own, his tongue going deep as he staked a claim on her that she didn't think she would ever be free of.

Then she broke.

Utterly. Completely. Her internal muscles tightening around his erection as she gave up everything. All of her thoughts. All of her control. She was broken open, for him, *with* him.

He growled against her mouth, his erection pulsing deep inside of her as he came, as he found his own pleasure, his own release.

She had been right to be afraid of this. Had been right to be afraid of him. There would be no going back after this. There would be no rebuilding those walls inside of her. No pretending that she hadn't known this pleasure, that she hadn't known this man. It wouldn't be something she could simply walk away from as if it had never happened.

And perhaps that was the problem. Perhaps it was what they had both always known.

They lay together for a moment, his heart pounding heavily against her chest, the room seeming to spin above her.

She'd done it. She'd had sex with Liam Donnelly.

And she truly didn't know what she was supposed to feel.

He rolled away from her, breathing hard. Then he sat up on the bed, his back to her. She rolled over facing him. And all the breath rushed from her body.

Finally, that whole tattoo was visible to her. And it was *the* tree. She was certain of that.

But it was more than just the tree. It was the girl, blonde and barefoot, leaning against the tree.

Grassroots Winery was inked on Liam Donnelly's skin. And so was she.

CHAPTER ELEVEN

LIAM FELT LIKE he had been kicked in the chest, so when Sabrina's tiny fist connected with his back, it took him a moment to realize that he had been hit in reality, and not just metaphorically.

"What the hell?" came her venomous-sounding growl.

"What?" he asked, getting up off the bed slowly and turning to face her. She was naked, beautiful, those pale pink nipples on display. But she was also angry. Angrier than he could remember ever seeing her.

He had seen her naked and shell-shocked before, that was true, but he had never seen her this righteously furious, blue eyes blazing.

"Explain that tattoo," she said. "The tattoo you have of the tree. The tattoo you have of *me*."

Oh shit. The tattoo. Why the hell hadn't he realized she was going to see that? Why the hell hadn't he realized…

Because somehow you managed to get it without acknowledging what you were doing. Because you're so deep in your own bullshit that you thought maybe she would be too. That it really wasn't a big deal.

The lights had been on the entire time, but somehow now he felt like they had been wrenched up so that they were even brighter. Somehow now, it felt like he was exposed in a way he hadn't been before.

He had been naked in front of a lot of women. And the response had always been positive. He wasn't shy in the least.

This was different. This was like reading pages from a diary he had never intended to keep. Like he was a damned teenage girl.

"It's a tattoo," he said, finally, flatly.

"It's *me*," she said.

"I have a lot of tattoos," he said. He got out of bed and walked into the bathroom, discarding the condom before returning to the bedroom. "About different things. Different things I've done."

"Right. But you didn't care about me, did you, Liam? It was easy for you to leave? Easy for you to accuse me of having baggage while you had stepped away from all of it carrying nothing. But you're a liar. You have it all on you permanently. It's just so self-righteous. You told me to let things go. You're telling me not to think... not to feel anything, and you have it all emblazoned on your body. What did you think? That I wouldn't notice?"

"I didn't think," he said, the words clipped. "Honest to God. I got the tattoo a couple of years after I left. And I thought about the tree, because trees are strong. And they have roots. And they can withstand storms. And then, when the guy was making the design I thought of a blonde woman. Standing at the base of the tree."

"Just a blonde. Any old blonde," she said, waving her hand around.

"I didn't let myself think about it," he bit out.

"Incredible," she said. "Let me ask you a question, Liam, does anybody buy your bullshit as much as you do?"

"It doesn't matter. It's just a tattoo."

"It's just the entire past permanently etched into your back," she said, flinging her hands wide. "Right. Not a big deal at all."

"Maybe it is," he said. "Maybe it's part of my life I didn't want to forget. Your father giving me the money…"

"Right. My father. Not me. But he gave it to you because of me. I'm everywhere in your past. And you're everywhere in mine. You're all up in all of it. And what happened to me afterward… You made me think that I was being ridiculous. That something was wrong with me. Everybody did. But it does all come back to you. It does. Whatever you say, whatever anyone else says."

"Convenient that you're freaking out at me now," he commented. "You know, now that we've already had sex. Now that you got what you wanted. But you're scared now, aren't you? Because you let yourself have it. You let yourself do it. So now you have to get up in my grill and blame me for more things."

"I don't have to. You showed all that guilt to me when you turned around."

"Why does it bother you so much? Do you feel vindicated?"

He didn't even know what fight he was having right now. Because her words were burrowing down beneath his skin and tearing strips off him. Because it was forcing him to look at those past decisions he made. At everything he had let himself believe. Liam Donnelly, the one who saw everything clearly. Who had known he had to leave Sabrina because it was for her own good. Who had known that taking the money for college was simply the right thing to do, because without it he would have nothing. Who had known that earning all that money was just something he had to do, not something that would fix him.

He had said all those things with confidence. To himself, to other people. To his mother as he wrote her that giant-ass check to pay her back for all the years she had spent raising him. To settle a score, he had told himself, not to flip her the middle finger. Not to try to prove to her with one last gasp she had been wrong about him.

That he mattered. That his life had mattered and that she should be damned glad her neglect hadn't killed him.

All of those walls, those structures he had built up around himself were going up in flames, bright blue flames that looked a lot like Sabrina Leighton's eyes.

"I do have a right to be angry," she said. "Because I've been carrying this on my shoulders the whole time. And it's right there on yours. Right there on yours and you're pretending that it isn't." She huffed out a laugh. "I have been… I ruined *everything*. I ruined everything, and you let me think that I did it for nothing. For something I made up. Something only I still thought about."

Suddenly, something snapped inside of him. Anger, unreasonable, unquenchable anger flowing through him.

She was uncovering his lies, getting down to the truth, and he didn't like it. He didn't like it, because he didn't want to see them any more than he wanted her to. No one else ever bothered with this. They were content with his facade. The suit, the money. If they were lovers, with his skin, and the tattoos. Never what they represented.

But she wanted deeper. And he wanted nothing less.

"You ruined everything, right? Absolutely everything." He moved around to the end of the bed, pressed his hands against the mattress and leaned forward. "That has been a pretty convenient story for you this whole time, don't lie about that, Sabrina. Because what danger does it put you in to believe that? To believe that you are so powerful you're the one who destroyed all the things around you and you have to stay here and pay penance for the rest of your damned life. You might have been hurt, you might have been wandering around all wounded and ashamed, but it kept you safe, didn't it? You got to blame it on me. You got to cast me as the villain, and you, the unwitting tragic maiden."

"I'm sorry, I might have cast you as the villain but you cast yourself as the benevolent knight." She curled her legs up, rolled away from him and got off the bed. "The benevolent knight who took a payoff from my father and then ran off leaving me to pick up all the pieces."

"Who told you that you were the one who had to pick them up?" he asked.

"What?"

"Who told you all those pieces were your responsibility? You didn't cause anything. You exposed what people were already doing. Your father already knew your mother was having an affair, I would wager a guess that half the people in town did too. Certainly the men she was sleeping with knew. Your father let that sin become yours. And you took it on. You took it on and made it yours. And then you held it close all this time, and you used it as an excuse. For why you didn't go to school away from home. Why you haven't left."

She huffed, her hands clenched into fists at her sides. She looked like she was fighting the urge to strangle him, but he carried on, anyway.

"You might be hurt, but you're safe. And I think that's what you wanted. So go ahead and scream at me if you want but it doesn't change the fact that you have stake in what happened to your life, and what happened in everyone else's isn't your damn fault. You would rather blame yourself for all those things than for the one thing that you can actually control, which is what you do with yourself. So go ahead, Sabrina, blame me for that. For the fact that you were a thirty-year-old virgin, for the fact that you never left home, but you're lying to yourself."

They stood and faced each other, naked and ridiculously angry with each other. He could honestly say he'd never had a screaming match with a woman when they were both naked.

Hell, he hadn't been with any woman long enough to have a screaming match period.

Arousal began to work its way through into his anger. He didn't get mad, that wasn't what he did. He was a problem solver, and he was way too guarded to let himself lose his shit like this. But there was something about her. Something about this.

And there was most certainly no control.

He started to collect his clothes, pulling them on quickly and stalking out of the bedroom. He heard scrambling and shuffling behind him and realized that she was doing the same. He didn't stop. He didn't care.

"Are you just going to run away again?" she demanded.

He turned back around and faced her. She was standing in the doorway wearing nothing but a T-shirt and panties. He wanted to throw her down on the bed. To stop this talking nonsense and just get back to sex. Because at least that felt good. This felt like hell.

"I'm leaving because you're acting like a crazy person," he responded.

Leaving because the alternative really was having her again, and he had a feeling she didn't actually want that.

"Not because you're scared?" she asked, her chin jutting out, her expression defiant.

"No," he said.

"Because you know what all those tattoos tell me? You have every bit the amount of poison and pain that I do inside of me, but you don't want to deal with it. You shove it down deep. You put it on your skin. You just move it to the outside so that you can pretend that it's over. But you haven't forgotten it. I cannot believe you have me on your back. And you've slept with other women and… How did they never ask you about it?"

"I was never with anyone long enough for them to earn the right to ask me questions like that."

"Well, since I'm the girl in the back tattoo I suppose I have the right to question you."

He stalked closer to her. "I'm done being questioned."

"Why?" She planted her hands on her hips. "Because you don't like the answers?"

"How about you? How about you and your great martyrdom? How does that look from where you're standing on your high horse?"

Her face twitched, her lips pulling tight on either side. "Get out of my house."

"Too real for you?"

"I just gave you my virginity, asshole. I'm done with you acting like somehow you have this great perspective on my life, and on yours when I know that you don't. You're a liar, Liam. And I think you lie to yourself just as much as you've lied to me. I don't have any reason to stand here and talk to a liar."

He grabbed his truck keys off the counter and headed

out the front door, realizing as he started the engine that she didn't have a car there.

Oh fucking well.

She would have to deal with that herself. She would have to sort it all out for herself. It was not his job. Not even remotely.

When he leaned back against the driver seat, the tattoo felt like it was burning.

She was right. She was. There was no getting around that. Especially not when he had just had it shouted at him. He had tattooed her on him so that he wouldn't forget. Because there was something about her he couldn't let go.

The scent of vanilla made him ache and when he smelled it on another woman he could never bring himself to touch her.

Because there was more young love bullshit involved in his feelings for her than he wanted to admit. Then or now.

What was the point? What was the damned point of any of it?

Of gaining perspective on something it was too late to change, too late to fix.

Then he was just mad. As he drove back down the highway toward Copper Ridge and toward the Laughing Irish Ranch, he was just pissed. Because Sabrina Leighton had finally been his. And it had ended in recrimination and shouting. Just like last time.

He didn't know why she had to dig in like that. Why she had to make it about anything other than the orgasms they had just had. He could never forget.

And somehow, it hit him then that she still hadn't taken down her hair for him.

CHAPTER TWELVE

THE NEXT MORNING Sabrina woke up feeling stiff, awful and sore. Her entire body ached, her chest ached, her heart ached. She didn't quite know what to do about any of it.

Damned Liam Donnelly. Everything from the night before came flooding back as she padded gingerly into her living room and started the coffee maker.

She looked out the window and saw that there was no car in her driveway.

Dammit. She was going to have to get a ride to work, and she was going to have to explain herself.

She mentally cataloged who she wanted to come and get her. She was going to owe them an explanation, that was certain. And she didn't particularly want to give one.

She needed a nonjudgmental driver, and she wasn't sure that person existed. But she did know somebody she thought might be able to give good advice. Talk her down.

Someone who had certainly been disappointed by a man before.

She groaned, grabbed her cell phone off the counter and dialed her sister-in-law. "Lin? Are you busy?"

"I'm still in bed," Lindy said, her voice muffled. "What's wrong?"

"I need a ride to work."

"What?" She heard the sound of rustling covers and she imagined Lindy sitting bolt upright.

"I'm fine. I'm at home. I just don't have a car. I left it in town last night."

"I can give you a ride to your car," Lindy said, sounding more urgent than sleepy now.

"Maybe after work. But I just want to get in and get started on the day."

She just wanted something to feel normal. Anything.

"Okay," Lindy said, her tone hesitant. "It will take me about half an hour to get ready and get down there. Is that okay?"

She knew that regardless of her reassurance Lindy had not entirely bought the promise that she was okay.

"That's fine."

She hung up the phone with her sister-in-law and paced the length of her house. She was waiting for the coffee. She needed the coffee. First would come coffee, and then perhaps clarity.

Except she ached between her legs, and she knew exactly why that was. And that was an overriding bit of panic that seemed to defy the idea that clarity was anywhere to be found.

Finally, the coffee was done, and she downed her first cup, then moved on to the second. She was halfway through that one when Lindy arrived at the front door and walked inside without knocking.

Her sister-in-law had her keys held between her knuckles, her expression one of near comical suspicion. She was not her usual pulled-together self, but wearing leggings and a denim shirt, her hair slightly ruffled. "Is everything okay?"

"Yes," Sabrina said, eyeballing the keys.

"Blink twice if something is really wrong."

"There are no intruders in my house," Sabrina said, deadpan.

Lindy relaxed her stance and looked around shiftily. "It was just very weird to have you call me that early."

"I know," Sabrina said, curving her fingers around her coffee mug and leaning over the counter.

"You look…kind of a mess."

She nodded glumly. "I know. I did my best, but apparently regret is incredibly hard to wash off of your face."

"Oh, Sabrina. What did you do?" Sabrina made a strangled sound. "*Who* did you do?" Lindy corrected herself.

"Three guesses," Sabrina said, taking another sip of coffee.

"Liam Donnelly?"

"Not even a fair game, really."

"Oh, Sabrina."

Lindy sidled up to her and wrapped her arm around her shoulders.

"It was stupid," Sabrina said.

"We are often stupid where good-looking men are concerned. All of us." She squeezed her and then released her hold on her.

"I was supposed to be cured."

"In my experience that isn't so simple as you'd like it to be. Especially when there's a history."

"My brother?" Sabrina asked, wondering if that was what Lindy was referring to.

"Oh, trust me, once I knew that he had put his hands on another woman, they were certainly not getting anywhere near me. But he begged me to take him back, Sabrina, and it was really hard not to feel tempted to do that. Ten years. That's so much of a life. And part of me really wanted to fix it. When he accused me of destroying us over a mistake…"

"It made you wonder if that's what you were doing?"

"Hell no," she said, waving her hand like she was clearing the air. "That was when the moment of clarity came. When it slapped me. *He* cheated on *me*, and he was going to put the blame on the end of our marriage on me. And I knew that it was basically the sum total of all of our years together. Damien wiggling out of whatever problems we had. Trying to make sure we shared equal blame even when he was the one messing around on the side. And I just… I couldn't do it. Not anymore. No freaking way."

"Well, Liam never did anything like that to me. And we don't have near ten years' worth of history either. I'm trying to excuse myself. A thousand different ways. That until I knew what it was like to sleep with him I was never going to be able to let him go. But I think I just hurt myself more." She hunched over the counter, trying to ignore the stabbing feeling in her heart. "It hurts. It hurts so bad."

"What happened?"

"It's all of our past stuff. I know that you're well aware that my dad and I had a falling-out before you and Damien started dating."

"Right. But Damien and I dating just about caused a falling-out between him and your dad too. Because your dad is ridiculous."

"He is," Sabrina agreed. "I don't know if Damien ever told you what I did."

"No," Lindy said.

So Sabrina took it upon herself to regale her sister-in-law with the stories about her transgression, and Lindy listened, not saying anything.

"Jamison is an idiot," she said finally. "I can't believe he's been mad at you all that time for that."

"I humiliated him."

"He was a grown man and you are his daughter," Lindy said. "And the only person who did anything wrong was his wife. You made a mistake, and I know it was embarrassing. But you were hurt. Your dad interfered with your relationship."

"I was seventeen. It wasn't love, it shouldn't have mattered."

"But it *was* love," Lindy insisted. "And it *did* matter. It mattered to you."

"Seventeen-year-olds don't know what love is."

"I disagree," Lindy said. "I think seventeen-year-olds can feel love exactly the way that they can. That first time. That kind of wonderful, weightless, innocent way where you don't know how to protect yourself at all. It's a different kind of falling in love, sure. But don't dismiss your feelings."

Some of what Liam had shouted at her last night echoed inside of her. That she was more than ready and happy to blame him for her choices and blame herself for the pain of her family. That she seemed to be in some kind of deep denial where her own feelings were concerned.

And it made her wonder. What she might have done if she didn't have somebody else to blame. If she hadn't had the pain caused by Liam to hide behind.

If she had actually dealt with her own feelings, her own fears, rather than hiding behind her *martyrdom*, as he had called it.

"I did love him," she said. "You know, in that way. And losing him hurt me. And I got mileage out of that for a long time."

"What you mean by that?"

"I mean, I was able to use it as an excuse. I've never... I was never with anyone before last night." Her face heated.

Lindy's eyebrows shot up. *"Really?"*

"Because I was hung up on him. Because I didn't want to get hurt again. I blamed him. But I think mostly I've never wanted to risk myself. Not again. I can throw all that at his feet, but it's more than that. I know it is. I just don't know how to sort through it. I don't know what to do with it."

"Well, now you know. I guess that's a start. It's like Damien. Once I knew what our life was, and what it was going to continue to be if I gave in and agreed to a reconciliation, there was no going back. There was only going forward. That's where you are. I mean, I guess you have two choices. You ignore everything that he told you, or you decide that there is no truth in it, even though I think we both know there is. So you either start making some changes, or you go back to how it was. But you won't have an excuse this time. You won't have anything to hide behind."

She nodded slowly. "He sucks."

"I'm sure he does," Lindy said.

"I was fine before he came back."

"I don't think you were," Lindy said. "But then, who is?"

"I should have called Olivia," Sabrina said. "She would have been so appalled by my behavior that she wouldn't have been able to lecture me."

"She's a funny girl, that one," Lindy said.

"Yes, and infinitely less annoying when push comes to shove, thank you very much."

Lindy snorted. "Come on, drama llama, let's go."

Sabrina grudgingly followed her sister-in-law out of the house and out to her little red car, which they all called her midlife crisis car behind Lindy's back. No one would dare say it to her face.

It was definitely a cute car. And not one that Damien would have ever allowed her to spend money on. No. Damien liked big, new trucks that cost over fifty grand, and that he could pretend were practical in some way because they could haul heavy things. A zippy little car like that was not his thing.

But Sabrina enjoyed it. She enjoyed it the whole drive back to Grassroots. They turned down the paved, heavily wooded road and Lindy parked in the lot closest to the main dining area.

It was too early for the winery to be open, and yet Sabrina noticed that there was another truck in the lot. A very familiar truck.

"No," she moaned, pressing her head against the dashboard.

"He wasn't here when I left," Lindy said, her tone nearly apologetic.

"I'm not ready to deal with him."

"Well, see if you can come up with ways to make him less intimidating. Can you laugh at him? Was his penis unimpressive?"

"No," Sabrina said.

"How do *you* know? You've never been with anyone else."

"I have the internet, Lindy," Sabrina said.

"Well, failing laughing at any kind of genital tragedy I don't really have anything for you."

"The sex wasn't even bad," Sabrina wailed.

"I'm very sorry," Lindy said flatly.

"It was actually great."

"Now I'm just jealous."

"Well, you can have him," Sabrina said.

"You don't mean that. Do I need to put somebody else on this project?" She posed the question gently.

"No," Sabrina said. "I'm a professional. And Liam is a problem that I made for myself. I have to deal with it."

"Wow," Lindy said, "look at you. Not hiding. And then, you know when he comes back at you with something terrible and insulting you can bring this up as evidence that you aren't the coward."

"I am one, though," Sabrina said, her throat getting tight. "I wish I wasn't. And actually knowing isn't helpful at all because it means that I might have to do something about it."

"Yeah," Lindy said, her tone dry. "I really do relate to that feeling. Like suspecting your husband might be cheating on you and wishing you could just ignore it for a while. Because once you know..."

"I'm sorry," Sabrina said.

"It's just life," Lindy responded. "A sucky part, but we were never guaranteed a smooth ride. And good things have come from it. I guess that's just what you have to trust too. That good things will come from this. That even if it isn't a smooth ride it's going to be good in the end."

"I trust none of that," Sabrina said, opening the passenger door and getting out.

"Well, you don't have to trust it for it to be potentially true," Lindy said.

"You're way too optimistic," Sabrina said.

"Better than being a pessimist. Then you're angry about the bad things happening until they do happen, and you could have had a little bit of happiness in the meantime."

"Better than being blindsided," Sabrina pointed out.

"Is it? Would it make it hurt less?"

"Stop being logical," Sabrina groused.

"I'm going back to the house to finish getting ready," Lindy said. "Please don't kill him."

"I'm not going to kill him," Sabrina called back over her shoulder as she walked toward the dining area.

"That is a relief," a male voice said.

Sabrina looked up and saw Liam standing in the doorway, his muscular arms crossed over his broad chest. He was wearing a T-shirt, probably because he had been inside and it was warm in there. But it just seemed mean, as she didn't want to be harboring fantasies about licking those tattoos.

"I'm not going to kill you *now*," she clarified. "Later, much later when everyone has gone to sleep and I have an opportunity to hide the body…"

"Nice to see your sense of humor is somewhat intact. Or at least that it's made a reappearance this morning."

"Why are you here, Liam? Is it to have a fight with me? Because I would suggest that you don't actually want to be in a fight with me this morning."

"Is that so?"

She narrowed her eyes. "I'm mean and undercaffeinated."

"Well, that is a terrifying thought," he said, moving out of the doorway and heading into the dining area.

She followed after him. The converted barn was empty, the wooden floors shining from her recent polish, the rustic wood chandelier overhead casting a lovely, serene glow on the surroundings. She felt neither glowing nor serene.

"Are you just here to talk about…work stuff?"

"We have work stuff to talk about. We need to get that furniture ordered. We need to get everything ready to go. We have two weeks until Christmas festivities kick off really strong and copper rich. I think we can actually have the place ready to do a soft open by then. We can really kick it into high gear at Christmas. But it would be great to have it ready for the tree lighting, don't you think?"

"That might be a little bit ambitious," she said. "You know, considering that Christmas decorations go up almost as soon as Thanksgiving is over."

"True. But I think we can do it, don't you? Anyway, the sooner we get it done, the sooner we're done."

She knew what he meant by that. He meant them. He meant them having to work together.

"That is ideal," she said, grinding her teeth together.

"Okay, we talked about work. Now, let's talk about last night."

"Not here," she said.

"Where?"

"In hell?" she suggested lightly.

"I would prefer to handle it a little bit earlier," he said.

She let out an exasperated sigh and walked toward the back of the room, shoving the back door open. "All right," she said, "let's talk."

They moved out to the back deck area of the dining room. There were a few little tables placed out there, and beyond that a large, open field stretching to the base of a blue-tinged mountain range. The air was cold, but strangely clear for this time of year, the sky jewel bright in spite of the chill.

"I'm sorry I left you without a car," he said.

"Are you?" She narrowed her eyes.

"Yes," he said slowly. "In that I'm sure you had to deal with that this morning. But I don't regret leaving."

"Right, because you didn't like what I had to say."

He chuckled, rapped his knuckles against the side of the old barn. "You didn't like what I was saying either," he returned. "So I think we were about even."

"Okay," she said. Instead of no, absolutely not, we are not even, we will never be even. Which was what she felt. In her chest. Deeper than that, all the way to her soul.

"I need you to admit it," she said. "I need you to admit that what happened between us meant something. Because my entire life, and all the pain that has come after it was based on that feeling. You left me, convincing me that everything I felt was in my head. I have spent a decade not trusting myself, not trusting my feelings, and you... It did matter. I mattered."

"What does it benefit either of us for me to admit that?"

"Because it's true," she said, nearly exploding. "Doesn't the truth matter somewhere in all of this?"

"Not if we can't do anything with it."

"I can do something with it," she said. "I can maybe move on. I can heal."

"Is that actually what you want? Because I think if

you wanted it you would have taken steps to do it by now."

"Stop telling me what you think. Stop telling me who you think I am, what you think I'm doing, or how you think that it's my fear holding me back. This is about you. And until we clear up this piece I can't move forward with anything else. So I need you to tell me. I need you to tell me that I mattered to you. That I didn't have feelings for you all by myself. I need you to *admit* that you didn't leave me to protect me. You left me because even though you felt something for me you felt more for the money. Be honest, Liam. With yourself and with me. And once you are maybe we can move forward."

"Where do you imagine us moving forward to?" he asked.

"Just into…finishing this. Being able to inject Christmas cheer into the grand opening like Lindy wants instead of just wanting to pour wounded bile on top of it. Maybe that's all it will be. Maybe that's all we'll accomplish, but dammit, Liam, I need you to give me this."

He tilted his head back, his expression unreadable. Even angry, his green eyes glittering, he was so beautiful. She just wanted to reach up and touch him, to feel his whiskers beneath her fingertips. To press her palm against his cheek and trace that line down to his square jaw, to his chin. She wondered what it would be like to hold his face steady while she leaned in for a kiss.

She shook off those thoughts as quickly as they appeared. She could not afford to have them.

"I took the money instead of you," he said, the words like iron. "Because whatever I felt for you I didn't think it would be enough. Because I spent my entire life living with a woman who resented my very existence because of all that she couldn't have because of me, and I was damn well not going to subject myself to that again. I was not going to… I was going to prove that I was could change my life, that I could amount to something. When that opportunity presented itself from your father I took it. I hesitated, but I took it. Because I knew that you and I couldn't have a future. But that the education would be my future. That money…it was my future. I can't apologize for that, Sabrina, I can't. All I can apologize for is that you were hurt. But that's the damn truth of it."

"Why did you get the tattoo?" she asked.

"You're right. Stuff that I don't want to work out, I put on my skin. I got away from here, I went to school, things were going well. But I couldn't forget. Just because I made the choice, just because I felt like it was the right choice, doesn't mean it was the easy one."

"Why were you so sure we couldn't have a future?"

"Because I can't have a future with anyone, Sabrina. I knew it then, I know it now." He shook his head. "My mother was abusive. To me. Not really to Alex. But I never wanted to go back to anything that looked like that. To any kind of family, any kind of house. I don't believe in it. Not for me. I never wanted to drag you into all that. I still don't. But I did. I did, because I assumed that you weren't a virgin anymore. Or maybe… Just because I didn't care for a while last night."

"Your mother abused you?" Suddenly, Sabrina felt ill.

"Doesn't matter. I can't change it. It's all a great big mass of messed up and there's nothing anyone can do about it. But when I say I don't want that kind of life I mean it. I feel like that's a line that men throw out a lot when they mean I don't want it *right now,* or I don't want with *you.* But that's not what I'm saying. So maybe it would be better to let you stay mad at me. But now you know the truth. I got a tattoo because I care. But there was nothing I could do with it then and there's nothing I can do with it now. So it's just another thing I carry with me."

Sabrina didn't quite know what to say. What did you say to something like that? Her life with her family hadn't been perfect. And right now, her relationship with her father was mostly nonexistent. Things with her mother were difficult, as always. Damien…well, he was particularly challenging at the moment.

But there had never been abuse.

She would never, ever, have thought that the strong, gorgeous man she had known then, that tattooed bad boy, had been through something like that. But that, she realized, was a girl's perspective. Standing here as a woman, looking at this man who had to keep track of events on his body…

She could see the damage that much more clearly. But perhaps that was in part because she could see her own. Way back when, she hadn't been able to see his damage. She'd been so caught up in her own.

Trying to be good. Trying to be quiet. Trying to earn affection from a man who would take it back so much more easily than he would ever give it.

Liam had been an escape from them. Her confidant, her fantasy. Her break from good behavior.

She'd seen those tattoos as symbolic to her journey, not to his. Those tattoos that—at seventeen—she had thought of as signs of his rebel status, were actually symbols of his vulnerability. Of his pain.

"I don't know what to say," she said, twisting her hands.

It was inadequate, and stupid. Because there were a thousand things she wanted to say, but she wanted to say the right thing. She wanted to say the thing that wouldn't cause harm. The thing that was right, that gave her information, but that also wasn't too invasive.

She wanted to know everything. She wanted to know nothing.

She wanted to know him, and she wanted to keep him firmly in her fantasies. The monster that had destroyed everything. The man that had brought her so much pleasure. It was so much easier when he was those things. Because she could be angry with him then. Because she could work out her sexual frustrations on him.

Introducing this, this dark, twisted childhood, made him more than a man. It made him human.

It gave context to those faults, those flaws, that she had decided simply existed to wound her.

More than that, it made Liam Donnelly's life extend beyond places where it had touched hers. It made him whole. It made him real.

And until that moment she hadn't realized that to her he *hadn't* been real. He had been a symbol. A symbol of rebellion gone wrong, of her feelings, of her vulnerabilities.

But perhaps, just perhaps, he was more than that.

Faced with this, it was somewhat impossible to deny.

"There's not much to say," he said. "I'm not selling you a sob story. I'm just telling you the why. Because you wanted to know. Because you wanted to know why I don't want to commit myself to a life of suburban hell. Because you want to know why I don't want kids, why I don't want to live in that situation where you're bound to people because of blood and vows and you can't just pick up and walk away if you need to."

Her thoughts tangled up on each other, wrapped around the words that she wanted to speak but couldn't quite bring herself to. The frustrating thing was she understood. Without asking for extra clarification. That growing up in a household with a difficult parent felt... You were powerless as a child in those situations.

You had to follow the whims of that parent or face the consequences. She knew that much, and she hadn't even experienced the same thing. Growing up in an abusive environment it had to have felt like an inescapable prison.

"I'm not going to abuse anyone," he said, as if he needed to clarify. "I just don't want that life. I don't want to be stuck. That's the great thing about money, Sabrina, you end up with a lot of mobility and a lot of power. Money doesn't make you happy, but it affords you the means to improve your situation, that's for certain."

"I didn't think you would ever abuse anyone," Sabrina said. "And I knew that's not what you were afraid of."

"You want to know," he said. "Don't you? You want to know what she did."

"Yes," Sabrina responded. Then she swallowed hard. "No."

"I've never told anyone about it before," Liam said.

Sabrina's eyes flew to his. "Never?"

"I don't know how well you know my younger brother Alex, but, believe me, he's the best of us. Brave. A hero for his country. He's happy. He always has been. He was such a neat kid. I mean, he went through the usual teenage rebellion stuff, mostly when I wasn't there, but as a kid he just seemed to enjoy being a kid. I hated it. I only had the money my parents could go out and earn, and our dad didn't care much for doing that. Mostly, he wanted to satisfy himself. Which meant fooling around with random women—not our mother—and sitting on his lazy ass, or working out in the garage on his motorcycle."

Sabrina had always been well taken care of. For all her parents' faults, her father had provided for them. She had never been hungry. Had never felt like needs weren't being met. At least, not those practical, physical needs. Her father was distant, and there were certainly emotional deficits, but she had a feeling you could only worry about those kinds of deficits when physical needs were being met.

"Sometimes there just wouldn't be food in the house. I collected all the change that I could and walked to the store once. I bought two frozen burritos. Made sure that Alex had something to eat. There wasn't much I could do about our situation, Sabrina. But I could make sure that Alex was taken care of. And that's not because I'm a saint, God knows. Just because it felt good to be able to control something."

"Why wasn't there food?"

"I don't know. Because my mom spent the money on alcohol? Because she went out to the bar and had dinner? My dad was probably being fed by whatever woman he was screwing around with at the time. My parents weren't home a lot, and if they were, they weren't paying much attention to us."

His face took on a strange, distant quality, his eyes going blank. "And if we were too much trouble, my mom would make sure we weren't in the way."

"How?" Sabrina asked gently.

"Well, we had a shared bedroom, but sometimes we fought. Or, Alex was little and he was having a nap, and my mom didn't want me to disturb him. So she would lock me in the closet in the hall."

He tensed his shoulders, stretching slightly, almost reflexively, as if he was fighting against some tight, imagined space in his head.

Sabrina's heart sank into her stomach.

"It wasn't that bad," Liam said. "Not at first. I could curl my knees up and pretend that I was a stowaway on a ship, or that I was hiding from imagined enemies or something. Sometimes she would do it all day. Or overnight. And that was hard."

"And Alex doesn't know? How did he not notice?"

"Because sometimes she would do it when we were supposed to be at school," he said, his voice hard. "And I missed a lot of school—it was hard for me to catch up. Just one of the many reasons I was never going to get myself a scholarship. I could have fought back, at a certain point. I was bigger than her. And eventually, I did figure that out. But it's your mom, right? And it takes a while for everything to even out. When you go from being a little boy to an adolescent with a little bit of physical strength." He shook his head. "I was never going to hurt my mom."

Sabrina took a step forward, reaching her hand out. Liam jerked away. "Why did she do that to you?"

"She hates me," Liam said simply. "She hates me from all the way up on that hill she lives in now in her custom house. The one that I bought for her. She hates me, because I'm the reason she was stuck with our father. Oh, she hated Alex too, make no mistake. Just not in the same way. She blames Alex for not being able to fix my dad. For not making him stay, because he eventually left. But she blames me for getting her ass stuck with him in the first place."

His gaze went to a faraway place, his eyes focused somewhere past the mountains. "She was going to be something. She wasn't going to be like her mother, tied down with a couple of kids. She was going to get away from that small town in Washington and go to school."

She hadn't done that, though, and Sabrina didn't need Liam to finish the story to know that. But Liam had. He had been driven to do it. Had taken that money from her father—something that had hurt her deeply up until this moment—and made the future his mother had always accused him of stealing from her.

"What was the longest amount of time you ever spent locked up?" she asked. Because she had to know.

"A few days," he said offhandedly. "Hey," he said in response to the distressed sound she made. "Other kids have it worse. Other kids get locked away for months. And they don't make it to adulthood to tell the story. I did. I was never in danger of dying, I was just uncomfortable."

"That doesn't make it okay. That doesn't mean... That doesn't mean it isn't awful."

He shrugged. "Maybe it is. But there's nothing I can do about it now. Nothing but what I did. Nobody forces me to do anything now, Sabrina. And I don't even owe your father any money anymore. I paid him back. With interest. No one owns me. I'm sure as hell never going to be in a situation that isn't of my own making again."

She had a feeling he had to believe that. That the alternative would be to slide into an abyss as dark as the closet his mother had locked him in.

She had a feeling he still wouldn't welcome her touching him. That he really didn't want her pity. She had a feeling this was a trade. A trade for what had happened last night. Maybe even for some of the pain he had caused her.

Whatever the rationale, it was not an invitation for her to get closer to him, that much was clear.

"Liam," she said slowly. "Your mom sounds like a bitch."

She hadn't planned on saying that, and she kind of felt guilty when the words left her mouth, because it was his mother and for all she knew he didn't really want to hear anything like that about her.

But he shocked her by laughing. "No kidding," he responded, rubbing his hand over the back of his neck.

"Where does this…" She tried to breathe past the tightness in her chest. "Where does this leave us?"

"Trying to finish this project before Christmas," he said, as if it was obvious. As if there was nothing else to even possibly consider.

She tried to force a smile. "Okay, then. Let's do that."

CHAPTER THIRTEEN

LIAM HAD AMPLE time to think about his little confessional with Sabrina over the next few days and the long weekend brought about by the Thanksgiving holiday. He also had ample time to think about what it had been like to have her soft, beautiful skin beneath his fingers, to think about how tight and hot she had been when he had slid inside of her.

That was the problem with the conversation they'd had out at the winery. It had erased so much of that anger he'd felt when he had torn out of her driveway like a bat out of... Well, that damned conversation... It was difficult for him to focus on it now.

And much easier to focus on how hot their night together had been. Well, it wasn't even a night, really. It was an hour of really, really good sex, followed by a screaming match that he was pretty sure had been due between the two of them, but had come at a terrible time.

But now, all he could think about was the sex.

And he kept thinking about it at inopportune times, like when he was supposed to be milking cows, and his brothers were standing in very close proximity, far too in tune to his distraction for his liking.

"What's going on with you?" Finn asked. "You're more cranky than usual."

"Not cranky." He scowled, adjusting the pressure on one of the milking machines.

"Right," Cain said, straightening and grabbing hold of a pitchfork. "You normally stare at the backside of a cow like you want to punch it."

"Actually, I kind of do. You guys have accused me of being merry sunshine more than once."

"This is different," Finn said, maddeningly sure of himself. Maddeningly correct.

"I'm antsy," he said honestly. "I want to get moving on the tasting room. We have to get it done before the Victorian Christmas festivities get kicked off."

"I thought Christmas was your goal."

"Well, we've upgraded. We want to take advantage of the influx of people that are going to be coming through town for this."

"And it has nothing to do with your pretty blonde counterpart? Because nobody is stopping you from going down and doing work."

"It's Copper Ridge," he said drily. "It's not like any of the places I need to get supplies from are going to be open. It may shock you to learn that the Farm and Garden is not having a Black Friday sale."

"Well," Finn said, "damn. I was hoping to get a killer deal on azalea flats."

"Sorry about your azaleas," Liam said, his tone dry.

"I don't think you mean that."

"I fucking don't," Liam responded. "But anyway, that's all. Antsy."

"Does that have anything to do with why you looked like you wanted to crawl out of your skin over Thanksgiving dinner?"

"No, that had everything to do with the fact that it

was the first time I've had Thanksgiving dinner in...I don't know. Alex and I maybe had Thanksgiving twice growing up? And that was just if our grandma decided to do something. And forced my mom to bring us."

He had found an excuse to go back to New York over Thanksgiving the year before. Really, he'd had to put some things with his old house in order, and sell some of his old things that he had decided he wasn't going to ever have brought to Copper Ridge. But, he had also lied about some personal plans. There was no reason he had to go back then, except that he had felt an underlying discomfort at the thought of being there.

This year, no good excuse had popped into his head. Plus, he was in the middle of dealing with the tasting room stuff.

Finn and Cain looked at him like he had grown a second head. He shrugged. "What?"

"I didn't realize," Finn said.

"Why would you? I don't like to talk about this bullshit. I know Alex doesn't. Alex probably had better Thanksgiving events in the army than I've had in my adult years. But that's my choice."

"What did you do for Thanksgiving when you lived in New York?"

"The same thing I did anytime I had a day off. Picked up some woman. Although, admittedly, if I was picking up a woman on Thanksgiving night she was probably a more dysfunctional woman than usual. But no more dysfunctional than me."

"You never hung out with friends?"

"I didn't have friends. I mean, not those kinds of friends. Not the kind that put the word *friends* somewhere in the name of the holiday and have jaunty get-togethers full of board games and butter. I just have the kind of friends that went out drinking and competed for different accounts at work. And would probably have poisoned my drink to make sure I didn't get the accounts if they'd had the opportunity."

"Awesome," Finn said. "That sounds super well-adjusted."

"Says you," Liam said. "Who was not necessarily the most well-adjusted when we arrived in town a little over a year ago."

"I still had Thanksgiving," Finn said. "Lane has always made Thanksgiving dinner for me. She used to make it for a group of friends, and Grandpa. So, toward the end there he just preferred if I brought him a plate, rather than making him join in on anything."

"I have Violet," Cain said. "We've always done holidays. Can't skip them when you have a kid, even when you want to. Most especially not after Kathleen left us, because I had to make everything normal. So, I had to learn to cook. After which I immediately learned to order Thanksgiving dinner in advance from a local restaurant."

"Fine. I'm the only cheerless, soulless one."

It had been strange, all of them sitting around the table like that. All of them together. Though the food had been good. And that he had definitely appreciated. He always did.

"You should have told Lane that was basically your first Thanksgiving. She probably would have done something extravagant."

"Four different kinds of stuffing wasn't extravagant?" Liam asked.

"Believe me, she could have gone further."

"I believe it. But I didn't really have any desire to make your pregnant wife work harder."

If there was one thing he knew for sure, it was that if Lane had had any idea about his lack of experience with family togetherness and holidays, it was that she would have bent over backward to make him feel initiated.

And he really wasn't comfortable with that. With anybody making a big deal out of him. Not when he hadn't earned it, anyway. Work stuff was different. He worked hard, and he expected rewards for that. But this whole just being a family and wanting to be together thing was strange.

He was learning where his brothers were concerned. But he was kind of just figuring out how to navigate the broader family. The women that his brothers had brought into it. And how domestic it all felt.

Domesticity was his nightmare.

The only real relief was the fact that he could extricate himself from it. Was the fact that he himself wasn't permanently entrenched in it.

"So you guys never had Thanksgiving?" Cain asked. "Did you have Christmas?"

"Not always," he said, shrugging.

"Neither of you have ever mentioned this."

"Look," he said. "It just wasn't that big of a deal. Anyway, we didn't have the money for holidays like that."

"I guess I always figured," Finn began, "that because you had Dad maybe you guys were a little better off. Financially, I know not emotionally."

"Whatever," Liam said. "We probably were. Emotionally. Maybe even financially, I don't know. It never seems right to complain about it."

"Sounds to me like you damn well should complain," Finn said.

Liam let out a long, slow breath. "Let's just milk some damn cows."

"Or we can finish having the damn conversation," Cain said. He leaned the pitchfork up against the wall and stood there, looking at Liam far too closely.

Liam had been the older brother in his household. He was the one that took care of his little brother. He was the one that shouldered everything. It was strange to be put in the position where that wasn't the case anymore. Where he had two older brothers looking at him, concerned, looking like they wanted to go out and draw some blood on his behalf.

It did some strange shit to his insides. He wasn't sure if he liked it or not.

"Our dad sucked," Liam said simply. "Whether he was there or not. Whether by virtue of his presence or his absence. I'm sure he's off sucking somewhere right now. There's no reunion on earth that's going to change it. There's no apology he could offer to any of you that would change the fact that he's just an awful human being. Trust me. I lived with him. All he did was drink, screw around with women, and baby his motorcycle like it was the child he actually cared about."

"Believe me," Finn said, "I have never harbored a secret fantasy of reconnecting with our dad. The little that I saw of him in my life was enough."

"That's for the best," Liam responded.

"What about your mom?"

He shrugged. "She didn't want us."

Finn and Cain exchanged glances. "Well, join that club," Cain said.

"That's the thing. I don't have the monopoly on messed up here. It's never seemed like there was any point in giving you guys a rundown on what Alex and I experienced when we were growing up, because I know it wasn't any better for you. I know it doesn't matter that we had Dad and you didn't. It doesn't matter... None of it does. It sucked for all of us, and here we are, doing better. Making better. End of story."

"Yeah, why do I get the feeling that that's not really the end of the story?" Finn asked.

"I don't know. Because you're suspicious?"

Finn shrugged. "Maybe I am. But, the fact remains that while my childhood was pretty bad, I had Thanksgiving and Christmas. At least, until my mom left me."

"Well," Cain said. "In fairness, after that you came to live with Grandpa. He gave you Christmas, didn't he?"

"He did," Finn said. "Even Grandpa."

"What did you get for a gift?" Liam asked, unable to imagine his grandfather wrapping anything in a bow, or being sentimental at all. The old man had loved them, which was more than he could say for pretty much anyone else they were genetically related to. But the old man had not been sentimental.

"Boot socks," Finn said. "And one time boots."

"Well, warm feet is something next to Christmas cheer, anyway," Liam said.

"Hell yeah," Finn replied. "Especially when you have to be out in the frost Christmas morning taking care of animals."

"Well," Liam said. "There you have it. Winner of most functional of all of our childhoods by far. The man who got boots for Christmas morning so that he could more comfortably do his chores."

Finn laughed. "I don't mind it. This is what I love to do. This job. I love working on the ranch. It doesn't matter to me if it was an unconventional life. It makes me happy. It's the reason I'm here. It's the reason I know Lane."

He had to admire his brother's certainty. Liam had yet to figure out how to be anything close to grateful for his upbringing. It was the reason that he... Well, it was the reason that he had a gigantic chip on his shoulder. Sabrina's father was the reason he had gone to school. And his brothers were the reason he was back here. His grandfather was the reason.

His mother was the reason he was about half a million dollars poorer. Because he'd felt completely bound to proving her wrong about him.

But he didn't have that blessed assurance that Finn seemed to have that the broken road he'd been walking on had been leading somewhere better.

All he had was sore feet.

"Yeah, well, I'm happy for you and your perspective."

"All that money and you haven't bought yourself any perspective yet?" Finn asked.

Liam shook his head. "No, I am neck-deep in cow shit instead."

"Well, I've found a lot of perspective in piles of cow shit," Cain said. "So maybe if you keep shoveling you'll find some of your own."

He doubted it. In fact, he felt a lot further from perspective than he normally did. Mostly, he felt... Well, he didn't know. And that was a helluva thing for a man who had been certain of his path in life for a long damn time.

From the moment he had been given that money, the

moment he had discovered that he could go to college, he had been certain about where he was going.

It was a damned lie to say he had left Copper Ridge and not looked back. As Sabrina had pointed out to him, with a good solid punch to the middle of the spine, he had the past permanently on his skin.

But he had wanted what was in front of him bad enough not to care about what he left behind.

Something about coming back here had screwed everything up.

Or maybe it wasn't here. Maybe it was just Sabrina. Because when it came to her he was caught between knowing that it was the right thing to never touch her again, and being desperate to get his hands on her again.

He wasn't used to contradicting himself, to not being certain. He doubted any amount of cow patties was going to solve that.

"Maybe," he said. Because he knew it was the only way for the conversation to end.

Because this was what older brothers did. He knew that well enough. It was what he had done when Alex had come back from dealing with Clara looking all heartbroken. When he had given advice on things he didn't know anything about. Because he had felt compelled to because wasn't that what older brothers were supposed to do? Protect, advise.

No matter what they knew or didn't know.

"Better keep shoveling," Finn said, clapping him on the back.

He looked at his brothers, who were smiling at him. And he knew that they weren't going to be able to advise him on any of this; more than that, he didn't want them to.

But it was nice to know they cared. It was a weird feeling. But it was nice.

And right about now he would settle for nice, since he sure as hell wasn't going to get satisfied.

SABRINA HAD BEEN correct about Christmas lights on the main street of Copper Ridge. The day after Thanksgiving they were all strung up in blazing glory, twinkling on the borders of each and every building, evergreen boughs with deep red bows hanging low beneath the eaves.

There was a woman standing in front of the large picture window at The Grind, drawing a design in white, red and green. A scripture and a wreath, it looked like.

Sabrina went inside the coffee shop and saw that the specials had been changed from pumpkin spice to drinks based with eggnog and nutmeg. She could not condone anything created with eggnog. But she did order a vanilla nutmeg latte to get herself feeling a bit more seasonal before she continued on down the sidewalk toward the tasting room.

The tables and chairs, and the display case were being delivered today, and she was going down to open it up in preparation. And she really hoped, perhaps unfairly, that Liam would decide he didn't need to be there for any of this.

They hadn't seen each other in close to a week, and she had to admit the distance was fairly welcome. Even though she had missed him like her heart was being clawed at the entire time. Which meant the distance was even more welcome as a result. She didn't want to miss him. She didn't want to feel anything. Nothing, nothing at all.

Sadly, she kept dreaming of him at night. Hot, sexy dreams full of all the things she now knew what happened between men and women. Yes, she had *known*. But it had been gauzy. It had been impersonal. It had not been hot, sweaty and very real. Had not made her ache between her thighs, or caused her to wake up slick and unsatisfied.

Awful. It was all awful.

She took a sip of her latte, which was decidedly not awful, and unlocked the front door to the tasting room, breathing out a long, slow breath as she surveyed the surroundings.

It was such a gorgeous little gem of a shop, and now that she had fully released her anger at the fact that Liam had been right about it, she could completely enjoy it.

She loved the way that the ornate moldings encased the windows, the way the original glass had a slight wave to it. Loved the wood floor, imperfect but all the more beautiful for it.

It was rooted in the history of the town, in the Gold Rush–era buildings.

Yes, it was all very peaceful. Without Liam standing in the middle of it.

A pickup truck pulled up to the curb in front of the little building and she rushed to prop the door open. She greeted the deliveryman and made light conversation with him as he brought the tables and chairs inside. He left them all laid out in the middle of the room and Sabrina took her invoice and wished him well.

She rocked back on her heels and surveyed her surroundings. Now she just had to get everything placed.

But thinking about that, about the discussion she had had with Liam about where the different tables and chairs could go, just brought to mind kissing him on the floor of the tasting room later.

Brought to mind kissing him. And then brought to mind what it had been like to do more with him. To get naked with him.

He was her only experience with sex, that one time her only frame of reference.

The horrifying thought that overtook her was that she was never going to be able to think about sex without thinking of Liam Donnelly.

She had set out to solve something, and instead she had perhaps broken it even further.

She growled, and kicked the leg of one of the chairs. It made a rough, skipping sound and she panicked, moving it quickly and looking down at that precious wooden floor. Thank God she hadn't scuffed it.

She needed to get herself together. Needed to stop acting like a baby. Freaking out about everything.

She needed to focus on the conversation she'd had with him last week. About his childhood. Think of him as broken and wounded. So that she could practice letting go. Practice forgiveness. Practice not just picturing him as a bad-boy hypersexual fantasy that made her knees weak and her pulse flutter.

Yeah, all that would be good.

She turned away from the door and started trying to figure out how she was going to move everything. She needed to get cloths to stick under the table legs, because she wasn't going to pick up the larger ones and move them to their position. The chairs she could move.

"Looking good."

She startled and turned around to see Liam in the doorway, his arms folded over his chest, his expression far too cocky to have simply been looking at chairs. He had been looking at her ass, she was sure of that.

Her face heated.

"You know what they say about people who sneak up on other people," she said.

"I am unfamiliar with any colloquialism related to that. Please enlighten me."

She sputtered. "Well, I don't know one. But there must be one."

"So," he said slowly, "you don't know what they say about people who sneak up on other people."

She huffed, planting her hands on her hips. "Well, since I don't sneak up on people I'm not the one who needs to know."

"But you led me to believe you knew."

"I'm sure they say…" She waved a hand. "That people who are sneaky are shady assholes."

He laughed. "I've been called a great many things. I've never been called a shady asshole before. But I'll take it."

"Not a compliment," she said. "Not a compliment."

"Oh well. My ego is just way too healthy to take anything as an insult. It all glances off. Gets turned into something positive in my head. I'm just that shameless."

She laughed reluctantly and rolled her eyes. "Yes, yes. Anyway. Obviously the table and chairs have been delivered. And we are still waiting for the big countertop freezer case. I have a feeling that's going to be a bit more of an ordeal to get in."

He arched an eyebrow. "Well, yes. The bigger it is the harder it is to get in."

Sabrina wanted to be mad at him for that juvenile reference, but instead she felt her lips twitching in response, felt a slight giggle rise up in her throat. Oh, that ridiculous man. "I would say that depends," she said, fighting back a laugh, her face getting hot.

"Would you now?" he asked, amusement testing the corners of his mouth.

"Yes, I would."

"From all your experience with…setting up shops?"

Sabrina cleared her throat. "Yes. I feel that as long as things are properly prepared it's perhaps not that difficult."

"Well, good thing I'm an expert in preparation."

She squeaked, then picked up a chair, keeping her focus on the furniture and moving it firmly away from him. "Stop bantering with me and move that table over by the window."

"Bossy today," he commented.

"Bossy *every* day. Also, we're not supposed to banter about any of that. No more bantering."

"It's going to be very boring setting up this dining room if we can't banter."

"I'm not here to entertain you," she said, trying not to laugh.

She didn't know what was happening. She had been all annoyed and everything before he had come in, and then he had frightened her and irritated her after that. She should be mad at him. Or at least, thinking of him as that broken, wounded sparrow she had attempted to recast him as. Somehow she was neither. She felt like they had a rapport. She felt as though they were…closer.

It stands to reason. You did have sex with him. And then he told you all about his childhood.

Yes, that was true. But, in the middle of all of that they'd also had a fight, and then they had spent a week not seeing each other. That should be the prevailing sentiment of all of it.

Yet, somehow she did feel a strange sort of companionship with him. A strange kind of closeness.

Liam Donnelly was annoying in infinite ways. And new ones kept popping up all the time.

"Well, if you're attempting to keep me unentertained, you're failing. Because, frankly, this is the most fun I've had in days."

"Oh, come on now, one of your sisters-in-law makes delicious pie and the other one is a fantastic cook. Don't tell me your Thanksgiving wasn't highly entertaining."

He patted his stomach, which was still rock hard. "Sure. It had its attractions. But I have to say, I'm not really used to the family gathering thing yet."

She laughed ruefully. "Sadly, I'm a little too used to them."

"Yeah, and to getting ice passed down the table along with your mashed potatoes, I hear."

Sabrina sucked in a breath. "Well. You do know my father."

"I've never been particularly bound by the idea of doing what's right. I mean, not that I don't care, it's just that it's never been something I've thought of either way. I try to do the best thing for myself while hurting the least amount of people. I think your dad is just so bound up in the idea of *right* that he can't see what's *good* anymore. You can go down a list of right and wrong and it can seem pretty simple until there are people involved."

"It's a nice sentiment," she said. "And I even agree with a lot of it. Except the part about you not caring what's right. I think we both know that isn't true. You're the man who shielded his brother from all the abuse going on in the house, to the best of his ability. How is that not right?"

He shrugged. "To my mind it was just what brothers did. At least, it's what an older brother did. It was my job. The problem is our parents were never going to stand on the front lines for us, Sabrina. That was something I accepted from a pretty young age. So I knew that if anyone was going to stand in the line of fire for Alex it was going to be me."

She regarded that face, that handsome, serious face that had spent way too much time frowning. "Yeah, and you don't care about what's right."

"Alex is the one that went off to serve his country, to be a soldier. I just went off and made a whole lot of money. I think we know who has honor when push comes to shove."

Sabrina let out a long, slow breath. "Alex is the man that you admire, the man that he is because of you."

"No, I'm pretty sure Alex is the man he is in spite of everything. In spite of my parents. And probably to a certain degree in spite of me. I was never perfect."

"You've never claimed to be, either."

"Why are you defending me now? Other conversations we've had, I'm the villain. Pretty much uniformly."

"I was wrong," she said.

"Why, because now you feel sorry for me?"

Sabrina let that settle in, let that hit her right in the center of her chest. Because it was true to a degree. Except that was oversimplifying it. She shook her head slowly. "It's not just because I feel sorry for you. It's because you told me all of that and forced me to think of you as a person."

"What *did* you think of me as? A goat?"

"No. I thought of you as a fantasy. A simple token. The representation of my failings, and also this kind of perfect, bad-boy fantasy. Like you're straight out of a teen movie, riding up on your motorcycle, shaking out my life. Wandering off in the distance with some really bass-heavy backing track in the background. Lyrics begging me not to forget about you."

"Are we *The Breakfast Club*?"

"We are not *The Breakfast Club*. However, I might have reduced us to that in my head. And that's not fair. I never thought about the other side of it. About what your life must have been like. It's so funny, I was this girl who had some unhappy things in her life, I did. But I didn't suffer. Not like you. I grew up at that beautiful vineyard, in that gorgeous house. There was always food."

"Even if your food was served with a side of stoic judgment," he commented.

"I was so obsessed with *me* that in my head your whole life began when you rode your motorcycle onto the winery property. When my teenage heart started to flutter at the sight of you I assumed yours began beating at that exact moment. In my head you existed for me, and I'm not sure that I ever really appreciated how much that continued to be the case all through my adult life. All throughout my memories of you. But you are… You've lived this whole other life since then. I lived a whole other life before. It was eye-opening to hear you talk about your past. I'm embarrassed to admit that. Embarrassed to admit how much I simplified you."

"Sabrina Leighton," he said, his tone tinged with a faint scolding. "Did you objectify me?"

She snorted. "Yes. I objectified you. I turned you

into an object of my sexual desire and forgot that you were a person."

"That's appalling," he said, totally deadpan.

"You sound horrified."

"I don't know how I'll ever recover," he said.

"The point is—" she looked down and chipped at her manicure "—it's a hell of a lot harder to be mad at you now that there are more…pieces to the puzzle. When you're the only one suffering in a scenario in your head it's pretty easy to be self-righteous. But you suffered. And I realize that now. When you first came back to town I spent a lot of time accusing you of not knowing me. But what I know for sure is that I didn't know you. I just imagine you the way that I wanted you. The way that was convenient."

He let out a slow, heavy breath. "Same," he said. "You know, as a beautiful object for a tattoo, and not as a woman that I left behind wounded. I tricked myself into believing that sex was the only thing that could make a bond between men and women. That was all I understood. So, deciding that allowed me to wash my hands of any pain that I might have caused you."

She looked around the room, then back at him. "Tell me honestly," she said. "Tell me honestly what you felt when you sent me away. I want to hear it from your side. Because I've thought about it from mine so many different times, and every time it ends with me wanting to die of shame."

"Well, that's not right," Liam said heavily. "Because shame is the last thing you should feel. You shouldn't be embarrassed about that. It was… Turning you away was the hardest thing I've ever done."

CHAPTER FOURTEEN

LIAM LOOKED DOWN at Sabrina and tried to catch his breath. This was ridiculous. Losing his shit like this over a woman. Over a virgin. But she was making him relive that night at the cabin near the winery. Making him remember what it had been like to come in from a long, hard day of work, and a long evening of drinking, and stumble into the cabin to find her sitting at the kitchen table, a long coat shrouding her body.

He had kissed her just the day before, and he had felt like a damn fool for it. Not just for doing it, but for the way it had affected him. Yeah, a damned fool indeed.

Twenty years old, and he'd already been with more women than he cared to count, and he knew for a fact that Sabrina was innocent. He had tasted it on her lips. Had known the moment her mouth touched his that she had never kissed anyone before in her damn life.

But she had kissed him. He had turned her away, and then she had gone to his cabin.

She'd stood up, untied the belt on her coat and let it fall to the floor.

And revealed the most beautiful body he had ever seen. Slim waist, slight curves, beautiful breasts that were begging for his mouth, for his touch.

And that pale thatch of curls at the apex of her thighs... Yeah, that had haunted his fantasies for years after. It had never gone away. Hadn't ever felt satisfied, until he had finally had her last week. Even then, he wasn't sure he would call what he felt satisfied.

He didn't know if he would ever be able to get enough of her, and that was terrifying for a man who knew he didn't want forever. To know that he would have to limit a thing that he wanted. Because he didn't do self-denial either. And that was a hell of a thing.

But then, Sabrina Leighton had always been a hell of a thing.

Right now, she was staring at him, with those beautiful blue eyes, and he didn't know how he was going to deal with everything that was rioting through him now.

"I wanted you," he said. "I walked in and there you were, so pretty, so perfect, and all I could think of was the way that your lips tasted against mine. But I also knew that you were innocent. That you were a virgin."

"I know. Because you told me that you didn't do virgins when you sent me away."

"And it was true," he confirmed.

"Yes, well, it was true last week too, but you took me up on my offer anyway."

"It may surprise you to learn, Sabrina, that I didn't imagine the most beautiful woman I had ever known was still a virgin at thirty."

She blinked owlishly at him. He would have laughed if he didn't feel so damned close to the edge. "I'm the most beautiful woman you've ever known?"

"Yes," he said, seeing no point in lying now, because the damage had been done with all the finesse of a wrecking ball.

"That can't be true. You basically went to the capital of beautiful people and lived there for years. And probably...you know...bed-hopped your way through it. And you want me to believe that I'm more beautiful than them?"

He shrugged. "It's chemistry, right? It's more than that simple surface thing. A lot of women are beautiful. A lot of men are good-looking. Chemistry is the thing that matters. And honey, if we had any more chemistry we would blow up the fucking building."

"I want to have chemistry with a nice guy," she said, her tone wistful.

He took a step toward her, his heart pounding heavily. He couldn't remember the last time he had been this strung out being so close to a woman. Couldn't remember if he had ever anticipated a kiss quite so keenly.

"No you don't," he said, brushing his fingertips beneath her chin and tilted her face upward. "You want a bad boy."

"No," she said breathlessly, "I did want one when I was seventeen and an idiot."

"You want *me*. And frankly, I think you even *want* to want me. I don't think you're distressed that you don't want another man. Otherwise, you would have had one. Thirteen years, Sabrina, and you are a beautiful woman. You could have anyone. But you want me."

"I could find a nice accountant," she said, her lips pursed.

"No."

"Some guy that's really good with spreadsheets."

"Honey, *I'm* good with spreadsheets. You're stereotyping. The sad thing for you is that I'm good with numbers, and I'm good with your body. I could probably explain how chemistry works too."

She narrowed her eyes. "I know how chemistry works."

"I don't mean the kind you learned about in school."

He leaned in just a little bit closer, his lips a breath away from hers, and then the door to the shop burst open. "Can you open both of these doors?" a man asked without any preamble whatsoever.

"Yeah," Liam said, not bothering to make a quick move away from Sabrina, not bothering to disguise what he had been about to do. Hell, he wasn't ashamed of this. He didn't have to hide from anybody anymore.

"Great. We'll bring it in. You know exactly where you want everything?"

"Yes," Sabrina said, recovering herself and clearly not appreciating Liam taking charge. "I can direct you when you unload it from the truck."

"It will take a few trips. It's in quite a few pieces."

"Fine."

For the next hour he and Sabrina stood by while the refrigerator case got set up. The actual countertop they were going to put over it was going to take another week to be finished. Something about needing the exact dimensions to customize that particular type of counter to the space. They would also be building some cabinets around part of the case.

But once the men had left, the space was starting to look much more like it was intended to.

"I need dishtowels or something," Sabrina muttered, looking around.

"For?"

"To move the tables without scuffing the floor."

"Or why don't you let me pick up and move the tables, and you can follow me with the chairs. I promise, I will do your bidding."

"Yeah, I don't believe that." She picked up a chair, and then they began to work together to set up the dining space.

"I think we can actually do this," she commented.

And she looked so…happy. He wasn't used to seeing her happy, not around him. Maybe she was a very happy person, but he had never made her particularly happy, a thought that made his chest twinge.

So he did the only thing he could think to do. He bent down and kissed her. Quick, gentle.

When he pulled away she was standing there looking stunned. "And that was for?"

"The chemistry."

"I didn't think we were going to do any of that… Anymore."

"Here's my question for you, Sabrina. Do you think that's reasonable?"

"I'm not entirely sure I know what reasonable is anymore. I don't think I have any brain cells left."

"To my thinking this can only go a couple of ways. Either we resist each other the entire time we work together over the next month, or we resist each other badly. And every time we screw up there's a whole lot of shouting and self-flagellation. I would like to introduce a third option."

"Why do I feel like the third option is going to be the one that means we can do whatever we feel like while pretending there aren't going to be consequences?"

"Because it is," he said. "Thirteen years, Sabrina. Thirteen years we both waited for this. I think we deserve it, don't you?"

"That's an interesting choice of words. I'm not sure I deserve any of this, and it's not because I think I'm bad. It's because I'm not sure… I'm not sure what any of this has to do with deserving anything. It just is. I certainly didn't set out to earn it. But maybe that's okay?"

"If I kiss you again how long is it going to take to get you talked out of those clothes?"

Her cheeks went pink, as pink as the little shoes she was wearing, and he was surprised when she didn't get angry, when she didn't slap him.

But she didn't.

"Honest question," he said.

"I don't know," she said, sounding woeful. "You ruined my life, you know."

"So I've heard. At length."

"No. I mean *recently.* Because every time I think about sex I think about you. And I have a feeling it's going to be like that for the rest of my damned life."

"Right. So, damage done. Hell, I would posit that the damage was done thirteen years ago."

"And you think that the two of us sleeping together until we're done with this project is going to fix something?"

"I don't know. I just know that it's already broken."

He didn't know if it was good logic, but to his mind it was logic that was difficult to argue with.

"This feels like penis logic to me."

"It probably is. But that doesn't make it bad. It just makes it of one particular slant."

She let out a long, slow sigh. "Lindy already knows. I mean, she knows that we slept together once."

"Okay," he said.

He had a feeling Lindy was the type of woman who

wouldn't think twice about eviscerating a man who crossed her, or crossed someone she loved, and he was currently in a working relationship with her that required him to see her on occasion.

"Don't worry," Sabrina said. "She won't kill you if I tell her not to."

"Well," Liam said, "that's appreciated."

"It's just that…Lindy knows, and Clara I'm sure assumes, but if we could otherwise not advertise it, that would be good."

"Is that a yes to my proposition?"

Her shoulders sagged. "You're right," she said, sounding a little bit distraught. "You're right, whatever I think we're going to do, whatever I want to have happen… It's not going to. I'm going to try to resist, and then what? I'm going to try to resist you and I'm not going to be able to, and I'm going to get angry at myself for not resisting, and then I'm going to shout at you. Exactly like you said. If there was any way I could see this going differently, trust me, I would take it. But I can't. I can't imagine it. So…why not? Why not just give in? You're right, if I already associate you with sex and attraction, and I have all this time, how is it going to get worse?" Her gaze turned sly, her blue eyes narrowing. "And, after all, you already have me tattooed on your back."

"Touché," he said.

"Not going to let that go for a while."

"I have a request," he said.

"I'm not going to guarantee it will be granted."

"That's fine," he said, moving closer to her, bracing his hand on the back of her neck. "I want to see you with your hair down again. You wear it up every day, and you even kept it up when I had you the other night. I want to run my fingers through it. I want to see it loose around your shoulders. I want it like I remember you."

"Like your tattoo girl, you mean?"

"Hell, if I loved it so much I put it on my skin, it seems like I've earned it."

"I don't think you've earned a damn thing, Liam Donnelly. But you sure feel entitled to a lot."

"Maybe so. And maybe that's a failing of mine. But I feel entitled to you." He wrapped his arm around her waist, drew her lush body up against his chest.

He hadn't been lying to her when he said he liked the way she looked now even better. Those fuller hips and breasts. He liked the maturity in her face. He liked the evidence that she was a woman.

"Maybe that's the problem," he repeated. "That I felt entitled to you from the very beginning. That I have felt like you should be mine. As I got to know you, as you got under my skin. It felt right, even when I knew it would be wrong. Even when I knew it was impossible, and I shoved it down deep. Figured it was harmless to let our friendship be what it was. Because I didn't actually understand that I could build a connection with a woman if I wasn't sleeping with her. But there's never been anything harmless about you, and every little thing I've ever told myself was just another lie. Something to let me excuse my behavior. To let me get close to you."

"Liam," she said, her blue eyes darting to the window, "people will see."

"Then they'll see," he said.

"I just told you I need things to stay…"

"Why?" he asked, pressing his thumb against the corner of her mouth. "Because people will know you have a lover? And that bothers you?"

She shifted uncomfortably. "No... I mean, if it isn't going to last, then what's the point?"

"I'm not going to sneak around," he said. "I have earned the right to not be hidden away."

Her eyes rounded, wide, and he could tell that she was reading the deeper implication in the words. An implication he hadn't really meant to place there, but there it was, nonetheless.

He had spent a childhood being locked away, hidden away at another person's will, and he would be damned if he endured it again.

Even for her.

"Fine," she relented. "No sneaking. But no announcing either."

"Fair enough."

"Oh, except I really don't want my sister, Beatrix, to know."

"I haven't seen Beatrix since she was a kid," he commented.

"Yeah, well, she's not a kid anymore. Mostly. But Bea is...well, she's Bea. And she's very sweet, and I don't..."

"You don't want her to know that you're fucking for the sake of fucking?"

Her cheeks turned bright pink. "Not especially."

"Fair enough."

"Believe me, it won't take a whole lot of subterfuge to keep it from Beatrix. She is a lot more interested in traipsing around finding rescue animals."

"Oh, please tell me she takes them back to your parents' house," he asked, grinning.

"Actually, Beatrix lives in *your* old house on the winery property."

"Wow. Did *anyone* side with your brother?"

"Just my parents. For a man so committed to doing the right thing, my father seems to have a lot of sympathy for people who commit adultery."

"Interesting."

"That's one word for it," Sabrina said.

"Should I come over to your place tonight? I wouldn't mind bringing you over to mine, but I live with my brothers."

"Yeah, that's kind of what I mean by not announcing. I would rather you came to my place. Anyway, you left condoms there."

He chuckled. "Good. I would hate to have to go run the gauntlet of people we know to pick up more." He had one on him now, but he intended to need more than one the next time they were together.

Sabrina groaned. "I guess Clara probably more than suspects we're together."

"Yes," Liam said. "Which means that Alex knows about us too. And, if my brother Alex knows, then the rest of them almost certainly do."

"Which means that Alison knows," Sabrina said. "And Lane."

"Which probably means that Cassie from The Grind knows."

"And Rebecca West," Sabrina said. "And her husband, Gage, which opens up an entire other vault of people who probably already know that we slept together."

"Small towns," he said, shaking his head.

"They are a pain in my butt," she said.

"But you haven't left."

She looked out the picture window, at the illuminated street. The glow from the Christmas lights were reflecting off the picture window, glowing on her beautiful face. "No," she said, her words half-filled with wonder. "I guess I haven't."

"Why exactly is that?" he asked, looking at her profile, ignoring the strange ache in his chest.

She turned to face him, her lips pressed into a flattened line. "I don't know."

"I have a hard time believing you've ever done anything without knowing the reason why," he said.

"Then I guess you don't know me all that well," she said. "I feel like half the time I don't know the reason why I do anything. It's maddening. More than maddening, it's…I don't know."

"Why did you stay here? Because yes, I know that losing your father's money made it difficult for you to go to college that wasn't somewhat local, but not impossible, I would imagine, given your grades."

"It's for all the reasons that you already guessed," she responded, twisting her hands. "I was afraid to leave. More than that, I was afraid that if I left I would…somehow sever the ties between me and my family that were already so badly near broken. I just couldn't face that. I don't know. I guess I just…"

"You wanted to stay and fix everything. You wanted to stay and fix everything because you feel like you're the one who broke it. And if you're the one who broke it, you're the only one that can put it back together, right?"

She tilted her head to the side. "Maybe. Maybe that's it. Or, maybe that started being the reason. I don't know. Now though, I do have a life here. I do. I want to stay and support Lindy. That was… That was not a unifying move on my part with the family."

"Sure. It was an easy decision for you to make because it was for someone else. Not for you. That's your big struggle, isn't it? Doing something for *you*."

He had a feeling she was about to tell him where to shove his concern. Instead she straightened and looked up at him with luminous blue eyes that touched him in places he wasn't sure he wanted to be touched.

"Yes," she said slowly. "I suppose that's true."

"Why? I know that you like to blame me. But we already broke down the fact that just isn't the case. It's not all me."

"I guess not. But like you mentioned, you certainly made a convenient whipping boy. I just... If I was never good enough for him... For my father, no matter what I did, it was hard for me to believe that I really deserved anything when I was so far outside his favor."

"But you didn't apologize either?"

"I did. Kind of. It's complicated, he and I. Complicated and yet somehow not. He was never going to approve of me. No matter what I did. I know that, Liam. I know that as sure as I know that it isn't even my fault. That somewhere in all of that I just somehow want to prove that what I'm doing is right. But I'm making good choices. I want to make him see. That I don't have bad instincts when it comes to people. That I don't have to be quiet to be good. I want him to tell me that. Even if that's not reasonable. Even if it's never going to happen, there's a part of me that's holding out for that. And if I leave, if I'm not performing my life in front of him then how am I going to prove my worth?"

He reached out, brushed his fingertips against her cheekbone, against that soft, perfect skin. "I don't know. I don't even know where my father is. My mother... I wrote her a check for half a million dollars, Sabrina. I figured that it would show her. That she would know then that she had been wrong to treat me the way that she did. Because that son that she blamed for all of her poverty, and all of her sadness, I was the one that lifted her out of it. And I did it better than she ever could have done for herself. I wanted to show her that. I wanted her to believe it. But you know, somehow she never did. That moment when I handed her the check with all that money on it and her face was blank, I realized that I was never going to get what I want, not from her. I gave her the thing she'd said she wanted all that time and…it still didn't matter."

"So what do you do? With all that. When you've done everything you possibly can to earn your parent being proud of you and they still aren't? What the hell are we supposed to do with that?"

"Are you happy?" he asked. "Your life, as it is right now. Does it make you happy?"

She looked around the tasting room. "Right now I…I wouldn't choose to do anything differently than what I'm doing."

"Then I suppose that has to be enough."

She nodded slowly. "Well, there is one thing that I would like to be doing that I'm not."

"And that is?"

"You."

"That can be arranged."

He kissed her then, gently at first, but then deeper, harder, forcing her lips open with his tongue, delving deeply, tasting her. The slick glide, that heady friction making his stomach feel hollow and his body hard

"I want you," she whispered. "I want this. I want to not be… To not be so afraid anymore." She pressed her palm against his chest, let her fingertips drift over his muscles. It burned him, even through the fabric of his shirt. "I want to make some decisions for me. Rather than making decisions because of anyone else."

"Is that so?"

"I want to be selfish." She looked up at him, licked her lips, and he felt the impact of it all the way down to his toes. "Is that bad?"

"You can be selfish with me if you want."

"Good. Good. I want to be selfish with you."

She stretched up on her toes again, curled her fingertips around the back of his neck, those delicate fingers in his hair sending a shock of something through him he couldn't readily identify. But then she was kissing him again, and his thinking was greatly hindered. All he could do was feel. Feel her delicate hands roam over his body, touching him as if he was something singular and new.

He supposed for her he was. That was a hell of a thing. Knowing that he was the only man she had ever touched like this. It had been the first time they were together, and it was now.

"Still not the best idea to do it here," he said, his voice rough, the words coming out of a tortured rasp.

"Probably not."

"Your house. As discussed."

"My house," she said softly. "Only, this time maybe I'm not going to leave my car parked here. You know. So I don't get stranded again."

"Well, there's no danger of that either way."

"There isn't?"

"No," he said. "Because this time I'm not leaving."

CHAPTER FIFTEEN

SABRINA WASN'T SO nervous this time. No, she was something much closer to excited than nervous as she got out of her car, and Liam got out of his, and they both walked toward her house. She paused in front of the front door.

"I'm an old-fashioned girl," she said, wanting to tease him for some reason, and not quite sure she could pinpoint why. Except that she enjoyed talking with him when they weren't fighting. It was a strange and new experience. And pretty damned wonderful.

"You're an old-fashioned girl?" he asked, a smile tugging at the corners of his lips. "What does that mean? I'm going to have to take your petticoats off before I get to see those pretty breasts again?"

His casual, easy way with that kind of talk left her breathless, a shock of heat skittering down her spine.

"I don't mind working for it, I have to tell you," he said. "I'm just wanting to make sure I understand the definition."

"No," she said. "No petticoats. But, since we were out together, I expect to get a kiss good night at the door."

"You better not expect this to stop at the door."

She lifted a shoulder, enjoying the way his face grew tight, his eyes gleaming with a feral light. "Well, I don't know."

"Honey, I will take you up against the door."

"It's too cold!" she protested.

"It won't be. Not once I get going."

He advanced on her and she looked up at him from beneath her lashes, feeling like the minx she'd never ever been before. "Do I get my kiss?"

"You don't have to ask twice."

She moved away from him, pressing herself against the door, her palms flat against the cold, wooden surface. And he approached her like a predator, those blue eyes on hers with laser focus. Her heart began to flutter, her entire body on edge. He was so beautiful. Perfect. She wanted him. All of him. More.

But for now, she was just going to take this kiss and enjoy it. If there was one thing that was true about herself and Liam Donnelly it was that they had skipped several steps on their way to the bedroom. They had gone somehow faster than most people, and a lot slower. There had been a kiss, and a thirteen-year gap, then an explosion that had been something beyond that.

But no dates. No sweet, good-night kisses.

Right now she would have her good-night kiss. And then she would have the rest.

He planted his palms on either side of her head, staring at her intently. Her heart thundered gloriously, her entire body ready for whatever else might happen. For whatever he had planned.

Slowly, he drew his fingertip along the edge of her jaw, to the center of her chin. He tilted her face upward, his eyes never leaving hers. Then he raised his thumb, tracing the lower edge of her lip, back around up to the top. It was slow, slow and torturous, delicate and ruinous all at once. She didn't know what to make of it. But then, she wasn't entirely sure she knew what to make of him. She never did.

It was strange to look at him like this. To fully appreciate the man he had become.

She remembered the young man, that twenty-year-old that had completely captured her teenage heart. She remembered all that had attracted her to him then. His unique sort of attractiveness that bordered on pretty, that had appealed to her in a way no other man ever had. And then there were his tattoos, which took him just to the edge of threatening.

That softness was all gone. What might have been called pretty at one point had hardened. The lines around his mouth, around his eyes, changing things. The added firmness to his jaw. The slightly more austere set of his mouth.

All of that worked to appeal to the woman she had become now. He had been perfect for her then, all she had wanted. All she could imagine. But she was different now.

So was he. Somehow he was just the right kind of different.

There was a deep sort of magic to that she didn't want to question. One that made her feel off-kilter and terrified and exhilarated all at once.

"You're doing it again," he said, his voice husky.

"What?"

"Thinking. Way too damned much for a woman who should just be waiting for a kiss."

"Then make my brain stop working."

He flexed his hips forward, his hard cock brushing up against her hip as he brought his head down next to hers, brought his mouth a mere breath away from her own.

He just stood like that. Frozen. Not closing the distance, not making the move. Teasing her. Tormenting her. Without words. Without touch.

It was so wonderful and awful and she didn't know what to do. She wanted to lift her hands and grab his face, force him to close that distance. But she also wanted to see what he would do. Wanted to surrender to this experience. To surrender to him.

Finally, lightly, ever so lightly, his tongue traced the seam of her lips.

She let her eyes drift closed, her entire body shivering as he took small, indolent tastes of her mouth, completely unhurried, seemingly unaffected by the heat that was currently threatening to consume her where she stood.

He was cool. Controlled.

She was melting.

Then he moved his hand, his thumb once again placed at the center of her lower lip, where he pressed down, parted her mouth and took advantage of the forced invitation.

He kissed her. All consuming. Drugging. So deep she felt like he was reaching places in her soul never before touched.

She couldn't think. Not now. She could only feel.

The hot, dynamic man up against her front, the hard, immobile door at her back. Trapping her against this man that would surely consume her. Destroy her, leave her spent, drained of everything she had if she but gave him the chance.

Suddenly, somehow, that wasn't so terrifying.

The idea that she could pour out all that she was into him, and leave herself some sort of empty vessel to be filled as she was now.

To rebuild herself, brick by brick.

To create a new Sabrina. A braver Sabrina. One that wasn't so lost in what other people wanted. So torn apart by what they wanted her to do. By who they wanted her to be.

She wanted what she had said to him to be true. That she was living a life she wouldn't change. Because if that was true, then perhaps she was enough. Then perhaps the decisions she had made so far were enough.

Perhaps they weren't so bad, and perhaps she wasn't either.

He kissed her until she was shaking, until her core had turned to molten lava sending a destructive, honeyed heat through her body that was as sweet as it was deadly, reducing her limbs to water where she stood.

Unbidden, her hips began to roll against his, seeking satisfaction for that deep, hollow need that was building there. And he responded by pressing all that delicious hardness against her. They were lost. Right then and there, against the door of her house, caught up in a good-night kiss that was really just a beginning.

She had told him that it was too cold out here for him to do any sort of taking, but now she questioned that. Because now, she felt nothing but heat. Nothing but desire. The cold had nothing much to do with what she wanted to happen next. Or what she thought should wait. She was lost totally and completely in her need for him. In her need for what might happen next.

For that oblivion. For that re-creation of Sabrina that she was so certain could come with a proper flick of his wrist. With the invasion of his body in hers.

The first time had been simply that. The first time. In her mind she had made it all about getting that first time finished. Finding a way to reclaim what he had stolen from her. Getting it out of the way so that it was no longer hanging over her head.

This time was something else. Something different.

It wasn't about the novelty of sex, about finally losing something. This was about finding something. Oh, how she needed it. Desperately.

"Inside," he growled.

She nodded, reaching into her purse with shaky fingers and pulling out her keys, unlocking the door and releasing it.

As soon as they were both inside, as soon as that door was closed behind them again, he pulled her back into his arms. She dropped her purse onto the floor, wrapping her arms around his neck and clinging to him as he kissed her with a deep sort of passion that overtook everything. Overtook sense. Overtook reason.

He wrapped his arms around her waist, drew her tightly up against his body as he kissed her, as he took them down to the floor of her living room. Not caring that it was hard wood, and that it was biting into her shoulder blades, and was most certainly doing the same to his knees.

"Liam…"

"I can't wait anymore," he growled, his tongue thrusting deep into her mouth as he wrenched her shirt up over her head and then went to work on her bra.

"Condoms," she mumbled, her own clumsy fingers tugging at the edge of his shirt before managing to get it up over his head.

"I have one."

"You do?"

"I made sure to grab one the last time I used a gas

station bathroom. And it hadn't been sitting in my wallet for longer than a couple of hours. Safety first."

She blinked. "Classy."

"I didn't want to be without the next time this happened between us. I didn't want to stop." He paused for a moment. "If that bothers you…"

"It was for me?"

"Hell yes it was for you. Do you think I want anyone else? I don't. I can't even remember anyone else." He kissed her neck, kissed her collarbone. "I don't want anyone else. I haven't been able to be with anyone else since I saw you. Since I saw you again. You think that was going to get better once I had you?"

"I thought that was the idea behind…having me."

"Hell no. The idea behind having you was to be able to have you as many times as I needed to."

She trembled beneath his touch, as those large, callused hands moved to cover her breasts, thumbs skimming over her nipples before he let his fingers glide down her midsection, her waist, to the closure on her jeans.

He made quick work of those, and her underwear, leaving her totally bare to his voracious gaze.

Except for her socks.

"Cute little fuzzy socks," he said, kissing his way down her inner thigh, pressing his mouth to that tender place on the inside of her knee, then down her calf, down her ankle. All the way to her gray sock that had jaunty, fleecy snowflakes on it.

She felt suddenly childish, and not near enough woman for a man who was quite so much as he was.

"Don't," he said. "Don't compare yourself. Don't

second-guess yourself. Don't do whatever the hell it is you're doing. Just stop."

She clamped her knees together as he looked up, and she felt suddenly self-conscious about his view. He reached up and grabbed hold of her hand, drawing it down to his lips. Then he nipped one of her fingers. "Don't," he said, his tone full of warning.

She shivered, letting her knees fall open again as he moved his hands down to the edge of that sock.

Slowly, with all of his attention focused there on her foot, he drew it off. She shivered.

Then he moved his attention to her other leg, pressing a kiss to her knee, her calf, her ankle. And then focused his attention to the next sock.

She didn't know why it was erotic. She had no clue at all. Except that perhaps it was just all that attention. All that focus. Given to the most mundane of tasks that she herself had performed approximately five thousand times.

The removal of socks, of all damn things.

And he was turning it into something new. Something earth-shattering. Something she would never do again without thinking of him.

Those rough fingertips skipped her ankle as he removed the final sock, and cast it down onto the floor, leaving her completely naked now.

Though, frankly, the socks had done nothing for her modesty anyway. But it was a more naked feeling to be without them.

Then he reached up, grabbing hold of her knees and spreading them, parting them slowly, deliberately.

"You are so beautiful," he said, his voice rough. "This

was what I wanted to do back then. And this was what I wanted to do all night after our first time."

He reached up, sliding the edge of his thumb along the crease in her most intimate flesh. She was wet, so wet for him, and with the way he was looking at her she couldn't even be embarrassed. Dimly, she felt like maybe she *should* feel embarrassed.

Except no. She had purposed to be selfish. For her own pleasure. For her own needs. She was going to take it.

Not that he was going to leave her much of a choice.

He was like a man possessed, a man on a mission.

Being the focus of Liam Donnelly's extremely intimate mission made her feel like the luckiest woman on earth.

He moved his other hand between her thighs, one thumb on each side of that sensitive bundle of nerves there, moving just around where she needed him most, teasing, tormenting, building that sensation of being hollow, aching for his possession.

She was ready to beg him. Oh, how she was willing to beg.

There was no such thing as pride. Not here. Not when it came to this.

But it didn't make her feel weak. Instead, it made her feel strong. Because she knew that this man, this strong man, was willing to prostrate himself before her because of what her body did to him. Because as weak and needy as he made her feel, he also made her feel strong. Because his own need was written there, across that hardened, world-weary face.

She had been a virgin. He was her first experience of this kind of intimacy. But she wasn't his.

And yet, somehow, she had captured him. Captured his attention.

It would be tempting to write off what she felt, the intensity of it, because of her inexperience. But if that was the case, then his must not count either.

And he was no virgin.

He had a wealth of knowledge and experience, had likely welcomed countless women into his bed, and still, he was desperate for this. Desperate for her. After going all this time without sex because of her.

It was singular. She knew that with confidence.

She felt powerful.

Even as she trembled.

She watched as he undid his jeans, took them off, retrieved his wallet with the condom a minute before rolling it onto his glorious length and returning to her body.

"I'm sorry," he said, his voice rough. "Sorry."

She didn't know what he was apologizing for until he dipped his head and kissed her, curving his arm around her waist and lifting her butt off the ground as he positioned himself between her legs, that thick blunt head reaching the entrance to her body.

That he thrust into her. Deep, hard and without preamble.

She gasped as he filled her, arched herself against him, stunned by the still unfamiliar sensation of the invasion. Aroused by it too.

For some reason, tears sparkled in her eyes as he swore, as that large hand squeezed her ass and brought himself down more deeply inside of her.

She had a hard time understanding how something so raw, so animalistic and…dirty in some ways…was also beautiful. Transformative.

But it was. It was somehow everything. Just like the man himself.

He shuddered, lowering his head, pressing it against her neck. And then, he began to move inside of her, his body a symphony of movement and muscle that played over her like a classical piece. Winding itself around her, creating a need that it soothed just as quickly.

She was filled by him. Transported. Both wholly connected with her body and somehow separated, lifted above it as well.

She rolled her hips against him, taking him deeper, not afraid, not nervous like she had been the first time. If it hurt, she was all right with that. If the floor was a bit uncomfortable, a bit too hard, then she welcomed it.

How else would she withstand the pure joy, the intensity of the pleasure, without a bit of pain to balance it all out?

Because surely she didn't deserve something so incredible. Something so powerful. Something with the ability to shift the very foundation of her being. Emptying her out and filling her again.

But then, she was past the point of worrying whether or not she deserved it. This wasn't about what she deserved. Wasn't about what he deserved.

It was just about the simple fact that on some level she felt as though her body had been created for this. Created for him. And his for her.

Then somehow, the moment she had seen him there at Grassroots Winery when she had been a seventeen-year-old girl she had known he was the answer to those empty places inside of her. That he was the fulfillment of it. Of that quickening heartbeat, of all those tender promises that had begun to bloom inside of her untried body.

Yes. She felt that with certainty the transcendent logic. That transcended everything.

This was right.

It was him. And it was her. Them together. As it had always been meant to be.

That certainty burst through her like light through the trees as her orgasm flooded her with warmth, with beautiful, transformative, awe-inspiring pleasure. Wave after wave of perfection that made her cling to him, cry out his name, made her feel like she was flying into a million pieces, held together only by the powerful strength of his arms.

He shuddered against her, that big body coming apart, his muscles trembling, shaking. She feared he might shatter too, and if that happened, there would be nothing holding them together. Nothing at all.

After that, they simply lay there. On the floor that was much too hard, breathing in gasping, broken sobs.

Then he gathered her to his chest, pulling her against him as he picked them both up, carrying her into her bedroom.

He laid her across that pink comforter that had embarrassed her the first time. Had made her feel like she was announcing her inexperience.

She didn't mind now. Didn't mind at all that it represented her resolute solitude since he had left.

Didn't mind that it telegraphed clearly that he was the first man ever to share the bed with her.

Because she was happy about it.

She wanted it to be him. Only him.

Maybe her brain was in an orgasm fog. Maybe she was a little bit muddled. She honestly didn't care.

Right now, she had been stripped down to her essence. Nothing but feelings. Tomorrow, she knew the dread would creep back in. The hard lessons learned. The things that made it difficult for her to be this vulnerable with another person. But for now, it was eradicated by her pleasure.

By the intimacy of his skin against hers, of laying in her bed naked with a man, pressing her entire body, forehead to forehead, chest to chest, their bare legs entwined with each other's.

Yes, right now she was lost in that.

Tomorrow she would be found, she was sure of it.

But she wasn't looking to make it happen any faster than it had to. Not in the least. Not at all.

She had fantasized about this. Falling asleep with him. Probably, she had fantasized about that more than she had fantasized about sex back when she had been seventeen. Mostly because she had been a little bit fuzzy on all the details about sex.

She was not fuzzy on those details anymore. But this was the first time they had fallen asleep together.

She let that warm her heart as her eyelids began to get heavy, and as she drifted off.

CHAPTER SIXTEEN

LIAM AWOKE WITH a start. It took quite a few moments for him to work out where the hell he was, and why he was lying on a pink bedspread.

Then, it hit him with the force of a freight train.

Sabrina.

He had gone back to Sabrina's house last night. They'd had sex on her living room floor. And then he had carried her into her bedroom where she had fallen asleep. He had woken her up at some point, and they had made love again before falling back to sleep.

He had never slept at a woman's house before. He had never spent the night with one.

He wasn't a man who had relationships. Wasn't a man who had ever wanted to get involved in any kind of entanglement.

It was too messy. And since he didn't want forever, not even a short-term relationship, he had never seen the point.

But he and Sabrina had reached an agreement last night, about doing this until the tasting room was finished, and so he figured somehow, this was all right.

Except Sabrina was not in bed. Which meant he was just sitting there sleeping underneath a pink blanket for no reason.

He sat upright, not bothering to get dressed as he walked out of her bedroom and into the kitchen.

Sabrina was standing there, her back to him, nothing but a T-shirt covering her curves, barely concealing her ass. Yeah, waking up to a woman wasn't so bad. Particularly when it was her.

"Good morning."

She turned around and her eyes flew wide when she registered his appearance. And probably a little wider still when she realized he was naked.

He gloried in the way her blue gaze drifted over him. As though she had never seen anything quite like him. And he realized that she hadn't. Not really.

That appealed to him more than it should.

"Good morning," she murmured. "Luckily I don't have a whole raft of people over for breakfast. Or they would be getting a show along with their pancakes."

"Do you often throw breakfasts at your house?"

"No," she said, tilting her head to the side. "Although, Sabrina's pancakes and all-male revue might have some legs."

"Hairy ones, anyway," he said.

She snorted. "How are you this morning?" she asked, picking up a mug of coffee and tapping the sides.

"I would be better if you would take your hair down."

"I don't take it down when I sleep, it gets snarled."

He leaned in, his nose touching hers. "I want to snarl it."

"Well, then you would have to de-snarl me," she said, sounding huffy. "I don't think you want that."

"I see I've got snarly Sabrina this morning. Well, I have to admit that I don't really mind her. But then, I've met a few different Sabrinas, and I can't say that I mind any of them."

"Stop that," she said, scowling meanly and wrapping her hands around her mug like little claws. "Don't be charming."

"Should I go back to being an asshole?"

"I did find certain things easier when I didn't like you."

"That's…" He frowned. "Not very flattering."

"I'm not *trying* to flatter you."

"Mission accomplished." He made his way over to the cabinet and pulled a mug down, and Sabrina continued to stare at him, looking wide-eyed and a little bit shell-shocked. "What?"

"Sorry." She took a sidestep out of his way. "I'm just not used to a naked man rushing past me in my kitchen on his quest for caffeine."

"Are naked men usually on quests for *different* things in your kitchen? Buried treasure. Truffles perhaps?"

She lifted a brow. "I promise you, that has never happened either."

"Never?"

"Never has a naked man rooted for truffles in my kitchen. Of the chocolate *or* fungal variety."

He chuckled. "Good to know. I have to say, I like that a whole lot more than I should."

"You like what more than you should?"

"The fact that I'm the only naked man to have ever wandered around your kitchen."

"Possibly not *ever*." She spread her hands wide, one still gripping her mug. "I don't know who lived here before me and what they wore or didn't wear in the kitchen. Certainly, I've dashed out to the kitchen in the buff before. That's the perk to living way off the beaten path. You don't exactly have to worry about the neighbors appearing in the windows."

"Except maybe raccoons."

"That's fine," she said. "The raccoons aren't going to take any illicit footage and put it up on the internet."

"You don't know that." He poured himself a measure of coffee and took a sip. "Raccoons do have little hands. I bet they could operate a smartphone if they could get ahold of one."

"Well, then maybe I have some amateur porn floating around online. Slightly more explicit after last night."

He was firmly happy to be part of her more explicit moments.

"I have to go to the winery this morning," she said softly. "But later I might want to go to the shops and take a look at some decor. I think Rebecca West is going to have some things to really finish off the tasting room."

"I could join you for that. Although, I'm not sure what I'm going to offer on the decor front."

"It's *our* project."

"That it is."

He surveyed her for a long moment, feeling a strange tightening in his chest that spread down to his gut, down to his groin. That lower tightening he understood. But the other stuff... He couldn't put a name to that. Or maybe, he just didn't want to.

Either way, he wasn't going to.

"Why don't I go up to the winery with you?" he asked, again, not quite sure of his motives.

She hesitated. "Discretion..."

"Lindy already knows. And it isn't like Beatrix is always hanging around. Or that she would draw the right conclusions even if she were."

"True."

"Anyway, it would probably be good for me to be there, because I need to get some serious inventory taken, and all the cheese orders that I need to place with my brother and sister-in-law finalized. I have my computer in my truck."

"All right," she said. "You win. We can ride together. Especially since we're going down to town later."

"I promise to be conveniently out of the way."

"Great. You can use my office if you want. It's not fancy. Little more than a coat closet, some might say."

"I can handle that," he said.

And if the idea of spending the whole day with her made his chest get even tighter, he was going to ignore that too.

SABRINA WAS FLUTTERY by the time she got her apron on and got herself situated in the dining area. She wasn't expecting it to be a big crowd today. After all, the weather was getting colder and lunching at wineries tended to be a bit more of a summer activity. They were definitely busier in that high season, when the roads weren't as frosty and treacherous, and when more people flooded both Gold Valley and Copper Ridge for tourism.

Though, both towns commanded their share of tourists that came in for Christmas festivities, and that was one reason that getting a shop in town was a good idea. The rural drives got harrowing when the weather cooled off. Especially when the day didn't manage to get above freezing at any point. Then it all just builds and builds. It hadn't gotten that cold yet, but Sabrina could feel it in the air. That crisp edge to the pine that reminded her of Christmas. Snow, and bitter cold.

She was working with Olivia in the dining area today, and was hoping that her transgressions were not written all over her face. It was a conversation she didn't particularly care to have with the other woman.

She needed Liam to stay in her office. She could not handle him parading around like a very pretty, tattooed ornament announcing her sins.

But when Olivia did walk in she looked ashen, her face drawn and pale, her brown hair scraped back into a tighter bun than usual, one that was a little bit lopsided, which Olivia never was.

She was always the picture of ladylike elegance, even working a fairly demanding job.

"Olivia," Sabrina asked. "Are you all right?"

"I'm fine," she said, sounding dull and listless.

"You don't look fine at all."

"Bennett and I had a fight," she said finally. "We never fight. Ever. We get along so well people are always commenting on it. It's like we're made for each other. That's what everyone says. His family is so wonderful, and he's so wonderful... I don't..."

"Why did you fight?"

"We fought because I want to get engaged. And he said he wants to wait. I was so thinking that he was going to propose this Christmas. But now that he's not... I just..."

"Olivia," Sabrina said, her stomach twisting. "Has it ever occurred to you that maybe...maybe he's not perfect for you?"

"No!" She blinked rapidly, holding back tears. "No," she said again, this time a bit more boldly. "He is. We've known each other since we were kids. First I was just a kid to him. And he went away to school, and then so did I. When I got back it *finally* happened. *We* finally happened. It's what was always supposed to happen."

"Except it's not happening," Sabrina said, as gently as she possibly could.

Olivia narrowed her eyes. "You're one to talk. You spent how long playing dramatic opera heroine over the same guy? One that wasn't even *here*?"

"You don't know anything about Liam," Sabrina said, knowing that wasn't fair, because everybody within a two-mile radius of her had gotten a pretty definitive impression of what the deal was with her and Liam from the moment he had come back into town. All because of Sabrina's own behavior. So the fact that Olivia was commenting on it now wasn't totally out of left field, and it wasn't unreasonable for her to think she had a bead on it.

Sabrina had set herself up for that by performing the way that she had.

Still, it made her mad.

"Do you love Bennett?" Sabrina asked.

"Of course I do. I've always loved him. I have loved him since I was in first grade and he was this tall, handsome, amazing older boy that was completely out of my league. I loved him all that time."

"What does it feel like when you imagine your life without him?" Sabrina asked.

"I can't imagine my life without him. If I try, it's like a big blank nothing in front of my face. He's what I've always wanted."

It was like a strange, idealistic version of how Sabrina had felt about Liam. Like he was this object that had at one point been meant to fulfill her fantasies. And then had destroyed them, and therefore ruined her. Thus symbolizing the realness and validity of her pain.

"What does it feel like when he kisses you?"

Unbidden she thought back to Liam. To last night. The way he had kissed her up against the door, and taken her down onto the floor. The utter desperation that had filled her. The need. It made her heart clench tight now even thinking about it. Her heart and…other things.

"It's nice," Olivia said. "I like to kiss him."

"What will happen if you don't?" Sabrina pressed.

"What does that mean?" Olivia looked petulant and more than a little frustrated.

"When he's right there, and you want to kiss him… What does it feel like will happen if you can't? If he doesn't kiss you?"

"I don't understand. Nothing will happen. I'll want a kiss, and not get one."

Sabrina put her hand on her chest unconsciously, rubbing at a strange sore spot that felt like it was expanding beneath her breastbone. "Does it feel like dying not to? And when he does… Is it like breathing?"

"No," Olivia said, her voice flat. "It's like kissing."

Sabrina stared at her; she didn't mean to, but she couldn't help it.

Olivia made an exasperated noise. "I know I'm *supposed* to be with him. I've known him forever. There's no need to be desperate about it. I know some people have that craziness. That match and gasoline thing, but we have…something else. It's that certainty."

"It doesn't seem very certain today," Sabrina pointed out.

She wasn't trying to be cruel, it was just that it seemed very much like the only thing holding Olivia to Bennett was the fact that she thought they were supposed to be together. Whatever that meant. And if she didn't feel that certainty, that impending proposal, there was little else keeping her there.

They had no passion, so the glue was that assurance.

It was such a strange combination compared to her and Liam. The only certainty with them was that it would end. It was the attraction that kept them coming back together. In spite of the fact they made no sense.

"What do you think would happen if you broke up with him?" she asked gently.

"I don't *want* to break up with him. I want to marry him."

"Well, the fact he's been with you all this time indicates he probably wants to marry you too," Sabrina said. "I'm not advocating for playing games. I just think you might need to show him what might happen if he doesn't. Show him what life looks like without you. If he feels the same way about you that you do about him he's not going to want that. It's not blackmail, it's just sometimes when you have something you need to lose it in order to appreciate it." Or, as the case was in her experience with losing someone you cared about, feel like your entire heart had been ripped out through your throat.

"I don't think I'm brave enough to do that," Olivia said, frowning.

"Good morning."

Sabrina turned to see Clara Campbell walking into the room carrying a tray of many pies. "These are from Alison. She didn't feel good enough to drive up and Lindy wanted to have them for guests today."

"All right," Sabrina said. "Morning sickness?"

Clara nodded. "It hit her with a vengeance. And Lane

had to have the shop open, plus, the guys had to be out riding the range and all that cowboy stuff. So I volunteered."

"Very giving of you," Sabrina said.

"Oh, totally," Clara countered, setting the pies on the counter. "Of course, I was offered a pie for my trouble. And the chance to come and visit a couple friends that I don't see often enough."

She lifted her hand and her engagement ring sparkled, and Sabrina saw Olivia eyeball the diamond hungrily.

"How are things?" Clara asked.

Both she and Olivia made noncommittal grunting noises. Then Olivia turned away.

"I need to go check on a few things. Get a couple bottles from one of the storage rooms. I'll be back before you go," she said.

Clara waited until Olivia was gone. "What was that about?"

Sabrina lifted a shoulder. "I think your engagement ring is giving her hives. Bennett still hasn't proposed."

Clara sighed heavily. "I'm not sure Bennett is going to propose."

"That's what I'm afraid of. She cares for him so much…"

Clara twisted her engagement ring. "Does she? Or does she just care about the idea of him?"

Again, that phrase struck Sabrina in a way that was a bit too relatable. She knew what it was like to hold the idea of someone up as the truth. Knew exactly what it was like to feel like you knew a person without actually knowing them.

"I don't know. It's hard to tell with her. She's a tough one to read."

"Speaking of people being tough to read," Clara said, turning her blue eyes to Sabrina. "I want to know what happened with the condoms and Liam Donnelly."

"Really? It's the *condoms* that you're curious about? Not the Cheetos? Don't you want to know what I did with those?"

"To hell with your Cheetos, woman. I want real details."

Sabrina sighed heavily. "Fine. We had sex."

Clara's eyes widened. "Are you going to be my sister-in-law?"

Those words, though spoken with levity, felt like a knife straight through Sabrina's heart. "No," she said, rubbing at the sore spot again. It felt like it was growing at a far-too-rapid rate. "Liam and I are not going to… That's not going to be a thing."

"Why not? He and Alex are so close…"

The strange thing was, Sabrina felt like he and Alex weren't all that close. She understood why Alex might think so. She even understood why Liam might think so. But Alex didn't know anything about what Liam had been through. Not really. Liam had kept it from him. She had to wonder if Liam was actually close to anyone.

Or if all the things that he held back about himself kept him at a very safe distance from the world.

"Yeah, sorry. I can't get married to him just to become your sister-in-law. As convenient as it would be. Because you know I love you dearly."

"But you don't love *him*?"

The denial hovered on the edge of her lips, but she found she couldn't quite say the words. So instead she just shrugged. "We're just taking care of unfinished business. It was a long time coming. The fact of the matter is we are going to be living in the same town for the foreseeable future, and we need to be able to be around each other without sniping. Plus, we are working on a project together."

"And somehow having sex is going to make it seem like you guys are less awkward around each other?"

"Well, I don't know about that, but we're not fighting every time we get near each other. So, I guess that's a thing."

"Sure."

Silence settled awkwardly between them and Sabrina reached around for a topic that was not Liam, or her uncertain feelings about him. "Your bison are good?"

Clara shook her head. "You always talk about bison when you're uncomfortable."

"Only with you. It's not exactly my go-to topic with anyone else." Sabrina smiled. "Since you're the only bison rancher I know."

"More people should do it," Clara said. "It's fun."

"Fun. I'm not sure most people would consider bison fun."

"Well, then those people shouldn't have bison."

To Clara's credit, she didn't press for any more details about Liam. Olivia reappeared a while later as promised, but it served the purpose of keeping the socialization brief. And Clara did not ask about Bennett.

When they left, Sabrina felt oddly heavy. Because Clara had asked her a whole bunch of questions she didn't know the answer to. Or rather, a whole bunch of questions she didn't want to think about.

How she felt about Liam being the first one. There were feelings. There had always been feelings. If there weren't, then him coming back would have made her feel nothing more complicated than a pulse between her thighs.

But it had always been more than that. It had always been deeper. Much to her chagrin.

She and Olivia worked steadily over the lunch rush, which was more a steady trickle of people than it was a true rush. Then at the end of her shift she wandered back into her office, not really conscious of what she was doing until she opened the door and saw Liam sitting there, his shirtsleeves pushed up to his elbows, revealing muscular forearms and those fascinating tattoos. The ones that she wanted to hear an entire biography on. His hair was messed up, as though he had run his fingers through it a few times. He looked rough and masculine, too big for the space, and almost comical sitting in front of the slim, silver computer.

He looked every inch the cowboy. Not even working on spreadsheets could make him look bookish.

"Hey," she said, leaning up against the doorway and looking down at him.

He turned his focus to her, those green eyes never failing to make her feel like all the breath had been stolen from her lungs.

"Hi."

"Are you…about ready? The little rush of the day is over, and I can leave now if I want. Today just isn't going to be very busy."

"Sure." He closed his computer and stuffed it into a soft sleeve.

As he did that, his muscles shifted and the ink on his arm moved right with it. His hands were large and battered from all the work he did outside, but more than capable of handling something delicate. Like a computer.

Or her body.

"You're like a cologne commercial," she blurted.

He looked up at her. "I'm what?"

She giggled. *Giggled.* What the hell was wrong with her? "I mean…because you're rugged, and manly, versatile."

His eyebrows shot upward. "Versatile?"

"Yeah. You can do math or fix fences instead. Good on the ranch, better…"

"In bed?" One side of his mouth lifted upward in a lopsided smile and made her heart turn over.

"Well, that wasn't how I was going to finish that sentence. That would not get past Standards and Practices."

"Standards and Practices are boring as hell."

"Well. Boring or not, it isn't going to make it to print if it's inappropriate."

"Honey, I only know how to be inappropriate. And I think you like that about me." He moved over to her, wrapped his arm around her waist and pulled her in for a kiss.

She was about to protest, because they were at work, and someone could walk in. But then, she forgot to protest, because she forgot the moment his lips touched hers.

She wrapped her arms around his neck, and he braced her with one strong arm curved around her waist like an iron bar. She clung to him, her breasts pressed against his chest, her knees going weak.

"Ahem." Sabrina jumped out of Liam's arms, brushing herself off as she looked up and saw Olivia standing in the doorway. "I wondered who you were talking to."

"Just… Working on… Spreadsheets. With Liam."

"Really?" she asked, sounding snippy.

Liam looked between Olivia and Sabrina. "I'll meet

you at the truck," he said, excusing himself and walking past Olivia. She knew that he wasn't abandoning her; rather he was doing his part to make the situation less awkward so she could speak freely.

"So," Olivia said, her voice like acid. "You're sleeping with him."

"Not…right now. Right now I'm standing here with you. And I'm not asleep."

"You have slept with him. Had sex with him."

"Yes," Sabrina said. "But I don't see what the big deal is with that?"

"Nothing," Olivia bit out.

She turned and walked out of the office. "What? Olivia… Whatever is happening, I'm not going to be the victim of your sniping and silent disapproval for the next few weeks, so you might as well tell me what the problem is."

"Everyone has someone."

"You have someone," Sabrina pointed out. "You had someone this whole time. In fact, a year ago, you were the only one of us who had a boyfriend."

"I mean… The way that he kissed you. The way that he looks at you."

"Bennett looks at you like you're a princess," Sabrina said. "He calls you princess. You mean…a lot to him."

"Yeah. But he doesn't want to… He doesn't look at me like he wants to eat me."

"Well, if that's something that bothers you then you need to talk to him."

"I can't. I can't talk to him about that." She sucked in a sharp breath. "He'll say that it's my fault."

"Why would he say that?"

"Because I won't sleep with him. Not until we get engaged."

Sabrina was stunned by that. She really shouldn't have been. Olivia had alluded to the fact that she was opposed to sex without a commitment before, so it really stood to reason. And Sabrina should have put two and two together and come up with celibate. It was just that she hadn't, because the two of them had been together for long enough that it didn't seem feasible.

"So you've been waiting to have sex with him until he gets engaged to you."

"That is what I just said," Olivia said. "And I stand by that decision. It's what I want. It's how I want to do things. I just… I'm jealous. I'm jealous, because what you're doing looks like more fun than what I'm doing right now."

"Olivia," Sabrina said softly. "If you're making that decision for reasons that are important to you then you should stand by it," Sabrina said. "And you'll be happy that you did. Because standing by what you believe in isn't a bad thing. Especially not if acting in a way you don't think is right would just fill you with regret later." Sabrina tried to force a laugh. "How much fun can you have when you feel guilty?"

She was the one who had posed the question, but she felt like there was no simple answer to that. Since, in her experience, a little bit of shame made things interesting.

That delicious lick of naughtiness that she felt when Liam touched her only added to the thrill. Of course, she'd never had a physical relationship with anyone in the context of a regular relationship, so maybe it was always like this. She wouldn't know.

"I just thought that he would propose. I thought that

it was almost there. That's what I felt like. Like the light was in sight at the end of the tunnel. It was going to be a big fat Christmas light. A big romantic Christmas proposal. And I ruined it, because I asked him, and he said it wasn't happening yet. He said that when it was all coming together, and it was the right time, he would let me know. But it's not now. I thought it was now." She sniffed loudly. "I wish I had never asked him."

"It wouldn't have been better for you to be blindsided when he didn't ask you come Christmas, honey," Sabrina said, wrapping her arm around her friend. "I don't know anything about relationships. I spent thirteen years hung up on Liam. So I do know what it's like to be completely stuck on one man no matter what. No matter what anyone tells you to do, no matter what logic dictates you should do. I'm not judging you. But I'm not sure that loving someone should make you this miserable."

Liam made her a special kind of miserable. Her chest hurt as much as her body felt good. But she didn't love him.

Wasn't love supposed to look like what Bennett and Olivia had? Steady, certain? It might not be fireworks or excitement, but it was the kind of thing that would last, surely.

"My parents had passion," she said, her stomach turning just talking about them like that. But it was true. And it was the only real advice she had to give. "And my mom has always been fickle. She's never been faithful to my father. And he stays. He stays, even though he's hurt and bitter. I would rather have comfortable and certain, and slow over any of that. I know it seems like it's taking forever now, but you want to be married to him forever, right?"

"Yes," Olivia said, the word watery.

"Then you don't need to hurry on into forever. You'll have a ton of time. And then it will be worth the wait."

Olivia nodded and Sabrina felt a sense of disquiet in her chest, a strange feeling of guilt. Like she had said the wrong thing somehow, except she believed what she had said.

Yes, what she and Liam had was hot enough to light bedsheets on fire. But not everybody needed that. And that wasn't the same thing. It wasn't love, it was just lust. It wouldn't last, it would burn itself out, and if Olivia was averse to those kinds of relationships, then she really wouldn't miss it.

"If Bennett is truly the one, the one that you want, the one that you know that you're supposed to be with… That he really will be worth waiting for." She released her hold on Olivia and walked outside.

It was gray, the fog hanging low, the December frost fighting hard to cling to the evergreen trees that surrounded the winery grounds.

She took a deep breath and watched it float away and join the mist. She hoped like hell she had given good advice.

There was only one part of that equation she knew for sure. That if you were supposed to wait for a certain man… Well, then you were.

Sure, with Liam it was all sex, but her body had certainly been intent on waiting for him.

And speaking of, her body gave a little internal leap when it saw him standing out there leaning against the truck looking all sexy and rakish and disreputable. Not at all like the smart choice. Not at all like certainty or true love.

No, he was every inch that bad-boy fantasy that she had long craved and then some.

Physical. Not love. Certainly nothing for Olivia to envy. Although, Sabrina wouldn't trade her for all the shoes in her closet.

"Is she okay?" he asked.

"She has the *I want to get engaged* blues, and I think any relationship happening around her is being taken as a personal affront."

"I see. Well, I don't see, but I expect that's okay."

She laughed. "Yes, it is."

"As long as you're happy."

She looked around at the winery, the winery she had been barred from essentially until recently, the one that she loved with all of her heart. At the manicured grounds, the rustic barns, the stately pine trees. And then she looked back at Liam.

Who looked right here. Who felt right with her.

Just lust. Just lust.

"I'm very happy."

CHAPTER SEVENTEEN

"Is ALISON JOINING us for dinner tonight?" Lane asked, directing the question at Cain.

They were all sitting around in the kitchen, some of them in the island, some of them at the table in the corner, Alex, Clara, Lane and Finn, Cain and his daughter, Violet. But not his wife, Alison.

"I'm not sure. It depends on if she's able to get up."

"Not so smug now," Finn asked, "are you?"

"Hey," Cain said. "Do not give us grief about her morning sickness. She didn't say anything, I was the one being cocky."

"Yeah. Well, I'm just saying. You are acting like there was nothing that was going to throw you for a loop."

"I didn't know she was going to be sick all day. It's morning sickness. You're supposed to be sick *in the morning.*"

"I guess your new baby doesn't have a watch in the womb."

Violet, who was seventeen and plagued by life, scowled. "I can't believe my stepmother is pregnant. It's embarrassing."

"Are you happy you're going to be a big sister?" Lane asked.

"Of course I'm happy. I just don't like having to explain to my friends that my dad got someone pregnant."

"You find it horrifying now, Violet," Clara said, "but believe me, when you're old like us you'll be glad that kind of thing is still happening."

Violet wrinkled her nose. "I might have to go join Alison in a sickbed."

"How dare you?" Liam asked, directing the question to Cain. "How dare you pursue happiness and have a new child when your daughter is so humiliated."

"A little humiliation is good for you." Cain winked. "It builds character."

"Then I have the most character of anyone I know," Violet said.

"That's actually true, Bo," Cain said.

She made a wretched face and then went back to eating the lasagna that Lane had made.

"How is everything coming with the tasting room?"

"Just about done," Liam said.

"Why hasn't Sabrina joined us for dinner yet?" Lane pressed.

Liam shot a look at Clara, and then looked back at his sister-in-law. "Why would she?"

"Because you have more than a business relationship with her, and don't you dare get mad at Clara, I would have guessed anyway."

"Fine," he said. "We're having more than just a business partnership." He looked at his brothers, daring them to say something.

"You say that like we didn't know," Finn said. "We've known from the beginning this was going to happen."

"Great."

Cain reached across the table and slapped a dollar bill down in front of Finn. "You win," he said. "I thought that he could hold out. I was wrong. Apparently my faith in our brother's self-control was misplaced."

"You absolute jerk," Liam said.

Finn grinned broadly and pocketed the money. "Being an unfaithful louse really pays sometimes."

"You did not place bets on me," Liam said.

"No," Alex responded. "They didn't. Or, if they did, they didn't tell me. And they didn't invite me into the pool, which is offensive, because I would've beaten them both."

"No, you wouldn't have," Finn said. "You're his little brother. You worship the ground he walks on. You would have had way too much faith in him."

"I'm realistic about him," Alex said.

Liam spread his arms wide. "I am sitting right here."

"Yes, you are," Cain said, waving. "Hi."

"I'm sitting here too," Violet said, her lip curled in disgust.

"I'm sorry, Violet," Alex said. "Do you need to go sit at the kids table?"

"Duh, Uncle Alex, I know that you guys are gross."

"Okay then, don't act offended."

Liam shook his head and went back to eating his dinner, ignoring the buzz of chatter coming from his sister-in-law and his sister-in-law-to-be. They were clearly overexcited because they thought that something permanent was going to happen with Sabrina and himself. And maybe, if they were different people, Lane and Clara would be correct. But he had an aversion to relationships a mile wide, and he figured Sabrina wasn't much different. The way she had talked about her parents… The way that her family was…

It just wasn't for people like them.

So many people had the fantasy of the house, the picket fence, that kind of togetherness and love and laughter. It all just made him feel like he was being strangled with a noose. He hated it. Hated the very thought.

"Hey," Alex said once the dinner plates had been cleared. "I want to talk to you for a little bit."

"We can talk here," Liam said, folding his arms over his chest and looking around the dining area.

"I'd rather not," he said. "I'd rather go to the living room."

He gave his brother a sidelong glance but followed him from the room the whole crowd was in into the living room. He kept his arms crossed, rocking back on his heels, fixing his gaze on the rock fireplace that spread from floor to ceiling, before shifting to the large windows that during the day overlooked an expansive view of mountains and trees.

"We set a date," Alex said. "Clara and I. We're going to have the wedding in May."

"Congratulations," Liam said, and he meant it. He wanted Alex to have that normal life. That normal life that he knew he wasn't going to get.

He considered it one of the very few true accomplishments in his life that Alex had been able to heal enough to go on and find love. He really did. If it meant that Alex lived with a slightly different memory of their childhood than Liam did, that was fine with him.

It was preferable.

"Yeah, well, I just wanted to make sure you were going to be in town then."

He looked away from the glass that was mostly reflecting his own cranky expression, and turned his focus to his brother. "Yeah. I'll be here."

"Good. Because I want you to be my best man."

Liam just stared at his brother. "A best man?"

"Yes, asshole. Who did you think I was going to ask?"

Liam shrugged. "One of your soldier buddies. You know, one of the guys who actually had your back in the trenches, instead of the guy that gave you wedgies when you were smaller than he was."

"My best friend in the military is dead. And even then, he was my brother in arms, and he was Clara's brother. But he wasn't my brother. *You* are. You were there all my life. You're the only one who was there all of my life. You're important to me, dammit."

"You're already engaged, Alex, you don't need to gear up to propose to me too."

"This is called brotherly love, jackass."

Liam huffed out a laugh. "Yeah. I'll be your best man." It made his stomach turn over, made his chest feel strange. Both a little bit too small for his vital organs, and also numb. "Do I have to wear a suit?"

"I figured you already had a suit."

Liam chuckled. "I do."

"So, it's also cost-effective to use you."

"Well I'm glad to be the cost-effective choice."

Alex hesitated for a moment. "You've always been there for me. You're the reason that I'm with Clara now. Without you, without that talk you gave me, it wouldn't have gone the way that it did. You've always been there for me. In more ways than I think I even know."

Alex was skating closer to the truth than Liam would like him to be, but he didn't really know what to say about it. He wasn't going to say anything.

"Hey, it's nothing. I'm your big brother. I'm there to

give advice that I don't even believe, I'm there to protect you. Whatever."

Alex let out a long, slow breath, his expression looking tortured. Liam had a feeling it was because their exchange was involving genuine emotion. And that was torture for the two of them.

"You're my hero, Liam," Alex said.

Liam felt like he had been punched in the chest. He didn't know what to say. Not about any damn thing.

"Come on, soldier boy," he said. "I'm not a hero. You are."

"No. Don't do that. You were my hero. All of my life. You took care of me. Always made sure that I got off to school all right, and things like that. And I know I was angry at you for a while for leaving. But I was just angry at everybody."

"No. You had every right to be angry at me. I left you there, and you weren't ready to be by yourself. You were still living in that hell and I just took off."

"That was an excuse," Alex said. "An excuse that I gave to myself so that I could stay mad. About everything to do with Mom and Dad. About everything to do with our childhood. Because I was scared. I was scared shitless, quite frankly, when I started having feelings for Clara, and that made me an angry son of a bitch. I lost a lot of people. But you are still here. Now that I have my head out of my ass I really appreciate that."

"There's nothing much to appreciate," Liam said. "It's just older brother stuff."

"Whatever. You're still my best man. Now, can we never speak of this again?"

"I would prefer it if we didn't," Liam responded. He turned to leave, his hand stuffed into his pockets. Then he stopped, giving that weight in his chest its full moment, its full breadth. Then he turned back to face his brother. "You're my hero, Alex. I hope you know that. You're the bravest son of a bitch I have ever known. You put your life at risk for this country. You've lost a hell of a lot. And then when push came to shove, you were brave enough to let go of all of that and go after Clara. You're my fucking hero."

Alex cleared his throat, his Adam's apple bobbing up and down. "Thank you."

Liam nodded once, and walked out of the room.

CHAPTER EIGHTEEN

THE TASTING ROOM was ready for its grand opening. Mid-December, and everything had gone along according to plan. Better than according to plan. It was all ready. The menus were made, the tables were set, the countertops were in. They had a register, they had an official schedule. They had an adorable little Open sign with a pun.

It was all absolutely perfect. A gorgeous little gem to add to the already sparkling town of Copper Ridge. Sabrina smiled gleefully as she walked down the cheerfully decorated street.

She looked up at the banner proclaiming the dates of the Victorian Christmas events. The first one would start this weekend, and coincide with the tree lighting, and the Grassroots Winery Tasting Room would be open for business that evening.

She was downright giddy. And her giddiness wasn't just down to the tasting room. Things with Liam were... incendiary. They were together whenever they could be, though, he often opted not to spend the night at her place, citing the fact that he needed to be back at the Laughing Irish to get work done early in the morning.

She had a feeling it was an excuse. Just like at this point keeping her hair tied back so that it didn't get tangled was an excuse for her.

She didn't know why she was being such a weirdo

about it. Except that he had asked her to take it down, and she had made an issue out of it. So, they were both clinging to the issue now.

Also, it had something to do with the tattoo. Something to do with not turning herself into that idealized girl he had once known.

It would keep her safe, she was certain. Or at least she needed to feign certainty.

Because she had a lot of feelings for Liam Donnelly, she couldn't deny that. Couldn't deny that there was a hell of a lot of caring happening, and that her heart was involved in ways she would rather it wasn't.

He was more than a fantasy now. More than a bogeyman that lived in her closet. He was a man. A man with flaws, a man with a hard, hurtful past. A man that she knew intimately.

She was familiar with every inch of that gorgeous body. But she didn't know what all the ink on his skin meant. She had purposefully kept herself from asking.

For the same reason she kept her hair up, really.

There was no reason to think of any of that now, though. She had a grand opening on her mind. She paused at the space between the shops, where a cross street ran through, where the town Christmas tree was already set up, the lights strung over the evergreen boughs, waiting to be lit.

She let out a long, slow breath and watched as it floated away on a cloud.

"Fancy meeting you here."

She didn't have to turn to know that it was Liam. But still, it made her heart leap. "We planned to meet here," she said.

"So we did," he responded, smiling broadly. "Still, pretty damn fancy."

"What is?"

He grabbed her hand and spun her toward him, drawing her up against his chest. On Main Street. In front of God and everybody.

"Your coat," he said, looking down. "I like it. It's very...pink."

"It's fashionable," she said, running a hand down the smooth wool.

He leaned in, pressing his forehead to hers. "I like all the little buttons. But mostly, I like thinking about undoing them."

She turned her head to the side, her heart thundering hard. "Liam Donnelly," she said, breathless, "you are shameless."

"Which, you have to admit, is one of my better qualities."

"I will admit no such thing," she said, taking hold of his hand and trying her best not to melt into a puddle when he laced his fingers through hers and continued to hold it as they walked down the street. "It would be unseemly."

"Well, we can't have you looking unseemly," he said.

"Indeed." She sniffed dramatically and they continued to walk on down the street together. This was kind of going against her let's-not-announce-that thing, but she didn't really care at the moment. What did it matter if people knew? Liam Donnelly was such a large part of her life, such a large part of her history. She had never been able to pretend that he'd meant nothing to her. And after this... Well, after this she would be no more able to pretend that he was just part of the town scenery.

Just thinking about that made her heart sink. Made her feel wobbly and sad. Because there was no way that she was ever going to feel neutral about him. She had accepted that, fully. And any vague idea she'd had about working him out of her system was ridiculous. There would be no working him out of her system. He was part of her. He had been from the moment she met him. She had a feeling he would continue to be. That he would always have a place in her heart, that he would always own a part of her soul.

That didn't mean that forever was in the future. It didn't even mean she wanted that. She didn't. She was almost completely certain.

But she was slowly accepting that the ache Liam made her feel was simply part of who she was. That he was part of her story. She was never going to be able to tear those pages out. And at this point, she didn't want to.

She was remaking herself, it was true. At least, she was working on it. Figuring out how not to be so afraid. Figuring out who she was apart from all that guilt that she carried around because of what had happened with her father.

Someday, when she dealt with all of that—and she was definitely going to—it would be due in part to Liam.

So why not hold hands with him? Why not have the physical satisfaction and feelings of closeness while they had it?

"I'm so excited about this," she said as they made their way around the corner and into the front door of the tasting room.

Everything was set, all the stock was in place, shelves full of breads and crackers and various things from both Lane's shop and Alison's bakery. There were wine racks full of bottles from Grassroots, and refrigerator cases full of Laughing Irish cheese. It was everything they had planned on it being and somehow more. Because it was real. It was something she and Liam had built together. A physical piece of evidence of what they had accomplished. Of how they had changed something together.

It felt symbolic. To how she personally had been changed by her association with him.

He looked at her and flicked the lights on, and it illuminated the space. The wooden floors that had been polished to a honey-colored glow, the glorious blue walls, and the slightly wavy glass windows. The old-fashioned fixtures that they had installed to keep with the original, early Copper Ridge theme.

"It's almost perfect," she said, turning around in the dining area.

"What else does it need?" he asked.

She wrinkled her nose. "I thought you were the experienced one."

He chuckled. "I am. We both know that."

"I'm not talking about your sexual exploits," she said, waving her hand at him.

He feigned shock. "Neither was I."

"Sure you weren't." She looked around the room again, and then out to the decorated street. "Well, it clearly needs a Christmas tree, Liam."

"I suppose it does," he said. "So, you know what that means."

"What?"

"We have to go get a Christmas tree."

CHAPTER NINETEEN

Liam didn't know who he was, not at the moment. Not considering he had sent Sabrina back to her house to acquire warmer clothes and a pair of mittens, something more practical than that long, elegant wool coat and her gray high-heeled boots. While he had gone over to Pie in the Sky to procure pies, to The Grind to get quiche, and then over to Rebecca West's store, the Trading Post, where he acquired a plaid blanket and picnic basket.

He was being *romantic*. He was never romantic. He was crass, he was good in bed, but he was not romantic.

Sabrina deserved it. He wanted to give her things. And he didn't even know what exactly he wanted her to have. Just more.

Sometimes he felt like he wanted to give her *everything*.

And then, more disturbingly, sometimes he felt like he already had. Because the essential problem with that realization was that it came along with one that reminded him he didn't have all that much to give. That if what he'd given her so far was everything, he was a damn sorry excuse for a man, and not one who deserved to be called a hero by his younger brother.

He shook his head, turning into her driveway and putting his truck in Park. He picked up his phone and texted her, letting her know that he was there. It would have been much more romantic, much more gentlemanly, for him to walk up to the door to signal his arrival, but he was kind of at his limit. Or at least, he needed to be.

Sabrina appeared a moment later, that blond hair resolutely pulled back still, this time, he suspected in a braid, as she was wearing a little knitted hat. She had also changed into a short, shearling coat and woolen mittens. And boots. With pom-poms.

And she was still sexy. With fucking pom-poms.

He sat resolutely in the truck, and she climbed in, looking rosy cheeked and excited.

"Where we going?" she asked.

"We have to find some snow," he said, pulling out of her driveway and heading away from Copper Ridge, away from the ocean. "I figure we would head up to Pyrite Creek, and if there was nothing there, we can go on up as far as Saddle Horn. I have four-wheel drive."

"That sounds very adventurous, cowboy," she said, putting her feet up on the dash. The little pom-poms on her boots bounced.

He felt a corresponding ache in his cock.

"Well, you have to be adventurous if you're going to hunt Christmas trees. Especially if you're after the elusive silver tip."

"Excellent," she said. "What is a silver tip?"

"You don't know what a silver tip is?"

She waved a mittened hand. "A pine tree is a pine tree."

"A pine tree is most definitely not a pine tree, country girl. I'm the one that went and lived in New York City for a while. You would think that you would be educating me on different pine varieties."

"They are green," she said, holding a hand up. He

had a feeling that she was holding up her index finger like she was counting off. But he couldn't tell. Because mittens. "They have needles," she said, her hand wiggling, confirming his theory about her fingers. "They are trees." It wiggled again.

"And you are cute," he said, grabbing hold of her hand and giving it a shake before turning his focus back to the road.

"That felt dismissive," she said, making an indignant noise.

"Is calling somebody cute dismissive now? I could call you prickly. That would also be true. Is that less dismissive?"

She made a sniffing sound as he drove on until they came to the pyrite gulch ranger station. Then he pulled off the highway and turned into the driveway.

"We need to get ourselves a permit before we go hunting Christmas trees," he said.

"That," she responded, "I do know."

"Well, thank God for that," he said. They walked into the small outpost, and Sabrina jumped slightly when she looked to the left and caught sight of the large, taxidermic cougar that was standing sentry.

"I can't believe that's still here," Liam commented.

"You are familiar with the…" She gestured toward the beast. "Him?"

"Yeah. It's been here since I used to come visit my grandpa."

She treated him to an expression he couldn't quite decode. "Tell me more about that."

But that was when a ranger came out from the back and asked what he could do for them. So, Liam set about to getting the five-dollar permit, and acquiring a map that would show them where exactly they could pull trees from.

Then they took both and headed back out to his truck. "I still want to know," she said when they got back in the truck.

"All right," he relented. "Starting at about twelve I used to spend summers in Copper Ridge. I guess you kind of knew some of that. My grandfather decided that he wanted to get to know his grandsons, since his own deadbeat son never seemed to take much of an interest in us. He tracked us down. And he brought us back to the Laughing Irish, and he worked us to death."

She laughed. "Clearly he didn't work you to death. Or you would be a great deal more diminished than you are."

"It's true. Death has a way of diminishing a man. So, maybe it was only half to death."

She snorted in response, and then he continued on with his story.

"Alex and I lived up in some crappy housing development in Washington. Not the big city by a stretch of the imagination, but not this. My grandfather taught us about ranching. He taught us about taking pride in building something with your hands. He taught us that we could do more than our parents had showed us. I'll be grateful for him for that forever. He was one of the biggest influences on me. And even though I didn't go straight into ranching, he's the reason that I got hired over at Grassroots when I was twenty. I didn't know what to do. I didn't know where to go. I also didn't feel like staying on the ranch like Finn did was really what I wanted. So, Callum put a good word in with your dad.

Who I imagine regretted trusting the old coot forever thereafter."

Sabrina laughed. "Well, I imagine he did."

"We all came out for Christmas break one winter. And Grandpa took us sledding. He drove us up this way, sat on his ass in the truck with the heater on and a hot coffee while we gave ourselves hypothermia in the snow. When we were older we'd come up and do ATV stuff. So yeah, I've been up this way lots of times."

"It's a shame you couldn't be here all the time," she said softly. "Did your grandfather know? I mean, did he know about what your mother did?"

Liam shook his head. "No. He didn't know. Nobody did. Like I said, Alex doesn't even know. Not the whole story."

"Why didn't you… Why didn't you tell?"

He paused for a long moment, mostly because he didn't have an answer. It was a question he'd asked himself more than once. Why hadn't he just told somebody? Why hadn't he told somebody at school? Why hadn't he told his grandfather? Alex? *Somebody?*

And it all came down to the same thing. He could only assume he had done it because part of him wanted to endure it. Part of him wanted to prove her wrong. And part of him had been waiting to come back with that check and say, "I sure as hell matter." All of his life. Even though that hadn't been the specific fantasy from the time he was a little boy, proving himself had always been a part of him. A bigger part of him than he had realized until much, much later.

"I suppose," he said slowly, "it's for the same reasons you haven't written off your dad. Because even though you know it's not your fault part of you wants to fix it.

I know part of me wanted to fix things with her for a long damn time."

"You gave her money," she said gently.

"I did. Damned lot of money. And she's used it. But I don't think she was ever impressed. I think she just felt like it was what she deserved for putting up with me. She's angry. She's angry, and she resents her children. She always has. Alex is a war hero. She's not proud of him. She damn well should be."

"And you're so successful," she said softly.

"That doesn't really matter. That's just money."

"It's hard work. And for you, it was sacrifice."

Leaving her. Hell yeah, that had been a sacrifice. But it was one that he'd had to make. There had been no other option. At least, not one that he could see then. Back when he had imagined...

Dammit all that he had imagined the money would fix it. That it would fix everything. That it would turn him from a blight on his mother's life into something that mattered.

It hadn't. It just still wasn't enough.

"It wasn't good enough."

"I understand that," she said. "Bastards."

He laughed, and turned the truck off the main highway and onto a dirt road that was marked with wooden sign.

"Yeah. We are unappreciated in our own time."

"We are," she said. "Except...I appreciate you."

He looked over at her, and felt something stretch between them. Something raw and intense. Something different than sex.

He cleared his throat. "You're not so bad yourself."

"Thanks."

They went on in silence until the gravel road became frosty, until frost turned into a light dusting of snow, growing deeper and deeper up on the sides. Until they were completely surrounded by a full-on winter wonderland. Dark green trees dusted in white, all of the foliage beneath completely concealed by a thick, white blanket.

"This seems like a good place. And hopefully I can get my truck out of this slush later." They pulled off the road, and the wheels of the truck sank slightly, sliding. "Should be fine," he said, smiling over at her.

"If I die in a snowbank because of you, Liam Donnelly, I swear I will come back as an evil specter and haunt you."

"You haunted me for thirteen years, Sabrina, so, that's a pretty pale threat."

The corners of her lips did something funny. Pulling up, and a little bit to the side. Not quite a smile. Not quite a frown. "What does that mean?"

"Exactly what I said. I quit a job once." Got out of the truck and walked around to the bed, retrieving the blanket, a tarp and the picnic basket.

Her eyes widened, as she jumped down out of the vehicle, the snow coming up nearly to the tops of her boots. "What's that?"

"Lunch," he said, grabbing an ax out of the back of the truck too and putting it on top of the picnic basket, holding them both with one arm.

"Between the tarp and the ax it looks a little bit like a murder," she pointed out.

"You have trust issues."

"Yes," she confirmed. "I do. But then I'm pretty sure you knew that already. Now, why did you quit a job? What does that have to do with haunting me?"

"Wouldn't you rather know what I got for lunch?"

"No. I want to know this."

"Fine. I had an office job, and I worked in the same department as a woman named Sabrina. I swear to God every time someone said her name all I could do was think about you. There's always been this whole…thing about you. And I've never understood it. But you got underneath my skin back then, and you did something to me. Even then. I don't suppose I have to understand it for it to be true."

She looked up at him, her blue eyes glowing. "I couldn't forget about you either. But then, you know that."

"I know you were mad at me," he said, his voice rough. "And I was kind of mad at me too. But I also always thought it was for the best. Because whatever that was… We could've destroyed each other, Sabrina. I believe it. I wasn't a good guy. I wasn't a nice guy. All that stuff with my parents… I was so angry. I was nice to you, I liked you. I did. But that couldn't have lasted. It just couldn't have."

"You would have resented me. Just like your mother did. For holding you back. Because I would never have been able to leave my parents. And I would've been mad at you for making my relationship with them difficult."

He nodded slowly. "I'm afraid so. But that doesn't mean that I left you and never thought of you again."

"I kinda figured," she said. "You know, tattoo standing as evidence."

"I had the tattoo already by then. And yeah, I'm an expert at lying to myself about why things matter and why they don't. That's how you survive spending a bunch of your childhood locked up. That's how you survive having your own mom look at you like she kind of wishes you would just die already. You get really good at telling yourself lies."

They said nothing after that, they just continued to walk down through the snow. He walked up a steep incline, helping her on up over a ditch and up the side of a hill where the trees were thicker. They dodged roots and hidden plants until they came to a spot that was relatively smooth. He laid out the tarp that he had brought, and then he put the plaid blanket on top of that. Then he set the picnic down. "I figured we could have lunch and a Christmas tree," he said.

She treated him to a shy smile and sat down on the blanket, grabbing hold of the picnic basket and pawing through it.

"Now you're interested in what I brought you."

"I was always interested but I'm more narcissistic than I am hungry. And I'm pretty hungry."

He chuckled. "I brought some mini pies from Alison's. And quiche from The Grind. Thermoses with coffee."

"You're kind of blowing me away here, Donnelly," Sabrina said, a smile tugging at the edges of her lips.

"I'll make a note of the fact that you can be bought for a quiche."

"A quiche and a mini pie. Plus a thermos of coffee. Don't make me sound so cheap."

"Perish the thought."

Perversely, he felt like he could have sat and watched her eat quiche and pie all day. Her cheeks were bright pink from the cold, and so was her nose. The way she ate, sort of mouse-like and delicate all at the same time, fascinated him. But then, her mouth fascinated him.

Because he could see no reason not to, he reached out, wrapping his fingers around the back of her head and drawing her head in close, and kissed her.

When they parted, she breathed out, her breath a blooming, white cloud. Her lashes fluttered, her eyes opening slowly. "Wow."

"Good kiss?"

She winked. "Good quiche." Then she shoved in his chest. "Okay, the kiss was pretty good too."

"In fairness, the quiche had bacon in it."

"Yes, in absolute fairness to your kiss, it did."

He kissed her again, and this time she didn't make any commentary afterward. Then they put their food away and walked along the road in search of a tree.

"How about this one?" he asked.

She tilted her head to the side. "It's too skinny."

"You don't want it to be too fat. You'll run out of room."

"But if it's too skinny it will look sad and sparse."

"What about this one?" he asked when they walked a few more paces up the road.

"Too short."

He moved over to stand next to it, wrapping his hand around the trunk and demonstrating that the tree was in fact a couple of inches taller than he was. "It's got to be at least six foot six. And you're going to put a star on it."

"The ceilings are almost nine feet," she pointed out.

"I have a feeling you're going to have to make some compromises," he said. "These are wild-caught trees. These are not carefully cultivated trees. They are imperfect. As God intended."

"Why is that superior?"

"Because it's natural," he said. "Not shaped or force-fed by man."

"That doesn't make any sense."

He gave up trying to explain the superior integrity of wild trees to her at that point, resigned to the fact he was going to have to find one she thought was pretty enough. "This one?" He gestured to one down the road and up a slight incline.

"We will have to go investigate," she said.

She walked up ahead of him, and he diverted his attention from the tree to the shape of her figure. To the rounded curve of her rear as she skipped off the road and leaped over the slight ditch between the road and the mountainside, and began to hike upward.

He followed after her, holding on to the ax, being careful not to fall down and chop into his hand.

"This one!" she said, flinging her hands wide.

He moved to stand beside her and the silver tip that she had selected. He had to admit it was pretty perfect as wild-grown trees went. Tall and full, without being too dramatic. And the parts that were uneven could easily be trimmed.

"Okay. Stand back."

"Do I get to watch you chop it down?"

"You sound excited about that."

She nodded. "I have some lumberjack fantasies that I would very much like to watch you play out."

"Really?"

"Yes. I buy very specific brand of paper towels for reason. You know. For the very brawny, flannel-clad mascot."

He arched a brow. "I feel like you should have let me

know about the paper towel thing and your lumberjack fetish a little earlier."

She blinked. "Why? So you could have called things off before you started sleeping with a crazy lady?"

"No. I would have put on some flannel and chopped some wood for you earlier. I have a feeling this will go well for me later."

She laughed and he took his position next to the tree and began to hack at it with the ax.

He looked up at Sabrina and had to laugh at the look on her face. Her blue eyes were wide and she had her mittens pressed up against her mouth as she watched him work. He didn't think a woman had ever looked at him like that. But then, for years he had attracted women because he wore expensive suits. Because he was in bars where men who made lots of money went after work. Because he had a nice penthouse and could buy them designer clothes and jewelry.

It had nothing to do with things like this. The strange, simple act that seemed to make her eyes sparkle and her cheeks flush pink. Something that could be accomplished with a five-dollar permit and a twenty-dollar ax.

There was something exposing about it, something deeply uncomfortable. Like she was looking through him. Like she could see him. All of him.

The tree started to list to the left, and he quit chopping, pushing it forward so it was lying against the mountain, then finishing it off at the base before picking it up with one hand.

Sabrina helped him carry the tree back to the truck. Well, she didn't contribute much, but she wrapped her mittened hands around the top, and he hefted most of the weight and put it in the bed.

When they got down into town, he parked the truck against the curb in front of the shop and unloaded the tree. He brought it into the tasting room, setting it up in the corner and putting it in the holder that he had bought earlier at the Trading Post. He also produced the box of ornaments he had purchased there too.

"You took a pretty bold risk," Sabrina said, approaching the box. "Making assumptions about what sort of quiche I wanted and about what kind of ornaments I might like."

He smiled. "I don't think I took a big risk with either. I've had breakfast with you a few times recently, so that was a pretty educated guess. And, as far as the ornaments go I just asked Rebecca what her favorite ones were."

"Pretty slick, Donnelly," she said, pulling out a few of the glass ornaments that were in the box. They were rustic, but elegant, and even though he wasn't an expert in that kind of thing, he had a vague idea of what would look good in a space like this, and what the clientele would respond to.

"Do you want some Christmas music?"

"That depends. Are you going to sing?"

"We are all better off if I don't sing." He pulled his phone out of his pocket and set it down on one of the tables, opening up a music app and selecting a premade list of old Christmas songs. He pressed Play and Bing Crosby's voice filled the room. "Though, I think Bing might be welcome."

She smiled. "Definitely."

While she laid out the ornaments, he took out a string of cranberries and white lights and set about to wrapping the garland around the tree, followed by the lights.

Sabrina hummed along to the music, and occasionally broke out into song. She had a nice voice. Sweet and soft. Something he could spend a long damn time listening to.

"I've never done this before," he said, grabbing one of the ornaments off the table and hanging it on one of the boughs.

"Never done what before?"

"I've never decorated a Christmas tree."

"How?" she asked, freezing with her hand right next to the tree, an ornament dangling from her delicate fingers.

"Well, my mother didn't like to celebrate Christmas. Or she just couldn't be bothered to do it. I don't know that she didn't like it specifically. But I guess it didn't fit in with her schedule."

"That doesn't seem fair," Sabrina said.

"Well," he said, "life's not fair, is it?"

"I guess not. But usually life isn't fair and there is still Christmas."

"I survived this long without Christmas."

"Well, now you're having Christmas. And you will have cheer. If I have anything to say about it."

He pulled the chair out away from a table and took a seat in it, crossing his arms and watching as she continued to hang ornaments. "I feel cheerful doing this."

He kept on watching her as the music filtered around them, the lights from the tree casting her in an ethereal glow.

He didn't have childhood memories of Christmas. When people talked about it in that tone of awe and reverence he had nothing to cross-reference it to. But he knew for certain that from now on this would be Christmas to him.

An empty shop, music from another time and Sabrina Leighton decorating a tree.

Once she finished she brushed her hands on her pants and stood back, admiring her work. "I think we need some wine, don't you?"

"Maybe some cheese too," he said.

"I'll get some."

"And I'll get the blanket," he said, heading out the front door and going back to the truck to retrieve the plaid blanket from earlier.

From the street, he looked into the windows, at the twinkling Christmas tree, and at Sabrina standing there. It was a good thing that they had installed some wooden blinds that would afford some privacy, because as far as he was concerned—as nice as it was to look at the view when he was outside—it was all a little too public for what he had in mind.

He made his way back inside, and Sabrina was just finishing pouring two glasses of red. She had a little plate with cheese that he imagined had been prepared at another time.

"Another picnic, huh?"

"Something like that," he said.

He took the wine from her hands and sat down, setting the glasses off to the side. She joined him on the blanket.

She reached out for the wine and he took that opportunity to intercept her, pulling her forward and kissing her. "I have to admit," he said. "I'm not all that hungry for food."

"Well…" She looked up at him, her eyes glittering. "Well."

He kissed her again, deeper, his tongue sliding against

hers. She was so sweet. So perfect. He would never be able to get enough of her.

And he knew beyond a shadow of a doubt that this would all be part of Christmas for him forever. Tasting her. Touching her. Feeling her against his body.

Suddenly, he couldn't wait. Not anymore. Not to be skin to skin with her. He needed her. Needed her with a ferocity that far surpassed anything else.

He pulled her sweater up over her head and smiled when he saw that she was wearing a black lacy bra, which he was going to go ahead and claim for himself.

"For me?"

"Might be for the UPS guy."

"Don't be silly. You didn't get a delivery today."

He reached around and unhooked the bra, letting it fall down to the floor, exposing those pale, perfect breasts. He lifted his hand and slid his thumb across one tightened bud, rubbing it gently, reveling in the small, kittenish sounds that she made.

He lifted his other hand, cupped her, squeezed her, then wrapped his arms around her and held her against him as he continued to kiss her, moving his hands over her back, down to the waistband of her jeans. He moved one hand around to the front to undo the button on her pants, and draw the zipper down. And then he pushed the other beneath the waistband, grabbing hold of her ass.

She clung to him, clung to his sweater as he continued to kiss her, touch her. Then he maneuvered her so that she was up on her knees, so that he could shove her pants and underwear down over her hips, shifting her so that he could get them off completely. So that she was entirely naked, and he was still fully clothed.

Then he laid her back on the blanket, her pale skin

a lovely contrast against the red. The lights from the Christmas tree shone over her skin like stars. Yeah, suddenly he saw a much bigger point to all of this. To the decorations. To everything.

He put his hand on her stomach, her body soft like silk. He slid his fingertips down beneath her belly button, tracing a line to her upper thigh, then traveling back upward across her stomach and down her other thigh, forcing himself to stay away from that lovely thatch of curls, all pale and pretty and begging for his attention.

Normally, she would say something to him. Tease him for teasing her. But instead, she simply watched him, simply looked up at him, all perfect and trusting and a hell of a lot more than he deserved.

He wanted to tell her that she shouldn't trust him. Or if she did, that the one thing she could trust was that he would disappoint her. Would probably hurt her.

The way she'd looked at him when he'd been chopping down the tree, like he was the fulfillment of something…there was only one way for that to end. Because he wasn't her lumberjack fantasy. He was just himself, and he wasn't a prize all on his own.

But he could give her pleasure now. And he was the only man who ever had. So there was that at least.

He continued to tease her, running his hands along her body, over her curves, teasing them both by denying either of them more intimate contact. She was restless, arching beneath his touch, begging for more without words. The fact that she said nothing spoke of her trust in him. That he would make it feel good. That eventually he would give her everything she needed.

He pulled his sweater off, throwing it to the side, then he made quick work of his jeans, grabbing his wallet and setting it off to the side so that they could more easily access the condom later. He grabbed hold of her, pulling her up into his arms, so that they were both in a sitting position, her knees on either side of him.

She slid her hands up his chest, up to his face, grabbed hold of him and kissed him as she rocked against him. He pressed his palms against her back, placed at the center of her shoulder blades, her bare breasts pressed up against him as they continued to kiss.

"Can I take your hair down?" he asked, his voice rough, the words strained.

"Yes," she whispered against his lips.

He reached back, sliding the hair tie off her hair, slowly, ever so slowly undoing the braid, relishing the feel of the soft strands between his fingers.

She kissed him deeper, and he rocked back slightly, her hair coming forward, blotting out the light, leaving everything black. Shrouded in darkness there was nothing but her. Nothing but the feel of her touch. Nothing but the feel of her soft fingertips skating over his bare back, nothing but the slick slide of her tongue against his. He felt like the lights were behind his eyelids now, little bursts of brightness that hit every time she shifted against him.

He curved his arm around her waist and laid them both down slowly on the blanket, bringing her over the top of him.

He gripped her hips, moved his hands slowly upward, to the small indent of her waist, to her rounded breasts, and back down. And then, finally, he pressed his hand between her thighs, slid his fingers through those sweet, slick folds, felt her desire all over him. Her need for him so clear, so beautiful he could scarcely breathe.

He stroked her, and she rocked against him, letting her head fall back. He looked up at her, at the beauty of her pleasure, at the intensity of the desire written over that beautiful face.

She was wild. Wild in the way he remembered her. The way he had tattooed her on his skin. As though he had seen this moment. But he hadn't. This had never happened back then. But it was like it was written somewhere on his soul. And he had felt compelled to capture something he had never even experienced before.

This creature. This Sabrina. Uninhibited. Beautiful.

He let his fingertips slide up to the line of her jaw, drift along to her chin. He slid his thumb over her lower lip and she shifted, drawing it into her mouth and sucking it in deep. His cock jumped, need pouring through him like a flood. He didn't know if he would survive this. He didn't know if he could survive her.

When he had come back to Copper Ridge he had been greeted—or rather shunned—by starchy, uptight Sabrina, and now he was here with this Sabrina. Truly, they were one and the same, and that was the really amazing thing. That he had earned this moment, earned this trust from her in spite of everything.

He was filled with a sense of being unworthy. Utterly. Completely.

With a shaking hand he reached out and grabbed his wallet, pulling it toward him and getting the condom out. "I can't last," he said, the words coming out strange. He knew that he should last. That he should give her more than this. But he was past finesse. All of those bedroom skills he had taken such pride in and for so many years were gone, apparently. He couldn't turn this into a well-practiced game that he knew all the steps to. Couldn't reduce this to anything. He was just living it. Experiencing it. Unable to do anything but throw himself at the mercy of the tide.

Of what she made him feel. Of what she did to him.

He wished like hell he knew what it was. He wished like hell that he knew whether or not he would survive it.

He shifted her back slightly, tearing open the condom and rolling the latex over his length before positioning her over him again. She gripped his shoulders, tilting her hips, teasing them both with the slick slide of his arousal through her damp folds. She lowered herself onto him slowly, her fingernails digging into him as she took him inside of her. She leaned forward, that long, beautiful hair brushing against his chest as she did. Sending lightning bolts of pleasure straight through him. He had to grit his teeth, gripping her hips tight to keep himself from coming then and there.

He was close. So close. But he needed it to last. For her.

Needed it to last because he didn't want this to end.

She lowered her head, kissing him deep, and he felt a deep, soul-shattering echo of need rock him, reach right down to his core, to everything that he was, and grab him tight. It was something more than arousal. Something more than sexual desire. It held every part of him, not just his dick.

And then she started to move, establishing an unsteady rhythm that spoke of her inexperience, that spoke of the fact that he was her one and only lover. And it made it all the better. This thing, this raw, intense joining that had nothing to do with anyone or anything but Liam and Sabrina. As if there had been no other lover for him either. As if it was only her.

As if a piece of him had waited for this.

Which didn't make any damned sense, but then, none of it did.

None of it made sense at all. If it was sex, if it was about skill, then he would be able to put that in its place. If it had simply been about having her, solving the mysteries of what it was like to be with Sabrina Leighton, all of it would have been answered a few weeks ago. And yet every time they were together it was more. It was something else. It shifted, it changed. It wasn't anything he could grab hold of. It was an endless well. And every time he expected to find the bottom of it, it just kept on going. On and on, forever, into the darkness, and he feared that he would never find the end.

And suddenly, he was at the end of his control. She was tormenting him, teasing him, running those fingertips over his chest, and he couldn't take it anymore. He grabbed hold of one hand, then the other, forcing them behind her back, gripping her wrists with one hand, pinning them to her lower back.

He growled, thrusting up inside of her, taking the control. Or maybe that wasn't right. Maybe he wasn't taking control at all. Maybe control didn't exist here. Just need. Just desire. It was something that he had to do. Something he had to have. Her. He would never get enough of her. It would never be enough. Never be deep enough. Never be hard enough. Because no matter how many times he had her, no matter how good the sex was, there was a hole in his soul. That's where it was. And she made it burn.

He closed his eyes, blocking everything out. Blotting out everything but her. She rolled her hips forward, a low moan on her lips, and then he felt her internal muscles contracting around him. And he couldn't wait any longer.

It was like dying. Like a damned heart attack. As much pain as it was pleasure.

She leaned forward, kissing his lips lightly and he growled, bucking up inside of her one last time as he spilled himself completely, as he gave himself up to her. Surrendered to her.

She collapsed over his body, one delicate finger tracing a line just above his nipple, to the center of his chest. He opened his eyes, looked up and saw the Christmas tree. He wanted to laugh, but he didn't have the strength.

Instead, he threaded his fingers through her hair, using them as a comb. "So that it doesn't get snarled," he said, pressing his lips to her forehead.

She didn't laugh. Didn't say anything. Instead, she just took a deep breath that seemed so all encompassing he could feel it in his own chest.

"I think we're ready for the opening now," she said softly.

His chest seized tight, because he knew what that meant. It was what they had agreed. That after the opening it would all be over.

"Soon enough," he said. "The tree lighting is in two days."

"Yes," she said, "it is." She shifted restlessly against him, as though the same thoughts had occurred to her. Silence stretched on, tension filling the air. "Liam," she said, almost rushed. "Tell me about your tattoos."

SABRINA FELT STRANGELY DESPERATE. But then, maybe there was nothing desperate about it. Because they had been talking about the tree lighting, and both of them had a tacit understanding about what that meant. They had agreed that they would see each other like this until after they were done setting up the winery. Technically, they were finished. And the grand opening would be on the night of the tree lighting. After that… After that they wouldn't be together anymore. And if she had any questions about him they wouldn't be answered. She needed to know this. She needed to know him. As much as she possibly could. Somehow, it felt important. Somehow it felt like a key. A key to knowing herself.

"Tell me the truth. Tell yourself the truth."

She expected him to tell her to go to hell. To tell her that it wasn't any of her business. And yet, he didn't. Instead, he wrapped his arms around her, shifting slightly beneath her, trapping one of her legs between his thighs. Then he rolled them over, so that he was on top. So that he was in the dominant position.

He was doing it to feel like he had some control, to put her on the defensive, and she knew it. She liked it anyway.

"The tree…" he said slowly. "Well, that was for the winery, but it was also for Copper Ridge. It was the first place that I felt roots. I thought the tree was a good symbol of that."

"And me?" She touched the center of his back, where she knew the now-familiar tattoo was.

"At the time, I just told myself it seemed right. But I got it so I wouldn't forget. So I wouldn't forget why I had gone to school. Why I had to succeed. You made me happy. And I left you for that. So it had to be damn well worth it. I didn't do it so I wouldn't forget you, Sabrina. I knew I wouldn't. Every time I smelled of vanilla."

"Vanilla makes you think of me?"

"Always."

"What about this one?" She brushed her fingertips over the streak of light that on was his arm, running along the winding river and rock scene.

"That is a will-o'-the-wisp. My grandpa used to tell stories about them. It's a fairy fire, often directed by a malicious spirit. It leads travelers off their path. Usually to their deaths. It's supposed to remind me to stay where I'm headed, no matter what."

Her heart tightened, her stomach twisting. "What about the bear?"

"Protection." She moved her fingertips up to the top of his shoulder, down the bear's back. "Mostly, he just reminds me that I have to protect myself."

"The ocean is Copper Ridge too, isn't it?"

"Yes," he said slowly. "The mountains, that too. And the Celtic knots are for the family. Our name. The piece of my father, even though he's not here. Mostly, my grandfather. My brothers. We're all linked together, whether we want to be or not. Family. Even though it's complicated."

"You're such a funny man. You seem so detached. So distant from everyone else, but you feel it the deepest, don't you?"

"I've never quizzed anybody else on how they feel. We don't exactly talk about our feelings. Not a Donnelly forte."

"Of course not," she said.

Suddenly, she didn't feel like they were lying there skin to skin. Suddenly, she didn't feel like they were in the same room at all. She felt like he was about a hundred miles away from her, and like he had done it deliberately.

She needed practice being okay with that. Because

after the tree lighting it would all be over. And she needed to learn to make her peace with that. To make her peace with the woman she had become because of this relationship. And to make her peace with the pain that would come from it ending.

"Do you have a brush in your purse?" he asked.

"A little foldable one," she said, frowning. "Why?"

He shifted her to the side and stood, grabbing hold of her purse and opening it up, producing the little travel brush that she left inside. "I doubt that finger combing is going to be good enough."

She looked at him, still feeling confused.

"Sit up," he said.

She complied, and he came to sit down behind her, wrapping her hair around his hand and brushing it in a long, smooth strokes. Her heart clenched, and her eyes filled with tears. And she tried not to make a sound as he brushed every single tangle out of her hair, as he destroyed each and every one of her defenses. Tried to keep silent as tears slid down her cheeks.

She had been right. It had been better to keep her hair up. To keep her guard up. But she hadn't. And now it was too late.

Because she had gone and fallen in love with Liam Donnelly. Again.

CHAPTER TWENTY

WHEN SHE WOKE up the next morning she was tangled in Liam and thoughts about the end.

Not the *end* end. But the end of them. And then back to the beginning of them. And everything that had happened at the end that time.

They had gone back to her place after they'd decorated the tasting room, and then made love again before going to sleep. She wasn't sure how she felt. Twofold. A little bit tender and overly emotional. She loved him. There was no denying it. And he had changed her. Changed her in some profound ways that she didn't want to fight.

She was determined that this time she wouldn't be unraveled by their ending. She was going to make something of it.

She had resolved this with him, in a way. Had put him in the place he would always be in her heart, one she couldn't deny, one she didn't even want to deny.

But she felt she had to reconcile the other things from her past as well. It was time. Time to not be so afraid. Time to make the changes that she wanted.

She brushed a kiss over Liam's temple and got up, dressing quickly and then staring at her car keys for a moment before taking a deep breath.

Without even getting a cup of coffee she went out

and got into her car, starting the engine and letting it idle for a moment as she mentally went over what she was about to do.

It was early, but her dad would be up. He was always up early in the morning.

She knew that much, even though she barely knew him anymore. He was dependable that way. Steady in his routine.

It wasn't lost on her that she was somewhat that way herself.

A smile touched her lips and she pulled out of the driveway, heading toward the gated lakeside community that her parents lived in.

As she drove the familiar road, she thought of all the ways she was like her dad. She had been afraid, for a long time, of being ruled by passion. She had taken steps to protect and defend herself. And in the end, had hidden behind the walls she had built rather than confronting him. Rather than dealing with the hurt, with the wrongs done. It was what he did. What he had done for years.

She had been angry about it. Angry at him. And yet, she was more like him that she had given herself credit for.

All that fear. That fear, and the deep-seated terror that she might not be doing the right thing.

That was her father. Frozen forever trying to do the right thing while trying to protect himself. Staying in a marriage that made him unhappy because he didn't know what else to do.

It was what she had done. Stayed in positions too many times that had made her unhappy. Because they were safe in their way. At least it was a particular kind

of unhappiness that she could cling to. That was familiar. At least, it was something she recognized.

But she didn't want that kind of easily recognizable
misery. Not anymore.

It was going to start here. It had to.

She pulled her car up to her parents' glorious home,
their retirement, the first time they had ever lived in a
house that didn't have sprawling grounds and acres of
land to keep up on, and she breathed in deeply.

Then she killed the engine and got out of the car,
walking slowly to the door, questioning her sanity every
step of the way, but knowing there was no other way.

She rang the bell, then stood there, waiting.

Unsurprisingly, it was her mother who appeared at the
door, looking as vibrant as she always did, her makeup
on in spite of the early hour, already dressed to impress.

"Sabrina," she said. "I haven't forgotten a breakfast
date, have I?"

"No, Mom," she said. "I'm actually here to see Dad."

Suzanne Leighton looked uncomfortable with that,
but that didn't really surprise Sabrina. She and her
mother had a decent relationship, but they conducted
most of it out of the house. "You're here to see your father? Did you call him ahead?"

"No," Sabrina said, "because if I had done that he
probably would have told me not to come. And I needed
to. I truly needed to come and talk to him."

"All right," she said, ushering Sabrina into the house.
"He's in his office having his coffee."

"Well, at least he'll be caffeinated," Sabrina said.
"That's more than I can say for myself."

"Should I bring you some?"

"No. It would be better if we didn't get interrupted."

Sabrina took a deep breath and wandered the labyrinthine hall that led to her father's office. She raised her hand and knocked, and she heard his voice—as strong and intimidating as ever—bidding her entry.

She cracked the door open and stepped inside. "Dad?"

His head was bent down, gray now. She never pictured him gray. She was always surprised to see that he was. He looked up, his blue eyes flat.

"What exactly are you doing here?" her father asked, not even making a nod toward being friendly.

"I'm here to talk to you," Sabrina said, approaching his desk without waiting for an invitation. "And I think it's very likely that I should have come to talk to you a decade ago."

He looked down. "I'm not sure that we have anything to discuss, Sabrina."

"You're wrong. We have a lot of things to discuss."

That brought his focus back to her. "I have a feeling you want to dredge up old history, but I don't have the desire to do that."

"Why?" she persisted.

"Because I've been remarkably forgiving of your behavior, I think."

She laughed. She couldn't help it. The sound was absorbed by all of the heavy wooden bookcases, as if the sacred space of Jamison Leighton was simply not made to contain such a sound and had to swallow it up as quickly as possible. "You consider *this* remarkably forgiving? You can't look me in the eye. Our relationship was never the same after that night at the party, and you can't pretend that it is."

"I didn't say it was the same," he responded. "How *could* it be?"

"Why?" she asked, looking at him with new eyes. The eyes of an adult, and not one of a child.

She had his eyes, and she was more aware of that now than she'd ever been. They were so much the same.

Liam Donnelly had mortally wounded her pride and she had marinated in that hurt. Had stayed resolutely enraged at him.

Suddenly she saw her father for exactly what he was. Something so similar to her own self it was shocking. A man whose pride had been wounded and who was clinging to the pieces of it.

And he blamed her.

"You can't look at me because I embarrassed you," she said. "Is that it? You think that me embarrassing you was the worst thing I could have done?"

"Sabrina," he said, "you behaved abominably. You embarrassed all of us."

"Yes, I'm well aware of that. I have replayed the situation in my mind over and over again, Dad, I'm well aware of how it happened. But I was young, and I was hurt. I was hurt because you paid a man that I was in love with to leave me."

"But I was right. He did leave."

"Yes. You were right. And I was devastated. You didn't comfort me. You didn't even try. You just…leaned back into all that righteous fervor of yours and decided that it didn't matter if there was any compassion as long as you were technically correct. But that wasn't enough for me. I was seventeen. I worshipped the ground that you walked on."

"That can't be true," he said, his voice rough.

"Why can't it be true?"

"If you worshipped the ground I walked on you would

not have fallen for a man who was so unsuitable for you to begin with."

"Why?" she asked, genuinely confused.

He turned his focus away from his computer completely, facing her full-on now. "Because if you knew what you did about your mother then you should know what it means to fall for someone who will never love you back in the same way," he said, his voice hard. "And if you did not learn from that, then I must come to the conclusion that you thought me a fool as well. You certainly must have, for you dragged all of the secrets out into public. You must have hated your mother. And you…you must have despised me most of all. You must've found me to be a ridiculous old man."

Those words almost knocked her back. "You thought… All this time you thought that me knowing she was unfaithful made me…look down on you?"

"How can anyone look at a man who is continually betrayed with any respect?"

"I could," she said. "I did. You were my father, and whatever she did didn't make me think less of *you*. You were only trying to do your best. You were trying to do what was right. I do understand that. But there was no softness in it, Dad. And I needed softness. I didn't need your rigid clinging to perfection."

"I could have done what I wanted," he said, his voice rough. "When your mother fell pregnant with Damien I could have opted not to marry her. The first time she was unfaithful to me I could have left. And then we wouldn't have you. And we wouldn't have Beatrix. And we wouldn't have this life together in our retirement, which has been remarkably better than those early years we spent together. I did what was right, I saw it through to the end and I am convinced that at the end of the day it was the best thing."

Which meant he thought cutting her off to save his vision of his life was the best thing too. "Rightness. Morality without quarter. Without compassion. Without love."

"I was never harder on you than I was on myself. Because I see myself in you. And I could see you going on that same path, and I did not wish it for you."

"So you cut me off when I made a mistake?"

Her father heaved out a sigh, and for the first time she thought he sounded weak. Diminished. Like there was a crack in that booming, intimidating voice, and it made Sabrina feel slightly cracked as well.

"I couldn't face you," her dad said. "Because you knew my shame. You knew what a failure I was. That for all of my talking about what was right I could not keep my house in order. I could not make my wife care for me. You worshipped me when you were young. I could not stand to see that broken."

"So you broke it yourself?"

He paused then, for a long moment. And she was certain it was the first time she'd ever seen her father speechless. That was the beauty of all of that moral certainty. There was a response for every occasion.

Yet he seemed to be searching for one now.

"I suppose I did," he said, looking past her.

"And you were too damn stubborn to apologize yourself? Too damned full of pride to fix this?" she asked, her heart beating faster, her hands trembling.

"Yes," he said, "I was."

"Do you love me, Dad? If I go off and join a dance troupe in Chicago, will you still love me?"

He looked away from her. "What kind of question is that?"

"It's a ridiculous one, because I don't know how to dance, but I just want to know if you love me. If you *still* love me. And if you will continue to do so if I make mistakes in the future, or do things that you don't approve of. Because I want to fix this, but I can't cope with the idea that I'll do this work only to lose what I'm working so hard to rebuild later when I inevitably can't be what you need me to be."

"I don't understand what you're saying."

"I'm saying—" she took a step forward, her hands pressed against her chest "—I want you to commit to loving me. If I'm going to try to fix this, if I'm going to try to mend this fence, and not stay angry at you for how much you hurt me, then I need to be sure that we're not going to find ourselves here again. I'm changing. And I need to know that you're changing too."

"I'm not sure I can change," he said. "But I would like to try to mend fences with you."

"Do better than try. Fix the fences. It cost me my pride to come in here, it's got to cost you something."

"Did you think that I stopped loving you?" he asked, his voice rough, shockingly so.

"No," she said, her throat getting tight. "Worse. I started believing you never really did. Because if you really love someone you don't just stop. It's not possible. It doesn't matter what they do, it doesn't matter what they say or shout in the middle of a crowded party. If you love someone it lives in you. It stays. And you just… It was so easy for you to stop seeing me as your daughter."

Silence hung between them for a long moment, and then, her father stood. He reached out and touched her hand with his. A light touch. Small. But the first real contact she had with him in years.

"I have always loved you," he said. "Very much. But I have not always understood what I was supposed to do with those feelings."

She choked on a watery laugh. It was either that or sob uncontrollably and she didn't want to do that. "I don't know if any of us fully understands what we're supposed to do with feelings like that." Her throat tightened, her voice getting thick. "But I guess we just have to try our best."

"My best hasn't been good enough," he said. "My right wasn't right enough."

A tear slid down Sabrina's cheek and she didn't bother to wipe it away. She was afraid to move. Afraid if she acknowledged the weeping it would never, ever stop. "Let's just try now," she said. "From now on let's just try."

"You're still going to be working with Lindy?" he asked after a beat.

Sabrina felt that like a blow. A qualifier. Of course there would be one. There always was. "Yes," she said. "Lindy is my sister, and I love her. And I would really like to figure out a way to have some reconciliation with Damien, because he's my brother and even if I can't agree with what he did I love him too. But, Dad, what's right is right. And if that's the case then Lindy is entitled to the winery."

"She could have stayed with him."

"I know you believe that, because it's what you did. But Damien didn't just cheat on her, he left her for another woman. He didn't want to be with her. Should she have fought to be with a man who didn't even love her?"

"I don't expect you to leave the winery," he said, finally.

She imagine that was the closest to admitting understanding as he would get.

"Good. I hope that you're able to come to the tasting room sometime. If you can't because it hurts you still that it's not in the family anymore, I do understand that. But I put the work into the opening. It's mine too. It means something to me."

"And you worked with the Donnelly brothers on that," he said. "I know Liam Donnelly is back in town. He paid me back."

"He is," Sabrina said. "He's part of the reason that I'm here."

A strange light reflected in her father's eyes. It almost looked like...hope. "Did you find a way back together?" he asked.

She shook her head slowly. "I don't think that's in the cards for us. But we've made our peace."

Her dad's shoulders sagged. "I really was just trying to protect you. Because I did see so much of you in me, and I could see you getting caught up in a relationship that would end up the way mine did."

"I understand that. I really do now. I understand that we are a lot more alike than we are different. Which is something I think surprises both of us."

"I always knew. And I tried to spare you. It's why I was so hard on you. But it seems that it wasn't necessary. Because you made good on your own."

"Thank you," she said. "I love you, Dad."

"I never stopped loving you, no matter that I didn't show it, I never did."

She had a choice then. To hang on, or to let go. To put

up another wall, or to let herself be open. To let herself take the chance at being hurt again. She knew what she would have done a few weeks ago.

Well, a few weeks ago she wouldn't have been here at all.

But she wasn't going to go back to hiding. She was going to be brave. It was good practice, because in two days she was going to have to do the bravest thing she could imagine. She was going to have to let Liam go.

So she might as well start practicing her bravery now.

"I believe you."

CHAPTER TWENTY-ONE

THE DAY OF the grand opening and tree lighting was chaos wrapped in tinsel. All hands were on deck down at the shop, preparing massive vats of mulled wine, special cheese platters and other items that would be given out as free samples. They had also prepared a best of Copper Ridge gift basket that would be on sale for a limited time to appeal to the influx of tourists that were coming through for today's festivities.

The tree that Liam and Sabrina had decorated the night before was lit up and glittering, and Lindy had brought down additional decorations to make the space look extra festive.

She had hung up mistletoe, and it took every ounce of Liam's self-control not to grab hold of Sabrina and test that mistletoe out.

He knew what they had said about their time together. About it only running up until this moment.

But he had a feeling that it wasn't going to go that way. Hell, why should it?

What they had worked. And it was good. There was no reason to end it now. No reason to end it until it wasn't fun.

Sometime after tonight he would have that talk with her. But he had a feeling they wouldn't even need to have it. It didn't make any sense that they would.

Feeling full of glad tidings of comfort and joy that he would have a gorgeous woman in his bed later, Liam took one last look around the shop and then walked out onto the unusually busy street.

His brothers and their wives and fiancée were in attendance; even Alison, who was looking a little bit pale, seemed to be getting into the spirit.

His niece, Violet, was there also, looking a bit more dour than swept up in the spirit of the season, but he had a feeling that was all about her street cred and not indicative of any actual feelings that she had about the situation.

There were carolers wandering the streets in clusters, the women in velvet dresses and the men in suits with bow ties and cloaks.

There were chestnuts roasting in an iron pot and being handed out free to various people, booths with different art projects for children and a chance for them to meet Father Christmas.

If Liam was ever going to have kids, this was the kind of thing he would want to bring them to. Because it was kind of thing he had never gotten a chance to experience.

Something made his stomach get tight, but he ignored it. He was getting pretty damned good at ignoring things like that. A lifetime of practice, he supposed.

Funny Olivia from the tasting room was also there, and so was her boyfriend, Bennett, who had brought along his friend Kaylee again. The poor woman seemed to be functioning as a very uncomfortable third wheel.

Liam was hardly an expert on friendships between men and women, since his relationships with women tended to be about one thing. But, given that, it was very hard for him to imagine that two people were as close as Kaylee and Bennett and didn't share a physical connection.

Though he supposed it was possible, and that he was an asshole.

He just doubted it.

Not that he was an asshole. But the other thing.

It wouldn't be dark yet for a couple more hours, and it wasn't until then that they would light the Christmas tree. In the meantime, it was all going to be carols and warm drinks, and children running around shrieking.

It was funny, because he had completed this entire operation thinking it was something he had done many times before. Being involved in the start-up of the new business.

But he had never done anything quite like this. In a place quite like this. He didn't look out into a tightly packed crowd and simply see an endless sea of people. It was something else. Something more. He looked out at that crowd and saw each individual person. People he knew, people he had at least seen before. And if he hadn't seen them before this they were still people he would probably see again. It was something unique. It was something that gave him the strangest urge to hide. Because he wasn't anonymous here. Nobody was. He couldn't simply blend in, another dark suit in a field of them.

No, here he was Liam Donnelly. In a button-up shirt, blue jeans and cowboy hat. One of the Donnelly boys.

For better or for worse.

He wasn't used to it. He didn't like it. This basic, simple existence that forced him to be…him.

He forced a smile, pushed his sleeves up and went back inside the tasting room, where Sabrina was chatting with customers and answering questions about wine and cheese pairings.

He watched as her pretty mouth curved upward into a smile, and he was reminded of the time they had sat in here and tested out those very pairings. When she had kissed that wine off his lips and he had gotten drunk on the taste of her.

That tattoo on his back burned. And he could swear he felt that line going from the tattoo through to his heart. He'd put the image on his back, where he couldn't see it most of the time, but he knew that it rested right behind his heart for a reason. Another thing he had tried to deny for a long time, but was having difficulty doing now.

She was... She was damn well part of him and there was very little denying that at this point.

He jumped in, helping serve free mulled wine to customers, offering service with a smile, because he was actually pretty damn good at that as long as it was a performance.

The girl from The Grind who had flirted with him just a few weeks ago stopped by, and about batted her eyelashes right off her face trying to get his attention. But he didn't care. No other woman affected him at all. No other woman but his. Sabrina.

She really did feel like his.

He looked over and saw that she had been watching the exchange, and noticed there was something wistful in her expression. Surely, at this point, she knew how he felt. Surely she knew that no other woman appealed to him more than she did.

If she had any doubt, he would have to make sure that he erased it.

He grinned at her, and she returned the smile, ducking her head and touching the back of her hair, which reminded him of how she had finally taken it down for him. How it had felt to sift his fingers through the silken locks.

He couldn't wait to do it again. Couldn't wait to have her tonight. His hunger for her bordered on obsession, and he was okay with that.

They worked until it started to get dark outside, and then the crowd inside thinned as people filtered out to the street to see the Christmas tree lighting.

Sabrina clasped her hands in front of herself and stayed where she was behind the counter, looking around.

"Come on," he said, sticking his hand out. "Let's go. We are going to go watch the Christmas tree lighting."

"Oh," she said. "I think we should probably stay here."

"No way," Lindy said, coming in from the back. "You go enjoy the festivities. Christmas still kind of bums me out anyway."

"But you were the one who said you wanted to have cheer and triumph, and Christmas-related revenge," Sabrina pointed out.

"And I do," Lindy said, flinging her hands wide. "I have. But, said revenge is centered on this space, and I'm fine staying in it for the time being. You go on and watch the tree lighting, and then come back so that I'm not slammed on my own."

"Okay," Sabrina said, taking Liam's hand without hesitation.

She looked up at him, and she had that strange, sad look on her face again. The one that he had caught sight of earlier. He didn't quite know what to think about it. Didn't quite know what it meant. But there wasn't a whole hell of a lot he could do about it either.

Not without digging into it. The problem was, he wasn't sure that he would like the answers.

So, he left it. Left it and led her out onto the street, down a couple of blocks to where the Christmas tree was.

Mayor Lydia West was making a speech about Copper Ridge, about its history and the unity in the tiny seaside town. Even with all of the antisocial weirdos. Well, she didn't say antisocial weirdos, but, he *thought* it. It was true enough.

Still, she was right. The sense of community here was real. Not because people were overly friendly, saccharine cardboard cutouts like you often saw in movies, but because this was the kind of place where people *had* to live together. To work together. You couldn't cut someone off without a hell of a lot of consideration, because you were bound to run into them again.

Bound to need to work with people who were related to them, or friends with them. Everything was wound up together here. A rural tangle that was tough to navigate if you weren't very careful with the various relationships all around you.

It was what he had been realizing earlier, standing there on the street, with no anonymity at all. You couldn't get lost in a crowd here. But you can sure as hell get found in one. That was tricky, it was exposing. And in some ways, it was comforting.

At least, he imagined it would be for some people.

He wasn't sure what it was to him.

He didn't know much of anything at the moment except that it felt good to hold Sabrina's hand. And when she moved in front of him and leaned up against him, the soft, sweet press of her body against his—and not just of her ass up against his cock—was like balm for a wound he hadn't realized he'd had.

"Okay," Lydia said, brightly, "I'm now going to turn over the lighting of the tree to Sheriff Eli Garrett."

The sheriff stepped up in front of the people and gave them a slightly abashed wave. Then bent down, plugging the lights in rather unceremoniously.

The tree lit up. Thousands of twinkling white lights blazed to light against the dark backdrop of the tree. Gold ribbons seemed to catch fire in the glow, and multifaceted glass stars sparkled like the real thing.

The choir began to sing "Hark! The Herald Angels Sing," and that tightness in his chest only grew.

Then, over the top of the music Liam heard a distressed sound. He looked over and saw Olivia Logan with tears on her face moving away from Bennett. She turned and started to stomp down the street, and Bennett said something to his friend, then went after Olivia, who seemed hell-bent on ignoring him.

Sabrina looked the same direction he did, a crease marring her forehead.

"Oh dear," she said.

"Any idea what that's about?" he asked.

Sabrina sighed heavily. "It's a long time coming, is what it is. They don't... They don't want the same things. I'm pretty convinced of that. But poor Olivia isn't."

"I see."

"She was really hoping he would propose before Christmas. And he actually told her he wasn't, but with his friend showing up and crashing what was probably supposed to be a date, and Olivia still smarting from the lack of impending proposal, I'm not that surprised that she's feeling done."

"Yeah."

It was a good thing that he and Sabrina wanted the same things. Namely, they didn't want marriage, or anything like that. They just wanted what they had. Another good reason to keep it going, really, since another reason that they should stick out this thing that was happening between them.

They weren't going to end up like that. Making a scene on the streets.

"We'll be all right finishing up tonight without Olivia," Sabrina said. "I just hope she's okay."

"Yeah," he said again, absently.

They finished watching the festivities, and then the crowd began to disperse slightly, people heading back into shops, and getting in line to see Father Christmas.

He and Sabrina went back into the tasting room and served up more mulled wine and cheese, and completely sold out of the gift baskets. They worked until the crowd started to thin and the moon rose high in the sky.

It was clear out, which was unusual. And without the blanket of fog to hold any of the heat in, the air was a particular kind of sharp, crystal cold that cut straight through to the bone. It was the cold that finally dispersed most of the crowd, leaving just a few stragglers talking and laughing out on the streets, and a couple of people left looking at different wine labels in the shop.

Lindy was leaning against the counter, her normally pristine blond hair sticking upward from its bun like antennae, dark circles spreading beneath her eyes.

"You look dead on your feet, Lindy," Sabrina said,

giving her sister-in-law's arm a squeeze. "You should go home."

Lindy looked around the now nearly empty shop. "It was wonderful, though, wasn't it?" she asked.

"It was really wonderful," Sabrina confirmed. "And we've got this from here."

Lindy looked skeptical. "I feel like I should stay."

"Who's opening up at Grassroots tomorrow?" Sabrina asked.

"Well. Me."

"Exactly. You have enough responsibility. And the whole point of hiring me is that you don't have to do everything. So go."

Lindy let out a slow breath, then straightened. "Thank you. I really do appreciate it."

Lindy gathered up all of her things and said goodbye, and then turned the open sign on her way out. Sabrina rang up the last few customers, and waved goodbye to them. Then she flicked the lights off. Leaving only the Christmas tree on.

They had been alone in the shop countless times, but it seemed different this time. Quieter. The emptiness more pronounced.

"That was fun," Sabrina said, twisting her hands, looking increasingly agitated. He hadn't seen her look like this for a few weeks. Not since they had first seen each other again after all that time apart. Not since they had first started trying to work together.

She shifted her weight from foot to foot, her focus on the Christmas tree. And then she finally turned to him.

"We need to talk," Sabrina said.

"We do?" he asked.

"Yes," she confirmed. "I went to see my father yesterday."

"Why didn't you tell me?" he asked, even as he realized he didn't have a right to that inquiry.

She shook her head. "It wasn't important then."

"But it's important now."

"Yes." She took a big breath. "It's an important part of my speech."

"You have a speech?"

"I have a speech," she said, lifting up her hand to tuck a strand of hair behind her ear. He could see that it was shaking. "Liam, if it weren't for the last month and a half I never would have gone to talk to my father. I would never have been brave enough. I was hiding. All this time I've been hiding. So cautious and afraid. So terrified that I would have to contend with all these feelings inside of me, feelings I've always had. And they scared me. They've always scared me. I used you, the memory of you, your ghost, to keep myself in my place. To keep myself from doing anything that might hurt me.

"I used my parents' marriage to give myself excuses for not wanting to be with someone. I decided that my passion, my desires were dangerous. You were right about me, you were right the whole time. I was scared. And you've helped me… You help me unlearn that. You help me undo it. So many years of locking myself up, and you've helped me fix it. Destroy all those walls that I built up inside of me. I couldn't have done it without you. I know it for a fact, because I was stagnant without you. And I need to thank you for that."

"You're welcome," he said, even though for some reason that didn't feel like the right response. Even though he wanted to just haul her up against him and kiss her and shut her the hell up because he could tell already he didn't like where any of this was going.

"So I just wanted you to know that. Because I know we are at the end now. Just like we agreed. I'm not going to ask you for anything more. I'm not going to ask for anything beyond what we decided on in the beginning. This is perfect. It really is. My journey with you is complete. I think I've learned everything that I needed to. About myself, about you."

She took in a shaking breath and he felt it vibrate through his chest. "I understand," she said, "why you don't want a family. I understand why you don't want love or marriage. What you went through was so awful, not even something I can remotely fathom. I get that you're... That you're broken in that way. And I guess..." She swallowed hard. "I even respect it. The damage that all of it did. I'm not going to stand here and tell you to just fix it. To heal it. Not when it's something I couldn't even begin to fully understand."

Liam was stunned. He didn't know what to say. He wanted to argue with her. Wanted to shout at her. Tell her they were not fucking done. They wouldn't be done until he damn well said they were. That he still got hard when she got close to him, and his heart beat faster every time he saw her, so how could they be done? But his mouth wouldn't work, his throat was stuck. It was like being locked inside of a dark closet all over again. Afraid to make noise, because if he did he knew it would only last longer.

All of that anger. All of that desperation, bottled up inside of him because he knew it would only make things worse. Because he had to behave himself if he wanted to be let out.

He was frozen like that. Even his heart refused to beat.

He was stunned. He couldn't say anything, and he had nothing to offer her. That made him feel...helpless, and he didn't do helpless. But he couldn't throw money at her and entice her to stay. Couldn't offer her a favor.

All he had was himself. And he was broken.

"We did it," she said, smiling, a thin, unnatural expression. "Thank you." She stretched up onto her toes and pressed a kiss to his lips.

It was like getting cut open, those soft, perfect lips slicing into him.

She walked back down, flat-footed, and gave him another smile. "I'll see you around though."

And then she turned and she started to walk away from him. Started to walk out of the shop.

And he was frozen still, frozen, useless.

That thought kicked something into gear. He mobilized, following her out the door, onto the now mostly empty street. The Christmas lights were still blazing, casting a golden glow onto the street. There were still some remaining carolers, singing glory to the newborn king, the sound wrapping itself around him. Strangling him.

"Wait," he said. "That's it?"

She turned to face him, the lights like a halo around her golden hair. "It has to be. Because it can't go on forever. And in some ways I want it to. But this is the difference between being seventeen and thirty. I understand now. I understand what we can have and what we can't. And I think... I want it all. Someday. A husband. Children. I can have that now. I know I can. And it's thanks in no small part to you. But part of all of that is letting it go gracefully. And right now I can. So right now I have to. Merry Christmas, Liam."

And then she stuffed her hands in her pockets and walked away from him. Like he had done to her all those years ago. She was leaving, just that easily. The only thing that had ever been Christmas to him, leaving him standing there on the bedazzled street with carols ringing in his ears.

And he didn't do a damn thing.

CHAPTER TWENTY-TWO

SABRINA'S BRAVERY WAS maxed out for now. It had simply given way to misery. A deep, unending misery that had reduced her to a puddle. She had cried all night, and then had barely dragged herself out of bed to sit at her kitchen table and cry some more.

Too bad she had to be at the tasting room in a couple of hours. And at the winery for stock before that.

She was not mentally prepared.

She had thought—on some level—that she would be able to handle the feelings that she was left with because she had lost Liam before. And she had been in love with him then, after all, so it wasn't anything she hadn't endured in the past.

But she had been wrong. Oh, holy hell had she been wrong.

She had loved him then, but as a girl. Now, she loved him as a woman. Knowing how long it could take to find someone like him, knowing that it was an impossible task or she would have done it at some point in the past thirteen years. Knowing what it was like to have shared her body with him. Her secrets. To have him share his secrets in return.

Yes, it was so much worse now. And it was nothing like anything she'd experienced before. Nothing could have prepared her.

She had built up that goodbye speech in her head, had convinced herself that she was going to walk away from their relationship stronger. And maybe, eventually, that would be true, but right now, it was all just crap. Right now, it was all just pain. Like being stabbed through the heart.

She had lied to herself. Had convinced herself that because so many things inside of her had changed, that because she had accepted that she would always care for him, even though they weren't destined to be together, that she would be okay when she pulled the trigger on the inevitable end. But she wasn't okay. She wasn't even close to okay.

She was devastated, all the way down to her soul.

But she had done the right thing. At least in the service of her pride. She hadn't gotten down on her knees and begged him to stay with her even if he could never love her. She hadn't told him that she was completely head over heels for him. Hadn't spilled her guts and opened up her chest and bled all of her emotions out onto the street. She should still feel better because of that. But she didn't. She wasn't sure she would ever feel better again.

She dragged herself away from her kitchen table and drove to Grassroots with burning eyes, and an onslaught of tears that was threatening to fall.

She wasn't going to cry. Not in front of everyone. With that resolute thought playing over and over in her head she pulled her car into the parking lot and parked, then put her jacket on and walked into the main dining room, keeping her head down. She didn't even realize she had forgotten to put her hair up until a stray lock fell into her face. She paused for a moment, feeling completely stunned.

What had he done to her?

She would never be able to undo it. That made her feel filled with a renewed sense of misery. But also... also awe.

"Good morning," Lindy said, looking at her with a strange, speculative expression on her face.

"Good morning," she responded, walking past Lindy and going into her office to dump her purse and her coat. She came back out, flipping her head back and brushing her hair out of her face. "I know we were completely out of the 2012 Cab after last night. Was there anything else? I'm going to get moving down to the tasting room."

"Do I have two totally drippy women on my staff now?" Lindy asked, folding her arms.

"What?"

"You look like you've been crying," Lindy said.

"I don't know what you're talking about," Sabrina said.

"Your eyes are red. Your hair is down, and your hair is never down. What happened?"

"Nothing," she said. "Nothing that wasn't planned."

"And what does that mean?" Lindy asked.

"*Nothing*. It just means that Liam and I are no longer...together."

"You broke up?"

Sabrina let out an exasperated breath. "I broke up with him. I mean, it wasn't even a breakup. We had an agreement that we were going to...see each other until after we were done opening the tasting room. The tasting room is open. And now Liam and I will no longer be…working together. So, there's no need for the two of us to carry on."

"Yes there is, you idiot," Lindy said, exasperated.

Sabrina frowned. "And what is that reason?"

"That you're *in love* with him."

"It's not enough. It's not enough. He's not in love with me. And he's not going to be. I just have to accept that."

"Why?" Lindy pressed.

"Because some things you can't save," Sabrina said, flinging her hands wide. "You of all people should know that."

"Yes," Lindy said. "You can't save a relationship when one party is actively sleeping with someone else. I do know that. But that's not your situation. He loves you."

"No, he doesn't. He likes sleeping with me. That's not the same thing."

"Heaven help me," Lindy said. "I'm surrounded by ridiculous women."

She stepped back to her office, and at the same time Olivia walked in, looking no better than Sabrina.

"Are you all right?" Sabrina asked, in spite of herself.

"No," Olivia said. "I broke up with Bennett."

"I thought you might have."

"I thought it would clarify things. I thought that… That it would make him… But I'm just miserable."

"Join the club," Sabrina said. "I broke up with Liam. And I am miserable."

Olivia looked like she might burst into tears. "I'm sorry."

"*I'm* sorry," Sabrina said. "I'm sure that my talk with you about Bennett didn't exactly help."

"Your talk with me about Bennett was part of my decision. But I think you're right. I think he needs to figure himself out, and I need to let him do that. I think it's the only way we're going to move forward. He's comfortable with me. And…I think this is exactly what we both need. Time apart."

Sabrina regarded Olivia closely. "Except you don't want time apart."

Olivia shook her head miserably. "I don't like being by myself."

"I was by myself for a long time before Liam, and I can say pretty confidently that I got used to being with him. And that I don't like the thought of not being with him. Of being alone. But I'm not sure that I can stand to be the only one in a relationship that's in love."

"I don't think he loves me," Olivia said. "Or I'm afraid he might not. And I need to see if that's true."

Sabrina sucked in a sharp breath. "I don't think there's anything wrong with that. If he wants to be with you, then let him be the one to make that choice."

She meant it. Bennett Dodge had been dragging his feet with Olivia for a couple of years, and if he wanted to be with her, he could sort it out. But that wasn't what she was doing with Liam. Because she really had meant what she had said to him. If he didn't want it, she wasn't going to hang around and demand that he figure out a way to wanted. It wouldn't be fair. It just…hurt.

"I'm going to try. I really am."

Lindy came back in, her expression one of slight disgust. "Ladies," she said. "There is no need to get ridiculous over a couple of men who don't appreciate what they had. Better that you sort it out now than after ten years of marriage. Trust me."

Olivia mumbled something that sounded like an agreement. But a half-hearted one at best.

"Look what we have," Lindy said. "We are fine just like we are. You don't need Bennett Dodge," she said to Olivia, then turned to Sabrina. "And you don't need Liam Donnelly. And I...I don't need anyone. Except for you two. Well, and Bea. Also, Dane serves a function occasionally. I could also use a masseur. And a maid. But I don't need a man. And neither do you. So, get it together."

Sabrina looked at Lindy, at all of her resilience. And she tried, with everything she had, to believe that someday she would reach that same place. Where she was completely satisfied with what she was building here with Grassroots. Where she wouldn't ache every time she thought about Liam.

But from where she stood right now, it was almost impossible to believe.

CHAPTER TWENTY-THREE

THE CHATTER AROUND the early morning breakfast table was getting on Liam's nerves. His brothers were so… content. So damned happy. It made no sense to him. It was something his brain couldn't untangle. He felt every inch a miserable son of a bitch, and they were drinking coffee and talking as if the world was just spinning like it always had. But it couldn't be. He didn't see how it could be.

Every night since Sabrina had broken things off between the two of them was a misery. He'd had nearly two weeks of it. And here it was, getting close to Christmas, and it wasn't getting any better. How could it? She wasn't here. She wasn't in his bed. Because…because she knew that he was broken. She understood.

She saw him.

She was going to go off and have babies with some other man.

Fucking hell. He couldn't stand it. He couldn't damn well stand it.

"You're even more unpleasant than normal," Cain said, elbowing Liam from his position next to him at the table.

"What the hell is wrong with you?"

Liam gritted his teeth. "Nothing."

"He's right," Alex said, who was joining them this

morning to help them deal with a new shipment of cattle. "You're a bigger pill than usual, which is really saying something."

"Shut your damn mouth," Liam said.

"What the hell is wrong with you?" Finn asked. "No more bullshitting. I'm serious. You're always off doing your own thing, you never tell us what's happening. I know there's something going on with you, we all do. So, get yourself together or tell us what's happening."

And it was like a lit fuse that had been burning for months, maybe years, decades, suddenly reached its end.

"You think you know me? You think you know there's something different about me? Except that's the problem. None of you know. None of you fucking know. And you know what? You should have. Someone should have. No one ever did anything for me. No one."

"What the hell are you talking about?" Alex asked.

Well, he had started. He couldn't stop it now. Even if he wanted to. He wasn't sure if he did. He wasn't sure what he was doing. What he wanted. Except it was all pouring out of him now. Like poison coming from a lanced wound, and he knew that there was no going back now. There was only going forward.

"I keep to myself because it's what I did to survive. All of us had a sucky childhood, and I've never seen any point in dragging my own personal drama out for everyone. But you really want to know? You really want to know why I keep to myself? Why I don't smile as much, or react to things the way the rest of you do? Why I went off by myself? And made all of the money that I could? To give myself all the control over my life that I could possibly have? I can tell you a story, then. You want to know the story?"

"I want to know," Finn said.

Alex was just staring at him, an expression of abject horror on his face.

He hated this. Hated that he was talking about it. Hated that it was all bubbling up to the surface. Because that meant it mattered. And he didn't want any of it to matter. He wanted to be done with it. He wanted it to be over. From the moment he had handed his mother that check, he had wanted it to be over.

That was his fuck-you. But it hadn't felt like it. It had just felt like more begging for approval. She hadn't even said she was sorry. Nothing. She had not given him a damn thing. No one ever had.

"Our home life wasn't good," Liam said. "Alex can attest to that. But there was more. There was more that happened. Our mother blamed me for her being trapped in that life. For her not having all of the things she thought she should have. She blamed me for the poverty. She blamed me for being stuck with our father. She blamed me. And she hated me. She didn't have the focus to give to either of us, really. Sometimes there wouldn't be food in the house. And Alex…I never wanted you to be hungry."

"I don't remember that," Alex said, his voice rough.

"You were always fed," Liam responded.

"What the hell?" Alex asked. "Are you saying that I ate when you didn't? That you starved for me?"

"I was your older brother. I didn't do anything big or special. I just did what had to be done, because none of the damned adults in our lives could bother."

"I never knew that, you stupid prick," Alex shouted.

"What the hell?" Liam responded, taken aback by his brother's barely leashed rage.

"How could you not tell me? I thought we were in all of that shit together. And it turns out you were in a whole different field of shit, and you didn't even tell me."

"How are you getting mad at me? I'm the one that kept your ass from starving. Our mom locked me in a closet for days on end sometimes, doing her best to keep me out of the way. And you're mad at me?"

Alex was white now, rage tightening his mouth. "Hell yes, I'm mad at you. Let someone in, Liam. Let someone fucking in. What the hell is your problem?"

"Have you been listening to anything I've said? All of it's my problem. Our mother. Our father, who couldn't be bothered to ever check in on his sons. Who looked the other way the whole time she did whatever the hell she wanted with me. That's my problem. Sorry if my trust issues are little bit too pronounced for you given all that I went through."

"You're a grown man," Alex said. "You could have told me any of that at any time, and instead, you just let it sit there. Then you let it get worse."

"Are you blaming me?"

"Hell no. But how could you not tell me? How could you not let me shoulder it with you? How could you... You let me be so mad at you. I felt like you abandoned me when you left."

"You were old enough to take care of yourself then," Liam said. "And I had to get out."

"Yes. I would have understood that if you'd explained to me some of the things that you went through. But you didn't."

"I never asked to be your hero, Alex," Liam said. "You wanted me to be. But I didn't see the point in making your memories of our life worse just to make myself look better."

"I would have... I would never have let that happen to you if I'd known."

"And then your life would've been awful too. And you wouldn't have been any better off than I am. But you... You've moved forward. I'm happy for you. It's a good thing. It's a damned good thing. Everything that I did was worth it for that."

"But maybe if it wouldn't have been you alone, we could have moved on together."

Cain and Finn weren't speaking at all, they were both just sitting there, stone-faced, their coffee mugs in front of them untouched and growing cold.

"Don't worry about me," he said to Alex. "It is what it is. I'm not going to have that life. It's not going to happen."

"Why? Because you don't want it? Because you sure as hell could have fooled me. I've seen you with her. I know that you love her."

"She doesn't want me," he said simply.

"How do you know?"

"Look. She left me. She left me because she knows that there's no future with me."

"And you fought for her? Or did you just stand there, all stoic and unruffled. Because you act like you don't care about a damn thing."

"What's the point? What's the point in fighting for something that you can't have? I gave that up. No point pounding against the closet door when you can't escape. There's no point begging to be let out when it isn't gonna happen until you're quiet." He shook his head. "I'm not going to beg for someone to love me. I did it enough when I was a kid. I'm done with it."

He stood up, making his way toward the door. "I'm going to go do our jobs. I'm done sitting around talking about it."

Alex stood up too, and then he looked over at Finn and Cain, giving them meaningful looks. Then he grabbed hold of Liam's shirt and dragged him outside, out to the front porch.

It was gray and icy out there, the sun not yet risen over the mountains. It matched his mood. As cold as his damned heart.

"You told me that I was going to have to man up," Alex said. "You told me to go after Clara when I was going to let her walk away. You told me to be a man, Liam, and I expect no less from you. Get it together. Fight for something. Fight for her. Fight for *you*. How long has it been since you've done that?"

"I did," he said. "You know I wrote Mom a check. I wrote her a check for a lot of money, and it still wasn't enough."

"Yeah. But you didn't want to give her money. You didn't want her to have a house. You wanted her to say she was proud of you. To tell you that she was wrong. You should have shown up with nothing more than you. Have you ever offered that to someone?"

"Why the hell would I?"

"Nothing else is ever going to fix it. Until you find the person that looks at you and sees that you're enough, nothing is gonna fix it. But first, you have to trust that you are."

"What is this? Therapy?"

"Maybe. If it has to be. You lead with things. It's all

about what you can do for people. Even when we were starting this whole ranch expansion with Finn. With the tasting room, you were offering to throw your money at it. That's what you do. You put all of these things out in front of you so that when it gets rejected it's not you."

The words struck him like a blow. Made him take a step backward. He could hardly breathe. Could hardly think past the pain pouring through his chest.

"You're enough, you're just too scared to test that. You can say your money's not enough. You can say your success isn't enough. You can say that your protection of me wasn't enough. You never have to see if you are." Alex took a step toward him. "Maybe it's time to test that. Maybe it's time to see. What are you afraid of?"

"You know damn well what I'm afraid of," Liam said.

"Say it. Feel it. Stop hiding behind all that…that Liam thing that you do. Where you shut everyone and everything out. You want family, you've got it. You know you do. With me. With Finn and Cain and Violet and your sisters-in-law. You want love… You want Sabrina? You go down there and you damn well demand it."

"She said she knows that I'm broken." If anyone had ever seen him, really seen him, it was her. And she'd walked away before he had a chance to disappoint her.

"Then go down there and tell her you aren't. Or maybe that you are, but you want her anyway. It's time. You have to do something. You can't just keep pretending you don't care. Not when you care more than anyone I know. I knew that there was something, but God help me, I didn't know it was that."

"Doesn't matter."

"Like hell it doesn't. I would've been there for you too. I would have. But I think that you didn't want to ask just in case. For once in your life, Liam, *ask* for something."

He didn't know what to say to that. Not to any of it. It was impossible. Impossible for him to do that. Because he would only get rejected. Because it would only end with him being told he wasn't enough. And that was what he believed, deep down in the bottom of everything. But it wasn't enough and he never could be. That was the worst thing. Standing in that corner office in New York, with all of that money, all of that power and still feeling small. Still feeling like there wasn't a damn thing he could do to fill that yawning void inside of himself. Like there wasn't anything that could be done to erase all those broken, destroyed things inside of him.

And here his brother was standing there just telling them to do it. Like it was that simple. To get on his knees in front of the woman that meant more to him than anyone ever had and offer himself. Only himself.

"You don't know what the hell you're talking about," Liam said.

"I do," Alex said. "I sure as hell do. My friend died for me, Liam. Left his sister behind, left everything behind for *me*. I didn't feel like there was any way on earth that I could compete with that. But you know what, she loves me. Clara loves me, and I didn't do anything to deserve it. I swear to God I didn't. All I do every day is get up, hoping to continue to be worthy of that thing that she gives me so easily. Like it's not even a struggle. I still don't understand it, but I sure as hell need it. I love her. I love her, even though she deserves love to come from a better man.

"Even if you don't understand it… If Sabrina can love you, you go and you take that. It doesn't matter if it makes sense. Enough things in life aren't fair, dammit, shouldn't this go in our favor? Just once? Just *once* shouldn't we have something?" Alex was breathing hard, his face seeming older than he'd realized his younger brother had gotten. "And if we only get a good thing once, it had better be the best thing. It had better be the woman you love. The woman who loves you."

Liam felt... He felt like he'd been punched. Felt drained. "And what if she doesn't?"

"Then that would suck. It really would. But I'm willing to bet that she does. And if she does, then I think it's worth anything to see, don't you?"

"But what if..."

"You go right back to where you've always been. But you'll have the answer."

"Somehow, that seems worse."

"Maybe it is. But it could also be better. So much better. Give it a chance."

Liam turned to walk away from his brother, and Alex stopped him. "You really were my hero, Liam. Even before I knew. You were always more than enough for me. You're my older brother. You're the reason that I'm with Clara now. You're the reason I'm half the man I am. It certainly didn't come from our father, sure as hell didn't come from our mother. It came from you. If you can see all that in me, then you should see a fraction of it in yourself. At least."

And then Alex was the one who walked away, and left Liam alone with everything.

Left him alone with a decision to make.

And the longer he stood there, the angrier he got. She had left him. Had told him that she understood. She had left without a fight. And he had... Well, he had spent a lifetime not fighting for things. Had spent a lifetime striving for material possessions instead of the love of people, because he didn't think he could earn the love of a person. But he was done with that.

The sun broke through the clouds.

He wanted Sabrina Leighton. He loved her. And he was going to move heaven and earth to make her his.

SABRINA WAS JUST closing up at the tasting room. Her mind and body felt frazzled. She felt raw, and fragile. But then, she had felt that way ever since she had walked away from Liam.

And now it was Christmas Eve, and it was even worse. Because it was Christmas, and it was supposed to be good. And there were some good things. Her father had come by the tasting room. And he had personally extended an invitation for her to come to their home for Christmas. She always did. But he never spoke to her. And he certainly wasn't the one who invited her. So there was that. The small inroads. The rebuilding of relationships.

But not the one that she wanted most.

She could rationalize all of those things inside her. Tell herself that it was just a lingering sense of missing him, because what they had had been fun. Because she did love him, even if her destiny wasn't to be with him forever.

But mostly, she was just starting to feel like she had played the coward all over again.

She had imagined it a brave and wonderful thing to do what she had done. To walk away from him nobly.

But in the end, it had all been about salvaging pride.

It had all been about not doing what she had done when she was seventeen.

She had been young then, but at least she had been willing to make a fool of herself for love. She was questioning herself now. Questioning how honest she was. Which was funny, because it was Liam she would normally accuse of lying to himself and everyone else. But she had built herself up this convenient, tall tower to hand down edicts from. To benevolently tell Liam thank you for setting her on the path of healing, without begging him to stay on it with her.

She blinked back tears, and turned around to lock the tasting room door.

"I thought I might find you here."

She turned to see Liam standing there on the sidewalk, his hands in his pockets. He was wearing an oatmeal-colored cable-knit sweater and she had the strangest urge to rush to him, to press her head against his chest, to curl into him.

But somehow she resisted.

"What are you doing here?" She blinked. "Are you here to check on the shop? Because…you still have a key, you know you're welcome to go inside whenever you want. Or did you need…accounting information…? Because I sent all of that over via email and…"

"Shut up." He advanced on her, his expression blazing with heat. "I'm not here for any of that."

"Oh," she said. "Then what are you here for?"

"I'm here for you," he said.

But before she could press further, she found herself being dragged into his arms. Found herself being pressed up against his chest just as she'd envisioned moments before, his lips crashing down on hers. She couldn't fight it. Couldn't fight him. Even though she wanted to scream at him, yell at him, pound her fists against his chest. Because how dare he? How dare he come back for her now and kiss her like this? How dare he offer more of his body when what she wanted was his heart? His soul. All of him.

She pushed away from him. "No. Don't. Don't tease me."

"Do I *look* like I'm teasing you?"

"I told you the way that it has to be," she said, knowing that she sounded desperate. "I can't… I can't do halfway with you, Liam. I can't. I have to be able to move on. I have to be able to find something normal."

"You only think we can't have that if you think we're broken." He grabbed hold of her chin, tilting her face up. His green eyes were wild, fierce. "I refuse to believe we are broken," he said, his voice bleeding the kind of raw emotion she had never heard from him before. "I refuse to believe that we have to be defined by everything that has happened to us. I don't want to be. I tried to escape it. I tried to be better than it somehow. I tried to be something more. Something different. I'm rich. I made a lot of money. I got really important in my job. It has never once fixed all the broken things inside of me. It was never enough. I can't pretend that if I offered it to you it would be. But I can offer you me. Just me. And the fact that I love you. Whatever the hell that means coming from me. I…I don't know how to love a woman. I'm not sure that I know how to love anyone. I don't have any practice at it. But I want to. Sabrina, I want to love you. For all of my life. I didn't give my heart easily. But I gave it to you a long time ago. It was you. It was always you. It could never be anyone else."

Sabrina had started shaking some time ago. Her hands, her whole body. He wasn't lying now, her Liam. Wasn't protecting himself with banter or his cutting remarks or well-placed smile. He was...well, he was shaking too. He was on the edge. He was not the businessman. Not that beautiful boy she had known all those years ago. He was just...Liam.

The businessman, the boy she had known and the boy who had been so desperately, and horribly, let down by his parents. The one who had been made afraid to give anything of himself. The one who had been locked away. Who had been neglected.

That was the man who stood before her now. The man who was opening himself up, risking himself. Offering himself.

Her cheeks felt wet, cold, and that was when she realized that she was crying.

"Liam... Maybe we are broken," she said. "I don't know. But if we are, then we're the right kind. Because we're broken just right, so that we can fit each other. And that's all I need. It's all that I want. I was too afraid to say this the other night. I was trying to be brave, trying to let us both off easy. But I think maybe that's not what we need. I think we need to do the harder thing. I think we need to figure out how we can make this work. Because that's what I want. I want this. I want you. Because I love you. I love you more than I want to be safe. I love you more than I want my pride. I love you enough to stand here weeping on the street." She laughed, watery and trembling. "And I was feeling really grown-up and mature because I watched Olivia doing this and told myself I wouldn't do the same but...I don't care now.

I'll cry a river down Main Street. I'll get on my knees and beg. Whatever I have to do. Whatever you need."

"You," he said, his voice rough. "Just you. That's all."

"You have me."

"Will you have me?" he asked. "Me and all of the things that make me who I am? Messed up and broken. All my tattoos, all those things I put on the outside because I was afraid to feel them?"

"Yes," she breathed.

"I'm going to feel it all now," he said, brushing her hair out of her face. "All this stuff I've been pushing away, all the feelings. And that might be a lot of trouble for you. Am I worth it? Am I enough?"

"More than enough, Liam," she said. "More than enough."

"I want this. I want you. I want to give you everything, and I've never wanted that in my life. You... You've shown me things, given me things, I never thought I could have. You're my Christmas, Sabrina."

"Your what?"

"My peace on earth. My hope. My joy. My love. All these things that I never understood until you. And you were that for me from the moment that I first saw you, but I wasn't ready. I wasn't ready then. To give everything. To ask for everything. But I'm ready now. I'm ready for this. Ready for you, finally. I wasn't right at first. I wasn't ready for what we could be. Now I am. I thought there was something I could do to fix the past. I thought I had to earn something, be someone different. For the first time I can recall, I want to be me. Because you love me, and I love you. That's all I need."

"Me too," she said, wiping tears off her cheeks.

"You know what scared me most about you back then, Sabrina?"

"What?" she asked, the word choked.

"You wanted me like I was. You never asked me to change. And before you…I was convinced I was going to have to reinvent myself to be worth anything. To be worth anyone's love."

"Oh, Liam…"

"I did. I made myself important, successful. And my hands still felt empty. My heart still felt empty. Because love wasn't there in that corner office overlooking Manhattan, Sabrina. It was here in Copper Ridge with you all along."

EPILOGUE

SABRINA DONNELLY PRESSED a kiss to the tattoo on her husband's back. Right against the tree etched into his skin, on the names that had been added to that tree over the past ten years.

Then she heard a shriek and buried her face more resolutely against him. "It can't be time for everyone to get up."

The thunderous sound of tiny feet headed down the stairs of the big house said differently. Not that she should be surprised. All the Donnelly children, just like their fathers, were early risers. And on Christmas morning, it was always worse.

For a start, all the kids were together in the main house on the Laughing Irish, as was Christmas tradition. And for another they were still buzzing from all the sugar they'd had the night before.

Liam rolled over to face her, a smile curving his lips upward, the lines by his eyes deepening. She loved every single one of those lines. And she knew he loved hers too. He told her often. They'd earned them together, after all.

Ten years, two kids and a whole lot of love.

Only a little bit of fighting, but when there was fighting, there was always making up. And Sabrina did like the making up.

"We probably have to get up now," he said.

"Let's make Violet deal with it," Sabrina said. "It will be good practice for her."

"She would scoff at that."

"Maybe not." Sabrina got up and started getting dressed. "I think there might be a proposal in her near future."

"I think so too," Liam said, grinning and getting up. Sabrina paused for a moment to appreciate every last one of her husband's assets. "Because Cain was twitchy last night and I have a feeling there was a man waiting to have a very serious discussion with him."

"That will be us in a few years."

"A few decades," Liam said. "And if Kelsey wants to become a spinster when she grows up that works for me too."

"Liar."

The two of them finished dressing and headed to the stairs hand in hand. Then walked into the massive living area that was already lit up, Cain and Alison's three kids sitting next to Liam and Sabrina's, three of Finn and Lane's brood of four sitting on the floor—the baby probably still in her crib awaiting liberation. And Clara and Alex's usually bright-eyed twins were lying on the couch wrapped in blankets, the six-year-olds a bit overwhelmed by the proceedings.

Liam wrapped his arm around her shoulders and held her tight. When she looked over at her husband, his eyes were suspiciously bright, the Christmas tree lights reflecting in them.

"What?" she asked, brushing her finger over his cheek.

"I love Christmas," he said, his voice rough. "Never

had one before I had you. And now…look at all this. It's my favorite. Christmas is my favorite."

Her heart felt large, full. Of her love for him, and for all the people in this house. She stretched up onto her toes and kissed him on the cheek. "You're my favorite, Liam Donnelly."

* * * * *

Love Copper Ridge?
Don't miss the all-new
GOLD VALLEY *series*
from Maisey Yates and HQN Books,
where true blue cowboys find love
with the last women they expect to.

Read on for an exclusive sneak peek
of SMOOTH-TALKING COWBOY…

CHAPTER ONE

OLIVIA LOGAN SUPPOSED it could be argued that she wasn't heartbroken, so much as she had broken her own heart. But it could not be argued that she had flattened her own tire.

Someone had left *something* sharp in the road for her to drive over with her little, unsuspecting car. Because people were eternally irresponsible, and Olivia never was. She never was, and still, she often got caught up in the consequences of said irresponsibility. Because such was life. That the idiot who left something treacherous on the road wasn't the one with the flat tire was another painful metaphor.

Olivia had had quite enough of life being a pain in the rear. If there was a reward for being well-behaved, she hadn't yet found it.

She got out of her car to look at the flattened tire in the back on the passenger's side, bracing herself against the frigid wind that whipped up right as she did so. The typical chilly, Oregon January weather did nothing to improve her mood.

And there it was. Silver and flat, sticking into her tire. A nail.

Of course. She was running late to work down at Grassroots Winery and she had a flat tire as well as a broken heart. So, all things considered she wasn't sure it could get much worse.

She scowled, then looked down at her phone, trying to figure out who she should text. Normally, she would have texted her boyfriend Bennett, but he was now her *ex*-boyfriend because she had broken up with him last month at Christmas.

She had her reasons. Very good ones.

She couldn't text him now, obviously, though. And she probably shouldn't text his older brother Wyatt, or his *other* older brother Grant, because they likely had loyalty to Bennett that could not be moved. Even poor pitiful Olivia and her flat tire.

She was pondering that, sitting on the outer edges of Gold Valley with her car halfway in the ditch, when a beat-up red truck came barreling down from the same direction she had just come from. Her stomach did a strange somersault and she closed her eyes, beseeching the heavens for an answer as to why she was being punished in quite this way.

There was no answer. There was only a flat tire. And that red truck that she knew well.

Oh, well. She needed rescuing. Even if it was from Luke Hollister. She moved closer to the road, crossing her arms and standing there, looking pathetic. At least, she had a feeling she looked somewhat pathetic. She felt pathetic.

Luke would stop, because despite being a scoundrel, a womanizer, and the only person who could beat her at darts, he had that innate sense of chivalry that cowboys tended to possess. All *yes ma'am* and opening doors and saving damsels from the railroad tracks.

Or the side of the road, in this case.

The truck came closer, and she registered the exact moment Luke saw her. Felt it, somehow. She took a step back, making room for him to pull off and up next to her car.

His truck kept going.

She took a step closer to the edge of the road, looking after him, and she knew the expression on her face was incredulous now.

"He didn't stop!"

She had been incredibly peeved that Luke Hollister had been the salvation she hadn't wanted, but she was even more peeved that he had declined his opportunity to be said salvation.

Then she saw brake lights, followed by reverse lights.

Slowly, the truck backed up, easing its way slowly up beside her.

Luke leaned across the seat, working the crank window so that it was partway down. And then he smiled. That slow, lazy smile of his that always made her feel like he had spoken an obscenity.

"Olivia Logan, as I live and breathe. You seem to have gotten yourself in a bit of trouble."

"I didn't *get myself* into any *trouble*," she said crisply. "There was a nail in the road, and now I seem to have a flat tire." He just looked at her, all maddeningly calm. "You weren't going to stop," she added, knowing she sounded accusing.

"True. But then I thought better of it. I'd hate it if you were eaten by wolves."

"There are no wolves here," she said, feeling impatient.

"They recently tracked one that came down from Washington. Just one though, so probably the worst that would happen is you'd get gnawed on, rather than eaten in your entirety."

"Well. I'm glad you decided to help me avoid a vicious gnawing," she said grumpily.

"I could change the tire for you," he said.

"Do you want to pull off the road, before we have this discussion?" she asked.

He looked in his rearview mirror, then glanced back at her. "There's no one coming. It's not exactly rush hour."

"There is no rush hour in Gold Valley."

But that didn't mean someone wouldn't be pulling up behind him on the narrow two-lane road soon enough.

He still didn't move his truck, though.

"Luke," she said, "I need to go to work."

"Well, why didn't you say so? Do you have a spare tire?"

"Yes," she said impatiently.

"I'll tell you what. I'll drive you down to work, and then when I head back this way back I'll fix your tire."

She frowned, suspicious at the friendliness. "Why would you do that?"

"Because I'm going that way anyway," he said. "You still work at the winery?"

She nodded. Grassroots Winery sat in between the towns of Copper Ridge and Gold Valley, and Olivia worked predominantly in the dining room at the winery itself. It wasn't, she supposed, the most ambitious job, which usually didn't bother her. She liked the ambiance of the place, and she enjoyed the work itself. But she had always assumed that she would marry a rancher, and help him work his land. Make a home for them. The way her parents had done. That seemed…silly now that she was single, and there was no rancher in her future.

But then, a month ago she was working there to bide her time until Bennett proposed to her. And now… Without their eventual marriage to look forward to she wasn't really sure what she was doing with herself. That made her feel small, silly. And anyway, she was the one that had broken up with him. Because of the fact that he hadn't proposed yet. After all that time. And she had been sure that by now he would have come back to her. Was sure that breaking up with him would make him realize that he had to commit or he could lose her. Except he seemed all right with losing her. And that was terrible, because she was not all right with losing him and that vision of her future that she had held on to for so long.

"How will I get home?" she asked.

"I could help you out with that too, but I'll have your car in working order by then."

She looked at him out of the corner of her eye. "Why are you being nice to me?"

That wicked grin of his broadened. "I'm always nice."

She let out an exasperated sound and then clicked the lock button on her key fob before climbing into the passenger side of his truck. She struggled to get in because of her skirt and nylons, but finally succeeded and shut the massive, heavy door behind her.

"Thank you," she said, knowing that she sounded ridiculously prim and not really able to do anything about it. She *was* prim.

She grabbed hold of the seat belt, then pulled it forward, having to wiggle it slightly to get it to click. His truck was a hazard. She straightened, held tightly to her handbag and stared straight ahead.

"You're welcome," he said, stretching his arm over the back of the bench seat. His other forearm rested casually over the steering wheel. His cowboy hat was pushed back on his head, shirtsleeves pushed up past his elbows, forearms streaked with dirt as if he had already been working today. Which meant that he had likely been out at Get Out of Dodge before driving down toward town. She wondered if he had seen Bennett.

"Were you out at the Dodge place today?" She tried to ask casually.

"You want to know if I saw your boyfriend," Luke said. Not a question. A statement. Like he knew her.

And this, in a nutshell, was why she didn't really like Luke. He had a nasty habit of saying the *one* thing that she wished he wouldn't. With a kind of unerring consistency that made her suspect he did it on purpose.

"He's *not* my boyfriend. Not anymore."

"Still. You're wondering about him."

"Of course I wonder about him. I dated Bennett for a year. I'm not going to just…not wonder about him suddenly."

"I expect, Olivia, that you could go down to Get Out of Dodge on your own pretty feet and find out how he's doing for yourself if you had half a mind to."

Olivia cleared her throat and looked at Luke meaningfully. Which he seemed to miss entirely. "I don't know that I would be welcome," she said, finally.

"Come on. It's been at least…six months since Wyatt has run anyone off the property with a shotgun."

Olivia sighed. "You're a pain, do you know that?"

"Now, is that any way to talk to your roadside savior?"

"Normally, I would agree, but I suspect that you're trying to irritate me on purpose. Otherwise you would have just answered my question." She settled back into the bench seat, looking down at the floor mats that were encrusted in mud. She had no idea why Luke had mats on the floor of his truck at all. It seemed ridiculous when the whole thing was covered in a fine layer of dust and small bits of hay.

She felt woeful on behalf of her black pencil skirt.

"You caught me," he said, sounding not at all contrite. "I am absolutely trying to irritate you. I would say that I'm succeeding too. You do know how to make a man feel accomplished, Olivia."

"And you know how to make a woman feel feral, Luke."

"You and I both know you've never felt feral a day in your life, honey."

She wanted to argue with him. Except, he had a point. But she was not going to give him the satisfaction of knowing that. Instead, she sniffed and looked out the window as they crossed into the town's city limits and drove in silence down Main Street.

He didn't want to come home for the holidays—
but can an unexpected reunion with a woman
from his past
make this cowboy's Christmas merry and bright?
Read on for COWBOY CHRISTMAS BLUES,
a GOLD VALLEY *novella*
from Maisey Yates and HQN Books...

COWBOY CHRISTMAS BLUES

CHAPTER ONE

GOLD VALLEY AT Christmastime hadn't changed at all since Cooper Mason had left town eight years ago. Every streetlight was wrapped in white Christmas lights, and wreaths and more white lights covered the redbrick buildings, window displays reflecting the season in each little shop.

He hated it. All of it.

And sure, he had come to terms with Christmas since Lindsay's death, because you couldn't exist in the world and not figure out a way to survive the season. But he had deliberately avoided this little corner of Oregon since then.

Because the last thing he needed was to be inundated with memories of his older sister and the joy she had taken in celebrating. The joy she had taken in everything, in spite of her illness.

Gold Valley was the same now as it had been eight years ago, and the same eight years ago as it had been when they were children. So it was easy now to envision her, rosy-cheeked and standing in front of the antique-toy store, her face pressed against the glass as she exclaimed over dolls and blocks, books and art supplies. Before sickness had stolen so much of who she was.

She'd been sixteen when she'd gotten sick, already dating Grant Dodge, who married her as soon as it was legal. Knowing she wouldn't live long. Their love story had made national headlines. A love story that was doomed already, which the public found so much more romantic than a love that might last a lifetime.

God knew why.

Cooper knew there wasn't a hell of a lot that was romantic about death.

He shouldn't have let his parents talk him into coming home for the holidays.

He always felt a little bit guilty about the way his visits home went. He avoided his old friends. Avoided people he'd been close to before. His football buddies from high school, Nate and Jason, who had wives and kids now. He hadn't seen Ben Preston in years. The older man had been his dad's mechanic and friend, and had been like an uncle to Cooper. Ben's chubby little girl, Annabelle, had always trailed around after him on the farm when they'd come to visit.

He didn't even know if Annabelle lived here anymore.

There was a time when she'd almost been like another sister to him. Now, he just tried not to think much about the past.

Cooper had lost touch with this place, and he'd done it mostly on purpose. Normally, he could outpace the guilt just fine. But sometimes...

He shook his head and went into the saloon, which was where he had spent most of his time this week. At least inside the Gold Valley Saloon there was some respite from the seasonal cheer. Some respite from the family home that was a shrine to Lindsay and all that she had been.

Here, it was just the bar. Just alcohol and people coming together for their own reasons. To escape real life, to visit with friends. To hook up.

Cooper snorted. He wasn't about to hook up anytime soon. He hadn't come back to this small town to cause trouble. He was way better off waiting until he left. But he couldn't deny that a little sex to take the edge off would be welcome.

But the gossip line in town was like a vine and rumors grew on it like grapes, and there was no way he wanted to get enmeshed in that. He had extricated himself. He had gotten out. He spent his days moving cattle around the country from ranch to ranch, never staying in one place very long. And that suited him just fine. He lived on the road, occasionally stopping to visit his parents. But never for that long. And never at this time of year.

He should have stuck to his guns on that one. But he couldn't resist his mom when she got emotional, and she'd been filled with conviction that he needed to come home for Christmas this year. Because it had been too long since he had. Because it had been Christmastime eight years ago when Lindsay had taken a sharp turn for the worse and passed away just before New Year's. And the memories were all oppressive now, even more than they usually were.

Cooper didn't want to think about it. Cooper wanted a drink.

He went up to the counter and took a seat, waiting for the bartender, Laz Jenkins, to come over and take his order.

And that was when she caught his eye. Standing over at the jukebox, looking down, caramel-colored hair falling over a face he couldn't see. A curvy figure, and a pretty delicious ass highlighted by the tight-fitting skirt she had on.

Not here to hook up, remember?

Yeah. He was not here to hook up. But that didn't mean he couldn't check out a good-looking woman.

"Can I get you something?"

Laz hadn't been the owner of the bar back when Cooper had lived in town, but the two of them had gotten acquainted over the past week. "The usual," Cooper said.

"Whiskey and lots of it coming up," Laz said.

That was another reason that Cooper felt comfortable at the bar. Laz didn't know his life story. That was another thing about coming back to town. He didn't know how his parents coped with it. Didn't know how Lindsay's widowed husband managed. To stay here in town where everybody was so keenly aware of the loss all the time. Every moment of every day. It was all they thought about when they looked at his family, he knew. When he or his parents walked out of a room, it was the thing they whispered to their friends.

That's Connie Mason. Her daughter died. Isn't that sad? So young.

Too damned young.

Right on cue Laz produced the promised whiskey, and Cooper took it down in one slug. Then turned his attention back to the pretty girl over at the jukebox. Yeah, he really would like a distraction. Particularly an hourglass-shaped one.

The woman turned then, and treated him to a view of what was a damned spectacular rack and a pretty face, as well.

She looked vaguely familiar, but then, living in a town this size most people looked familiar. Could be a clerk from a store he'd gone to earlier in the week, someone he'd passed on the street.

She looked up, her brown eyes clashing with his, and she bit her lip. It was a cute gesture. Seductive, and not accidental, he had a feeling.

Well, maybe Pretty Jukebox Girl was looking for a night of distraction herself.

It might be worth exploring. For a night. Nothing else. He left a twenty on the bar top and began to walk her way.

HE WAS COMING toward her. Cooper was coming toward her. She had come here tonight for him, so she supposed she should be excited. That she should be triumphant, because she had been working up the nerve to approach him for the past week, and she had spared absolutely no effort getting herself ready for a seduction tonight. Which was hilarious, since Annabelle Preston had never seduced anyone in her life.

Being in a relationship was one thing. She'd been in one for a long time. Too long. It wasn't like she didn't have experience. But setting out to a bar with the express purpose of seducing a man? That was…yeah, that was outside her scope.

Cooper had always been the most beautiful man. She had thought so for as long as she could remember. Back when her father had serviced the heavy machinery on the Mason family farm, she had often tagged along and taken the opportunity to stare at the brooding boy who captured her attention with such intensity.

Cooper had always been sweet to her. But like an older brother or something. Their dads were good friends in addition to having a professional relationship, and so they'd seen each other quite a bit when he lived at home and she was a child.

He hadn't ever *noticed her* noticed her, of course. She was seven years younger, and had definitely been a kid in his eyes.

She'd been so hungry to matter. Her father had always been so good to her, but he was all she had, and attention from someone like Cooper had been thrilling.

He had looked sad sometimes, and she'd known it was because his sister was sick. And even if she didn't understand everything when she'd been nine or ten years old, she'd delighted in making him smile. Or even laugh. Running around the ranch, while the poor guy was tasked with chasing after her.

She'd climbed apple trees in their front yard, filling her arms with as many as she could. And he would always shine them with his shirt and hand her the best, brightest ones.

One time he'd taken her to the barn so she could look at a box of kittens one of the barn cats had just given birth to. Seeing those strong hands, so gentle and tender, on such tiny creatures had made her feel... She hadn't really understood it.

She'd been thirteen then and he'd been twenty. He'd made her ache. Made her feel so much longing she hadn't fully comprehended.

At fifteen, she'd had a fight with her father and run away to the Masons' farm. She'd climbed into the loft and fallen asleep and hadn't realized she'd worried everyone sick. Then she'd awoken to a husky, masculine voice and had opened her eyes to see Cooper looking down at her. He was angry, because of how she'd frightened her dad, but…but seeing him look down at her like that…

She'd wanted him to be the one to wake her up forever after that.

The last time she had seen him she had been seventeen and all rounded puppy fat, to his chiseled twenty-four.

Even if she hadn't been a child to him *then*, she wouldn't have expected him to notice her that day. Because the last time she'd seen him had been at Lindsay's funeral. It had been a blur of tears and grief for her, so she knew it had been much more so for him. He'd been so still and stoic, all grim-faced and hard. She remembered hugging him, offering what little comfort she could.

He'd wrapped his arms around her and held on tight, the slight hitch in his breathing the only real show of emotion she saw from him that day.

She thought of that day far too often. Of how much she wished she could take his pain away. Of how much she wished she could be in his arms again, even though that was messed up because he'd been grieving and it shouldn't have affected her to be held by him while he was grieving.

He had been back intermittently since he had moved away, but never for very long, and he'd never sought her out. In fact, it felt like he deliberately avoided talking much to anyone in town other than his parents whenever he came back for a visit.

Then last night she had been in the Gold Valley Saloon, meeting up with a group of friends, and there he was. He had walked in and her entire world had stopped.

She'd been in a T-shirt and jeans, looking about as

plain as paper, because she'd just gotten off work, and he'd never once looked her direction.

And that was when she had made a decision. She was single, had been for almost a year, and she was ready. Ready to do something bold. Ready to make a change. Ready to stop *settling*.

So she'd decided she would come back to the bar looking…sexy. And she would get his attention. Because yes, she was ready.

Ready to be the kind of woman that Parker had said she could never be. Parker, who thought that she needed to make sure she wore outfits that didn't show muffin tops and who felt that most lingerie didn't suit her figure.

Parker, who thought that she was too doughy to ever be a sex kitten.

And yeah, tonight she was wearing Spanx. Which she knew could become an issue later. But she had to get the man into the bedroom before she could worry about how she would take the Spanx off gracefully with him in residence, and what he would think when he found out she wasn't quite as sleek as she appeared.

Yes. That was a problem for after she passed this first hurdle.

But he was coming toward her. And his gaze was hot, so she was hoping she was on the right track.

He was as beautiful as ever, and had actually gotten better-looking with time, in her opinion. He had filled out more, the shadow on his jaw darker than it had been back then, that jaw a bit more square. His forearms were thicker, his shoulders broader. He was bigger all over, really. More heavily muscled. She had heard that he did something with livestock, and she imagined that contributed to his physique. Whether he was eighteen or twenty-six, he appealed to Annabelle. She had a feeling he would appeal to her when he was forty. Fifty. Beyond. He was her special brand of catnip, and whatever the reason why, it was true.

She wanted her catnip.

She'd walked herself into a safe, settled life that had been a direct route to nowhere. A boyfriend of five years who'd done nothing but eat all the yogurt the day she bought it and criticize everything she did in that slow, subtle way that was like death to her self-esteem by a thousand paper cuts.

It had taken her time to figure out what she wanted after Parker had ended things—he had ended things with her, that had been another blow straight to her soft underbelly (very soft, according to Parker)—and now that she had...

Well, her revelation was shaped like Cooper Mason.

She wasn't looking for a long-term relationship, and God knew Cooper wouldn't be either. He wasn't that kind of guy. At least, he gave no indication of being that kind of guy, not in all the years he had lived in Gold Valley, and his rumored lifestyle certainly didn't conform to that idea either. But she needed excitement. She needed to seize something for herself.

She needed to stop acting like she believed that she was everything Parker thought she was.

She had started changing her life last year after the breakup. When she had gone ahead and bought the Western clothing store, Gunslinger, on Gold Valley's main street, a store she had worked at for most of her adult life. She had always dreamed of having her own store and it had fallen into her lap when her boss had informed her she was retiring.

She'd talked to Parker about that dream before. He'd told her—couched in concern, because his sharpest words were always wrapped in something soft, so that it took days to fully realize they'd had the power to cut her—that he didn't think it was the right move for her. That she was far too wishy-washy and she wouldn't want to be anyone's boss and she'd hate being in charge *actually* and on and on.

But she was pulling it off. Without him. Happily.

The business was going well, her professional life nicely improved. But there was the little matter of her confidence in herself as a woman. And fulfilling a long-held fantasy.

It was then she realized that she was standing there staring at Cooper while she engaged in a complex internal monologue.

"Hi," she said.

It was a far cry from a saucy opening line or a casual *how have you been?* Which would have been better. But oh, well.

"Hi," he returned, that voice rough like gravel and even sexier than she remembered.

"I've seen you in here a lot lately," she said, stumbling over her words.

"Yeah," he said, looking a little surprised. "I'm in town visiting my parents." He lifted his hand and pushed his cowboy hat back slightly, leaning up against the juke-box, directly across from her. The planes and angles of his face had gotten more chiseled in the past eight years, too. His jaw sharper, covered in golden whiskers, the hollows in his cheeks more pronounced. But his blue eyes were the same.

"Not here to stay, then?" She had assumed as much, but part of her had hoped.

He shrugged his broad shoulders. "No," he said. "My job keeps me on the road most of the year, so I don't really have a permanent residence. Suits me just fine."

She should have known that the rumors she'd heard were accurate. The telephone game in Gold Valley was pretty unerring.

"That sounds exhausting," she said.

"I like it," he said. "Get a chance to see a lot of new places. Meet a lot of new people."

"I suppose," she returned. "But you must get lonely."

A slow smile curved his lips upward, the kind of smile that Cooper Mason had certainly never directed her way before. "I'm never lonely."

"Oh," she said, the breath pushing out of her lungs, her stomach tightening.

Of course he wasn't lonely. She imagined all he had to do was direct that smile to any woman he encountered in any bar in any town, and she would turn her panties right over to him.

Suddenly, her mouth felt like it had been stuffed full of cotton.

"Can I buy you a drink?" he asked.

"No," she said.

All she needed was to get a drink in her and do something dumb. She was on edge enough as it was, and while she knew that most people liked to use alcohol as a social lubricant, she felt like she needed to keep herself from getting too socially lubricated. She wanted to keep herself from being an idiot as well as a long shot.

"Are you waiting for someone else?"

"I was waiting for you," she said, the words far too

honest, far too sharp, scraping her throat dry on the way out.

His smile widened. "I think I might have been waiting for you, too."

Oh. My.

He was waiting. For her. For *her*. Annabelle, who he'd always seen as a kid. But not now.

He *did* see her as a woman now. And he wanted her. And oh, holy night, she wanted him, too.

She knew it then. She knew it in her soul. That her Christmas present to herself—Cooper Mason—was about to get given to her.

It was working. It was happening.

Screw you, Parker.

"Sounds like we were waiting for each other then," she said, cringing internally, because she was really bad at this flirtatious back-and-forth.

"You want to get out of here?"

Well, that was quick. Granted, they weren't strangers. She knew Cooper, had known him for her entire life, even though she hadn't talked to him in eight years. She knew that he was a good guy. Knew that he wouldn't hurt her or anything like that. She trusted him.

Still, it was moving a little too smoothly. She hadn't anticipated him being right into it right away.

"We haven't even kissed yet," she pointed out.

Her heart was thundering so hard she could hardly hear his response, because her brain was simply echoing with the rhythmic sound of her pulse.

"I can fix that," he responded.

He braced one hand on the top of the jukebox, and curved his arm around her waist.

A man hadn't touched her in over a year, not since

her breakup. And she had only ever kissed two men in her entire life. So, having Cooper stand so close to her, his large hand resting on her waist... It was a lot to process. A lot to take in.

And then, before she could think any deeper, Cooper brought his lips down on hers.

His whiskers were rough, his mouth firm, and the whole thing a sensual assault that left her scarcely able to breathe.

This was it. This was what she wanted. This was need that went beyond settling. This wasn't just a kiss because she wanted a guy's kiss. *This* was a kiss because she wanted to kiss *this* particular man. In *this* particular moment.

She wasn't with him because she was afraid of being by herself. Because she was afraid that she wouldn't be able to do better. This had nothing to do with a relationship, with hoping for marriage one day.

No.

This was about desire. Real, deep desire. About a lifelong fantasy, not just vague general needs for sex or closeness.

And that fantasy was finally about to be fulfilled.

CHAPTER TWO

HIS JUKEBOX GIRL didn't say anything when he hurried her out of the bar after their kiss. Her eyes were wide, her pupils dilated, her lips swollen. She was obviously as into the connection between them as he was.

He didn't usually do totally anonymous hookups. But it was Christmas, and he hated Christmas in Gold Valley, which made it difficult to breathe.

The moment her lips had touched his he had felt like he had drawn his first full breath of air since walking into town more than a week ago.

So he was going with it. She hadn't asked his name, and he wasn't going to ask hers. Names didn't matter. She needed something from him, and he sure as hell needed something from her.

That was going to have to be enough.

"You got a place?" he asked when they were both in his pickup truck.

"Yes," she said, chewing her bottom lip. "You're staying with your parents, aren't you?"

He had mentioned that he was in town visiting his parents. "Yeah," he said. "Kind of awkward to bring home a date."

She laughed, a vaguely nervous sound. "I suppose so."

"Just give me directions."

It turned out she lived within walking distance, in a little house in one of the historic neighborhoods just a few blocks away. It was a small, simple structure with a pristine porch decorated with hanging flower baskets, empty in the cold, but charming nonetheless.

Hanging flower baskets were not the kind of thing he associated with women trolling bars for one-night stands, but then maybe he didn't really know anything.

Typically, if he met a woman when he was on the road they would go back to his motel room. So, for all he knew all the women he slept with had hanging baskets on their porches.

He'd never asked.

That made it kind of strange, though. A bit more personal than he was accustomed to.

She had white lights strung in swags across the roofline in addition to the baskets, and a little evergreen wreath hanging on the door. More Christmas. But for all he cared she could have a poinsettia on her bed, and as long as he got to have an orgasm.

Wordlessly, she got out of the truck and didn't wait for him as she crossed the driveway and went up to the front door. He killed the engine and followed her inside.

The house was as neat and charming as its outward appearance gave the impression it might be. A tidy Christmas tree with gold ornaments and bows was in the corner, little touches of cheer here and there. But luckily there were no poinsettias.

She moved to the center of the living room, standing next to a coffee table stacked high with books he had a feeling she actually read. She clasped her hands in front of her and looked around, her expression growing increasingly worried.

"I got a new bed after my boyfriend moved out," she said, shooting the words into the silence.

He lifted a brow, things suddenly becoming clearer. "Did you?"

"Just to make sure that we're clear," she said. "That it's a new bed."

"Honey," he responded, "I'm used to sleeping in motels. Those are not new beds. People have fucked in them."

Color flooded her cheeks. "I was just saying."

It seemed to him that she was out for a little bit of revenge sex after a bad breakup. Worked for him. He could easily call his sex revenge sex. Revenge against the world. But the world was a bitch and she didn't care.

"I don't particularly care who slept here before me," he said, advancing on her. Her pretty brown eyes widened, her lips dropping open. "I only care that I'm the only man you think about as long as I'm here. But I'm pretty sure that won't be a problem." She started to say something, but he pressed his thumb against the center of her lips, then curved his hand back, tracing the line of her jaw, sliding his fingers through her hair.

Then he kissed her. Deep and luxurious. The kind of long, sensual kiss that he hadn't allowed himself in the bar. Devouring. Raw and hungry, his tongue creating a slick friction against hers.

He didn't normally enjoy kissing, because as far as he was concerned it was just the sad appetizer that came before your steak. But this kiss was the exception. It was wet and hot, as soft as the rest of her.

Kissing wasn't his kind of thing, and come to that, this woman wasn't usually his type. He often went for leggy, willowy types in miniskirts and backless tops.

He didn't do challenging. He liked obvious. Bright, blonde and sleek, with glitter on top.

Jukebox Girl was different. Soft, curvy, a little bit more to hold on to. And he was damn glad to have his hands full of her.

She whimpered, arching against him, her full breasts pressing against his chest, as he slid his hand down to grab her ass.

Yeah, she was one sweet handful.

He kissed her all the way back toward a bedroom—maybe it was hers, maybe it wasn't, he didn't care—and then sat her down on the edge of the bed. He pulled back, jerking his T-shirt up over his head, more than ready to have her hands on his skin.

Her mouth dropped open. "Don't you eat McDonald's?"

"What?"

"You live on the road all the time—it seems like you would subsist on French fries and hamburgers."

"I kind of do," he responded. "Though I typically prefer bar food."

She waved her arm up and down. "Then how is it you don't have any fat on your entire body?"

He looks down at his flat stomach. "I work outside. It's hard labor."

Her face turned pink. "I'm wearing Spanx."

He frowned, not sure what that had to do with anything. "Okay."

"I'm not skinny." She said it like she was announcing her status as a convicted killer.

He passed his hand over the front of his jeans, over the very obvious bulge there. "Do I look like I care?"

She looked down. "Some men care."

Irritation spiked in him. She had mentioned an ex-boyfriend, and he had a feeling the ex was responsible for the horrible, crestfallen look on this beautiful woman's face.

He leaned forward, flattening his palms on the mattress on either side of her. "You," he said, "are hot as fuck. Spanx or no Spanx. Though, I have to tell you, I would prefer no Spanx right at the moment."

She flushed, a pretty pink color, and he gripped the hem of her shirt, pulling it up over her head and revealing breasts that were as generous as he'd been hoping they might be, shoved up a bit higher like they were an offering to him thanks to the black contraption she had on underneath, a one-piece-looking jumpsuit with a deep neckline that scooped just beneath her bra.

He pulled one strap down from her shoulder, then pushed the other down, tugging it to the top of her skirt waistband. Then he flicked her bra strap down, then the other. He kissed her neck, her collarbone, all that soft, glorious cleavage.

She sighed, her head falling back, her self-consciousness clearly forgotten. It didn't take much work to get her skirt, and the rest of that foundational garment, pulled off her beautiful body, leaving it mostly bare for his inspection. Generous breasts, a nipped-in waist, and rounded hips and thighs.

Everything looked great to him.

"You're the prettiest thing I've seen a long time."

Her blush extended from her cheeks on down. "That can't be true. There are...the other women. The ones you've...also seen naked."

He grinned at her. "Other women? Can't remember them."

"Well. The town is all decorated for Christmas. It's awfully pretty."

"Not as pretty as you. Trust me. Christmas trees and white lights, tinsel… Doesn't interest me at all. You, on the other hand… I find you very interesting. Now, I want you to take that bra and those panties off."

Her blush intensified, but she obliged him, reaching behind her to unhook her bra, casting it to the side before pushing the black lacy panties down her shapely thighs and kicking them to the foot of the bed. His stomach felt hollowed out, his arousal ramped up to such an intense degree that he was in physical pain.

"I don't have abs," she pointed out, shrinking back further onto the bed.

"You have everything that I need," he said, leaning forward, planting his palm on the bedspread and kissing the top of one of her thighs. She shivered and then moved away from him.

"What are you doing?" she asked.

He huffed out a one-note laugh and then gripped her hips, holding her still. "If you have to ask, then you just answered one of my questions."

"What?"

"Your ex is an asshole, I take it." He leaned in then, parting her thighs and tasting her right at the apex, sliding his tongue through slick folds until she whimpered. Her pleasure, her flavor, was salvation. A respite from the dull pain that had crawled inside his chest and hammered out a large yawning space inside him over the past week. Hell, maybe over the past eight years.

That terrible grief that was always there, that had pushed its way up to the foreground recently and refused to go away.

It had no place here. No. This was all about them. The world, the town, the damned Christmas lights… they had all fallen away.

It was just him, her and this bed. Her body. His desire.

He continued to pleasure her, sliding two fingers inside of her as he worked at that most sensitive place with his tongue. She was panting, gasping, and he thought that she might try to get away from him again, so he held on to her as tightly as possible, his blunt fingertips digging into those lush hips.

When she came, it was like the clouds had broken open and he'd gotten his first hit of sun in months. The first bright thing. The first good thing.

He moved away from her, shucking his jeans and underwear, kicking them on the floor. "Condoms?" he asked.

"Um… In the bathroom?"

That was more steps away than he cared to take. He bent down and grabbed his wallet, producing protection and rolling it on as quickly as possible. She was staring at him, wide-eyed, and he felt that like a physical touch. Then she sat up, clamoring to the edge of the mattress. She curved delicate fingers around his hardened length, glittering brown eyes looking up at him in wonder as she squeezed him.

He groaned, flexing his hips forward, thrusting upward into her grasp. She held him like that for a while, exploring his length, testing him.

"I'm done playing," he said, grabbing hold of the back of her head and bending down, kissing her hard as he pressed them both backward onto the bed, as he settled himself between her legs.

They had all night. They could play around later. But for now, he needed to be inside of her.

He felt like he had waited forever, even though it had been no time at all. They hadn't wasted any time talking, and yet he felt like he knew her. He knew that she should be a lot more confident in how beautiful she was; he knew that a man was responsible for making her feel like shit. He knew that she hadn't been pleasured nearly as extensively as she should have been in her life. Knew that she had a neat little life. Knew that she took care of her things, and that having undivided attention on her made her uncomfortable.

All that knowledge added up to something big. Made him feel like he'd been waiting for this moment for years rather than an hour or so.

He pressed the head of his arousal against the slick entrance to her body, dragging the broad head through her wetness before pushing in an inch or so, rolling forward slowly, teasing her methodically.

Teasing them both.

She whimpered, the sound building into a moan that came from deep inside of her.

Then he lost it completely. He bucked forward, burying himself to the hilt, swallowing her little gasp of pleasure as he did.

She gripped his shoulders, wrapping her legs around his waist, her lush lips pressed against his ear. "Yes," she whispered. "Harder."

And Cooper was a gentleman, so he obliged.

He bucked into her, losing all sense of time, of anything other than the red-hot pleasure that was racing down his veins, that was overtaking him completely.

She was hot, so hot and responsive, tight around his

cock. She met his every thrust, a sweet sound of pleasure on her lips each time he thrust back home. When
she came, she gasped, the expression on her face one of
wonder, like he had given her a gift. And damn it all,
he couldn't hold back any longer.

His control broke entirely, and he froze as his own
release took him over, grabbing him by the throat and
shaking him hard, leaving him nearly blacked out as he
pulsed deep inside her tight, wet body.

He collapsed against her, pressing his forehead down
on hers. She clung to him, her fingernails digging into
his shoulders, her heels pressed into the backs of his
thighs.

"Cooper," she whispered. "Oh, Cooper."

A rush of adrenaline worked its way through him, a
strange sensation prickling over his skin.

He had never told her his name. He was sure of that.
He lifted his head, looking down at the woman who was
currently staring dreamily up at him.

Eyes that were very familiar. An expression that was
very familiar.

A memory swam in front of his vision. Of waking a
sleeping teenager in the loft of his parents' barn. Those
sleepy, dreamy brown eyes had looked up at him just
like this.

And suddenly he realized that he was buried balls
deep inside little Annabelle Preston.

One of his father's best friends' daughters. A girl who
had spent ages following him around the family ranch,
all round chubby cheeks and hopeful eyes.

A woman he'd known since she was a child, and who
he had just screwed within an inch of both their lives.

Well, fuck.

CHAPTER THREE

COOPER HAD GONE still on top of Annabelle, and her brain was buzzing from the spectacular orgasm she'd just had.

She had never had sex like that in her life. She had never been with a man that looked like him, had never had a man do…that to her. She had never, absolutely never, come twice in one…*session.*

She was lucky if she got to come once.

But now, her fuzzy feelings were fading because Cooper was looking at her like he had just seen a ghost.

"Annabelle," he said.

His tone was so confused, his expression so dumbfounded. She couldn't make sense of it.

But…oh, no. No.

He had never once used her name. Not once tonight, until now.

He hadn't known who she was.

There were no words for the horror. The humiliation. He didn't want her. She'd thought…finally. And no. He'd just wanted sex. She'd trusted him with her body because she knew him. And she'd thought…he knew her, too. But he didn't.

Her stomach twisted, turning sour.

She pushed his shoulder, scrambling to get out from beneath him. "Who did you *think* I was?"

"Annabelle," he said again, moving away from her.

He was just staring at her, like she was a ghost still, but now possibly a ghost who had grown a second head. Which was not the look that you wanted from a man who had just banged you senseless.

It was ludicrous. She was naked, pressed against her headboard, her breasts heaving with every breath she took, her thighs parted slightly, because she still hadn't gotten control over everything.

When she realized *that* she snapped her knees together, angling to the side.

He was still naked, too, breathing hard, the muscles on his chest and stomach flexing, that very large, very masculine part of him looming in her vision, making it impossible for her to think straight.

"Yes," she confirmed. "*Annabelle.* But I thought you... I thought you knew."

"No," he said, shaking his head.

He sounded so disgusted, so horrified. She wanted to curl up into a ball and disappear from the situation completely.

"So, you just thought you were having sex with a stranger? You didn't even ask my name."

"I thought that's what we were doing," he said.

"I *knew* it was *you*," she whispered. "That's why I..."

Oh, no. This was horrible. Worse than having the boyfriend who had so firmly felt like settling tell her one day, after five years, that *he'd* been wasting his time with *her*.

Cooper Mason didn't finally see her as a woman.

Cooper Mason did not want her. Cooper Mason *the opposite* of wanted her, if his reaction to the entire situation was anything to go by. He was clearly disgusted unto his soul that he had ever touched her.

Except... He had been into it when they'd done it. He had been.

"I don't understand."

"*I* don't understand," Annabelle said. "I thought that we... I thought you... You didn't know who I was."

"No," he said, holding his hands up, "I swear to God. If I had I never would've touched you."

"Well, that's...horrible. And humiliating. And you are a gigantic tool," she said, grabbing a pillow and holding it across her breasts. He was not allowed to look at them if he was going to cast aspersions on her.

"Annabelle, I have known you since you were three years old. I would not have slept with you if I'd..." He stared at her harder. "You look different."

"I hope so, since I'm not seventeen anymore." She sniffed. "Also, I lost a little weight."

He shook his head, getting out of the bed and hunting for his clothes. "You're just not...not a woman to me."

"Clearly I am," she said.

"Not...not you. The person that I thought you were."

"That doesn't make any sense."

He took a step back. "I have to go."

"Cooper," she said, scrambling out of bed.

"This was not what I wanted," he returned. "It was a bad idea."

"Why does it change anything?"

"Because I'm not here for an entanglement. And I'm certainly not here to start something with a home-town girl who, when last I saw her, wasn't old enough to drink."

"I don't want to start anything with you," she said. "I wanted to have sex with you. I wanted to..."

She couldn't go on; it was too humiliating. Because

she had fulfilled her lifelong fantasy of jumping Cooper Mason's bones and he was actively disgusted that he had jumped hers.

She couldn't admit it. Not to him. Not now.

Couldn't confess that she had a crush on him as deep and enduring as the Tioga River when he looked like he would rather take a stick in the eye than even think about having sex with her again.

"I'm not a one-night-stand kind of girl," she continued stiffly. "But I'm in a space where I thought I would have one, because I just got out of a long-term relationship." She was only partly lying. A year was recent enough when the relationship was as long as hers and Parker's had been. "I figured since we kind of knew each other it made it less sordid."

"Not for me," he said, his tone hard.

"This doesn't have to change anything," she said.

"But it does," he responded.

"Well, now it does," she said. "Because you changed it."

He pulled on his underwear, his pants, covering up that gorgeous body of his. "Don't tell anyone this happened," he said.

"Oh, you don't want me to tell anyone," she said, doing her best to keep her voice even. "How will I ever keep it a secret that I had sex with Cooper Mason and then he ran away when he discovered it was me because he was so disgusted?" She flung her arms wide. "I'm dying to tell the world."

"Annabelle… I come back to town two times a year at most. I don't want complications. And I sure as hell don't want more ties to Gold Valley. There's a reason that I left. There's a reason I stay gone. I only come back for my mother, for my father. I figured you and I were just going to have a little anonymous fun."

"Well, it's not fun anymore, so get your tight ass out of here," she said, feeling humiliated and indignant and past the point of caring that her breasts were out and swaying all over the place with the force of her indignation.

"Annabelle, trust me," he said, pulling his shirt over his head, "this is to protect you."

"Bull."

"You're the last person in the world I want to hurt. And I don't have anything to offer you. I'm sorry, but I think it would be best if I left." He turned and began walking out of her room.

"Yeah?" she shouted. "Well, I didn't want anything from you but an orgasm, and I got two of those!" She heard the front door slam shut.

She sat down on the bed again, then flopped backward, too shocked to move. There was a deep, serious pain stabbing through her chest, but she felt too shell-shocked to cry.

She had just had the best sex of her life with Cooper Mason, and then he had walked out on her.

"Merry Christmas to me."

CHAPTER FOUR

"I HOPE YOU don't mind running some errands with me today," Connie Mason said, interrupting Cooper's particularly dark train of thought.

"No," he said. He could tell his mother was trying to keep her tone light, but he could also sense underlying anxiety there.

His mother had problems going out sometimes, among other things, and he could understand why. It was a small town and she always ran into people she knew. She didn't always like being asked how she was doing, particularly this time of year.

Sometimes going by herself, without a buffer, was impossible.

Not that she would ever want to admit that.

"I'm going to drop off my jewelry down at Gunslinger and pick up the money from the sales I've made over the last month."

His mother had gotten heavy into jewelry-making over the course of Lindsay's illness. Lindsay had been sick from the time she was sixteen, and her family had spent a fair amount of time in hospitals. Connie had gone even heavier into it after Lindsay's death.

"Great," he said. "We can grab some lunch."

He was distracted, and his mom didn't deserve to bear the brunt of that. But everything in him was still reeling from last night's shock. He had come home and had sex with Annabelle. As soon as he'd realized who she was, he had been unable to get the image of her as a kid out of his head. Of her as a round, sweet-faced teenager, giving him a hug at his sister's funeral, which had been the last place he'd seen her.

This damned town. It was like a tangled-up ball of yarn, and every time you thought you were grabbing hold of a new thread, you weren't. It was just more of the same damned tangle. Everyone, everything, every place, seemed connected. Every memory. There was no escaping it.

The worst part was he wasn't turned off now that he knew who she was. The sex had been so hot he felt permanently singed by it, but the fact that his partner had turned out to be little Annabelle Preston should have served as a metaphorical bucket of ice water. It should have made his memories less of a turn-on, not more of one.

He gritted his teeth. "Are you ready to go?" he asked.

"Almost," his mother responded.

She spent some time gathering up her jewelry, getting things together in that methodical way that she did everything. His mother was one of the biggest control freaks on the planet. Organized. Never anything out of place. But she hadn't been able to control the one thing she would have wanted to control the most.

He swallowed hard, hating the fact that his thoughts were so consumed with the past. But it was impossible to be consumed by anything else when he was in this place. Except for those few short hours he had been in Annabelle's arms.

Then he had been consumed with her. Utterly. Completely.

He pushed the images to the back of his mind and headed out of the simple farmhouse with his mom, helping her into his truck before getting into the driver's side and starting the engine.

His family home was on the outskirts of town, on a three-acre plot of land perfect for the kind of small operation his parents had. His parents had always kept a couple of cows, chickens and goats. Theirs wasn't a ranch that made a heavy profit, but something that provided the family with food and also earned a little bit on the side selling some of what the animals produced, and trading with the neighbors.

There were good memories here. The man he had become owed his roots to this place, his love of ranching cemented by his upbringing. He loved his parents. And part of him felt guilty that he didn't spend more time at home. Especially since he was their only remaining child.

But sometimes he thought his absence was good for them, too. Gave his dad a chance to take enough time for himself. To tie flies and go fishing. For his mother to make her earrings and spend time with her friends.

They got together at prescribed times of the year and dealt with the heavier things, but they got time away from it, too.

When they arrived on the town's main street he parked his truck against the curb, and his mother waited in her seat until he rounded to her side to open the door and help her out of the tall vehicle.

They wandered along the uneven sidewalk, lined with redbrick buildings that had been built in the eighteen hundreds. Gold Valley was a town that had sprung up around the gold rush, people headed to California, stopping in Oregon along the way and mining what they could there. It had a classic, Old West feel to it, carefully maintained by the city council and various ordinances that ensured the main street would never be too modernized.

There was exactly one neon sign in town, an old one from the 1950s that was officially the only lit sign allowed to exist in all of Gold Valley. The facades of the buildings might have remained the same for decades, but the businesses had changed. More coffee shops, more boutique clothing and a couple of fancier restaurants.

They made their way down to Gunslinger, which was housed in a narrow building wedged between the Happy Cow ice cream shop and the Gold Valley Inn, the premier date restaurant in town. Cooper pushed the door open, letting his mom go in first, and then followed behind, looking up and taking in the store. He'd been in it many times before, but it had been years, and it was laid out completely differently now, racks of stylish clothing in the center of the room, jewelry artfully showcased beneath a display case and a selection of specialty wool blankets against the wall.

But it was the movement behind the counter that caught his eye. And then he stopped.

Annabelle. Of course it was Annabelle.

Instantly, his mind was filled with X rated images from last night, not that they had been far from his consciousness before he had walked in. Before he had seen her. But now it was all he could think about. With his mother right next to him.

This just got better and better.

She looked up, and her eyes collided with his, going wide. Then she looked at his mother, the expression on her face deliberately blank. "Connie," she said. "I have your envelope."

"Good," his mother said. "I have more jewelry for you, too."

"Good," Annabelle parroted. "We need more. Your pieces are always popular."

She looked back at him, then looked away just as quickly, twisting her hands nervously, something he had seen her do last night in her living room, just before they had...

Well, he really didn't need to finish that thought.

Annabelle very pointedly didn't engage with him and he took that as his cue to busy himself. He really wasn't about to draw attention to the fact that there was any sort of connection between Annabelle and himself.

He moved away from them, pretending to look at the blankets on display while Annabelle continued to talk about the pieces that his mother had brought in. He needed to get himself under control, because everything in him wanted to reach behind the counter, grab hold of Annabelle and draw her up against him again. Kiss her again.

It was almost impossible for him to understand how he hadn't recognized her last night. Today, he would have. Today she looked more like the woman he remembered from all those years ago. Her brown hair was pulled back partway with a clip, the style looking carefree and natural. She looked softer, her makeup much less heavy, no lipstick on those full, pretty lips.

Last night, she had been all smoky eyes and crimson

mouth. Definitely not things he associated with little Annabelle Preston.

And, frankly, she had been nothing but a fine set of curves to him at first. His focus had been on her amazing body, and her face—while lovely—had definitely been a secondary thought.

Today, though, all of it was melting together. Who she was, the fact that she was *still* beautiful and the fact that her rack was *still* spectacular.

Coupled with the fact that he also knew exactly what her body looked like uncovered. And that it held up to the promise.

That was the trouble. She was soft all over. Soft and smooth, and he itched to touch her again. To be inside of her again.

It was enough to get him hard just thinking about it. Except he was in a cutesy Western shop standing next to his mother, and he was thirty-two old. That was enough to keep him under control.

"Cooper," his mom said. "You remember Annabelle Preston, don't you? She owns the store now."

Cooper paused and turned toward them. His eyes clashed with Annabelle's and her cheeks suffused with color. "Yeah," he responded. "I remember Annabelle."

He hadn't realized she owned the store. Which he supposed was another sign she was a grown woman. And accomplished at that.

He tried not to think of all the other ways he'd found her accomplished last night.

"She's so grown-up now," his mom said, not a trace of irony in her voice. "The last time you saw her she must have been a girl."

He really didn't need his mother to supply him with

this kind of information. He was well aware that Anna-belle was no longer a girl.

Was *intimately acquainted* with the fact that she was a woman.

"She is indeed," he responded, and the color in Anna-belle's cheeks grew deeper.

His mom looked up and out the window, and her ex-pression changed. "Oh, it's Opal," she said. "Hang on just a second, Annabelle. I have to go talk to her about a gift I'm making for her daughter-in-law."

With that, Connie rushed out of the store, intercepting an older woman on the streets, the two of them greet-ing each other as if it had been months since they had encountered one another, rather than the couple of days Cooper suspected it had been.

And that left him alone in the store with Annabelle.

"Cooper," she said, her tone icy. "Nice to see you."

"We both know you don't mean that."

"Well, I was going to try to be polite, but if you want honesty instead, no, I don't mean it." She sniffed. "Be-cause you're an asshole who abandoned me last night after having sex with me."

Guilt punched a hole in his gut. "It was a lot to wrap my head around."

And if he had stayed he would have wanted her to wrap her hand back around him, and he was trying to be chivalrous. Something he had damned little experi-ence with.

Annabelle looked like she might be considering blud-geoning him with one of the wrought-iron lamps sitting on the counter to her left. He had to wonder which she'd choose. The elk or the bison. The bison looked weightier, but the elk antlers were probably sharp.

"It wasn't a lot to wrap your head around when you thought I was a stranger," she said crisply, clearly deciding to talk rather than murder him with home decor. "It didn't take you any time to decide to go home with me in that case. As long as I was just disembodied female organs it was fine."

He frowned. "That's a pretty distasteful way of putting it."

"It is distasteful," she maintained, moving from behind the counter and busying herself straightening clothes on the rack.

"It's distasteful that I want to protect you? Because that's the issue here. You were… I mean, I remember you being a little kid and I had to catch you when you fell out of an apple tree. I put a Band-Aid on your skinned knee once, and I know that…somewhere in there you caught a case of hero worship. Trust me, Annabelle, I'm not a hero. And I would never have put us in this kind of position if I'd known."

Suddenly, Annabelle seemed to boil over, and he wondered if he would have to be ready to dodge a blow after all. She stamped her foot, her hands balled into fists at her sides. "Well, *excuse me*. Excuse me for thinking that you might actually see me as a woman. That you might actually want me. I am so done with this, Cooper. I am tired of being not good enough, not exciting enough. Is that the real reason this is a problem? Was I not sexy enough for you? Was it a massive turnoff when my foundational garment was removed and you saw that I didn't have a six-pack? Are my hips problematic?" She slapped her hands down on said hips in emphasis. "What about these?" She raised her hands, cupping her own breasts and shaking them. "Not exactly sample size."

"No," he said, heat licking through him like a match being struck, his body getting hard as his gaze was drawn to those pretty curves of hers. "You were not a turnoff in any way. I didn't mean to give you that impression and I'm sorry that I did. But the reality of the situation is I'm a man who lives on the road. I have no desire to have a family, or to have a wife. And I don't want any more ties to this damned place. It's not a happy place for me. I don't want to have a woman here. That's why I wouldn't have chosen to get involved with someone as complicated as you."

"Right." She rolled her eyes. "Complicated. Well, there's always *something* wrong with me. My ex, Parker, certainly made sure to drive that point home, as if I didn't already know that. And now I know I'm not even good enough for a little bit of sex."

"You're too good for it, Annabelle," he said, softening his tone.

"But you aren't? Whatever the hell woman you *thought* I was wasn't too good for it?"

"That's not what I meant."

"I'm not sure you know what you mean," she said, the words far too pointed.

Maybe she was right. Maybe all his excuses were BS. Maybe it all had to do with the strange, vague weight that settled in his chest when he thought of this place. The way that sex felt heavier because it had been with her.

Maybe it was that.

And there were no words to explain that. Nothing to throw out easily as a logical explanation. It wasn't logic. It was all that shit around his heart that ached and stabbed at him even when he wanted to pretend it wasn't there.

"Fine," he said. "If that's not good enough for you, then just try to understand that this is messed up. Your dad would punch me in the face, and it would be the kind of rumor that would never stop circulating around town. Though at least it would let me be something other than the guy with the dead sister. I could be the guy who screwed Annabelle Preston and then left her."

"Why is there no allowance in there for me to be the one screwing you? I wanted this. I...I have wanted it." She frowned, her cheeks getting pinker, her brown eyes turning glossy. "I spent five years with the same guy. Having mediocre sex and listening to all the ways I failed to impress him. When I saw you last night at the bar, I thought that you finally wanted me. That I could have a little piece of something that wasn't disappointing. That wasn't mediocre. That's what I wanted. I felt so... You made me feel beautiful. And then you took it away."

"You are beautiful," he said, not able to stop himself from taking a step toward her. "You can't doubt that I enjoyed being with you."

"Of course I can. Because you ran off. You said it would never happen again. And you told me not to tell anyone."

"That's because of who you are. Who I am. Really, it's because of who *we* are."

"Who's that?" she asked, sounding impatient.

"You're little Annabelle Preston and I'm..."

"No," she said. "I'm not *little* anything. I'm Annabelle Preston, and I own this store. I'm a grown woman, and you're a man. There is no reason that what happened last night shouldn't have happened. Your reasoning is bullshit."

"My reasoning is designed to keep you safe, Annabelle," he said.

"I don't want to be safe," she whispered. "I've been safe for too long. Safe is boring. And it's dull. Safe just kills you even more slowly."

"Well, I don't want to kill you at all."

"Funny I can't say the same," she said drily.

She was right. It was bullshit. Because here he was staring down a woman he wanted more than he wanted to keep on breathing, telling her all the reasons he couldn't have her again when he wasn't even sure he believed them anymore.

It was Christmas. He was back in Gold Valley, reliving all the pain from his past… Didn't he deserve something?

"I'm only in town through Christmas," he said, his voice rough.

She was looking at him with those far-too-familiar brown eyes, but that wasn't what was compelling him. No matter how deeply he tried to drill into his head that this was a woman he had known in childhood—a woman who was younger than him, less experienced and probably far too trusting of him because she had this idea that he knew who he was—he couldn't shake the fact that he was attracted to her.

And why the hell not? She presented a good point. She wasn't a kid anymore. The gulf between their ages was definitely narrowed by the years, and she seemed to want this as much as he did. Even if he shouldn't want it.

Her dad might still punch him out, but with the limited timeline, they might also be able to keep it a secret.

"I'm only here for the week," he repeated. "Six days

to Christmas. But I can sure as hell use some distraction during that time."

She blinked. "Are you…propositioning me?"

"Didn't you want me to?"

"Well, you were warning me away a few minutes ago, so it seems like a strange shift in tone."

"I want you," he said, closing the distance between them. "I shouldn't. But dammit, ever since I drove back into town it's like the past is closing in on me. My memories of losing Lindsay feel like they could be from yesterday, not from eight years ago. And the only time I felt halfway decent was when you kissed me. When I was inside you. I wouldn't mind feeling that good again."

"Oh," she said, lush lips rounding.

"But you have to understand that it's just for now. It won't be every time I come back. And when I leave…"

"You'll sleep with other women?"

"We won't be tied to each other," he said, liking the sound of that much better. Feeling like it made him less of an ass, as long as he made it clear that the freedom worked both ways.

She bit her lush lip, studying him for a moment.

"I'm not sure," she said, lifting her chin. "Because what I don't want is to be a pity lay. I don't want feelings or a relationship or anything either, but I want to be sure that if we're having sex, you're into it."

"Annabelle," he said, his voice rough even to his own ears. "I wanted you last night when I didn't know who you were."

"And you quit wanting me the minute you found out."

"Hell no. I still wanted you. Why'd you think I had to leave?"

She blinked. "I just thought it was because you were completely grossed out."

He chuckled, hard and bitter. "That would make things a lot simpler."

She looked like she was fully considering all these things, all the options. Perhaps even still the option of pounding his head in with a lamp. But when she finally spoke, it wasn't to make threats. "Well, if we can't have simple, maybe we can have hot?" She looked hopeful.

"Sounds good to me, though that could be because there's no more blood left in my brain." His reasoning was flawed, no two ways about it. But he was kind of past the point of reasoning. So what if it was Annabelle? It wouldn't matter in the end. He hadn't recognized her, because she hadn't been in his life for the past eight years. And when he left Gold Valley after Christmas, she'd go back to not being in his life. As long as they didn't parade around in public they could easily keep their parents out of it, they would keep the town out of it, and it wouldn't matter. In the end, it would just be a fond memory for them both. And until then he would have some much-needed oblivion in the middle of all this sharp, horrible Christmas cheer.

"Can you come over tonight?" she asked.

He looked at her, watched as the color in her cheeks intensified under his intense scrutiny. He wanted to kiss her. Didn't want to wait for privacy or the cover of darkness or anything. "You won't be able to keep me away."

His mother came back into the store then, Opal tagging along behind her. "I hope you don't mind, Cooper. I think we picked up a third for lunch."

"Not at all," he said, forcing his focus away from Annabelle and back onto his mom. Whatever she needed, he would give it to her. He was here to visit his parents, to play the part of good son. This arrangement with Annabelle wasn't his focus. It just made his time here bearable. Hell, more than bearable. It made it pretty sweet.

"Why don't we head to Bellissima?" his mother suggested.

"Sounds good."

He turned back to Annabelle and tipped his hat. "See you around."

"See you around," she echoed softly.

It was going to be a hell of a long day.

CHAPTER FIVE

ANNABELLE HAD NO idea how she made it through the rest of the day. She was jangly and jittery until the moment she turned the Closed sign around and started counting out the till.

Then she looked up and saw her father standing there at the door.

She sighed, feeling beleaguered, which really wasn't fair because she loved her dad. But she was really looking forward to seeing Cooper.

She rounded the counter and walked over to the door, letting him in. "Dad," she said, "what are you doing here?"

"I was driving by, saw that you were still in the shop. Figured I would stop in."

"Oh, that's... Thank you. I'm glad you did. And I'd love to visit. But I'm...kind of in a hurry?" To have sex with a hot man. She wouldn't say that last part. Even thinking it in front of her dad was uncomfortable.

"I won't keep you," he said, even as he wandered in a slow circle around the store, clearly willing to keep her a little bit. "I hear that Cooper Mason is back in town."

The back of her neck prickled, spreading up to her scalp. Was her dad psychic? Being raised by a single dad had always been tricky. She hadn't had a woman in her life to teach her about the softer things. But that also meant that she was close with her father. They had spent tons of time together when she was growing up, and she had spent a lot of that time on various mechanic jobs with him, talking to him about everything, even when it was uncomfortable things. Each was all the other had.

But she would not be talking to him about her recent relationship change with Cooper. Having a physical-only affair with the son of a family friend wasn't really the kind of thing she and her dad could talk about.

"I saw him at the saloon last night," she said, not seeing any point in lying about that because it would be too easy for her story to be contradicted. Plenty of people had seen them together last night. A few people had probably even seen them kiss. Though she doubted anyone would rat her out to her dad. Still, rumors did get around.

"He was always a good boy," her dad said.

She cringed, wondering just how much of a good boy her dad would think he was if he knew what they had done last night. Or how Cooper had treated her afterward.

"He's nice enough," she supplied.

"Really sad about his sister."

Her heart twisted. It was unavoidable. What everyone in town thought of when they thought of Cooper. When they thought of Connie and Jeff. Gold Valley was small enough that it was common to know pieces of the stories of half the people you walked by on the street. Especially the interesting pieces. The gossip-worthy bits.

Tragedy was interesting when it wasn't yours. A chance to make mournful expressions and then whisper about it intently behind your hand.

It was like a cloud that hung over the entire Mason family, over Lindsay's widowed husband, Grant.

She wondered what that must be like. To be so defined by such a terrible thing. To know that when you saw a person you knew in the grocery store, the minute you walked away they'd explain to their friend, *That's Grant Dodge. His wife died a few years back.*

She wondered if it was why Cooper stayed away.

"You okay?" her dad asked.

"Why?"

"You seem quiet."

"I was just thinking about Lindsay," she said truthfully. "It's sad what happened. I don't blame Cooper for not coming back often."

"You loved him when you were a kid," her dad said, smiling. "You had a crush on him that was clear as day to anyone who looked at you."

Heat raced through her. "Dad," she said. "That was a long time ago."

"Maybe, but it seems like yesterday. Besides, it was cute to watch you follow him around the ranch."

"Well." She cleared her throat. "I'm not a kid anymore."

"I know."

"I hate to move you along, but I really am in a rush. I'll see you for Christmas, though," she promised. "I'm going to cook a turkey. Stuffing. Mashed potatoes. Everything you like."

She had started cooking Christmas dinner the moment she had learned how. Because she had been very tired of frozen lasagna for every single holiday at that point.

"You're a good daughter, Annabelle," her dad said. "Do you know that?"

She forced a smile. "I do," she said.

As her dad walked out, she pondered those words and why they made her feel weird. Yes, she was a good daughter to him; she knew that. But for a lot of her life she'd just felt like she made things more difficult for him.

She had been the product of a one-night stand, and a mother who hadn't wanted a child. So her father had taken her on when he'd still been a teenager. And he had devoted his life to her. But she wondered. Wondered if she was the reason her father had never found anyone. If she was the reason he'd ended up a heavy-machinery mechanic, because practicality had been more important than schooling of any kind.

She shook her head. Shook off all thoughts of her mother, of all her father had given up for her. Because that was another dead end of terrible thoughts that made her feel sad and small. Inadequate.

Annabelle was a puzzle piece that didn't fit neatly into anyone's life. She understood that. But sometimes she wished it could be different.

Except for this week. This week, she was what Cooper Mason needed. She was going to be the bright spot. And that felt pretty damned good.

CHAPTER SIX

ANNABELLE WASN'T SURE if you were supposed to get a man refreshments when you invited him over for an evening of casual sex. She really had no idea what to do in this kind of scenario. She'd had that one long-term relationship. Just the one. Until last night, Parker was the only man who had ever seen her naked, and he had always taken great pains to let her know how disappointing it was. He was awful, and she knew that, but it didn't mean that her self-esteem was unaffected.

But Cooper wanted her.

Actually, the fact that he wanted her in spite of his reservations was cheering in some ways. She decided to get a bottle of wine down from the cupboard. As she was in the midst of battling with the cork, there was a knock on the front door.

Her finger still wrapped around the slim neck of the bottle, she walked over to it and threw it open. And then her heart stopped. Because there was Cooper, looking at her like he might want to eat her alive. And this time, he was well aware of who he was looking at.

Happiness burst through her chest.

She couldn't help it. Couldn't stop it. She didn't want to attach any particular feelings to this thing between them, not after his very stern lecture. But this man was her lifelong fantasy. The moment she had begun to understand what happened between men and women, she had begun to think about what it might be like to do that with him. To have those rough, large hands on her body.

But then the world had fallen apart, and he had left town. And she had nothing but the memory of that one long hug to fuel her.

Then there had been Parker, and she had been forced to reconcile the fact that reality was not as much fun as fantasy.

Until last night. Until she had finally gotten the man of her dreams. Until he had finally shown her that reality could be even better than fantasy as long as the sex was with the right person.

Physically. He was the right person *physically.* That was all. She'd always found him hot, so undoubtedly being with him fulfilled that natural desire she felt.

This time it probably wouldn't be as good. This time, there wouldn't be years of buildup leading up to it. They'd just been together last night. She'd had two orgasms. There was no way tonight would be as good. She didn't possess the strength for it to be that good.

"Are you going to invite me in?" he asked.

"Yes," she said, stepping out of the way as she wiggled her hand and tried to get the cork out of the bottle.

"Need help with that?"

"Please," she said, handing it to him. Their fingers brushed.

That brief, momentary contact was enough to send a sensation through her that rivaled the buzz that would come from a glass of the wine he was currently trying to open.

Whatever she'd just been thinking about tonight not being as good, she was most definitely wrong.

"I thought you might like a drink," she said lamely.

"Thanks," he responded. "You thought right. When I'm in town I always want a drink. Or ten."

She bit back the questions that were building inside her. He wouldn't want her to ask questions. Wouldn't want this to be about anything more complicated than the physical connection between them.

She sighed.

"What?"

She turned around to look at him. "Nothing."

"That was quite the sigh."

"Well. It's just been that kind of a day." She moved over to the couch and sat.

"Why?" Cooper sat down next to her, his knee brushing against hers.

Now he was pressing, and he was the one who had made the rule that they were keeping things casual. So now she was just annoyed that she hadn't pushed him for more information when she'd had the chance. When the opening had been natural. "Just the nature of retail." She waved a hand.

"But you like it. Or you wouldn't have bought the store."

"Did you and your mom spend your lunch talking about me?"

"Of course we did," he said. "She was eager to fill me in on the gossip. And on the fact that you bought the store from Freda Lopez when she married Quinn Dodge."

"Yes. These days, he and Freda are mostly living in New Mexico, enjoying the dry heat—which sounds vile to me—and his son, Wyatt, has taken over Get Out of Dodge."

"I'm up to speed on that," Cooper said. "You know my mother would never leave out pertinent information."

"Of course not."

He lifted a brow, regarding her closely before speaking again. "She also said that your ex-boyfriend, Parker, was a terrible human being."

She might have guessed Connie would bring up Parker. Her dad hadn't been short on opinions about him, and he'd most definitely shared them with Jeff and Connie. "She's not wrong," Annabelle said.

"Why were you with him?"

She shrugged. "It felt better than being alone at the time." Her throat had gone prickly, tight. "I was in college, and I was still a virgin, so it seemed like maybe it was time to fix that. I met him at a concert in the park—he was new to town. He asked me out. I went on a date with him and I liked him, and then we slept together. We just kept sleeping together after that. And I guess when you add meals to that it becomes a relationship. It most especially does when he moves into the house you bought. Before you know it…well, before you know it, it's been five years of your life."

"Right," Cooper said. "I wouldn't know. I'm definitely not an expert on relationships."

"I thought he was the best I could do," she said. "And a lot of what he said to me confirmed it. Then last year he broke up with me."

"He broke up with *you*?"

"That's always how it goes, right? I gave him…so much time. And he never really intended to give me anything in return. He was just waiting for something better to come along." She tapped her fingertips on her wineglass. "But I suppose in the end beggars can't be choosers. At least, that's what I always told myself."

He set the bottle of wine down on the side table in the living room with a heavy thunk. "Let's get one thing straight right now," he said, closing the distance between them and gripping her by the chin, tilting her face upward so that she was forced to look at him. "He was lucky to have you. Whatever he said to you…he was an ass."

"I know…"

"*Do* you?" Those blue eyes were hot and intense on hers, and she almost couldn't look directly at him. He was too beautiful. That sculpted face, lips that she knew were perfect for kissing. A little bit of golden stubble on his jaw. His eyes…oh, those blue eyes.

He was too beautiful and too perfect to be this close to her.

She didn't get touched by beautiful, perfect men. And yet, here he was.

She looked away. "I had enough confidence to put on some Spanx and seduce you, didn't I?"

"You did," he said, sliding his thumb across her chin. "I'm sorry if the way I acted after that did anything to dent that confidence. Believe me when I tell you the reasons I shouldn't be with you don't have anything to do with you."

"Right. It's you," she said, her heart twisting at the reminder—yet another one—that this was temporary.

"It's cliché, maybe," he said. "But it's true."

"Why?" Now she was going to ask. She was going to ask because he had started digging into all of her stuff, so it seemed fair enough to her to dig around his.

"I don't do relationships," he told her. "My job doesn't allow it."

The way he said it, so flat and hard, she knew there was more than he was saying. That he chose a job that didn't allow it on purpose. That he was on the run for a very specific reason. But of course, he wasn't going to say that he didn't do relationships because his *heart* wouldn't allow it. That losing his sister had been difficult and he wasn't over it.

You didn't get over loss like that, though, she knew. Sure, she hadn't lost anyone to death, but her mother had never wanted to be a part of her life. She understood what it felt like to have a hole in your life. That no matter how much you loved the people you still had, it couldn't be ignored.

"Okay," she said.

"You, on the other hand, apparently *like* relationships."

"Correction," she said, "I *did*. Or I thought I should. Now, I'm only in the market for a little bit of sex. So while I appreciate you trying to protect me and all...this is actually just what the doctor ordered."

"A few orgasms?"

"With a hot man," she said seriously. "I know that... it was pretty obvious I had a crush on you when I was a kid."

His eyebrows shot up. "Was it?"

She sputtered, "Well, my dad said it was."

"I didn't think of it like that. You were just a cute kid that liked to hang out with me. Are you telling me that your motives weren't pure?"

"I idolized you," she said. "You'll be happy to know that I don't idolize men anymore."

"Well," he said, "that is a relief."

"These days I just want to jump you."

"Also a relief."

"Good. Because I think we should get to that."

The talking worried her. The fact was that the more minutes they carved out together, the more likely it was there would be a hole left behind when he left.

They'd both had enough of those kinds of holes. They didn't need anymore.

He wrapped one strong arm around her waist and brought her up against his chest, kissing her, deep and long, glorious. She didn't want it to end. She felt the kiss all the way down. It made her feel dizzy. Made her feel light and heavy at the same time.

It had to be the kiss. Not him. Not her feelings for him.

"You're right," he said. "We should."

CHAPTER SEVEN

IT WAS ONE thing to accidentally have a one-night stand with Annabelle Preston. It was another thing entirely to choose to make that one night more. To choose it knowing who she was.

Knowing that the woman he held in his arms now had once been the girl who had followed him around with bright eyes and a hopeful smile.

To know that some asshole had crushed that smile, dulled those eyes.

To know that maybe, if he were careful, he might be able to fix some of that damage.

Cooper wasn't a savior. Never had anything made that more clear than when Lindsay had gotten sick.

She had known—for most of her life—that she was fighting a battle she couldn't win. That no one could save her. Not her parents who had loved her, not the husband who had married her anyway, knowing that he was signing on to be widowed.

And certainly not her younger brother

Who had seen her as the bravest, most beautiful person in the world, reduced in memory to her death, rather than her life. Who had watched as her every breath seemed to steal life from her body instead of give it.

While he could do nothing. Nothing but watch.

No, he wasn't a savior. He had never saved anyone. He couldn't even save himself.

But perhaps he could do something to fix what that jackass Parker had done to break off those pieces of Annabelle's self-esteem.

Perhaps he could put some of them back in place.

Right. Pretend that you're being noble when you really just want to get off.

That was the same voice that was happy to remind him that he wasn't a hero. No, he wasn't.

But maybe there could be some altruistic mixed in with the selfish here. Just maybe.

He kissed her, guiding her down onto the couch rather than leading her back into the bedroom. He filled his hands with her abundant curves, pressed his palms over her breasts, drew his thumbs over her tightened nipples. She was beautiful. And he had absolutely no issues with how long he had known her, not in this moment.

She was a woman. And he was a man. They both wanted this. They both understood what it was. A little oblivion to get through the season. That was what mattered.

He moved his hands down her body, taking in the shape of her waist, the soft curve of her hips. She blushed when he glided his hands up underneath her shirt. Cooper didn't have any experience with women who blushed. It was a strange sight, and one that lit his blood on fire even if it shouldn't.

He felt all that smooth skin beneath his touch, brought his hands up to unhook her bra, taking it off along with her shirt. She was beautiful. Full breasts, soft to the touch. He leaned forward, drawing one nipple deep into his mouth, relishing the sound of pleasure she made as he did.

He could spend all night sating himself with her.

But as he finished undressing her, pleasuring her until they were both mindless, until her harsh cries signaled that she was ready for more, he was aware that he had chosen this. That he had chosen her.

And all the entanglements that came along with her. Whatever he said, wanting her had somehow been stronger than the need to stay unconnected.

He undressed quickly, sheathing himself with protection and sitting down on the couch, then lifting her and bringing her onto his lap so that she was straddling him. So that he could get a show along with his pleasure.

He looked at her, at all those gorgeous curves on display. He took stock of every last inch of her, and he did it slowly. If he was going to do something morally questionable, he might as well savor every second of it.

She was blushing, her skin turning pink all over, and he followed the rosy trail with his tongue. She was moaning again by the time he finished, by the time he pressed his hardened length to the entrance of her body and thrust up inside her.

"Show me how you like it," he rasped.

She grabbed on to his shoulders and moved experimentally, clearly not quite comfortable with this new position.

Much like the blush, he reveled in that, as well. And much like the blush, he didn't care if he shouldn't.

Then she seemed to relax, letting her head fall back, letting her eyes flutter closed. And she began to move, riding him like she hadn't a single inhibition in the world.

Like she wasn't ashamed of anything. Her body, how much she wanted him. That turned him on even more.

And then there was no more thinking. There was just him, wrapped up in her, the soft press of her breasts against his chest, her fingernails digging into his back, the tight clasp of her body around him.

All around them was Christmas. She had a Christmas tree; she had lights all around the room. He didn't ever have that sort of thing. Hadn't allowed himself to be surrounded by it in years.

But somehow right now it didn't seem so bad. Didn't seem quite so awful, quite so tied to things in the past that been corroded by grief.

This—being with Annabelle—felt shiny. It felt new and beautiful and bright.

He hadn't felt anything beautiful and bright in a long damn time. Christmas or not.

Pleasure was building in him, a dull roar thundering in his ears as lust overcame the feelings that were expanding in his chest. And thank God. He didn't want feelings. To hell with feelings.

He was going to embrace the physical. Because that was easy.

Except nothing felt easy as his orgasm roared up inside him, as she found her own release, trembling and shaking in his arms, her internal muscles pulsing around him, sending him straight over the edge.

No, there was nothing easy about that.

About a climax that left him broken, undone. Made of jagged pieces when it ended.

But then, he would never have said he wasn't broken. Would never claim the pieces inside him were anything but jagged.

She just made him so acutely aware of it. How sharp and damaged he was, compared to her soft perfection.

That was the problem.

Not so much the revelation that he was damaged, but the contrast to the woman he held in his arms. Because when he was on the road, when he never stopped moving, never settled in, never tried to build a connection to someone, it didn't matter.

He didn't have to examine it. He didn't have to know the person in his arms, in his bed for the night.

And because of that, he didn't have to know himself at all.

It could be a haze of double yellow lines, and the blend of pine trees whisking together into a blur of green. Of alcohol-soaked evenings and soft female skin.

But none of it was personal. None of it *lasted*.

Annabelle Preston was personal, and she could never be anything else.

He pulled her into his arms and held her there, listening to her breathing hard, feeling her skin, damp and sweaty against his. But not from running across a field or climbing apple trees. From making love to him.

Yeah, that was personal. And right now being in her arms felt too good, too right. And even if he knew he should pull away…he couldn't.

ANNABELLE HAD NEVER even thought of having sex on her couch. In full view of her coffee-table books, which were about civilized things like baked goods the pioneers made and shoes through the ages.

No, she had never thought of doing something quite so hedonistic. Because she had never been overcome by the need to be with someone before. By the need to have him inside her. By the need, the desperate need, to find release in his arms.

But she was overcome now. Or she had been. Now she was just a puddle. Naked and lying across her couch, completely unashamed.

"About that wine…" she said, looking to the bottle.

"What about it?"

"Well," she said, "I thought I would have needed to banish my inhibitions, but apparently you do a good enough job of that all on your own."

He lifted a shoulder, the muscles in his torso flexing. "It's a gift."

"Well, I'll take that. Consider it my early Christmas present."

"That seems like more of a gift for me, honey. The chance to have you uninhibited."

He got the cork out of the wine bottle and poured a glass for her, then a second one for himself.

And that was how she ended up sitting naked on her couch drinking wine. Which bordered on being almost as hedonistic as the sex. Almost.

"So," he said, "are you going to tell me why you feel like you need wine to let go of your inhibitions?"

He was staring at her with those gorgeous blue eyes, and she didn't know why he wanted to know anything about her. He was interesting. Mysterious. He had gone a thousand places beyond Gold Valley, and she'd never really gone anywhere. She didn't know why she would be interesting to him. She had never been interesting to anyone else.

"My boyfriend really wasn't a nice guy," she said, tucking her hair behind her ear and straightening. Which made her feel even more exposed, so she rounded her shoulders forward slightly. "But I spent so many years with him that it wasn't obvious to me. It wasn't like it was years of razor-sharp insults cutting into me. It was more a constant stream of low-grade disapproval, battering against me and leaving bruises. It was just…a lot of little things. And they added up and made me feel terrible about myself." She swallowed hard, then took another sip of wine. "And it's… You know, my mother just…gave me to my father when I was a baby. Like I was something from her closet that didn't fit her. That easy. So I can't help but feel that I'm deeply uninteresting to everyone. Wine makes me feel more interesting. I mean, in theory."

"You don't need wine to be interesting," he said, the vehemence in his voice shocking her. "It sure as hell had nothing to do with you. And in my experience, the way the people act has a lot more to do with them than it does with you. As somebody who's spent a fair amount of time running, I can tell you that whatever was happening with your mother…that's her stuff."

"Is it?"

"Sure as hell," he repeated.

"You're very certain."

"I am. Like I said, I'm an expert on that kind of thing."

"So that's what you're doing?" she asked. "Running?"

She wasn't sure what had made her press. It was funny. He had always seemed above her in some way. Because he was older. Because she had admired him so very much. But there was something about being naked with a person. It was an equalizer.

Even that was kind of funny when she thought about it, because his body was perfect by the standards of the world. Honed, muscular, not a spare ounce of fat anywhere. And she was…well, she was not perfect by those same standards.

But he was here, when he could be…well, anywhere else in town. With anyone else. And that made her feel like maybe there wasn't so much wrong with her after all.

He had been inside of her. He had wanted her. Still did. That made her feel like she deserved some answers. Like in these quiet moments in her living room, with the lights from her Christmas tree shining softly around them, they could share more than just their bodies.

"Just moving. Continually. Sometimes more quickly than others." His lips turned up slightly, his smile rueful.

"Is it hard to be back here?" She hated asking him about Lindsay. Mostly because she knew he couldn't escape it. She had witnessed it earlier when she had talked to her father. That loss was what was most closely associated with Cooper and his family.

But she wanted…she wanted to talk to him, not about him. And that, she thought, might be different enough to make him open up.

"It's hard to be anywhere," he said. "Eight years and it gets a little bit easier, I guess. But there's always a hole. Out there… Lindsay was never part of that life. I made a life that she had never been in, so that I wouldn't be so aware of her absence. Here… I only know Gold Valley with her in it. And I don't like it as much without her. I know our family home with her. Christmas and Thanksgiving, when we were kids, and then when she and Grant got married. We walked to school together every day. She was my big sister. She taught me how to tie my shoes. She protected me. And I couldn't protect her when it mattered most. And sometimes it hits me, like a punch in the gut. As fresh as it was the day she died. As fresh as it was when I fully understood what it meant that my sister had cancer. When the cancer came back, and back again."

"I'm sorry," she said. "It must be tough to be reminded all the time."

"And it's hard to remind everybody around me."

She didn't say anything. She simply looked at him.

"I feel like being here stirs it up. For me, for everyone. When I'm gone life kind of goes on. When I'm here…it seems to me that it's all fresher. I'm sure that if Grant ran across me I would remind him of her. It's not like Grant hangs out around our family homestead. And I know it's for a reason." He rubbed his hand over his face. "I know I remind my parents of her."

"That hardly seems fair."

"There's nothing fair about any of this. But I'm not complaining. I'm here. Lindsay is gone. It would be pretty damn selfish of me to complain about the fallout of her death when I get to go on living, wouldn't it?"

"I don't know," Annabelle said. "Maybe. Except you are alive, and being selfish is part of being alive. So it seems fair enough."

"It's just easier. Easier to stay away. Because out there…nobody knows my story. And here, everybody does."

"It's not your story," she said quietly. "It's something that happened in your family. Something that happened to your sister. It's a loss that you experienced, but it's not your story. If that's your story, then I have to be an abandoned daughter. And I don't want to be that. I don't want somebody else's issues to be mine."

"Life doesn't give you a choice," he said. "That's the tricky thing. You just have to keep going."

"Keep running, you mean."

"It's served me well enough."

"Don't you ever get lonely?"

He appraised her, his blue eyes growing hard. "Lonely is sitting in a room with two people that you love, having something hard that you share between you and not being able to talk about it. Lonely is walking down the street knowing people would rather talk about your past to their friends than talk to you about how you feel. Lonely is playing at looking fine all the time so that your parents don't worry about you. Lonely is what happens when I'm in Gold Valley. Not when I'm anywhere else."

She could feel it then, the distance beginning to stretch between them, and she wanted to reach out and do something to close it. Wanted to get beneath his skin.

Hero worship was one thing. That was what she had felt when she had been a little girl, and he had been so tall and strong and perfect. Like a superhero in a cowboy hat.

But now that she was with him like this, she could see that he wasn't a superhero. He was something better— he was a man. A man that she could touch. A man who wasn't invulnerable, but who went on anyway in spite of all he had been through.

But he was alone, and she wished that he weren't.

She wished he would let her be there for him.

And she fought against the feeling that she wasn't pretty enough, or compelling enough, or special enough to be the one he needed. She was here. And she wanted to make herself into that person. That was the person she wanted to be, not just now. Not just for him. But forever. For when he left.

She didn't want Parker to define who she was. She didn't want the mother who had given her away without ever knowing her to define the way she thought of herself. Not anymore.

"I don't want you to be lonely," she said, leaning in and brushing her fingertips over that beautiful sculpted face.

He wrapped his fingers around her wrist, holding her steady. "I'm not right now."

He kissed her then. Kissed her until she couldn't think, until she couldn't catch her breath. Until she felt the distance melting between them. She didn't know all the right things to say. She had never lost anyone to death the way he had. But she knew what it was like to feel isolated. To feel like the people around you couldn't understand what you had been through.

She knew what it was like to feel like she wasn't strong enough. Like she didn't have any control. Cooper hadn't said those things, but she could sense it. Somehow. He had lost his sister, and there had been nothing he could do about it. She couldn't imagine how that must've felt. But probably even worse than knowing she never had a chance to try to convince her mother to stay.

You won't be able to convince him to stay.

She ignored that voice whispering in her ear. She didn't need to convince him to stay. She only needed this week. It was all she expected. She knew that it would end. She knew what to expect. She wouldn't be upset at the end of this.

He was giving her the kind of pleasure she had never experienced before, and he was already making her feel stronger. She just wanted to do the same for him. That was all.

As he moved their glasses of wine to the side and picked her up, carrying her toward the bedroom they hadn't made it to earlier, she repeated those words over and over again. As if that would make them true.

She needed them to be true.

After Christmas Cooper would be gone, and she would have to find a way to live with that.

CHAPTER EIGHT

IT WAS THREE days before Christmas when Annabelle reminded Cooper that it would probably be a good idea to acquire gifts for his family. She had to get some things for her father, and she had convinced him that the two of them should go together.

As much as he didn't relish the idea of the town seeing them together as a couple, he supposed that the two of them being together in a general sense wasn't all that strange.

Well, no stranger than Cooper being back in town to begin with.

Carolers dressed in Victorian clothing were walking on the opposite side of the street. A horse and cart, decked with boughs of evergreen and red bows, were parked near the town Christmas tree, waiting to offer rides to people who had come to enjoy the Victorian Christmas festivities the town held every year.

There was a dusting of snow on the ground, the lights twinkling against the frosted brick as the temperatures stayed persistently low in spite of the fact that the sky was clear and the sun was shining. It didn't matter. It was still frozen.

Annabelle, meanwhile, glowed brighter than anything on the main street of Gold Valley. Her long dark hair was loose, covered by a knit cap, and her cheeks were rosy. She was smiling and greeting people easily as they walked down the street. He admired that easiness. Didn't envy it, necessarily, but wanted to keep on being close to it.

That was the thing about her. They had spent the last couple of nights together, and it wasn't a problem for him. Didn't make him feel itchy. Didn't make him feel as though he needed to get some distance anytime soon.

No, there was something peaceful about being with her. A feeling he hadn't known he could possess. One he hadn't known he wanted.

The other thing that was changing after the past couple of days was the way he saw her. Not as two separate entities. Not as the girl he had known and the woman she was, but as both of those things. Like now, with her practically skipping down the sidewalk, exhilarated to be out in the cold air, happy to be greeting townspeople…

That was when he saw the girl who used to run across the fields. Climb trees. Pick apples. Like she had never once fallen and scraped her knee. The same woman who drove him crazy at night, who put on a show for him with that gorgeous body like she had never been hurt by her jackass ex.

And he liked both parts of her. He liked her quite a lot, and he couldn't remember the last time he had liked anyone.

Particularly not someone he was sleeping with.

"I guess you can't get your mom jewelry," she said.

"I can't?"

"She makes her own."

"Yeah. True. But that doesn't mean that she can't enjoy someone else's." He paused and looked inside one of the shop windows, at a set of topaz earrings on display. "It isn't like artists only hang their own paintings up in their houses, right?"

"I don't know," Annabelle said, frowning. "I'll have to ask some of the artists that sell their work to the shop."

"When did you buy the shop, anyway?"

"Oh, that was a breakup gift to myself."

"Quite a big gift."

"Yes. But it was kind of a big breakup. And it was something that I really wanted. Something that he didn't think I could do. I wanted to prove that he was wrong."

"I would say that you have," he commented.

"I hope so. And you know…the longer I have it—the longer I have this whole life without him—the less it's about proving anything to anyone. It's just about enjoying myself, really."

"You should enjoy yourself," he said. "God knows without you I wouldn't be enjoying myself this week."

"Well…that's nice."

"I'm serious," he said. "Your smile lights everything up. This street…me. I don't know how to explain it."

She looked down, a slightly embarrassed expression on her face. Hell, he was a little embarrassed, too. He was practically spouting poetry on a public sidewalk. "I make you feel happy?"

"Hell yeah."

"Out of the bedroom?" She tossed him a saucy smile as she stepped inside the little shop and walked over to the earrings he had been considering a moment ago.

"I'm smiling now, right?" he asked.

"Yes," she agreed. "You are."

"I'm happy." He was. Not in an easy throwaway fashion either. This was something new. Something he'd forgotten he could feel.

She looked down for a moment, a small smile playing at the corner of her lips.

"They are pretty," she said, turning her focus to the jewelry, diffusing the tension.

"They are," he agreed. "I think Mom will like them."

"Can I ask… I don't want to be nosy."

"I don't believe that at all."

She rolled her eyes. "Well, I don't want you to think I'm being nosy. But I want the answer."

He chuckled. "Of course."

"I see your mom quite a bit. She sells jewelry to the store, and she comes in a couple of times a month to collect her money. But sometimes…I can tell that it's very hard for her. Sometimes she doesn't stay and talk."

"And sometimes she doesn't come when she says she will?"

She nodded. "Sometimes."

"My mom has pretty intense anxiety. She's always had it. But it got worse when Lindsay got sick. And then worse still when she passed. She said to me once that you think tragedy is something that happens to other people. And then when it happens to you…you lose all sense that there was ever a safety net there. I think that's how she feels. Like she's walking on a tightrope and there's no safety net under there. Sometimes I think she's more keenly aware of it than others are."

"I didn't realize."

"Nobody ever wants to ask about it. I think because no one wants to upset her, or me, or my dad. You know, my family does it to each other too. We don't talk about anything too deep so that we don't upset each other. Sometimes I wonder if that does more harm than good."

"That makes sense to me," she said. "All of it. I didn't

used to talk about things that were bothering me with Parker. I just… I thought that I was being sensitive. I thought it was me. I don't think I would take that any-more." She looked up at him, her brown eyes glittering. "I'm learning to ask for what I want. To say what I want."

"I sure appreciate it."

"Well. It's easy with you."

"Why?" Suddenly he had to know. Why she liked being with him. Other than the fact that he made her feel good during sex. That was all that should matter. Except… More about her mattered to him. More than just how soft her skin was, and how wonderful it felt to lie naked beside her. Walking down the street with her felt just as good—hell, standing in this jewelry store felt just as good, and it shouldn't.

"I'm not really sure," she said, a small smile touch-ing her lips. "Maybe because… When I was a kid you were someone I could always…trust. If I ran, you ran after me. If I climbed a tree and I went too high and I fell down, you caught me. That time I got angry and ran away and went and hid in the hayloft…you were the one who found me. And…whatever you feel right now, about being here…you are here. It's easy to feel secure with you. In you. And…that's the most important thing I can think of."

Her words, so honest and simple, made his chest feel tight. He didn't feel like the person she had just de-scribed. She made him sound steady and faithful. She made him want to be. But he had decided a long time ago to keep on moving, to keep connections to a minimum.

But this connection he was finding with her was so different than he had imagined something like it might be. It made him wonder if the key to peace was really out there on the road.

Or if it was somewhere much closer to home.

She looked at him again with those soft brown eyes, and he did his best to ignore the hitch in his chest.

"Let's buy those earrings."

CHAPTER NINE

"PLEASE, COOPER." HIS mother's voice was almost as un-expected as his phone ringing in the first place.

Cooper was naked in bed with Annabelle, and he knew that he shouldn't be. He'd spent the past few days with her, ignoring his responsibilities. He should have gone to visit his parents yesterday, and the day before. Because he was here to visit his parents, not screw himself into oblivion at every opportunity. But here he was.

His mother had called early this morning, her voice sounding distressed, and no matter how much he wanted to, he didn't think he could deny her request.

"I always bring flowers for Christmas. But for some reason I just... I don't feel like I can make it this time. It's supposed to get easier. But Lindsay is still gone. I can't... I can't face it. Not this year. But she needs her poinsettias."

He'd thought his mother had seemed agitated the other day, and he felt like this confirmed she was in an anxiety funk right now. It wasn't something any of them verbalized, but his mother, the organized control freak who hadn't been able to control a disease hell-bent on taking her daughter from her, had bouts of major anxiety that were often triggered by unexpected things.

Not that Cooper would ever know what those things

were, because she kept it all locked down until the moment she couldn't.

Until moments like these.

Cooper had never returned to the place where they had sprinkled his sister's ashes. Not since the ceremony. Not once. He knew where it was, though. The location was emblazoned in his memory like everything else from that horrible day. That day that was supposed to be a celebration of her life. A life that was gone.

"I'll go with you," he said, keeping his tone measured.

"I can't go." She sounded frozen, and it made him feel like there was a block of ice in his own chest. But there was nothing he could do but this. This one thing she'd asked of him. He could count on his hands everything his mother had asked him to do in the past eight years.

Coming home for Christmas was one. This was another.

He was here. How could he say no?

"I'll be by soon to pick up the flowers," he said, his tone sounding wooden to his own ears, the words tasting like metal.

He ended the call and looked to his side to find Annabelle studying him. He shifted uncomfortably, not quite sure what to tell her.

Well, the truth, he supposed.

"That was my mom. She's having… She has a lot of anxiety. She tries to combat it with the earrings. She tries to keep herself busy. But clearly, nothing is helping today. She likes to take flowers to my sister's gravesite on Christmas Eve. But she doesn't feel like she can make it today."

"Is that in the cemetery?"

"No. Her ashes are in the mountains. So she wants me to take some flowers up there."

He didn't tell her that it was a place he never went to. He would deal with that shit when he was able to process it. He would deal with it hopefully after he had done what his mother had asked him to.

"I can come," Annabelle offered, her touch on his arm soft and reassuring, the look in her dark eyes so genuine and sweet it made him feel like a terrible person for not wanting to take her up on it. For wanting to say no immediately and forcefully. But maybe it would be a good thing to bring her. Maybe then he wouldn't have to think much about where he was and what he was doing. He could drop off the poinsettia and leave.

"Sure," he said, keeping his tone casual, as if this wasn't out of the ordinary at all. "We can get dressed and drive over to my parents'."

Annabelle got out of bed and started to collect her clothes, which had been strewn all over the floor. Then she paused. "Cooper, where do your parents think you've been the last couple of nights?"

He lifted a shoulder. "I assume they think I found someone to sleep with."

"But they haven't said anything to you."

"No. Because I'm thirty-two years old. And they're pretty used to me not being around all the time."

"I know," she said softly. "I would just think that they would wonder."

"Well, if they are, they're going to have to go on wondering."

He was being short with her, and she didn't deserve that. He should tell her to just stay home, but he wasn't going to.

They dressed silently and then she got into his truck, where they continued the silence as they drove from Annabelle's neighborhood, down Main and out of town toward his parents' place. "I won't be long," he said, getting out and heading toward the house.

She was probably right. There would probably be questions. And it was entirely likely that his mother would spot Annabelle out in the truck. But, whatever. It would all be over soon enough. And then explanations wouldn't matter at all.

After Christmas he would leave. He would leave this town. He would leave Annabelle. He would go back to the way things were, and he would forget. He was tied to Gold Valley as long as he had his parents. Was tied to it by his remaining family, and by the fact that his roots were here. But he did a pretty damn good job of pretending that wasn't the case most of the time.

He would forget. He would spend months not thinking about it. Roaming around from town to town and state to state, wherever his work took him.

He didn't have any reason to enmesh himself any deeper in his hometown. And he wouldn't.

He went up to the door of his parents' house and knocked, even though that was kind of silly, since they were expecting him. Since he had grown up there.

But as he stood there with his knuckles smarting slightly from the way they had connected with solid wood, he reflected on the fact that it was basically a commentary on how things were. He came back. But it wasn't the same. It wasn't home. Not anymore.

He heard his mother tell him to come in, and he pushed the door open.

"Hi, Mom," he said, stepping into the kitchen, where

she was sitting at the table, her hands wrapped around a mug of tea. She looked like she hadn't slept. She had probably been up all night worrying about Lindsay's poinsettias. And the fact that she didn't think she could deliver them.

"Everything okay?"

They weren't supposed to talk about things like this. Even though he knew his mother struggled with this kind of anxiety, and that sometimes it prevented her from doing the things she wanted to do. That it came out of nowhere. That she was sometimes completely felled by random bouts of depression and grief for varying lengths of time.

They didn't talk about it. Just like they didn't talk about how badly everything still hurt. Not really.

They operated as three completely independent people rather than a family.

As if they had lost their glue.

Loving someone who was sick was a strange thing. The world revolved around that illness. And their family had revolved itself around sadness and hospital visits. Tests, all clears and relapses. In many ways, that hardship, that illness, had been a glue of sorts. And when it was over...

They hadn't known who they were anymore.

"I just can't seem to get myself together today," she said, looking as pale and worn as the faded yellow curtains behind her.

"That's okay." He crossed the room and placed his hand over hers. "I can do it for you."

She smiled up at him, squeezing his hand. And he felt like...like he actually might have fixed something. Even if it was a small something. Even if it was a fix that wouldn't last. Today, he was here, and his mother had let him know what she needed. He was able to come through for her.

"Where's Dad?"

"He's in his shop."

"He doesn't want to go up?"

She shook her head, her lips tight. "Your father doesn't go there."

He felt something stab through his chest, hot and sharp.

Neither he nor his father could bring themselves to visit the spot where Lindsay had been put to rest. It was only his mother that went. Only his mother that brought flowers. She carried that, all on her own. He wondered if his father was even conscious of that. Or if it was another casualty of their lack of communication. Their inability to share with each other. The ways that they had pulled away since they had lost Lindsay.

"It's fine," he said. "I'll do it." He saw the poinsettia sitting on the counter, and he was crossing the room to get it when he heard footsteps behind him.

He turned to see Annabelle standing in the kitchen doorway, looking sheepish and a little lost, her dark hair disheveled, like she'd just rolled out of bed. Which she had. With him.

"Good morning, Mrs. Mason," Annabelle said.

"Annabelle," his mother said, surprised. "Is everything all right? Are you here with your father?"

"No," Annabelle said. "I just... I came with Cooper."

His mom looked between Annabelle and him, and he was shocked enough by the announcement that he forgot to be irritated.

"I thought you were going to wait in the truck," he began.

"I would have," Annabelle said, leveling those brown eyes on him. "But I was… I wanted to make sure you didn't need help carrying anything."

"It's fine. Just… Give me a second."

Annabelle nodded and slunk out of the room, and his mother looked up at him quizzically. "Is that where you've been the last couple of nights?"

"It doesn't matter," he responded. "It's not going to turn into anything more."

"It's Annabelle Preston, Cooper. And she's not going to be anything more to you?"

"How can she be? I'm never home. I don't have a home, not really. I'm not signing on for the…for the family thing. She's a great girl…"

"Her father would kill you," Connie Mason said, her blue eyes full of concern and no small amount of anger.

"He doesn't need to know. I didn't intend for you to find out. Because…there's no point. It can't be anything."

Silence fell between them, uncomfortable and thick. And normal. Sadly, just normal. Because none of them knew how to talk to each other anymore. They wanted to protect their wounds, and not harm anyone. It had turned into a silence that might be worse than anything else.

"You're really never coming back to us, are you?" she asked.

He frowned. "What do you mean? I come back to visit whenever you ask me to."

She sighed heavily, looking down into her teacup. "Not really. Not all of you."

He had about a thousand things to say to that. That he didn't have all of *them* either. That it was completely understandable they had all changed. That if they hadn't, there would be something wrong with them.

But words wouldn't come. He didn't know how to talk about his feelings. He sure as hell couldn't figure out how to do it on command.

"I can't," he responded. Then he grabbed hold of the poinsettia and turned away, walking back out of the house into his truck, where Annabelle was just reclaiming her seat.

It wasn't until they got back on the highway that he turned to Annabelle. "Why did you come in? I told you I would only be a minute."

"And I didn't want to wait. Sorry. I hope I didn't make a whole lot of trouble for you. I just… I was worried something was wrong."

They started driving down the highway, headed to the remote place where they'd sprinkled Lindsay's ashes.

"Something *is* wrong," he said. "My sister is dead. I have to take flowers to her grave on Christmas Eve. My mom is right," he continued. "It doesn't get easier. It only gets worse. People say time heals, but I think it all just gets more final. And the longer you go hurting like you do, the more you realize…it's going to live with you forever. That's a hard pill to swallow."

She said nothing for a while. Finally she spoke.

"I imagine it comes in waves," she said softly. "I know… I know it's not the same, the way that my mother abandoned me. But it's the closest thing to that kind of grief that I have. And sometimes I think I'm fine. But then sometimes I see a mother and child together and the longing I feel takes my breath away. Sometimes, when I'm with friends and they talk about the ways their mothers irritate them I feel jealous. This kind of horrible acrid jealousy that I can't overcome. And I never knew her. I never got the chance to love her. The only thing that I even care about is the theoretical idea of having a mother. There's not a specific one that I even miss. I can't imagine how it must be for you."

His stomach tightened, her words landing on tender places inside of him. That longing. He understood it well. Not just for his sister to be here, but for the family he'd once had. A family that had been centered on sadness and heavy things since he was fourteen and his sister had been diagnosed.

A longing to be someone who wasn't touched by grief.

But the longing felt eased just then. In this moment, with someone to share with. He hadn't talked to anyone in so long, and he talked to Annabelle. She talked to him. It was as strange as it was wonderful.

"The worst thing of all is knowing that something terrible is going to happen and there's nothing you can do to stop it," he said, turning the truck off the highway and up a long, winding dirt road that he knew would eventually lead to the place where his sister's ashes were.

"I know..."

"No," he said, cutting her off. "Nobody does. It's the helplessness of it. The finality. You can't argue with that kind of sickness. You can't argue with death. A long illness like that... You hope for a miracle. You wait for one. Because obviously this kind of thing happens to other people. It doesn't happen to you. Not to your family. As long as somebody is ill you can sit around and make bargains with God. You can hope that you'll be an exception to the statistic. But death...you can't argue with that. And after so many years of arguing against illness...it's just... It's almost impossible to accept. But the hope is gone. It makes you want to go back and stop hoping like that sooner."

"But that wouldn't change anything either," she said softly. "And then you're living without hope."

"Hope didn't change anything," he said, hearing the harshness in his tone. "So what's the point of it?"

They were silent as they continued on up the dirt drive all the way to the top. When they reached a dead end, he parked. He grabbed hold of the poinsettia that was sitting in the bench seat between them, all bright and defiant in the face of death and winter. "It's this way."

They walked silently together up a narrow, worn path that led to a creek shrouded in trees. This was the resting place that Lindsay had chosen before she died.

Suddenly, the unfairness of that hit him fresh, like a slap in the face.

It was the first time he had been up here in eight years, and of all the realizations he had expected to have, this one felt like it came from nowhere.

At twenty-six years old, his sister had picked out the place she wanted her ashes to go. Had had to make that decision because she knew that she wasn't going to beat her illness. Knew that her time was rapidly running out.

It wasn't fair. None of it was.

It wasn't fair that she'd had to do that. That she'd had to find it in herself to think of those things. To accept her prognosis with the grace and dignity she had.

He didn't think he would have accepted anything of the kind with grace and dignity. Hell, he knew he wouldn't. He hadn't accepted that she was going to die. Not at all. Not until it was too late. And even then...

He didn't like being in this place where he had to accept it. Where he had to be fully aware of it. Where he couldn't pretend that she might still be back home waiting.

As if sensing his thoughts, Annabelle said nothing. She simply stood beside him. Looking down at the fast-moving creek, her cheeks red from the cold, her hair blowing in the breeze.

Suddenly, he was so damned tired of silence.

"Lindsay loved it up here," he said, his voice shattering the cold winter air like it was a pane of glass. "She said it's where she and Grant had their first kiss. I suspect it was more than that, but she said *kiss*."

Annabelle laughed, the only warm thing in this frozen landscape. The only warm thing inside him.

"Of course, I didn't want to hear about any of that. But I'm glad she had him." He gritted his teeth, emotion swelling in his chest.

He had no idea how his former brother-in-law had survived the pain of losing her. And he didn't know, because he never asked. Because he just left. And he sure as hell never talked to the other man about that kind of thing. They didn't really make an effort to see each other, but every so often they had a drink.

He'd called Grant once when he'd come into town, and Grant had made some excuse about finishing his last stretch at the power company before going to work full time at his family ranch.

"She was loved," Annabelle said. "I know she still is."

He nodded. "More than most, I think."

"I'm sorry," Annabelle told him. "I'm sorry that there's nothing deeper or more substantial to say. But I don't understand why things like this happen. I don't understand why you or anyone else should have to deal with something like this."

"There's no answer," he said. "That's the problem. I can't make sense of it. I'll never be able to make sense of it. Though…being with you helps."

"Does it?"

"I didn't think anything could," he said. "Mostly, coming back…there's too much bad to make the good worth it. But not right now."

"Is that why you don't like being here?" He knew that she meant Gold Valley, not here specifically.

"It feels final when I'm here," he said. "It reminds me that there's nothing left to hope for. That there's no more wishing and praying for an illness to go away. She's gone. And…so is my hope."

"I think you're wrong about that."

He frowned. "No. I'm pretty sure I'm right."

"No, I…I know what you mean. She's gone. And that's a terrible thing to face. But there's still hope left in the world."

"Useless hope," he said. "Hope that doesn't change anything."

"Except how you live."

Neither of them said anything after that; they just stood there. And it surprised him the most that he felt strangely at peace here. He had expected something different. Had expected to be overwhelmed by grief. Had expected for everything to feel final and wrenching and awful as he stood here leaving poinsettias for his sister.

But it didn't. Instead he felt connected to her in a way that he hadn't in years. In a way that went beyond the pain of loss. He could picture her like she'd been when they were kids, running through the trees, her blond hair a tangle of curls in the wind. And even the way she'd been as a teenager. Even after she'd been sick. She hadn't only been sick. She'd been more than that. She'd fallen in love with Grant. She'd lived as big as she could.

"Do you want me to leave you alone for a bit?"

He thought about it. And he realized he didn't want her to. Before Annabelle he hadn't felt any peace since coming back to Gold Valley. He was afraid if she left his side now, she'd take it right back with her.

"Stay. I'm alone all the time."

She stood next to him, rested her head on his shoulder, and they simply stood. No words. Nothing. Just standing together.

Tonight was Christmas Eve. It was their last night together. Tomorrow would give way to the chaos of Christmas and then to him leaving.

But tonight. They had tonight.

And in spite of the heaviness that he felt at the thought, he felt something else, too.

He refused to call it hope.

CHAPTER TEN

SOMETHING HAD SHIFTED between them out there at Lindsay's memorial site. It wasn't really a grave. It had been beautiful, a mountain haven with a creek running through it and majestic evergreens all around. Beautiful and sad.

But not just sad.

Cooper had actually talked with her, shared with her, and she felt...

She loved him.

She realized that now. She always had. She could call it lust, hero worship, all those things. But it was more than that. Of course it was all clear as everything was coming to an end. She realized it when she really shouldn't have. Because he was leaving and there was nothing she could do about it. But as she had been talking to him out there at Lindsay's memorial site, when she should have been filled with nothing but bleak sadness, she'd had a revelation.

There were certain things in life you couldn't choose. No matter how hard you fought them, they wouldn't change. From her mother's abandonment to his loss, there were simply things you couldn't control. But you could control whether or not you gave up. He was right. Hope didn't always change things in the end. But hope, *love*, were what made life worth living.

She wanted to hope. She wanted to love.

For too long she had let other people write her story. Tell her that she wasn't enough. Her mother by her actions; Parker by his words.

But she was done with that. She deserved to live big because she wanted to. Deserved to have everything because she thought she did. She simply wasn't going to let the negativity of others define her.

Of course, she had no idea what to do with her newfound revelation. No idea how to go about broaching the subject with Cooper. Maybe she couldn't. Maybe she would just have to carry her love inside her. But whatever ended up happening, she wasn't going to regret the way she felt.

"Do you need to talk to your mom?" she asked when they were back on the road.

"No," he responded, his voice rough. "Let's go back to your house."

So they went.

When he made love with her this time, it was like a storm tearing through both of them. Like all the emotion that had risen up in that moment at Lindsay's resting place was bubbling over.

He was like a man possessed, and she was happy to let him take what he needed.

She clung to him, held his face in her hands, kissed him as he cried out her name when he found his release.

Her name. No one else's. *Hers*, because maybe to him she mattered.

She had to.

"I've never been up there with anyone," he said roughly when they were finished, his fingertips idly tracing shapes over her bare skin.

"Never?" she asked.

He rolled onto his back, staring up at the ceiling. "Actually," he said slowly, "I've never been up there at all. Not since her funeral." He shifted, looking over at her. "I avoid Gold Valley, as you might have noticed. I can't always, because when my parents ask me to visit I do. But I avoid it when I can. But going up there... No one ever asked me to. So I didn't. I was afraid it would take me right back to how it felt that day. But...I'm glad I went. Today I'm glad."

She put her hand on his shoulder. "I'm glad I could be there with you."

The words that had poured through her the moment they started driving down from the mountain began to well up inside of her. She wanted to tell him. Because she wanted more than this. She wanted more than just Christmas Eve. She wanted a lifetime of them. A lifetime of him.

And yes, it had been years since they'd been in each other's lives, and they had only spent a week together since. But didn't they both deserve to have something good? Didn't they both deserve some hope?

"I'm glad you're here with me, too."

"I love you," she said, unable to hold the words back. "I just... I thought you should know."

She didn't say anything after that. And neither did he. The silence stretched out. "Aren't you...aren't you going to say anything?"

"You don't love me," he finally said, the words hard.

But he still didn't move. Was still lying naked next to her in bed.

"I do," she responded. "I have. And I only fell for you harder this past week. You...you make me feel beautiful.

Like I'm enough all on my own, and that's what makes me want you. You don't make me want you because you've made me afraid I can't have anyone else. You don't try to get strong by making me feel weak. Parker manipulated me into being dependent on him. That's not what you've done. I had to get rid of him to become a better version of me. Being with you... I'm that better version of me with you, and you seem to like it. I didn't know that was possible. And you don't have to love me back, but you don't get to tell me how I feel."

"I can tell you anything I want," he said.

"You're so difficult. Just stop this. Stop running. Stop keeping yourself in the darkest place you can."

"We talked about this, Annabelle. I'm not going to stay here."

"Then I'll...I'll go with you."

"You're going to come with me, on the road. You're going to help me move cattle. You're going to sleep in disgusting motels and drive for long hours, camp on the side of the road if necessary?"

"Why not? I know what it looks like to stay here and be safe. To hide away in this little house. I know what it's like to live here with a man who thinks I'm chubby and silly and much less than he deserves. But I don't know what it's like to demand what I want. So, I'm giving it a try. I want to make this work with you. I've always cared about you, but over the past week I've fallen in love with you."

"It's the sex," he said flatly, getting out of bed, creating space between them.

"I've had sex and not been in love. I didn't love Parker."

"Then it's sex combined with that leftover hero worship of yours. It's not love."

"It is. And I want to find out how much more it could be. How much deeper it could be." She took a deep breath. "Because I thought a lot about what you said earlier."

"You thought about what I said a couple of hours ago?"

"Yes," she said. "And stop it. Stop trying to put distance between us by being an asshole. Just let me say what I'm going to say. The only reason you're even commenting is that you're afraid I'm going to tell you something you don't want to hear."

"And yet you don't seem to be taking the hint."

"I'm choosing to ignore it, because there are things you need to hear. You told me yourself that loneliness was sitting in a room with other people and not being able to talk about what's in your heart. Well, I'm going to talk about what's in mine. And if it hurts your heart, I'm sorry. But you need to hear this. You need to feel something."

"I've had enough of feeling," he said, his words jagged.

She shook her head. "I don't think you have. I think you're scared that there's a hell of a lot more that you could feel, Cooper. And you don't want to. But I think it's hope that makes life worth living. And it's love. And maybe none of it changes the outcome. Maybe in the end there are fights you can't win no matter how much you love someone, no matter how much you pray it could be different. But the alternative is to live without any joy. The alternative is to live without believing in anything, and I can't face that world."

"You're right, you know," he said, his tone hard. "You can't actually understand what I've been through."

She let that go. She didn't let it hit her. Didn't let it hurt her. He was just trying to protect himself, and she understood that. She even agreed with him to a degree. But it didn't mean that she had nothing to offer him. Just because she hadn't been through the exact same thing didn't mean she was wrong.

"So that's what you want. To go through life caring about nothing, being connected to nothing."

"Like you said," he responded, "what's the alternative? The alternative to living with hope, the alternative to believing in something, is to care about nothing. Nothing but what feels good right now. Nothing but what you can hold in your hands right this second. And I'm fine with that. I'm fine with holding you in my hands right this second, Annabelle. You're beautiful, and you're soft, and I love the feel of you. The taste of you. But I'm not going to build something new inside myself just to let life knock it down again. I'm not going to hope for things that might never be. If you want to spend tonight with me, you got it. Because I'll commit to that. What's here, what's now, what's real, I'll grab on to that with both hands. But I'm not going to pin my happiness on something that can be taken away."

"Are you happy at all?" she asked, scrambling out of bed after him.

"Happiness," he said, moving even farther away from her, "is a naked woman in my arms, and a drink waiting. That works every day. Guaranteed to chase the blues away."

"And it doesn't matter where it is? It doesn't matter what woman? It makes no difference at all." She was feeling desperate now, her heart thundering so hard it was making her dizzy.

"None," he shot back, bending over to collect his clothes.

"Stop it," she said, grabbing his shirt out of his hands and holding it up against her chest. "Stop being a coward."

"I am not a fucking coward," he spat. "I'm…"

The heat seemed to drain out of him then. Like he couldn't finish the sentence. "You're a man who's been wounded," she said. "And is afraid of being wounded again."

"No. Don't play this game. You're not the little mouse that's pulling a thorn out of my paw, Annabelle. There is no thorn. At least, there's not one you can reach. If it's there, that bastard worked its way all the way through my system and embedded itself into my heart a long time ago and there's no getting it back out."

"Okay," she said, the word coming out as a whisper. "Maybe you're right. There's a thorn. Maybe it will always be there. But maybe something else can exist alongside it. And isn't that better than just having a thorn?"

He reached out and took his T-shirt from her hands, pulling it over his head and covering his body. "I'm never going to try and find out."

He collected all of his things, picking up his cowboy hat last and pressing it down onto his head. Then he pulled the brim down, giving her one last look. "Merry Christmas, Annabelle."

It echoed that first night they had been together. That first night he had abandoned her. It had felt terrible then.

But now it felt devastating. Now it felt like she might not be able to breathe ever again.

This was the cost of love. Of putting herself out there. Of deciding that she was worth the kind of risk that she was asking him to make.

She waited for those feelings to fade away. Waited to feel like an idiot. To feel like she was a doughy, sad little girl who had been asking for something she didn't deserve.

But that feeling didn't come.

She still felt justified. She still felt right.

Cooper had wanted her. She was the one he had talked to about his loss. She was the person he had brought up to the place where his sister had been laid to rest when he could have easily gone by himself.

And she was the one that he felt compelled to fight against.

She scared him. If she didn't, then there would be no reason for him not to carry on an affair with her when he was in town. Fear was the only explanation. And he was only afraid because he *did* feel something for her.

In the darkness of that moment, it gave her hope.

And that was when she knew that if she was right about nothing else, she was right about hope.

Even if it didn't change anything, it was the thing that could save you.

The thing you could hold on to when there was nothing else.

And now that she had nothing but hope, she clung to it as tightly as she could.

CHAPTER ELEVEN

WHEN COOPER STUMBLED back in the house early the next morning, drunk and needing to be delivered by the only taxi in town, his father was sitting at the table, where his mother had been the previous morning.

"About time you showed up," he said.

"Why were you waiting up for me? I haven't come home any other night this week."

"It's Christmas. So I figured you might."

"Well," he said, spreading his arms and taking a stumbling step forward, "looks like you were right. Here I am."

"Yeah," his dad said. "And likely to be hungover during dinner tomorrow."

"It's kind of a tradition for me. I know I haven't spent Christmas with you in a while, but I don't usually do the holidays sober."

His dad sighed, his blue eyes, so like Cooper's own, reflecting a deep weariness. "What's going on, Cooper?"

"We talk now?" Cooper asked.

"Only if you want to."

"Not particularly. Talking won't change a damn thing. Nothing will."

"Oh, maybe not. But it might make us feel better."

Cooper let out a frustrated breath and sat at the

kitchen table across from his dad. "Why? We've never talked before."

"There's a reason we asked you to come for Christmas this year, son. It's because we wanted to try and fix this thing between us, and I don't think your mother and I did a very good job of that. We waited for time to heal, and it hasn't. You figure after all this time it'll heal itself. But it didn't. And we thought we'd better get to making some of the healing happen."

"You want to be a family again?"

"We've *been* a family," his dad said slowly. "A family that got blown apart. A family that's been having a hard time coping with the hand we were dealt."

"Why would we have anything but a hard time with the hand we were dealt? It's a bullshit hand. I don't want to play it. But nobody asked me."

"I don't want to play it either, but what choice do we have?" His dad leaned back in his chair. "I lost my daughter, Cooper. And nothing prepared me to deal with that. Nothing on earth could. But somewhere along the way I lost you, too, and that I don't like at all."

Cooper pressed his palm over his face, his head starting to ache already. "I never wanted to make you feel like that. But…I just don't like the reminder that she's gone."

"None of us do. But your mother and I stay here because if we left we wouldn't be as easily reminded of all the time we had with her."

Cooper was stunned by that. He had never thought about it in the reverse. That without the house, the town, they wouldn't be as aware of her life. He had been so focused on making sure he wasn't continually aware of her death.

"We hoped for a miracle for so long. What did we get?"

"We had Lindsay. For the years that we had her. All that sweetness and joy she brought, no matter what was happening with her health… She was special. I hope you have children someday, Cooper. I hope you understand how much they seem like a miracle. She was my miracle all on her own. You were my miracle. You are."

Cooper felt like someone had stuck a broken bottle straight through his chest and twisted hard, the jagged pieces tearing through his already wounded flesh. Touching that thorn deep down in his heart and making it ache.

"If you knew," Cooper said. "If you knew when she was born she was going to die when she was twenty-six years old, do you think you would have loved her the same?"

The clock on the kitchen wall ticked three times.

"I hope so," his father said. "With everything I have, I hope so. Because no matter how much it hurt in the end, loving her is one of the best things I've ever done. It's one of the best parts of me. For years we were afraid cancer would win and we didn't pull away. I would have bitterly regretted it if we had. If we hadn't used the time that we were given."

Cooper thought of Annabelle. He thought of what she had said to him about hope.

"The end might have been decided already, might have been out of our hands, but everything that happened before that…that was up to us. I'm glad we gave it everything we had. No matter how much it hurt in the end. No matter how much it still hurts."

"It's just been my goal to try to not feel pain like that

again," Cooper said, pushing up from the table and staggering backward.

His father studied him quietly. "Are you feeling anything else?"

That question hit him hard, like a sucker punch to the jaw.

He wasn't sure if he had felt anything else for a long time. Nothing but what he had told Annabelle. Nothing but what he could hold in his hands on a given day.

But that was such a small amount. It saved up nothing for the future, and it gave him no joy from the past.

And he was starting to realize how little depth it gave everything.

But depth meant pain in about a thousand ways, and Cooper sure as hell didn't feel inspired to embrace it.

What he wanted, what he *really* wanted, was something that he couldn't get from life. Not really. He wanted a guarantee.

It's why he'd rejected Annabelle. Not because he didn't have feelings for her. But because the feelings were so strong they scared the hell out of him. He wanted to know that if he went headfirst into this thing with Annabelle…if he let himself love her…that he wouldn't lose her.

That nothing would happen to come between them. To splinter the bond they had built.

Because that was what the loss of Lindsay had really taught him. That when you encountered the rough things in life you didn't just lose one person. You lost everything.

Your place in the world, the way that you saw yourself. The way that others saw you, too.

And there was no guaranteeing that it would be all right. There was no fixing it.

He felt like numbness in comparison to all that loss was a blessing.

"I'd rather live the way I'm living now," he said. "At least I can breathe."

"I ask myself sometimes," his father said, his voice rough, "if there's any point in breathing just to breathe. But then I remember I was given a next breath. And I figure I have to enjoy it. Even when I don't want to. Even when everything is hard, I can be thankful for that breath. Don't you think if Lindsay were here instead of you that you would want her to love? That you would want her to go on with her life with Grant and be happy? Bet you wouldn't want her to lose everything because you did."

"Maybe," he acknowledged. "But I'm not sure it's that easy."

"Of course it's not that easy. It's why I have to remind myself to do more than breathe. It's why I failed at it many times over the course of the past eight years. It's why your mother and I haven't been able to fully reconnect with you, even though we want to. It's why sometimes your mother can't go up and leave the flowers, and why I've never been able to. I'm not saying we do it perfect. I'm not saying it's easy. I'm just saying that it's the hope I have."

"Hope. Hope is bullshit."

"Hope is what makes things possible," his father said. "Otherwise you're just breathing until you die."

The older man got up then, leaving Cooper sitting at the kitchen table with nothing but his impending headache to keep him company.

Was that true? Was he just living until he died because there was nothing else to do?

If so, that was a bigger pile of bullshit than hope itself. Because his dad was right. At least he had the luxury of breath.

But loving Annabelle…

That really would mean coming back here. Because she had a business here. She had a life. It would mean buying himself a plot of land, settling down. Where the grief could touch him again. Where he would have to contend with the person he was.

Where he might have to work to become the person he was supposed to be. The person who was touched by grief. Touched by loss.

And who lived anyway.

A stronger version of himself. A better one.

But it was going to take bravery and strength he didn't know if he possessed to become that man.

Annabelle deserved nothing less. So he supposed he had to figure it out.

Because that, he realized, sitting there drunk as hell on Christmas Eve at his parents' kitchen table, would be the real tragedy.

To have love, right there, and to decide not to take it.

To have lost love not because life was unfair, not because sometimes the world was cruel and hard, but because he was a coward.

To not have *Annabelle*. The woman who skipped down streets decorated for Christmas with a smile on her face. Who loved him, even when he was grim. Who made him feel like he could be that man she saw. That man she'd seen as worthy of adoration when she'd been a kid, and worthy of her love now.

She had shone a light in his darkness, had brought peace to all that noise in him. And he had run from it, because that was terrifying. Wanting another person like this. Needing another person.

It was opening himself up to the possibility of pain again. But…the alternative was life without his light. And now that he'd had it…he knew how dark it all was without her.

He couldn't go back to that.

So he was going to have to figure out how to grab hold of what she was offering.

All that movement that he had been pretending to make for the past eight years was actually an exercise in running in place emotionally. So now he had to figure out how to move forward. And he had a feeling it was going to start with staying put.

CHAPTER TWELVE

ANNABELLE HADN'T BEEN heartbroken when Parker had ended their relationship. Mostly because she hadn't been in love with him. It had been a relief in many ways--though her prevailing emotion had been anger, because it wasn't fair that he had gotten to be the one to detonate that tired five-year relationship of theirs that had certainly not fashioned either of them into the best version of themselves.

No, she hadn't been heartbroken then. But she was heartbroken now. On Christmas morning, attempting to ready the early-afternoon dinner that her father would be coming over for, she was heartbroken.

She had known that it was going to end. She had. Cooper had warned her. But she had thought it would end because they both mutually decided it would have to.

She hadn't expected to fall in love. Not this quickly. Not this intensely.

Five years and she hadn't fallen in love with Parker, not truly. A week was all it had taken to become completely enmeshed in all that Cooper was.

But then, she supposed she had been in love with him when she was a girl, and all it had taken was a slight shove to make her fall completely.

She had known the boy that he was, smiling and

handsome and always kind to a little girl who had felt like her place in the world was tenuous.

And he had grown into something else. A man who was hardened by the pain that he had experienced, but who was still good, all the way down.

Plus, he had abs for days.

Not that his abs were the reason that she loved him, but they were certainly fun to touch.

The memory almost made her smile. Except then she had to contend with the fact that she wouldn't be touching those abs ever again. That was just sad.

They were strange, though, these feelings inside of her. Because they were painful, and they sliced deep, but they didn't undermine who she was.

This didn't undermine who she was.

It was a strange thing, to go through this kind of heartbreak and feel stronger for it even the next day.

Maybe it wasn't the heartbreak so much as the fact she had stood up for what she felt she deserved.

She would feel more triumphant later, she was sure.

Later, when Cooper was a trial that she looked back on, when this was a defining moment in her past, when it didn't hurt like there was ground-up glass in her heart every time she breathed.

It was her thorn.

But unlike Cooper she would be determined to have more than just the thorn.

She would find a way to have a rose, too, dammit.

Whatever it took.

Idly, she carried on mashing potatoes, glazing a ham and getting everything ready for dinner.

It was extravagant, far too much for two people, but they were always able to have leftovers for a week afterward, so it made all the effort and expense worth it. Really, it was worth it simply because she got to spend time with her father. Her father, who had always acted as though she mattered. For a moment, she mourned the fact that his sacrifice, the way that he had treated her, hadn't been sufficient in the end to make her feel like she was enough.

It should have been. Her dad deserved more than that.

And when he came over, when they were sitting down to dinner, she said just that.

"I'm not sure that I've ever adequately thanked you," she told him. "For everything that you did for me. I imagine a single man could have been doing things that he enjoyed a lot more than taking care of a child all those years."

Her dad put down his fork and knife, abandoning the ham that he'd been focused on a moment before. "Are you thanking me for raising you?"

"Well, yes. We both know that you didn't have to. Mom didn't. No one was forcing your hand."

He let out a long, slow sigh. "I didn't give anything up to raise you that I didn't get back ten times over, Annabelle. The world is a hard, strange place, and when you're young you have an idea of what the perfect life looks like. Success, house, spouse and children. That normal life. But what I learned quickly having you was that normal paled in comparison to what I got."

"It's not really the dream, though," she said, "is it? Having to work a physically demanding job and raise a child on your own."

"That's the thing about dreams, Annabelle. They're just dreams. They're not real. They might be nice to think about, but they can't put their arms around your neck and hug you. You can't have Christmas dinner with dreams. Reality is harder. But it gives more back."

They lapsed into silence, and Annabelle started to eat again.

"So," her father said, his tone light, conversational. "Are you going to tell me what's going on with you and Cooper Mason?"

She looked up, blinking rapidly. "What?"

"His mother said something about him not being home the last few nights, and that you were with him yesterday."

"I…"

"He's a good boy," her father said, reiterating what he had said earlier that week. "And I know how you feel about him."

"How I feel about him?"

"You always lit up when he walked in, little girl. Always. You loved him then—I bet you love him now."

"But he doesn't love me."

"He's scared. That's different."

"It might not matter in the end if it's different or not. If he can't see a way through it."

"That's the real trouble with dreams," her father said. "Nobody fantasizes about what it takes to get there. Just about having what they want. But there's always a cost to something great. Always. To raising a beautiful, wonderful daughter, so that you can sit around a Christmas dinner table with her. Finding a woman that you can love forever. Those things come at a price. Happy photographs on the wall don't tell you that, but it's true. There's no such thing as perfect. There's just life."

She thought back to the thorn again. "The roses always come with thorns."

"Isn't there a song about that?" her dad asked.

"I think so." They smiled at each other, and both of them stilled when there was a knock on the door.

"I'll get it," Annabelle said, getting up from the table.

She hurried to the front of the house and flung the door open, her eyes going wide when she saw Cooper standing there. He looked awful. There were dark circles under his eyes, the grooves on either side of his mouth deeper, or at least they seemed to be. And still, he was gorgeous in his navy blue Henley that showed off his broad chest and lean body. Still he was handsome, even unshaven and tired looking.

He made her heart twist, made hope bubble up inside of her. That hope that was as much an enemy as a friend right now.

She was beginning to see his point on the subject.

"What are you doing here? Because if you came here to pick up a T-shirt or a CD or something..."

"A CD?" He lifted a brow. "Did we break up in 2005?"

"I don't know," she said, sniffing. "I was just making a point."

"I'm not here for a CD. Or a T-shirt."

"Good. Because you didn't leave either of those things here. You never even brought a CD over in the first place."

"I know," he reiterated, his tone patient. "I'm here to talk."

"It's Christmas," she said.

"Yes, it is. And I'm sorry that it's Christmas. I mean, I'm sorry that I'm interrupting."

"I was eating ham."

"Then I'm even sorrier. But I still have to interrupt."

She twisted her hands and stepped out onto the porch, ignoring the cold bite of air that greeted her. She jerked the door shut behind them, her wreath making a jingling noise that was severely at odds with the portentous feeling in her soul.

"What are you doing here?" she repeated.

"I had to see you," he said. "I went out drinking last night. And I love drinking, Annabelle. Drinking is one of the only things that has gotten me through the long nights in the past eight years. Drinking and moving. One foot in front of the other, always grinding through the miles, measuring my life in them. No attachments. Nothing. But that's not living," he said. "That's just breathing. Breathing and drinking. It's refusing to be changed by what happened. That's not fair. It makes me angry, that people only think of Lindsay when she was sick. When she died. That people don't just remember her being alive, but they look at us and they remember that she's dead."

He shoved his hands in his pockets, looking down. Her eyes followed his, to the toes of his scuffed-up cowboy boots. The evidence of all the hard living he'd done to try and push the pain inside him away.

He looked back up, those vivid blue eyes meeting hers. "But my tribute to her isn't any better. I don't live like she was ever here. I don't live like that loss mattered. Because I'm too afraid to sit in one place and let it change me. I wanted to change everything around me, so I wouldn't have to have the lights turned on inside me. Wouldn't have to see who I was or what I'd let her loss turn me into."

He shook his head as she continued to stare at him in silence. "I talked to my dad last night. We really talked.

For the first time since she died. And he's not much better off than me, but the one thing he said was we have to do more than breathe. He's right. We do.

"I want to do more than breathe. I want to live. I want to live with you, Annabelle. Because you're the first thing I wanted enough to make me realize that if I didn't change I was going to be miserable forever. Numb was fine until you. But you... I want to feel it. And you're right. I might not be able to get the thorn out, but there has to be more to me than just that. Otherwise why am I here?"

Annabelle let out a long, slow breath. "I was just talking to my dad," she said. "He's inside. He's still eating ham."

"Okay," Cooper said, clearly not exactly sure where she was going with this.

"He said... He said that dreams are just pictures. Not the whole journey. Everybody has an idea of what's perfect, but they don't like to think about how you get there. And it seems to me like if we...if we do this, if we're brave enough to do this...everybody might look and see the picture, but you'll know that you had to walk a hard road to get there. That you had to do the brave thing. Scale a mountain to get to that perfect picture that we can hang on a wall. You're brave, Cooper."

"I feel like a coward," he said. "Honey, my knees are shaking."

"Mine, too," she said, taking a step forward and closing the space between them. She pressed her fingertips against his cheek.

"You were brave enough to be the one to say we should do this in the first place. It's your bravery that made me want to be even half that strong." He cupped her chin. "I love you, Annabelle. I haven't said that to anyone in a long time. I love you. And even if I can't guarantee what will happen in this world, I can guarantee that I'll love you through it. I think that's a choice I'll never regret."

"I love you, too." She wrapped her arms around his neck. "You made me feel like I was worth it."

"You always were," he whispered. "Always."

The front door opened, and her father appeared.

"This looks promising," he remarked, crossing his arms and leaning back against the doorjamb. "I was hoping you would come to your senses, Cooper," he added. "I keep telling Annabelle you're a good boy. And I would hate to have that proved wrong."

"Me, too," Cooper said, not taking his eyes off Annabelle. "Me, too."

"Well," Annabelle said. "We have enough dinner for…everyone. I know that your parents don't do Christmas in the same way they used to. But, do you think they would want to join us? For once we won't have any leftovers."

He smiled, then brushed his thumb over her cheek. "I'll give them a call."

EPILOGUE

GOLD VALLEY AT Christmastime had changed completely in the years since Cooper Mason had come back to town.

Oh, not in a way that anyone passing through the main street of town would notice. There were the same white lights. The same bustling choir dressed in Victorian dresses walking down the street every weekend in December.

The street stayed the same. But what had changed was everything that mattered.

Annabelle set the ham in the center of the table and smiled. "Time to eat."

It wasn't like everything was happy all the time, but when they felt sad, they talked about it. They didn't shove it under a rug. They dealt with it. His dad had been right…you couldn't sit around and wait for time to heal. Sometimes you had to work at it. But it had been worth it.

For the past three years they'd all shared Christmas together. His parents, Annabelle's father, and he and Annabelle. They were family now after all.

He'd married Annabelle at Christmastime two years ago.

It was funny how he'd dreaded Christmas for years, but now it was the holiday his whole life centered around.

It was when he'd met Annabelle. When he'd married her. It was the time of year that healed them all, bit by bit.

That made them all aware of what they had, more than what they were missing.

Annabelle straightened and gave him a small smile, tucking her hair behind her ear. She had flour on her cheek. He wanted to lick it off. Which was insane because flour didn't taste good. But she did. He just always wanted to lick his wife. "Can you come help me with the mashed potatoes?"

"I didn't know mashed potatoes could be troublesome," he said, getting up and following her into the kitchen.

"They aren't," she said, smiling up at him. "That was a ruse."

"I'm shocked," he said, feigning horror.

"You are not." She moved in closer to him. "I have a secret to share with you."

"Are you going to tell me what my present is?"

She shook her head. "No. Though this is a little hint about a gift you're getting next year."

"Oh, yeah? What's that?"

She stretched up on her toes and pressed her lips to his ear. "Next year there's going to be an extra, very small person at our family Christmas."

His heart clenched tight, joy bursting through him. He smiled and pulled her up against him for a kiss.

Right then, he was so full of hope, so full of love, he could hardly breathe.

Hope, he realized, changed everything. Without hope, he wouldn't have come back home. Without hope, he wouldn't have been able to dream of this moment, wouldn't have been brave enough to take a chance on a better life.

"I don't need another Christmas gift as long as I live," he said.

"Why is that?" she asked.

"Because I already have everything I could ever want. Family. Hope. Love." He kissed her. "And you. I have all of those things because of you."

She smiled, tears in her eyes. "Not bad for a girl who used to think she wasn't important."

He looked at her. So easy to see the girl she'd been, the woman she was, the mother she'd be. His Annabelle, who had been so many things to him over the years.

"You're so much more than *important*," he said. "You're everything."

* * * * *

When it comes to sweet and sexy romance,
no one does it like *New York Times*
bestselling author

MAISEY YATES

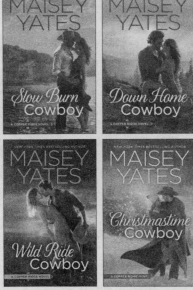

Come home to Copper Ridge, where sexy cowboys
and breathtaking kisses are just around the corner!

Order your copies now!

www.HQNBooks.com

PHMYCRS17R

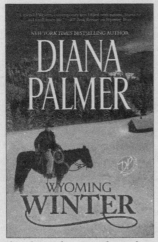

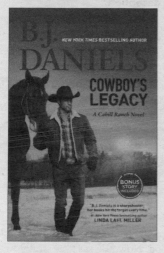